FALLING FOR YOU

Giselle Green was born in London and grew up in Gibraltar. She studied Biology at King's College London, and has an MSc in Information Science. She is also a qualified astrologer with a particular interest in horary, a form of medieval astrology. Her debut novel, *Pandora's Box*, won the Romantic Novelists' Association New Writers' Award in 2008 and has sold across Europe. She lives in Kent with her husband and their six sons.

By the same author:

Pandora's Box (Avon, 2008)
Little Miracles (Avon, 2009)
A Sister's Gift (Avon, 2010)

GISELLE GREEN

Falling For You

First published in Great Britain by

Yule Press
9a Tunbury Avenue
Walderslade
Chatham
Kent
ME5 9EH

www.gisellegreen.com

A Paperback Original 2012

1

Copyright © Giselle Green 2012

Giselle Green asserts the moral right to
be identified as the author of this work

A catalogue record for this book is
available from the British Library

ISBN 978-0-9571152-0-0

Set in Minion by Shore Books and Design
Blackborough End, Norfolk PE32 1SF

Printed and bound by CPI Group (UK) Ltd, Croydon, CR0 4YY

Acknowledgements

Firstly, a big 'Thank You' goes to Eliott who's been an enormous help in getting me to think differently about how I approached this book. Your input has been invaluable. Many thanks to Catri for editing, to Nigel for layout and well done to Debbie for the fantastic cover.

   To all the friends I've spent time with over the last two years at my 'writing retreat,' Clare, Jan, Cara and Catriona, thanks as always for the pleasure of your company. And last but not least, my grateful thanks go to Matthew for IT assistance along the way.

To Michael,
who already knows
how to make his dreams come true.

'He that has light within his own clear breast may sit i' th' centre and enjoy bright day'

Milton

Rose

I swore I would not do this again and yet …
Here I am.

The door handle to her old room sticks a little, feels stiff in my fingers as I turn the knob. It's not going to open, is it? The truth is, part of me doesn't even want it to open. I want it to remain shut. I don't want to go in there and yet if I do not … I feel a little rush of acid to my throat as it makes that old clicking sound it used to make before the catch releases and then I know it's open. It's open and I just stand there, hovering on the threshold, my heart going ten to the dozen because I know it's been five years, five long years since anyone's even stepped foot in here and I swear to God right now it feels no different than if I were about to open her coffin.

I step in, just a little bit, and the smell of the air inside catches me by surprise because it doesn't smell of her anymore. It doesn't smell of scented candles burned right down to the wick, none of the old high notes of bergamot or sage, none of the lingering sweet scent of cinnamon incense sticks. It smells - musty. The door makes a loud creaking noise as I push it open wide. It's late and I stop for a moment, listening out in case I've woken Dad upstairs but no sound comes. Thank God. I move a bit further into the room, looking for the light switch.

She's gone, hasn't she?

She has. I'm not sure right now if that makes me feel more

relieved or sad. If she's gone - I take in a deep breath - then all she's done is exactly what I mean to do, which is to leave Clare Farm. That's why I've come back here tonight, to do the one thing I swore I'd never do again.

I blink, as the soft light from the one lamp in the room lights up the old familiar surfaces. Her basket of coloured candles is still there by the window; her gemstone crystals of every shape and hue, they're still there, collecting dust; the framed picture I drew for her one Mother's Day of a gathering of butterflies spread out across the sky; the besom she used to clear the energy in the space before she worked her spells.

That's still leaning up against the wall. I hesitate, and then I pick it up and examine it a little more closely, feeling the smooth bamboo of the handle with my fingertips, imagining I am back there watching her holding it again. It's just a broomstick, really. The old-fashioned kind, with the long bits of straw on the end. A broomstick that I will use in a moment to sweep round the space where the spell will be worked, just like I always used to see her do.

Is this wrong?

All I want is the chance to leave home, just like everyone else. All my best friends left Merry Ditton this September, most of them went to Uni and that's where I should have gone too. It's where I would have gone had things been different. A year ago, I already had the Uni offer I'd set my heart on. I've worked so hard, achieved all the grades. My ship was all set, ready to sail …

When I walk over to the drawer under her dresser the little dish of salt I will need to draw my magic circle on the table is still in there; the box of matches. I sprinkle the salt into a circle and then I take a few bright Holly berries from my pocket, roll them onto the table. I push them with my fingertips over to the bottom, the south end.

Red for the South, the element of fire, for passion and for courage and … and get up and go.

2

And I have to go. I thought I could be patient and stay here as long as I was needed, that I'd be able to catch up. But then - this week I met up with some of my old friends, freshly returned from their first term at Uni and I realised something that I hadn't even begun to see up to now; that I will never catch up. Even in just the few weeks they've been away, they've all moved on. Subtly, in some strange and almost indefinable way I couldn't quite put my finger on, they'd all changed, stepped somehow from my orbit and left me behind. And the longer I stay here, the further behind I am going to slip. In a few years' time it won't matter what my plans for the rest of my life once were; I'll be like one of those rockets that fails to launch on Guy Fawkes' night, a damp squib that went out with a whimper while everyone else of my age was busy lighting up the sky.

Ouch. When I strike a match from the box the tip hisses and flares into the darkness, then goes very small, burning my fingertips as the match shrivels to black. The second match I try takes an age to light the wick on the candle. A cold stream of air goes past my back now and almost immediately, the flame goes out. *No, damn it.* What's wrong with these matches of hers - are they all damp? *Help me out here, Mum.* I grit my teeth and light it up again. I have got to do this, it's got to work and it has to be now. *You've got to help me out,* I can feel the frown deepening with tension on my forehead, *because I can't do this alone anymore.* I want - I want my chance in the world, just like all the others have got. I want my own life and a career and maybe even a boyfriend ...

Red for passion ...

The wick on the candle grows large and yellow suddenly, throwing bright wobbly light across the table, catching me by surprise. I didn't mean that last bit. I feel my face flush with an uncomfortable warmth because I know I put far more energy into

3

that thought than I should have. No. I shake my head abruptly. I didn't set up the circle tonight to ask for a boyfriend.

The candle light does a very strange thing now, elongating itself into a long thin taper and I tell myself there must be some current of air in the room that's causing it. And why has the air in the room suddenly gone so very cold?

Of course it's gone cold. It's nearly midnight on the 23rd December. The heating went off two hours ago and they're predicting snow.

I focus on the candle again, what it means. The thing I set my heart on, long ago; the future I desire to move towards, now. I have to be specific, I remember, if this is going to work. So; I close my eyes and see myself back in the grounds of the college I want to go to. I see it as it was the first time I ever laid eyes on it. I see it as it is. I see it as it will be.

I want my offer. So I imagine myself receiving it. I see the paper, thick and expensive, with its yellow, green and blue letterhead in my hands.

Dear Rose Clare,

We are very happy to be able to offer you a place to study Law at Downing College next year...

But it isn't quite as simple as that. I can't go away if there's no one here to look after Dad. If only he could have his health back then everything could go back to the way it should be ... My eyes skim over the circle I've drawn on the table. Should I ask for his health? My eyes narrow as I hesitate over how I should frame my request. I don't want to wish for something that cannot be.

My attention lingers over the west quadrant of the circle. What shall I wish for you, Dad? What do you need? I fill a little dish with water from a bottle. I place it in the West. I will wish for him to find closure; anything that might give him some peace.

I take a new match and I light the green candle. This one

4

lights up easily and I take that as a good omen. In my mind's eye - because you have to visualise the thing you want, you have to make it as real as real can be - I see Dad as I'd like to see him again; at peace with himself, smiling

A bright swathe of bleached light from the full moon falls across the table now, reminding me that there are energies afoot, that I have to be careful. I know full well what can happen when someone who has the knack and knows what they are doing, evokes magic. That's why I don't touch it. That and the fact that Dad would certainly be upset if he knew. Mum was as dear to him as life itself but he never got on with that side of her nature. He never understood it. For most of my life, I've kept well clear myself. I don't dabble as our home-help Mrs P would put it. Or, as she more prosaically commented on one occasion, 'conjure up spirits.' But what does she know? I've come back to it tonight because I'm desperate. I let my head hang in my hands for a moment. I've got to be desperate if I'm back here doing this again, haven't I?

No, I haven't forgotten what happened the last time I tried it.

Lawrence

22nd December West Camp Village, Jaffna

'Will it hurt, Lawrence?' Nine-year-old Sunny leans over and touches the place at the end of his plaster cast. The place where his foot should be, but we both know that very soon what's left of it is going to have to come off. I put that plaster cast on Sunny myself, only a few weeks ago. The injury was bad, but I expected that in time and with some surgery, it would heal. Now one of the doctors with the UN medical corps has picked up the tell-tale signs of a pre-gangrenous condition this morning. He's ordered an amputation, and the news has come as a shock. What am I going to say to Sunny?

When I look through the flaps of the Medic-Aid station at the row upon row of uniform white plastic sheeting tents stretching out into the distance, the larger question superimposes itself; what am I even still doing here? I came to Sri Lanka intending to do a three-month voluntary stint and nearly one year on I'm still here...

'Lawrence?'

'It'll hurt a bit,' I say carefully. 'But better just the foot than the whole leg, right?' *Easy for you to say,* his huge eyes, like lumps of soft brown sugar seem to reprove. Of course. I'm not a football-mad nine-year-old anymore. I couldn't possibly understand. He'll see me, at twenty-two, as ancient, as a fully grown adult who's got his life all sorted out ...

I resist the urge to put my arms around him and pretend everything will be all right. That's what his Mum or Dad would do. But they're not here and I'm not them. He's nodding now, being sensible, being grown-up with a professional like he has to be, but I get the impression any minute now there are going to be some huge tears rolling down his dusty face.

'How will I run after a ball?' he asks, 'When they take away my foot?'

'We will make you a new foot,' I say assuredly. 'You'll be able to run. Of course. Once you get used to it.'

'I might be able to run,' he mutters, 'but if I kick the ball too hard with my new foot it'll fall off.'

'It won't. Your new foot will be strong,' I tell him determinedly. I say it like it'll be the same. Like it'll be better. 'You'll need physio, naturally. Exercises. You'll need to work hard but ... ' I go over and pull back the curtains behind his bed, breaking off eye contact. 'With your new super-foot you'll be able to kick the ball harder than any of the other boys.'

'I will?' he looks unconvinced.

'Sure you will.'

'Will I still be able to feel the sand between my toes?' he demands now, 'On the toes of my new foot?'

I suck in a breath deep into my nostrils. I shake my head.

'You won't be able to feel anything. That's why you'll be able to kick the ball harder.'

He considers this for a bit.

The windows behind his bed are clear plastic. Right now it's early morning – maybe 7 am but there's still a huge full moon shining like a lamplight in a pale grey-blue sky. 'There you go,' I tap his shoulder gently so he turns round to look at it. 'There's a football waiting for you. A huge one.' For a split second ray of sunshine he smiles with his very white, crooked teeth.

'When I was small,' he says softly, 'I used to think one day maybe I'd grow up tall enough to kick that football right out of

7

the sky.'

He's just brought a lump to my throat. Man, I hoped he was one of the ones who was going to make it out of here okay. I thought he was, but I really don't know, now. If we can't locate some member of his family to take him in, it's looking increasingly doubtful.

I glance at the barbed wire fence along the perimeter of the compound that's still peppered with photos of the missing, and the large advert - '*Two hundred rupees for five fliers of your loved one*' catches my eye just like it always does. In this economy, two hundred is a lot of money when they're only up there for a month before relatives are asked to pay up again. Apparently, they do. I'm not sure whether to marvel at the resilience of the human spirit or be sickened that there's always some vulture ready to make money out of someone else's misfortune ...

I turn away from the window. I'm not supposed to get involved. I'm supposed to keep myself at one remove from the things that are going on here but I'm finding that increasingly hard. There are over two hundred thousand people in this refugee camp, all waiting for the day when they'll be told they can go home and for so many of them that day is just never going to come...

'It isn't a football, is it?' he says soberly now. 'The nurse here told me the moon was made of green cheese. I don't know green cheese. I think it's made of space rock. That's what I think. What do you think, Lawrence?'

'What do I think?' He's got a little bit of sticking-up hair on his forehead that makes him look like a hedgehog. I want to flatten it down for him before they take him into surgery. I want to go in with him but I know how crowded it gets in the op rooms here. Everything's improvised .The less people in there the better.

'I read in a book that the light of the moon is a trick. Did you know that, Lawrence?' He tells me solemnly. He's always reading. 'I read that no matter how thin or how full the moon seems to be – the truth is it's just a big old rock and it always stays the same.'

8

'I suppose it's an illusion isn't it, Sunny? We only see what the position of the earth allows us to see, that's true. But the moon is always intact. And ... once your foot is gone, you'll still be here, intact, won't you? Same as you ever were. You'll find a way, right?' His eyes grow suddenly sad again.

'What about my family,' he says after a while. 'Will they still recognise me when it's time to go home?'

'They'll recognise you.' I pat his hand and there are still splodges of green paint on his fingers because he was in the classroom yesterday. Sunny painted me a picture of his village in the hot dusty paddy fields of Vanni. He talks about going home all the time. He tells me his mother needs him to help her go out and pick the rice. He likes to watch the water buffaloes as they graze; the fields beyond them are jewel green, the sun as yellow as the yolk of an egg, and now he's discovered paints - the UN workers have been distributing art materials to the kids - he's determined he's going to capture it all. When he goes home. He's convinced that his Mum and Dad and all four of his sisters are still going to be there when he does.

But the truth is, despite my best efforts up to now, I haven't been able to locate a single soul who knows him. We've got systems in place to work out who belongs to whom; good systems - far better than the photos on the fence - but, two hundred thousand people, that's ... a small country's-worth of people. And so far, none of them are his. It is likely that his whole family got crushed under the house UN workers managed to pull him from. We don't know how many of them were in there at the time. He has no memory of the night his village came under attack, so Sunny lives in hope. The nurse Saila has come and is standing by his bedside smiling softly now. His eyes widen and I know that he's scared.

'Will you will go and find my Amma?' he begs me now. He's asked me to find his grandma before. He must have picked up by now that it's a next-to-impossible task. 'You will find Amma and then you will come back?'

'You know I'll come back.'

'You won't go back home to England?' He looks worried. Of course he's worried, but it's not about me.

'The only way I'll go back is if I take you with me,' I promise, just like I always do. Sunny's big dark eyes search out mine now from behind his toy monkey. Like that, he looks so much younger even than nine. *He's a kid, he's just a kid,* part of me rages. He shouldn't be going through all this. His life is ruined, blown apart because of a stupid war that he had no part in making...

'Tell me about your home,' Sunny delays, glancing at Saila. 'In the *North Downs of Kent* ...' It's something he asks me all the time. He knows I don't have to stay. I'm just a volunteer here. I could walk out and get on a plane home any time I choose. There are no rice fields where I come from, no grazing water buffalo, no monsoon rains. But there are other things.

'Close your eyes,' I say. He hugs Monkey to his chest and signals me to carry on.

So I tell Sunny again about the greeny-yellow fields of rape seed bordered like photo-frames by the fluttering petals of bright red poppies. On the other side of the cramped tent I can see them preparing the trolley they'll use with an IV feed to wheel him into surgery. He's picturing my world, he's got his eyes closed right now. He can't see what's about to hit him in his.

So I tell him about the shiny black of the crow's feathers and the pale cuckoo-egg blue of the sky over Merry Ditton on a wet spring morning. I tell him about the deep green of the moss that grows on the old oak guarding the entrance to Macrae Farm. The green is deeper, I tell him, than the untouched emerald green of the miles of jungle surrounding our refugee camp here above Jaffna.

The nurse is standing there, watching us, not moving, waiting for me to finish so she can take him away. I don't want them to take him away. I have run out of colours, so I move onto topography; how you have to make sure you've got good working brakes if you ever ride a bike down the impossibly steep Aslep's Hill. I tell him about the time when I didn't, I crashed. I ended up walking round like a cowboy for two weeks after that and Sunny laughs till tears come out of his eyes. This reminds me that I've never yet seen Sunny cry.

I tell him about my dog that I left behind five years ago; Sunny likes to hear the stories about how everyone in the world was scared of that dog apart from me. The nurse comes up alongside us quietly and Sunny gives a little yelp when she inserts the IV tube into his hand.

'Be brave, young man,' I tell him and he nods his head. 'Do you want me to take him for you?' I point at the fur monkey but he just tucks it in under the blanket, out of sight of any other passing kids. 'Okay then. I will see you in a few hours.'

I turn to the nurse, who wants a word before I leave. *Don't get involved, don't make it personal*, she's going to remind me, but it feels all too late for that …

'Get some sleep, Lawrence,' she advises. 'How many hours straight have you been on shift now?'

I shake my head. I don't need to sleep.

'I just need some caffeine that's all.'

'Lawrence Macrae,' Saila puts a firm hand on my arm. 'You need to get some sleep.'

Doesn't she understand?

'I'll be all right,' I brush her suggestion away. I've got to keep going.

Could I find Amma? Is it even remotely possible that any of Sunny's people have survived? 'Think positive,' I say to her. 'I'm planning to try my luck in East Camp. I hear they had a new influx of about fifty people last week from roughly the right area.' It's worth a shot. 'I *might* find someone from his family. It could happen, right?'

She sighs, resigned to the fact that I'm not going to go to my bed.

'I hope so.' She doesn't look convinced. 'It would be good if he could have someone here for him during the next few weeks.'

'I'll be here.'

'I know, but …' she hesitates, 'family is different isn't it, Lawrence.'

Of course it is. For most people it is.

'Who's carrying out the procedure?' I wonder suddenly.

'Wilhelm.'

Great. *That's just great.* I frown. A quick glance at Sunny's notes on the foot of his bed and I see it's the young Belgian guy who'll be operating on him. Why couldn't it have been Ranjavati? The Belgian surgeon isn't all that experienced. He's cutting his teeth out here, to put it crudely.

'Are you going to the staff social, later on?' Saila puts in tentatively. 'Tent 15A. A few of us have got hold of some beer. You'd be very welcome to join us and … I could fill you in on how the op goes?'

'Maybe.' She's the third person to ask me today. All female. She's nice, but I've made a point of not getting too close to anyone out here. Not in the relationship department anyway.

'I think my line manager would prefer it if I stayed away from the beer tent,' I pull a wry grin.

'I heard about that fracas,' she murmurs. Did she hear what I did to that guy, I wonder? The memory makes me feel uncomfortable. I don't drink. It's not my drinking that's the problem. It's what booze does to other people that I have a problem with. I watch as she straightens up the edges of Sunny's bed.

'How did your EO take it?'

'I'm not his favourite person right now. He's under pressure to put me on a disciplinary for it and that's put him in a difficult position. He's a good man and I'm sorry for that.'

She smiles slightly.

'You're a real enigma, aren't you, Lawrence?'

'Am I?'

'Yes. I see you go out of your way all the time to help people who are suffering - like this lad here - but then you're equally happy to …'

12

I feel my jaw tense. That guy in the beer tent the other night was blotto. He thought he was going to have some fun smacking his girlfriend around. I showed him different, that's all.

'He had it coming to him, Saila.'

Her eyes search mine for a moment. I swear I see her give a little shudder, but she decides to leave that topic.

'He's got to you though, this little one, hasn't he?' When she comes and stands by me she is so close, her shoulders are touching mine. 'Why is that, do you think?'

'You tell me,' I catch her gaze and hold it but she just giggles.

'He tells me you're going to take him home with you?'

Home? I am not going home. I turn away from Saila, frowning, as the tent flap goes up. The surgeon's just come in and her manner becomes professional now, brisk.

'I'm going to look for his Amma,' I tell her. 'I'll be in later, okay?'

Something about her last comment has stayed with me though, rankling under my skin. I am never going *home*. But why is it the thought of Macrae Farm has been in my mind so much lately? It bugs me. I've been catching echoes of it in my dreams.

As if something - or someone - is calling me back.

Rose

'The day you were born,' my father points a gnarled finger towards the window, 'there was a sky just like this one. Cold and so still and full of snow ...'

'In March?' I turn and look at him curiously, wondering what's brought this on. He doesn't talk much about his life before. I know it brings back mixed memories.

Right now I've got his tablet box on the table where I've been counting out the pills. Four little white ones, two large white ones and ... there should be one new red pill per day. I frown. We seem to be out of red pills. We can't be, surely? I rummage in the drawer and he turns to me, angling the wheels of his chair a little away from his permanent look-out post at the window;

'I'd been awake since 2 am, waiting to hear.' He stops and draws in a laboured breath. 'It was awkward. My wife knew about you,' he glances at me, suddenly pained. 'I don't think she ever loved me, but she threatened to divorce me if I visited you and your mother in the hospital. Promised me she'd sue for every penny. I knew she would, too.'

'Did she?' I let out a breath. He's never told me this before.

'Oh yes,' he dismisses that briefly. 'It wasn't pretty. I worked for her father. I knew I'd lose my job. It was wrong in so many ways and yet ...' he draws his shoulders up, as if to say - *I had no choice* - 'when the phone call came I ran out of the house so fast I left my wallet behind. The car ran out of petrol two miles from the hospital and I walked the rest of the way. By then,' he pulls a faint smile, 'it had already begun to snow. In mid-March! Imagine that. All the way down to you I kept seeing all the daffs and the tulips out everywhere, all those brave yellow-golds and crimson-reds suddenly shuddering under a mantle of ice ...'

I picture them. All those tender young shoots getting nipped in the bud, all the glorious colours that never got to unfurl that spring, destined to wither away on their stalks ... I close the tablet box with a snap.

'So you walked two miles,' I say. 'In a blizzard.'

'I'd have walked a thousand miles.'

I know. I feel a momentary pang of sadness for him. There's nothing that my father wouldn't have done for me and my Mum.

'Before that, I'd believed I had everything, Rose; a comfortable lifestyle with my wife; money, power. But suddenly the rest of my life - it all seemed like ... like grey dust, worthless ashes because there you were, this beautiful, vibrant new thing. I held you up high and counted all your fingers and your toes. Only a few hours old; you were so tiny I couldn't believe how perfect you were ...'

I smile at him, because I know he's trying to tell me that he loves me; he's always loved me, that he's grateful to have me in his life. I'm grateful to have him too. A dad who's always been prepared to go to the moon and back for his wife and his daughter; a dad who's only concern was always to honour the commitments he made to those he loved best in his life. I'm grateful for that, yes. But he can't know - I won't let him know - that right now I'm feeling something else, too. A little envy, perhaps? Because once, long ago, my dad found a way to escape from the thing in his life that was trapping him. He fell deeply in love with my mother, and that was what gave him the strength to leave his unhappy marriage.

But me - I push the tablet box back into its drawer, making a mental note about the red ones - am I ever going to escape my current situation? Will I ever get the chance?

'*If we're making you a new offer for next year you'll hear from us before Christmas,*' the interviewer's words, uttered as I left the room at Downing College two months ago, are ringing in my ears for the hundredth time. 'Before Christmas' she said. And it's already nearly midday on Christmas Eve. There isn't very much of 'before' left now. It's almost all gone.

'I knew then there was no way I was ever going to let you slip out of my life.' Dad's voice is suddenly apologetic, full of remorse. 'But I wonder sometimes, Rose. When I see how things have turned out for you, I wonder if I did the best thing?'

'Of course you did the best thing,' I tell him firmly. 'Feet up,' I say and I click the foot-rest on his chair into a higher position so I can slide one slipper off now, begin the process of gently rotating one ankle round in an anti-clockwise direction ten times before I do the other.

'You did it out of love,' I remind him. 'Because you loved Isla. You left your old life behind for me and Mum out of love, and that can never be wrong.'

'Maybe sometimes love can be wrong, though?'

I lift my eyebrows.

Can it? It makes me uncomfortable that he even asks the question. Is he saying now he regrets the choices he made eighteen years ago, the spring I was born? If he hadn't chosen to go with my mother then I'd have had a very different life, I know. So would he. If he hadn't loved Mum so much, he'd never have made her that promise he did before she died. He wouldn't be in a wheelchair now, would he? He wouldn't be trapped here, unable to go anywhere else, or ever get out of Merry Ditton.

Neither would I.

'Love is what's keeping you here right now, isn't it? That, and loyalty to me.'

I feel a slight burning in my face. I don't like him to talk like this. As if he were a burden. He's not. He's right that I'm here because he needs me but love *does* matter. Loyalty matters.

'Things'll all work out in the end, Dad.' When I pick up his

16

hands to tuck them back in under the blanket they feel so cold. The skin on the back looks papery and thin, almost translucent, and the sight of it catches at my heart. If I leave here, I leave him. And I don't want to leave him.

'I'll make it out of here when the time is right.' I feel a complete hypocrite saying that now. I was that desperate I even tried to cast a spell, didn't I? Only last night. A spell to get me out of here, but he mustn't know about that ...

The truth is, University offer or no offer, I'm never going to make it out of here unless he gets better. Dad's got limited mobility but he's often wheelchair-bound and there's no way he can fend for himself on just the six hours a week care the council have said they'd provide for him. When I explained that wasn't enough, a woman came round from the council and took us round Forsythe's home for the disabled elderly 'Just so you know you have an alternative' she told us both on our way out. But I saw her face. Forsythe's was so awful she must have known that what she was really saying was - *there is no alternative, if you can't manage things between you.* Because there is no way Dad is going to end up at Forsythe's. Not while I'm around.

No; I've been thinking about this. The only way it could work is if Dad's brother Ty would agree to have Dad at home with him and his family. He might, if Dad got on well enough with these new meds. It could happen. In my wildest dreams, it does. Ty's eighteen years younger than Dad, only forty, and a flourishing entrepreneur in his own right. They've got a big house. Heaven knows, they've got enough space at their house but I know space wouldn't be the issue. I figure if we sold Clare Farm maybe I could help pay for a carer who'd look after Dad most of the time so Ty and his family wouldn't feel too tied down by it all.

In my fantasy, that's how it all works out but I haven't actually asked Ty yet. I haven't said anything to Dad either. I know he won't want to move. He promised Mum that he wouldn't and he's a man who keeps his promises. I never made that promise though. I never said I'd stay here and yet ... how can I go? My head is beginning to hurt, now. I need to concentrate on these foot rotations, I'm losing count.

Five … four … three …

'You don't mind, do you Rose?' He's looking disconcertingly straight at me now.

'I don't mind what?'

'You don't mind that we've stayed on at Clare Farm?'

I mind. I've minded it every hour of every day since Mum passed away. But I know very well why we're still here.

'Why d'you ask?' *Two … one.*

I glance back over at Dad who's suddenly gone quiet and is just sitting there, looking at me in an understanding and sorrowful way.

'Because I know you've been wanting to get away from here for a long time ... I want you to,' he stops and puts his hands to his throat. His voice is deserting him again. It comes and goes, even with the new medication that's supposed to help. Sometimes he can't utter a sound for days, and then the only thing that's left is whatever he can tell me with his eyes.

'Postman might just be late,' Dad gets out eventually. He *knows* what I've been waiting for all morning.

'He isn't late, Dad. He's not coming. He has no letters for us today, that's all.'

'You may still get your offer, Rose.'

Dad, *please.* He's looking at me in that funny way he has sometimes, like he could make the world all right for me just by the wishing of it but he can't. He can't make everything all right. He hasn't been able to do that for a long time.

'You know,' he leans over and his hand touches my shoulder softly. '… why I never moved us away from here, don't you? It's because this was the only one thing left that I could still do for her, Love.'

'I know.' I give the end of one of his socks a little tug, pinch his toes before he gets too maudlin. 'Next foot, please.'

'And you know what would happen the minute we left this

place - *if* we ever left it?' I follow his gaze out beyond the window again and I feel my heart sink.

'They had the big diggers out again earlier. I saw them, three of them, making for the Topwoods,' he mutters darkly.

Treacherously, I think; *let them. Let them wrench every single tree in the Topwoods out by its trembling, earth-caked roots and let them build a block of new high-rise flats up there. I don't care about the sodding trees! The trees were Mum's pet project.* I look at Dad painfully. *They were never mine, Dad. They were never yours. Mum was the only one of us who was passionate about conserving the land and now she's gone.*

'You've done your best, Dad,' I remind him gently. 'You've kept your promise to Mum for as long as you've been able, despite your injuries. But - if they ever did build on that land,' I say casually, 'would you be prepared to leave?' The shock in his eyes leaves me with no option but to immediately back-peddle furiously.

'They can't erect any buildings,' I remind him neutrally. 'Not as long as we're living here. They know you're …' I correct myself - 'that we're keeping an eye out.' Like David and Goliath, I think. Only Goliath has the big diggers and between us, me and Dad couldn't even make up one half of a David.

'We're not going anywhere just yet,' I say softly. But when I stand up, I can't resist going over and hoisting up the sash window behind him, leaning out as far as I dare, to see furthur up the lane, because I still wish I was going somewhere.

Omigod, there he is.

The postman.

The flutter of anticipation struggling with the possibility of impending disappointment in my belly is poignantly familiar. It is, after all, Christmas Eve.

That Downing College offer, it's a dream, that's all. A pipe dream. But - it would be a sign that things could change in life, a sign of hope where I haven't been able to see any for such a long time.

'Those diggers were probably drafted up here just in case they're needed later. The Met office has forecast snow on the way, lots of it.' I put on a smile. 'It's going to be a white Christmas, did you know, Dad?'

It's gone so quiet and still and peaceful outside. I watch the postman trudge wearily round the steep bend at the bottom of Asleps Lane. He's right at the end of his round, he's got to be, his post-bag is hanging limp and empty, slung over his shoulder. Has he even got anything left in there? If he's trekked all this way just to deliver another flier for the Indian takeaway in the village I am going to *die!*

'Look, it's started,' I say, pretending to myself that I'm not desperate for the post, playing that game again, because the outcome - if I let myself care - could be so cruel. 'Looks like the Met office were right.'

And right now the sky is a bright grey, expectant. As if all the world were just like me, waiting for something, on the verge of something important and … something is coming. Is it even remotely possible that my wish could have worked? I don't know quite what's coming, yet, but there's change in the air.

Is it good change? I hear the soft thud as the post arrives downstairs on the mat.

When I stick my hand out of the window, on the end of my fingertips I can feel the first of the frozen snow drops that come spinning out of a dark-bright sky.

Lawrence

23rd December West Camp Village, Jaffna

I didn't find Amma.

I sit up, startled, rubbing at my face to try and get my bearings. Beyond the clear plastic window of the tent I share with Joaquin, it is early outside, morning already. When did that happen?

The digital clock we keep on the fold-away table between us says 6.20 am. *No way, man.* I run my fingers through my hair, confused.

I didn't mean to go to sleep, I wasn't supposed to. What's happened to Sunny? The operation will have been over hours ago. *Damn it!* I flick the torchlight on and scramble around for something to put on over my T-shirt. Outside is cold. It's still raining. How am I ever going to find out how his op went at this early hour? There'll be a nurse on duty but it's unlikely she'll welcome me barging in on them at this hour. He'll be asleep - dosed up to the eyeballs, probably.

But what if he isn't? What if he's awake and scared and he's wondering where I am? Hell, why did I ever lie down on my sleeping bag, even for five minutes? I should have known I'd crash. *I'm* the closest thing Sunny's got to having an adult who looks out for him. I should have been there for him when he came out of Recovery and I wasn't.

It's a long way to the Recovery tent from here and there aren't many folk about yet. The guy who puts up the fliers on the fence gives me his usual grin when he sees me looking, but I'm not one of the poor sods stuck here wondering desperately what I'm going to do next. I notice he's taking more fliers down than he's putting up, today. Maybe people round here are running out of money. *Or hope?* I put my head down and keep on walking, aware that my presence out so early in the morning has been noted. I'm collecting a few curious looks from the military guards posted here and there along the way, too. They're here 'to keep the peace' and to make sure that 'people don't panic and do foolish things'. Like try to leave, maybe.

But that's not my business.

I need to concentrate on how I'm going to get in to see Sunny. I have to show my UN paramedic badge a couple of times. I pretend I'm going to relieve one of the nurses coming off duty and the guards don't know any better. It seems feasible and they let me pass.

By the time I get to the Recovery tent the sun is just rising. The rain has stopped for a few blessed minutes but the air is still dank and misty. The nurses are having an early morning cup of chai at their station, and they ignore me. The patients' beds are still quiet, not much movement around yet.

But Sunny isn't in Recovery. I rub at my eyes fiercely, aware that I'm still barely awake. He's got to be here, though. I saw them yesterday, about to wheel him away for the op - there isn't anywhere else he could be.

Unless something has gone badly wrong. I feel a spasm of fear in my chest. Where is he?

One of the women at the nurses' station looks up then. She waves, beckoning me over.

'Lawrence, he isn't here,' I watch her pull out an admittance list, as if to make doubly sure. 'That little lad. They didn't operate on him after all.'

'No?' I stare at her, open-mouthed. 'Are you certain?' He

was prepped and ready to go. What could have made them change their minds?

'It seems a red light patient came in and knocked him out of his slot right at the eleventh hour.'

The tightness in my throat slackens off.

'They've put him in the standby-suite. It'll still happen today,' she assures me. 'The best thing is,' she lowers her voice, 'It means he'll be seen by Mr Lazerev, if he's on this morning …'

Lazerev. I don't know him. There are so many doctors here, and every time you think you've got the hang of who's who, they change. Everybody changes. Except me. I've been here too long, that's why. It's time to move on.

'Lazerev's the best,' she's saying but my head's pounding like a hammer. 'Shall I take you to him?'

'I'm good, thanks.' I've got to get a grip. 'Thanks,' I say again, as she gives me a sympathetic look. I get to the Standby suite just as Sunny's being taken out to the bathroom.

'Hey, Big Man …' I give him a high five.

'Lawrence,' he says ruefully. 'As you see, I am still here.'

'Still here?' I crouch down by his chair and touch his cheek with the back of my hand. Why is it that he touches me so deeply, this one particular child? It's a question that's perplexed me for some time. All patients are important, and we're taught that none should be favoured. Besides, they come and go. And yet Sunny matters. He matters more and I don't know why. His dark eyes take me in shrewdly.

'Did you find her?'

'I'll fill you in, later,' I promise him. 'If I hold you up now we'll both get in trouble with the nurse,' I look up and wink at her.

'Plenty of time to catch up later,' she flushes pink and looks down but she's smiling. 'We've got a schedule to keep to.'

'Ah, I assume you know that young man?' From his Russian accent, I take it to be Mr Lazerev who appears behind me just as she pushes Sunny out of sight.

'Lawrence Macrae,' I turn and introduce myself. 'I've been

working with Sunny for some weeks now.'

'Lawrence. He's just been telling me that you went out to find one of his family members is that right?'

'Correct.' Behind him the guy I take to be his Registrar shifts from one foot to the other and I get the sense the two of them have been having some sort of discussion about Sunny.

'May I ask if you were successful?' Lazerev glances at his colleague, then back at me. 'It might have a bearing on what we undertake today …'

I shake my head, ruefully.

'Pity.' He taps his notes with his pen. 'I've had a look at the damage. If we went for a ray amputation,' he's saying thoughtfully, 'we could save the whole foot, you realise. Just take off two toes and the corresponding metatarsal bones.'

What did he just say? My heart skips a beat. He could save the foot?

'My problem is that'd leave him with an open wound for three months. If we can't guarantee antiseptic conditions for the duration of the healing period we could end up doing more harm than good. It's a pity he wasn't on the Aid Abroad list.' He glances at the Registrar again who lifts his shoulders slightly, as if to say there's nothing to be done about that.

'Aid *who*? I'm sorry, I haven't heard of …'

The Registrar shakes his head slightly now, his face closed. 'No point wasting time pursuing that, Mr Macrae. As far as I'm aware, they closed the list two weeks ago.'

'Even so …' my mind is racing ahead of me. Antiseptic conditions – is that all they need to agree to go ahead with this ray procedure? I appeal to Mr Lazerev now. 'Think about it. This child has no family left. He's got nothing, no life to go back to at all. But if we could save his foot, if there were any chance …?'

'But you say you don't know of anyone who could take him in? Anyone at all?'

I almost shake my head. Sunny hasn't got anyone. 'There may … be someone,' I get out.

24

The Russian takes me in for a moment. 'Is there or isn't there?'

I consider the situation rapidly. If I say there isn't anyone they are going to go in and take off Sunny's foot, right here, right now. He will be disabled for the rest of his life. That will affect his chances of getting work, of one day finding himself a wife … under these conditions, everything, in short that goes to make a life.

'Possibly,' I stall. 'I've still one other avenue left to try.'

'In that case, I need a moment with my Registrar, please,' he says.

I nod, and step outside, exchanging the shady area inside the tent for the brightening morning so they can confer privately for a moment. What did I do that for? I haven't any avenues left to try. Yesterday I saw first-hand what the situation was like in the place where Sunny came from.

I have no idea how I'm going to turn this around.

While they talk, I sit on an old abandoned orange crate and try and get my head around what Mr Lazerev's just told me. *Could* they do that thing he was talking about, just take off the toes? It seems too good to be true. Yet - from what this surgeon says - it now seems a possibility. If we could secure the right recovery conditions. Who can I ask? *Who?* There's got to be someone.

But there isn't, is there?

I haven't been awake all that long and the memory from yesterday comes as if from a dull, faraway place in my mind. Yesterday I managed to hitch a lift with Joaquin when I found out his team were going out to Katkulam. That's a village near where Sunny comes from, about an hour away from here. Turns out the landmine clearers go there every Wednesday. Someone like me wouldn't normally be allowed to go and Joaquin did his best to dissuade me. He was adamant that I wouldn't find any relatives out there but I had to go look. I'd promised Sunny I would.

I went to Katkulam, I drag my mind back to follow the train

of events that brought me here. I went to Katkulam because none of the new lot of refugees at East Camp had ever heard of Sunny and I still harboured some forlorn hope of finding a survivor from a village near his home who knew him. I don't really know what exactly I was expecting to find. Some sort of abandoned village, maybe. A few craters here and there where the bombs fell. Some damaged houses. Lots of debris. A few chickens scratching around in the dirt, one or two mangy dogs, I don't know. I didn't find that.

When we got to Katkulam I thought Joaquin had just stopped at some random place to take a leak, that he'd chosen the dimmest and darkest spot to do it because he knows how that freaks me out. They all get a rise out of that, joshing me cos I'm not scared of bombs, I'm not scared of fighter jets or any man but I'm scared of the dark. After a time when my eyes got acclimatised to the poor light I started to make out strange shapes, dark and crooked amongst the foliage. They really scared the shit out of me. Turned out they were the bombed-out shells of houses that had got covered in jungle creepers.

Then everyone got out of the jeep. Someone pulled at my elbow and told me I had to put my face-protection gear on. Everybody was taking great care about where they put their feet. I thought at first they were larking around but Joaquin assured me they weren't. They warned me to make sure I only stepped in their footsteps and nowhere else and that's when it dawned on me that they really weren't kidding. I'd known why they were out there but I'd imagined there'd just be the odd device planted here and there. It wasn't like that.

'This whole place,' Joaquin spread his arms out, encompassing as far as the eye could see, 'It's littered with UXOs. Unexploded ordinance,' he explained as my eyes must have widened questioningly. 'Landmines.'

It was unfathomable. The place was barely even recognisable as a village. Another few months and there would be virtually no sign left that anyone had ever passed this way let alone lived here.

No chickens. No dogs. No stubborn old people who'd refused to move still eking out an existence somehow, which is what – in the back of my mind – I know I'd been wildly hoping for.

Definitely no Amma.

I'd sat on the jagged edge of a broken wall and watched the landmine operatives carefully staking out the edge of one of the paddy fields and the entire thing felt surreal. The home that Sunny was so longing to return to - his house with the bright red front door, his mother's washing blowing like a row of celebration flags over their plot where a small pig ran about, the parade of banana trees like tall green soldiers lining up out front - that place existed only in his memory now, only in his heart. I got a bad feeling, sitting there yesterday afternoon, that all the people he had painted for me, they might exist only in his memory, too. They might be all gone, all his family, crushed by their own houses and buried in the deep earth under the creepers and he would never see any of them again.

So, no, I'm pretty darn sure that Sunny hasn't got anyone who'll be able to help him now.

I stand up abruptly as I hear the nurse calling my name. Mr Lazarev and his Registrar are both waiting for me when I pop my head round the tent flap and he beckons me back in.

'You see now here you have given me a problem,' I can hear a smile in his faint Russian accent and I get the impression that - somehow - I might just have set the cat amongst the pigeons.

His Registrar is looking stiff and taut-faced. 'If there is nowhere the patient can go to recover, it would be *negligent* not proceeding with the operation as planned,' he mutters under his breath.

Mr Lazarev looks at me as if I might have had a chance to think up a plan in the five minutes while they've been having their conference. I haven't though. I swallow nervously. I haven't, but I may yet.

'Sir,' I spread open my arms. 'If you could delay the operation by just … one hour …' My thoughts are jumping so fast I can

27

barely stop my words getting tangled up, 'by one hour,' I repeat, 'then I may be able to find the antiseptic conditions you require for recovery.'

The Registrar opens his mouth to protest. 'Aid Abroad's last scheduled flight out of here is New Year's Eve,' he points out - a week away. 'And granted, a space might open up on the flight,' he stutters, 'though it's unlikely. But that is beside the point. There are dozens of forms to fill in, people to be informed, before someone can be accepted onto the scheme.'

'One hour,' I plead, avoiding his eye contact and appealing instead to Lazerev, 'Just one hour.'

'He'd need a sponsor,' the Registrar says tightly.

'I'll find one.'

'There are protocols to follow,' he protests. 'The process takes weeks – even months, which you do not have, so you see, delaying the operation only ...'

'I'll *find* someone. I promise you.' The words are out of my mouth before I can process what I'm saying. I'd never even heard of Aid Abroad up to a few minutes ago. I have no idea what it would entail. What am I saying?

'The sponsor needs to have been in the EU country in question for a period of at least two years to be eligible ...'

'I'll find someone then. Let me try. Let me make it happen.' *How the hell am I going to do that? I don't have anyone in the UK anymore who I could call upon to help at such short notice. I've let all my friends and contacts go there, severed all ties ...*

'All right.' Even the Russian is looking at his watch now. 'This boy is pre-gangrenous, you understand,' he silences us both. 'Blood poisoning is a risk, and we've already delayed twenty-four hours. Okay,' he says briskly, suddenly making up his mind. 'You have until this afternoon, Mr Macrae. If you haven't located any suitable recovery conditions for him by then, I'm afraid we'll have to proceed as planned.'

The Registrar bristles a bit because he thinks this is all an unnecessary delay. I can tell that underneath he's certain he'll yet be proved right.

'Go to tent 249, East Camp,' he tells me. 'Ask for the Aid Abroad co-ordinator, a man named Michel Lestat, but I warn you …'

'Thanks. Thanks so much …' I scribble the details down.

'Next op will be at 2pm,' he says pointedly.

'Got that.'

I went out to Katkulam yesterday to see what might be salvageable from the remains of what used to be Sunny's life. What might be resurrected. The answer is; not much. I wanted to bring him some good news. That's why I have to pull this off. What better news than the possibility that we can salvage his foot? I'm going to have to catch my line manager Dougie and pray that he's in a charitable mood, that he'll be willing to stick his neck out and somehow help me get Sunny on that last flight out.

The Registrar leafs through his notes. 'So we'll need to hear from you before twelve-thirty?'

That gives me - I glance at the time - four hours from now. It's more than I asked for.

'Gotcha.' He thinks I won't do it, smug bastard. He thinks - he probably *knows* - I've got no chance in hell.

29

Rose

I feel sick.

'Anything for me?' I've made a point of coming down the stairs slowly, one at a time. When I get to the little round porthole window in the bend of the stairs I even stop for a bit to watch the postman on his way. I tell myself I'm trying to figure out if he's cute but the truth is I'm just staving off the evil moment when I finally learn whether my letter has arrived or not …

'There's one for you,' our home-help Mrs P is standing in the hall holding up two letters at arm's length. 'It feels like a card.'

Stop feeling my letters, I think, panicking that she's going to sweep away my last little bit of hope before I even get to the bottom of the stairs. 'And this one's for …' she screws up her eyes and balances her glasses right on the end of her nose. 'Oh. He's made a mistake with this one. This should have gone to the Macrae Farm.'

Damn it. Is there really only a card for us, then?

'Let me have a look …'

I jump the last two stairs and virtually tear the letter out of her hand. She's right; it feels way too much like a card for my liking. It is a card. With a cheque for fifty pounds attached;

'*From Uncle Ty, Auntie Carlotta and Samantha. Buy yourselves a little something from us.*'

I swallow.

It is over and the prickling at the back of my eyes warns me that I'm about to break down in front of her. There is no Uni offer for me. They don't want me anymore and I've missed the boat. I don't have any offers from other Universities to fall back on. It was always Downing College - my longest shot - or nothing.

I turn away from her, pretending to read the card over again but for a long, wooden moment I just stand there, trying to take it all in, feeling as if I'm not quite steady on my feet, as if I'm swaying. It's a horrible feeling; a feeling that I'm plummeting down a long, empty chasm and there's this sinking dread that any minute now I'm going to hit the bottom.

'Rose?'

I swallow; shove the cheque back into the envelope, aware of her watchful gaze.

'Are you sure that other one's not for us? Let me see.' That one's in a large white envelope. It looks official. Oh, let her have misread the name on it, *please, please.*

'This one's got Rob Macrae's name on it. I'm sorry, Rose.' Underneath her measured tone I detect a trace of sympathy. She knows as well as Dad does what I've been holding out for.

'Look - why don't you see if you can catch the postman and get him to run it over to the Macraes - it's his mistake.'

Catch the postman? I look at her blankly. Why on earth would I want to do that?

It takes a few moments for the hard truth to sink in.

'You might as well,' she reasons. 'We can't keep it. And it's better not to harbour any grudges over the Season of Goodwill and all that …'

What is she on about? I don't care about the Macraes and whether or not they get their letter! Doesn't she get it?

But right now I have to get away from here and do *something, anything* other than just stand here enduring that look of pity in her eyes … When I haul open the front door the cold air hits me like a slap in the face.

'Hey, postman!' My voice sinks like a stone in the cold noon air whereas he - unburdened of the heavy load of the last two letters at what must be the end of his shift - has a new spring in his step, he's nearly at the lane.

'*Wait up!*' I run after him and all the tension and the pain and the hope-against-hope waiting of the last couple of weeks which comes out in my strangled voice is enough to stop him dead in his tracks.

'You put this through the wrong door.' My voice comes out a mere croak but I wave the letter at him. 'It's for the next farm up.'

'You're kidding me?' The disappointment on his face almost matches mine. It *should* have been for me. My offer letter. My sign that there's still a door open somewhere for me…

'I'm not kidding you.' I wish I was. He squints at the address as I hold it up for him to see.

Bollocks, he mutters under his breath. Second that, I think. But now my throat has started feeling horribly sore. I need to go back upstairs and get into my bedroom so I can cry in peace.

'You couldn't … take it over for me, could you?' His plea as I turn to get back inside stops me in my tracks.

What?

'It's just that I should've finished this shift two hours ago. I kinda got lost. Hand it to your neighbours when you see 'em, could you?'

'*Our neighbours* are a mile and a half up the road,' I remind him. Hell, it's cold! Standing here in my slippers I can feel the heat draining away from my toes as we speak. A speck of snow lands on my nose now and another on my eyelids. He's got a nerve to ask. He must know they're not just next door. Besides; he's not our usual postman - a festive season recruit I'm guessing - so he won't know that the last people on earth I'd ever want to go out of my way to help would be the Macraes.

'They're not friendly neighbours,' I tell him slowly. He doesn't need to hear the whole story. 'And they've got dogs.' Four dogs, to be precise. Two Rotties and two Pitbulls last I counted.

'I already made their acquaintance,' he does a little twirl to show me and I see that his trousers and his jacket have huge great muddy paw prints down the back.

'They went for you?'

He nods and I give a resigned sigh. Didn't anyone warn him?

'Bill - our usual postman - he normally leaves their letters in the box on the other side of the fence.' My nose is starting to drip. I want to go back inside but he carries on talking.

'He told me about that but I couldn't find it. I couldn't see any dogs either so I went in. It's kinda the real reason why I'm so late, actually. And why I made a mistake with the letters.'

'I'm not taking it over there for you, I'm sorry.'

His phone goes off now - beep-beep - and he puts me on hold for a minute while he reads the text he's been sent. Whatever he's just read, he doesn't look too happy about that, either. He's not much older than me, really. He looks cold and tired and my heart goes out to him because I know how he feels. If it were anybody else in the world other than the Macraes involved …

'Here,' I hand him back the white letter firmly. 'You'll have to leave it in the box outside like Bill does.'

'It's just that …' he hesitates and I sense there's something else coming. 'If you took it to them then you could pick your own one up while you were there.'

My heart skips a beat. There's another letter?

'Say again?' I get out.

'Well, I only had three letters left to deliver. There were definitely two for Clare Farm, so if you've got the one that should have gone to Macrae …'

He bends over to open up his post-bag and I think for one wonderful moment he might be about to look to see if my letter could still be stuck in there. But he only brings out his gloves and puts them on.

'You're saying you must have put our other letter through Macrae's door? You … you're not very good at this, are you?'

'It's not a vocation,' he admits, then he stops, seeing my face. 'I'm sorry. I thought those dogs were going to gnaw my shins off.'

33

I must have panicked. I'm *really* sorry ...' He's sorry. *He's sorry* ... it's what he's prepared to do about it now that really counts. I take in a deep breath and ask the question.

'Who was the other letter for, I don't suppose you saw?'

'Two were addressed to Rose Clare. One was for R. Macrae,' he looks at me apologetically. 'Only now that I've posted it through their door, I'm pretty sure I'm not allowed to ask for it back.'

You're not?

'It was for me? *Rose Clare?*' My voice goes high-pitched as I grab hold of his arm and he looks a bit startled. 'You're sure about that?'

'I am sure. I noticed because Rose is my granny's name. I thought you'd be a little old lady like her.'

'Thanks.'

'You're anything but, though ...' He smiles and when he does his teeth show, all even and white and I realise he really is rather cute.

And more importantly, he's told me something that's just rekindled my hope.

'Flattery's not going to get you out of this mess,' I'm saying but right now it's difficult not to smile back, it's difficult to stop my heart from thudding in a sudden whoosh of excitement because if he's right and there is another letter for me then ... it would be the best Christmas present in the whole world, ever.

If it's true.

'I don't suppose you noticed where it was post-marked?'

'Sorry. Only thing I did notice ...' he screws up his eyes now, recollecting something, 'Was that a reply seemed to be indicated - whoever sent it had hand-written something along the top. *Please reply by* - That sort of thing.'

'By when?' My heart has started racing again. *Could* it be from the lecturer who interviewed me? She'd hinted at the time she might need a quick response. Something about the fact that I was a re-interviewee, that I'd already been made an offer last year ...

'I … I couldn't say now. I'm sorry. You really need to get hold of it, don't you? I realise it's started snowing.' He glances up and the sky above us has become dull and leaden looking. 'If you've got someone who could run you up there … your dad?' he offers helplessly.

I blink. My dad was the victim of a random attack five years ago that left him with an inoperable embolism deep within his brain. He doesn't drive. He doesn't go out of the house anymore. He can't stand for very long and he rarely even leaves his room. Mrs P and her husband who drives her about wouldn't want to go up there either, I know that.

There isn't anyone. I shake my head at him.

'So …?' I'd go and leave him to it, but I need an absolute assurance from him now that he's going to get my letter back.

The temporary postman makes a strange noise in his throat.

'Are you going to help me get it back or aren't you?'

'Um. That text was from my girlfriend.'

Oh. Of course it was. I fold my arms and stare at my wet slippers while he gets out his sob story. He wants to go off-duty and he'll say *anything* now to get out of this.

'Thing is, we're supposed to be at this Christmas Eve gig tonight and I'm already running two hours late and …'

And what? I look at him crossly. Just because I haven't got anywhere to go out tonight doesn't suddenly make me responsible for this mess. All these things are his problem. Not my problem. My mis-delivered letter is his problem too. Except he doesn't seem to care about that.

'I'm really sorry, Rose. Look. Maybe the Post Office *can* do something about it. Ask them.'

'I thought you *were* the Post office …' I begin, but he runs on.

'It's just that - being Christmas and all - it'd surely be quicker to get it yourself? There'd be less red tape and all that? Give your neighbours a ring first. Maybe they'd be prepared to chain up those dogs for you?'

'I can't. Oh, for heaven's sake! We haven't actually spoken to them for … for years.' He puts his phone away, having the grace to look at least a little concerned.

'Will you be all right, Rose?'

I stick my face in my hands and the cosy daydream I'd been having a few minutes ago disappears into the icy air. I'm on my own with this one, aren't I? Just like I always am these days, for everything. I shake my head at him watching his face redden and then, before he can say another word, I turn on my heel.

'Hey, Rose …' he calls, but I ignore him.

He's not going to help me. He's got a gig to go to and he thinks this'll all be sorted with one quick phone call and a reconciliatory 'Merry Christmas' down the line.

If only he knew about us and the Macraes he'd understand.

The dogs are by far the least of it.

Lawrence

11.30 am   23rd December   West Camp village, Jaffna

'*Christ.*' Dougie lifts up his hand as I come into the crowded tent which serves as his office area. My boss is shaking his head at me. He's got his other hand covering the mouthpiece of his phone and he seems to be breathing unnaturally hard.

I stop where I am. To say that he looks upset would be understating it. *Fuck.* I take in the time on my wristwatch. If he's in the middle of some other crisis right now this is going to be damn inconvenient. I need his help, and I need it now, this can't wait. I take a highlighter pen and write in big letters on a piece of paper 'URGENT!' and hold it up for him to see. He just narrows his eyes at me.

'Macrae. With an M,' he's saying. 'No, not a Y. That's c-r-a-e at the end.' What's that? Who's he speaking to? I get my boss's attention, make a pointing motion with my finger.

Me?

He nods curtly and motions for me to sit. He goes quiet then, listening to whoever's on the other end of the phone for what seems like a very long time. It doesn't sound good. Who could be talking to him about me, I wonder? And Dougie doesn't look too great, either. He's put his hand to his head as if it suddenly feels heavy, his elbow propped wearily on the table. Whoever Dougie's got on the other end of that line, he isn't saying much in reply.

37

While I wait I become slowly aware of the itch as a trickle of sweat is running down my back, the fact that my whole body seems to have become as tense as a coiled-up spring. In the silence in his tent I strain my ears to catch the odd word here and there but all I can pick up is what sounds like one very long, very angry rant at the other end. It goes on and on. Man, this *really* doesn't sound good. It sounds like it's something serious, whatever it is. Very serious.

I rub at my face, and my skin feels tired and grubby. I haven't shaved yet today, I remember. I haven't had a shower. When I left my tent at the crack of dawn this morning that felt okay. Nobody much was about, the day hadn't properly begun and it didn't matter. Sitting in my boss's office with an atmosphere fit to rival an electrical storm brewing, right now, it feels like it does matter. Who the hell is that on the end of the line?

I don't let myself think of the worst it could be.

I came away from all that years ago. I came away and I've stayed away. Time and distance - and constant occupation, so that the mind's never allowed to dwell on the past - I've found these to be great healers. No, it won't be *that*.

The only other thing that comes into my mind is that Aid Abroad guy who I just went to see. Could it be him? I only left his office fifteen minutes ago. A jobs-worth if I ever met one. As predicted by Lazerev's Registrar, I got nowhere. I pressed my case, I admit it. I accused him of incompetence, of maladministration; damn it, he as much as admitted to me that there's at least one space on that last flight out of here on New Year's Eve. Sunny could be on that. But pen-pusher Lestat said it didn't matter; all the forms that have to be filled in, in triplicate, have not been filled. I told him I didn't give a damn. We're talking about a young lad's whole life here, but he wouldn't budge. I know there are protocols and procedures that have to be followed - there always are. And more than that, there are logistics that have to be sorted; Sunny won't just need a sponsor. He'll need medical care put in place, immediate assistance for when he lands, accommodation

38

and so forth.

But … I sit up rigid on the canvas chair that Dougie's just directed me to, and will myself to breathe normally while my precious minutes are ticking away … sometimes protocols and procedures can be expedited. Paperwork can be pushed through at miraculous speed. Helpful and willing voluntary medical staff can be located, I know this. I've seen it happen before, where there's enough goodwill and co-operation between people; miracles can happen.

I look up at my boss and the discomfort I've been feeling grows a little stronger.

What's Dougie so mad at me for?

I can see his jowl wobbling from here. He's usually this big-hearted Northerner, who can't do enough for you, nothing's too much trouble for him. Usually, we get on like a house on fire; he likes me because I work hard and I'm good at what I do. I'm damn good at it, actually. I get the job done and I don't clock watch. But right now he won't even look at me. He's got his eyes downcast, and his mood - I can feel it - is growing blacker by the moment.

I think back a minute. I didn't say anything so bad to that Lestat dude. I pushed it as hard as I could but I could tell fairly quickly he wasn't going to budge, that I'd need help. That's why I've come to Dougie, who's got the clout to move things if he wants to.

Man I'm biting my nails again, and they're already down to the quick.

'Am I in trouble?' I try and get eye-contact but his face is closed, his mind still on the caller. I've been in trouble before. If this is just about what I said to Lestat I can handle it. If it's about … that other thing, then that's a whole other deal. My whole life might be about to unravel if that ugly matter has somehow managed to find its way to the surface. I search his eyes for clues, but what I see there doesn't leave me much room for hope. Dougie looks absolutely devastated. Has someone found out who I am? The police have cottoned on to where I am - is that it? I thought - I'd let myself come to believe - that nobody cared anymore. It was a terrible thing I did, I know it was. But … time moves on. I've put it all behind me, made a new life - what else could I do?

Finally Dougie puts the phone down. Something in his voice is cracked and broken.

'Why did you do it, Lawrence?' I don't answer. Do *what* is the question? What does he know?

'Come *on*,' my boss stands up abruptly and he's a formidable six foot six. Eighteen stone. And getting angry. 'I want some answers, Lawrence, and I want them now.'

I bite my tongue. Fine. I admit I've lied to him about some things. At my job interview, some truths had to be stretched. Not about my experience, I'm fully qualified for this job, but about other things …

'That man almost had my ear off do you realise? He's doing his nut!' I stare at the ground, at the same pink and grey plastic sheeting that looks like a carpet that graces every tent down this row and I think; a detective who was looking for me, who maybe thought he'd caught up with me after all this time - he wouldn't be *doing his nut*.

'Who was it?' I ask mildly.

'Please. Don't come the innocent with me. You know full well who.'

I decide to take a chance.

'If that was the Aid Abroad guy, I wasn't rude to him. I was relatively polite. Look, the reason I'm even in here right now is to ask if you can help me with something. I haven't got long before they operate on Sunny and if I don't find someone who's prepared to put in place all the paperwork for him they're going to hack his foot off.'

My boss wipes his hand over his brow and gives me a dumbfounded look.

'What in hell's name are you talking about, Macrae? I'm referring to the captain of the Sri Lankan Camp Police force whose nose you broke a couple of nights ago. His CO has just got wind of it and is demanding your immediate release into his custody.'

Fuck. I make to get up out of the chair but then, with Dougie still towering over me, think the better of it.

'I'd forgotten about him.'

'You had, had you? I was rather hoping that was the reason for your unannounced visit to my desk this morning. Otherwise why wouldn't you have been on ambulance duty with the rest of the crew who were expecting you, I believe, over one hour ago?'

I'd forgotten about that too. Double fuck. I cover my face with my hands.

'You're really losing it, aren't you?' I feel Dougie's hand on my shoulder, for a moment compassionate. 'I warned you, Lawrence. I told you at our last assessment that I felt you hadn't been up to speed for a while now. Not your fault. I told you. We have to go off duty for a bit or we all get like this. It's called burnout.'

'I didn't go missing this morning.' Bugger it, I'm losing time here. Dougie's still seething from the bollocking that guy's just delivered down the phone about me, but I haven't got time for his anger or his compassion or even his attempt at a counselling session. If we're going to move on Sunny's case this morning we need to do it fast.

I get the feeling that the goodwill I was hoping for isn't going to be forthcoming, though.

'Just explain to me,' he pleads. 'Why *the hell* did you do it? I know you young men - you have to witness a lot of difficult things out here. It's no joke. But if you're spoiling for a fight why choose a high-ranking officer to deck? You've got to have known there'd be consequences.'

'I didn't know his rank, but it wouldn't have made any difference,' I mutter. 'He was knocking that girl about and someone had to stop him. No one else did.'

'Nobody's suggesting you didn't do the right thing to stop him, Lawrence. You just didn't have to break his nose. You didn't have to pummel him into the ground and leave him for a rag doll. The guy's due to get married in a week's time for Pete's sake!'

41

'To *her?*'

'Who cares who he's getting married to?' he glares at me. 'The only thing we have to worry about here is that this man's daddy is one important honcho in this vicinity. He's somewhat upset right now because his only son's wedding pictures aren't going to look so pretty. You can understand that?'

'Yes, Dougie,' I mutter under my breath. I need to talk to him about Sunny.

'You've got some serious anger issues, you know that, right?'

'Yes, Sir.'

'Yes, Sir,' he echoes, turning away from me in despair. 'Issues that could end up seeing you acquainted with the inside of a jail cell. Are you prepared for that?'

I'm well aware. I put my head down and keep silent. Dougie's rummaging around on his desk. I have no idea what for. I want to tell him about Sunny's predicament. I'm bursting to bring it up again but I think that might just be the straw that breaks the camel's back.

'I'm going to get the staff physician to sign you off on a breakdown ticket. That'll state you're unfit for any further duties at present but it'll also - with a bit of leverage - give me the excuse I need to put you on the next flight out of here before you're required to face the charges this blasted CO is going to make. Understood?'

I stare at him for a minute. If I'm correct he's just fired me, in the kindest possible way.

'Dougie, I ...'

'No.' He holds up his hand and silences me. 'I know what you're going to say. You broke the guy's nose, Macrae! Forget about that boy Sunny. You can't help him. Forget about everyone else out here, it's all over for you. This time round, anyway. You've been here a year already and it's two days before Christmas - isn't it about time you went back to say hi to your family at least?'

'*My family* ...' the words get stuck in my throat. Dougie doesn't know about my family. I start to shake my head but my boss isn't having any of it.

'Oh come on, lad! I've picked up from the beginning that you haven't been keen to return home but isn't it time you put whatever it was to one side? You can't stay here any longer.' He pauses, then, 'You've done these people a great service, Lawrence, don't let's run the risk of tarnishing your record just because we didn't recognise when enough was enough.'

I just stare at Dougie for a moment. His choice of words has just cracked open some long-sealed memories. This isn't the first time in my life I've been forced to move on. I'd hoped things would be different here, that I'd get a chance to settle, maybe?

But that is not the story of my life.

'Your hound gone off roaming again, boy?' My father's observation had seemed innocent enough. I should have known it wouldn't be.

But on the first morning of the week my life fell apart I wasn't thinking about that. My dog Kahn - part-wolf and part Alsatian - had always been a free spirit; running off for a few hours was just something he did at times. All my tired brain could register at that moment was if Kahn had gone AWOL, I wouldn't need to take him out for his morning walk before I left for work.

'He'll be back,' I told my father. He had to be. Kahn was the one thing from home I was planning on taking with me when I left Macrae Farm. Only Dad didn't know about my plans yet, did he? My plans to take Mum and Pilgrim as far away from Macrae Farm and him as we could possibly go. My plans that we should just disappear, find some place where he could never discover us, live out the rest of our lives in peace and free from fear. I'd glanced at him uneasily as he shook open his animal-feed catalogue. I knew I couldn't afford for him to even suspect what my plans were or there'd be hell to pay.

The thought crossed my mind.

'Kahn wasn't with the others at the feeding bowls last night either, was he?' Could he have been missing for longer than I'd

realised?

Dad didn't respond, just commented to no-one in particular; 'I see that Bailey's trying to salvage what's left of his rare-breed stock.'

'Pity. There are only three of his type of pig left in the world now, aren't there Dad?' My younger brother had looked up from his toast, his round face aiming to please. Pilgrim didn't know we were leaving, yet. Mum just nodded, affecting interest, carried on her ghost-like activities around us in the background of the kitchen, stirring the pot. I glanced at her over the top of Dad's catalogue, waiting for a co-conspirator's sign, the slightest raise of the eyebrows, anything, that'd say to me 'We're on the same team and working together so we can leave; soon we won't have to listen to this rubbish ever again …'

My father was an enthusiast, as well as a trader. On the farm, the Large Saddlebacks and the Tamworths still rooted around in their pens; officially, he was a pig farmer though it was an open secret that the pig farming had never been where he made his real money. No, my dad had 'other concerns', mostly illegal ones and it was this empire that he'd assumed me and Pilgrim would eventually want to become a part of. Dad had made no secret of his displeasure that I'd already refused to start work for him that summer. I'd gone for a holiday job at a local dog breeders in the next village down, instead.

'It's a pity, isn't it, Lozza?' my brother had turned to me that morning, wanting to include me in his commiserations, "... about Bailey's pigs?"

I remember my father glanced over the top of his catalogue to see if I'd respond as well, make some appropriate comment that'd show I cared.

I didn't. My father knew I wasn't interested. Not interested in his pigs, not interested in his money, not interested in him. It bugged him, that. I knew it bothered him deeply that I wanted nothing to do with him. That I wouldn't yield; that no matter what he did he was never going to fashion me into his own mould. I put down my mug, looked away from him, stared out towards the fields *beyond the open window.*

On the first morning of that final week all I knew was that I had to get us away from there. I had to keep my focus on that goal. I was going to work and save and keep my head down and before the new term started for my brother I'd have all of us out of there.

I hadn't bargained on what was about to happen next.

Rose

I slipped out of the house quietly.

Dad was asleep and Mrs P was pottering around in the kitchen. I left her a note by the door to say I'd be back soon, and she won't leave the house till I return. I figured the less I said about where I was going, the better. They won't like it. But I couldn't hang about waiting till January for the Post Office to get my letter back. If I wait till January, that's too long, it'll be too late.

It's already gone one o'clock.

By the time I turn to look over my shoulder at the patchwork of fields and country lanes spread out behind me all I can see is everything getting covered over with white at a rate of knots. I'm going to have to step on it. I'm at the juncture on the hill where the road forks to the right. It joins the narrow footpath towards Macrae Farm away from the main road and at the moment it looks like really dodgy footing.

I stop for a moment, punching my hands together in my gloves, stamping my feet to keep the momentum going. I both want and don't want to go to the Macraes in equal measure. If I go ... I imagine myself powering up the hill, arriving at the Macraes, knocking on their heavy wooden door which doesn't have a doorbell.

How's it going to be, to stand there at their doorway and when they open the door say to them, just as you would to a *normal* neighbour - 'There's been a mix-up with the letters; you've got mine and can I have it back please?' How would that feel? Could I do that? The strange thing is, even though they're our nearest neighbours they haven't had any contact with us for so long I doubt any of them would even recognise me.

I couldn't have been much older than eleven the last time Rob Macrae came down to Clare Farm. He'd come to Dad a few months previously claiming he'd got this opportunity to get a National Trust grant to restore an old ruin on his land – but only if he owned enough of the original land that went with it. He said in order to get the grant he'd need to buy Topfields and Topwoods - two pieces of adjoining woodland that belonged to Clare Farm. Convinced it could only be good for Merry Ditton if the ruin were restored, Dad had agreed to sell the land to our neighbour for a pittance. That was before someone tipped Dad off – it turned out Rob Macrae's real intention was never the castle project, he wanted to sell the woodland at Topfields off to some developers who were after it. Dad had tried to pull out of the sale.

I guess that's the first time we learned what Rob Macrae could be like when crossed. I remember him storming over to ours in his four by four, coming up and hammering on the door with three of his mutts in tow, all of them unmuzzled. I hid behind the telephone chair in the hallway and Dad never asked him in. I can still recall our neighbour's blue eyes blazing in the doorway, that red hair which he used to slick back with hair oil, the barely disguised threat in his voice when he warned my dad;

'Back off, Clare.' He'd looked over towards Mum, then, something unmistakably nasty in his eyes. 'I don't lose any sleep over the likes of *you* …' He made me cringe, but Mum wasn't scared of him, I could see that. She looked him steadily in the eye until, in the end, it was Rob Macrae who had to look away first; something about her unseated him.

But the way he said those words stuck in my mind for a long time. The implication that 'the likes of us' were somehow so beneath his contempt as to be not worth a moment's consideration; that he was a man who - given the opportunity -

would be ruthless.

My parents fought back with every means they could, of course. They lodged objections with local planning, gained some support in the village, but whatever the rights and wrongs of it, it was pretty clear a lot of people in Merry Ditton were reluctant to get on the wrong side of the Macraes. In the end, the matter was ruled in their favour.

I wipe the snow out of my eyes.

That was the year Mum joined forces with her eco-activist friends, setting up camp in burrows they dug out under Topwoods. It was a form of protest that would effectively halt any tree-removal work for as long as they remained there. That was when the real rot set in between our families; sometimes I think that maybe if that hadn't happened, then … what happened after wouldn't have occurred either.

But … I can't think about that now. I can't. What's done is done. I *know* what the Macraes are really like, and I know that Dad would be dead set against me having any contact whatsoever with them. Even now, my phone is buzzing. It's home. Mrs P has discovered my note, no doubt, and that's her, wanting me to return. But I am not going back yet.

Sod that.

I am just going to go and do it. With any luck the Macraes will all be out and it'll be one of their farmhands who opens the door. I might not even come across any dogs. It is so quiet and still and the snow keeps on falling. It's landing on my nose and cheeks, I swear I'm actually breathing it in. In the silence my own breath sounds very loud in my ears. It sounds uneven and way too fast, and inside, with every step I take, every fibre of me is calling - *just get out of here, Rose, don't go up that way, walk away now.*

But I can't. I can't walk away from the only chance I may ever get to leave this place.

I'm about one hundred metres in, when I become aware of the crunch of another set of footsteps ahead of me round the corner. There is someone else on the path. I stiffen, stop walking, listening out as hard as I can and now I can hear that whoever it is, they also have a dog with them. I can hear it snaffling around and - suddenly, as it must have become alerted to my scent - there's the sound of a low snarling noise coming from its throat. *Shit.* I've changed my mind.

I've changed my mind! My legs have turned to water but I can't get away now, it's too far to track back onto the main road before I'm spotted.

'Get back here Tosser, you stupid Mutt, there's no one ...' The bull mastiff appears first, tugging fiercely at its ginger-haired owner who's yanking back on its leash. The path is too narrow for me to pass by him easily, and I can see from the enjoyment that rapidly replaces the surprise on his face that he's thinking exactly the same thing.

'What have we here, Tosser? A trespasser, I think.'

Inwardly, I'm cringing because we both know that's exactly what I am. The Macraes have signs up everywhere to the effect that trespassers on their land will be 'dealt with.' The dog starts up a low growl in its throat and the owner yanks it down into a sitting position. Then he kicks it, hard, with his boot for good measure giving me a sick feeling in my stomach. It yelps and falls silent.

'Gotta show them who's boss, don't you?' His piggy blue eyes, scrutinising, don't leave my face for one second and it dawns on me that he's trying to figure out who I am.

I know who he is, well enough. Pilgrim. Me and my friend Shona used to sneak up to the top of Asleps Hill when we were kids and watch his antics on his dad's farm when he thought no one was looking. *Why* we used to find that entertaining I can't imagine now - it was the danger, I suppose; what might have happened if we'd been caught. Children always like to run away from monsters don't they? Whatever the reason, I know him far better than he knows me and he was a spiteful and mischievous kid. Apart from size he hasn't changed all that much physically and I don't suppose he's that different inside, either. I suppress the shudder that runs through me at the memory.

'And you are …?' he demands now. Across the cold air I can smell his breath. I can smell the fustiness and the farm-smell on his clothes.

'I'm your neighbour,' I tell him.

'Are you?' He fumbles for a cigarette in his jacket pocket, an automatic reaction to cover up his surprise, I'm guessing. He holds his hand protectively over the light for a few seconds.

'Don't see much of you, do we? How's your dad?' He arches his eyebrows curiously, as if we pass the time of day like this all the time, as if he has a right to ask.

'He's - *fine*,' I breathe.

'Is he fine? Thought we heard something about Jack Clare going into Forsythes Oldies home at one point.'

'Well, he's not going to Forsythes.'

'Heard some talk that you might be selling up, then?' He blows a long line of smoke just short of my face. 'My old man nearly made you an offer …' A small smile crosses his face and I remember that they've wanted us out of here for years.

'We aren't going anywhere, Pilgrim.'

'Pity.' His piggy blue eyes don't leave my face for one second and the horrible thought crosses my mind that he might already know more than I do – what if he's seen my Uni letter and he *knows* I'm not going anywhere?

'Is it?' I ask uneasily.

'Pretty girl like you shouldn't be stuck on a farm all her life - what's your name again?'

'Rose,' I tell him through gritted teeth. I don't want to tell him my name. I don't want to stand here pretending to be civil. I don't want anything to do with him. 'Look, I know this is your land but I'm not trespassing. I've got a very good reason to be here. If you'll just let me pass …' I make to slide past him but he steps smartly in front of me, so I can't.

'Hold your horses, *Rose*.' He tries to grab hold of my elbow but I shake him off. 'Whoa,' an unpleasant look crosses his face.

50

'*That* wasn't very friendly was it, Rose? And you have such a sweet name, too. You're a Rose with thorns, though, eh?' He composes himself now, pleased at his own wit.

'You're not thinking of showing any of those thorns to me, are you, darling?' He makes to chuck me under the chin and I take a step back in horror.

'Shove off, you creep.'

'That's not very neighbourly of you, is it?' He pulls an annoyed face at my reaction. The dog starts up its low growling again and this time he doesn't silence it.

'I've got to ...' I swallow, hard. 'Look. I need to speak to your parents. Let me by or let me go, you can't keep me here.'

'Whatever's the rush though? What does she want to see the folks for, eh, Tosser?' He looks at me curiously. 'It must be something very important, I'm thinking?'

'Important enough.'

'Important enough to tell me, then.'

I frown. I don't *want* to tell him. My letter feels far too private and too personal to share with him and yet I suppose I'm going to have to if I want his co-operation.

'Postman mis-delivered a letter.' I give a little shrug like it's important in a boring sort of way - like a bank letter or something. 'I need to get it back, that's all.'

'A letter? That's it?' He sounds disappointed. 'Still, this letter of yours - is it important enough for you to pay Pilgrim a little toll to let you pass?' He pushes his gloved hand through his snow-filled hair and it dawns on me that he thinks he's a looker.

'Toll?' Is he after *money* now? 'I haven't got any ...' then I see that he's puckering up and it isn't money he's after at all. He's got me boxed in so close up against the brambles I can smell the beer on his breath. I actually think I am going to throw up.

'The only thing I'll give you is a kick in the goolies if you don't let me pass,' I glower at him, but it's pure bravado. He's got the upper hand because he's stronger than me and he's got the vicious dog and we're all alone up here. He knows it, too. I can

51

barely move. He laughs, and I know that logically, now's the time to start feeling what he wants me to feel - scared - and to quit gracefully, but for some reason his stupid smirking only makes me feel madder.

'You think … you think everyone in your family can do what they like around here. That you're immune to any come-back for anything you do, but you aren't. You think you Macraes aren't ever going to have to *pay* for what you did to my dad?' *Shit - where did that come from? I didn't mean to say that.* His face is about an inch away from mine and up to this point he is still smirking,

'… *What* did you just say?'

'Because you will pay for what you did to him. One way or the other, I promise you that.'

'Oh! Rose,' he laughs delightedly. 'I like a little spirit. Thing is, my family were cleared … Ow! Dammit. My … my…' He puts his hand in between his legs now as if he's suddenly experienced a sharp pain in his privates. He jerks his head back up, looking at me in shock and horror, but it was nothing to do with me. I didn't touch him. I wouldn't want to touch him with a ten foot barge pole.

He steps back a fraction.

'Steady on now, Rose! No evidence was ever brought forward to suggest we had anything to do with what happened to your dad that night…'

'No it wasn't. But *I know* your family had everything to do with it. People round here might carry on as normal, pretending that you Macraes are just a regular set of people, because it suits them to think like that. I know different.' He's breathing much harder now than he was a minute ago. He throws his lit fag down into the snow and crushes it in with his foot.

'Oh yeah?' He lifts his chin now. 'What do you know, Rose Clare?'

I shrug, feeling my face flaming because he's right. I can suspect all that I like but I have no evidence, nothing to bring them to book with. I don't have to let on, though. Let him squirm a bit. I'm dicing with danger here, being reckless, I know I am - but what have I got to lose?

'I'll tell you what I know,' he hisses into my ear. 'I heard your mam was a witch. That if you looked at her the wrong way she reckoned she had the power to turn you into a toad,' he sneers.

'*Some* people already are toads.' I give him a withering look. 'She couldn't turn them back into people, either.'

He stares at me blankly for a moment. Then;

'Hell!' He bends over double suddenly. 'What the ...?' He looks up at me and there's a confusion of fear and superstition in his eyes. 'What do you think you're doing, woman?'

I'm not doing anything. He's drunk, clearly. I can't account for his pain. His dog has stopped snarling and has started whining piteously now.

'Nothing.'

'... because I've heard things about you, too.' He turns away from me, wincing. 'My dad used to watch you and your mam up to your shenanigans on them Topfields. You're no regular girl either, are you, Rose Clare?'

'What're you talking about?' What have I got to do with anything? He's just a stupid drunk.

'Look. I never had *nothing* to do with what happened to Jack Clare. Hear that? Nothing. So don't you go taking your pay-back on me, understood?'

I stare at him blankly for a minute. What does he imagine I could possibly do to him, anyway?

Use the dark arts?

I slide out of his way while he's still hunched over in pain and push aside the uncomfortable memory that I did threaten this man with a kick a moment ago. I didn't touch him, but I've heard Mum say often enough that 'energy follows thought'.

Huh, well - I glance up at the leaden sky - if this is power, Mum, it isn't the kind of power I want in the world. My education's the only thing that's going to give me that.

I glance at him surreptitiously. Maybe I can get out of here? Leg it now, while he's … indisposed? I would, but he sinks down into the snow, moaning, suddenly.

'Get me an ambulance,' he gets out through gritted teeth. Then he looks up, a beseeching expression replacing the angry demand on his face. 'Stop it, Rose Clare. Leave me be,' he says through puffs of breath.

'I am leaving you be, you idiot!' 'My mum was a healer, not someone who hurt people,' I throw at him, but he only puts his hands up over his face, as if to ward me off. Well, let him think what he will. I don't *like* it, but it's got him off my back usefully enough.

I'd laugh in his face except it really isn't funny. It isn't funny that we have to live on the doorstep of people who are so bigoted and superstitious and stupid and it *really* isn't funny that - even after all this time - the legacy of misunderstanding my mum still lingers on.

'Come on Rosie-red. See what you can see …!' We're standing on the edge of Topfields, Mum and me, gathering cowslips. I'm twelve years old and I don't want to be here, too old for this already but her own enthusiasm never wanes.

'Come on,' she urges, pressing more flowers into my palms but my hands are already full. She wants me to make a cowslip flower ball, a totsy. I look down at the sorry bunch of flower stalks we've gathered, their drooping heads of golden bell-shaped flowers already wilting in the heat of my palms.

'Look,' she says, her deft fingers opening up one of the tiny yellow flower-heads. She shows me the profusion of ruby-red seeds underneath, laughing with delight at it. It's pretty in its own way I know that but I don't care. Doesn't she see I am growing up? I think; I don't want to play with these weeds any more. I'm only here because I want to talk to her about the skiing trip that's being organised at school. How all my friends are going and that's what I'd really like for my birthday next spring and how you need to think

about these things in advance.

'Make a totsy, Rose. Let's find out who your true love will be.'
'No.'

'Come on, don't be scared.' She's standing in front of me, her long black hair billowing out in the breeze behind her and she's laughing, confident because all this is her arena; the fields and the open air and all the small flowers of the earth, this is her playground where she runs free and I wish that she would stay here, that things could go back to being the way they used to be but I'm growing older and she's moving on and I don't think things can ever be the same.

In a few days she'll go back to her friends and continue with the woodland vigil she's been keeping for the past four weeks in underground tunnels they've dug out in the land under Topwoods. Like badgers in a burrow, she says to me. I tell her that sounds dark and smelly and muddy but she only laughs. Some of them have made houses up in the trees too. They do it to protect the woodland because as long as they're there the trees can't be torn down to make way for development. She wanted me to go and spend some time there with them, understand what it is they're trying to do but I won't so she came back home for a few days instead.

But she won't stay.

Even now she's got me doing things I don't really want to do, being places I don't want to be, like up here. Mum doesn't worry about other people, but all I ever think about when she drags me up here is how close we are to Macrae land. How we shouldn't stray over the boundaries because I've seen Rob Macrae looking over at us often enough. He parades up and down sometimes with his gun, shooting at pheasants, glaring at us. I don't like it but all Mum will say is not to worry, she's put in protection. That's all she ever says. None of these people are ever going to hurt you, my Rosie, she says.

'Titsy Totsy tell me true,
who will I be married to?'

She laughs, and her laughter is deep and open. It seems to me that it rings out over every blade of grass in the flower meadow beneath us. I am sure it echoes in the topmost branches of all her beloved trees, and then … her open hands fly up underneath mine. She forces my hands up, pushing them so fast that all my flower stalks go sailing merrily up into the air. They go so much higher than I thought they would. My face turns upwards to watch them, the sky is full of powder puff clouds, a momentary backdrop of deep, cold blue and then my flowers are scattering all over the ground like golden raindrops and she's standing there, watching me, an intent look on her face.

'What did you see, Rosie-red?'

'Nothing.' I fold my arms, drawing an exaggerated sigh but we both know that I saw something. I know she saw it too. I saw … something that was nothing, a shadow so fleeting it could have been only a fleck in the corner of my eye.

'Let it settle,' she says softly. I don't want to speak to her about this. It feels as if she is intruding in a place that should be mine. Step back, step back … I feel an upset deep in my stomach now, a sadness I cannot place. I don't want to go to these places she goes to, even if it's true what she says; that she could teach me to go there, that I could. I don't want to be a hedge witch, Isla. I don't want to. Leave me alone! I turn my head away from her.

Away from her prying gaze, I run through what I know I just experienced in my mind.

I saw a man running through Topfields. A man with dark hair. He was running for his life. Shall I tell her that? I hardly saw him, but I felt … I felt him, I felt all his sadness and his fear and all his goodness rolled into one. Quick as the flick of a switch, as the flowers rained down all around us, titsy totsy, I knew that he was the one who should be mine.

I am twelve years old, only twelve, but there's a place in my heart that's far older than that. I didn't properly see him. But in those few fleeting moments I recognised him. My mate. My companion. My love.

He should be, but … but what is it that I didn't see? I couldn't *see it. There was something else, I know that, but it was veiled from me. I'm not sure I want to know, either.*

'What did you feel?' She knows. I can hear it in the compassion in her voice. And I sense that she knows even more than I do; she knows what will become of him, too.

'I didn't see him,' I tell her stubbornly. 'Titsy totsy - it didn't work. It wasn't like I thought it would be.'

'Magic never is,' she says softly. She comes and pushes the hair away from my eyes, holds my face so gently in her hands, so tenderly. Then her eyes narrow, as if she's seen something, realised something, her voice gets thinner and I get the feeling her next words are the saddest thing she'll ever have to say to me;

'Perhaps you are one of those who'd do as well to stay clear of it, after all.'

Rose

'I'm sorry, all right?' Pilgrim is still on his knees in the snow, begging me to get him some help. 'I didn't mean nothing by what I just said. Just … phone someone. I'm in pain, woman.'

'Phone who?' I can't see an ambulance coming up here under these conditions. Besides, from his voice he doesn't sound so much hurt as he does angry and scared. I stand back for a minute, considering; what the hell am I supposed to do now? I've no inclination to waste time rescuing this obnoxious git, but if he really is in medical difficulties then I can't just leave him, can I? Even Tosser the dog has run off. Dammit. Though if he calls me *woman* one more time he really is going to have to take his chances alone.

'Well, will you *look* where the man's got to?' Two well-muffled figures come up the path behind us now - a large man and a girl. The feeling of dread that they might be more Macraes dissolves instantly as I recognise Shona's red bobble hat that I gave her last Christmas.

'I have never, ever in my life been so glad to see anyone …' I tell her feelingly as she comes up for a frozen hug.

'Dad needed to come up here to borrow a specialist wrench from Mr Macrae,' my old friend explains. 'Some posh guy in a Bentley broke down with all the family in the car and they begged Dad to get some emergency repairs done. Pilgrim was supposed to bring the wrench down and meet us on the hill …' She's still looking at me in frank bewilderment. 'Otherwise there's no way we'd have been up here, Rose.'

'What's wrong with him?' she nods her head in Pilgrim's direction and pulls an unsympathetic face. She's already heard enough expletives to realise he's more furious than in real agony. I pull her a little further out of earshot.

'Christ knows. I only met him ten minutes ago and he suddenly started writhing in pain. He's *mad*. He seems to think I've put some sort of hex on him.'

'Oh, Rose …' she looks at me sympathetically.

'He brought up my Mum, too. How unnecessary was that? He said he'd heard things about her and that I must be like her and …' I look at her painfully. I'm suddenly aware of a sick feeling in my stomach. Shona shakes her head.

'You're not a witch, Rose. Don't let anybody put you into that box. Just because your Mum was a pagan - that's just stupid and superstitious to put that on you. Those Macraes are all idiots anyway, you know that.'

'I know.'

'He only said it to make you feel bad, Rose. Don't let him get to you.'

'He *said* it because he believes it,' I tell her uncomfortably. I saw that look on his face a moment ago. He wasn't faking that. He might be superstitious and stupid, but that's what he believes. That's what all the Macraes believe, no doubt. We aren't living in the sixteenth century anymore but it's still horrible.

'Who cares what he believes?' she shrugs. 'Look. My mum always said if you'd had any powers you'd have used them years ago to make all those Macraes jump off a cliff!'

'True. I don't know if I'd have had the self-restraint to deploy my mum's abilities so wisely. Maybe that's why I never wanted to be like her.'

'Well. You aren't, are you?'

'No.'

'Well then.'

We glance over to the others

'He's been lifting those weights again, haven't you, lad?' Shona's dad Matt Dougal is a gentle giant. He lifts my tormentor up from the snow now. 'You were warned you'd rupture something sooner or later.'

'Ouch, *Fuck!* Take it easy Dougal. Take it … ow!'

'You'll be all right, lad. Just got to get you back inside. You've probably torn a ligament.'

'He likes to keep fit,' Shona says cynically. She pulls me to the side now, walks me back towards the main road, her arm locked comfortingly in mine.

'What are you even doing up here, Rose?' She pauses. She knows my history. We've been friends since the age of four, and there's no way I'm pulling the wool over her eyes.

'I thought you Clares didn't have any truck with this lot?'

'We don't,' I shake my head miserably. 'But there's a letter of mine that's gone astray. It's at Macrae Farm. I have to get hold of it, Shona.'

'You *have* to? And in this?' She opens up her hands and her gloves are immediately encrusted in white. 'An important one, I take it?' her eyebrows arch curiously.

'I'm hoping it's my Uni offer. So, yes. Really important.'

'OMG! Your Uni offer?' she grips my arm in excitement. 'You won't be able to reach the Macraes this way today, though. The hill's already iced up. We had to come the long way round through the village to come up your side of the path and we'll have to go back the same way. God knows how he's getting back up. His Dad will have to send a tractor!'

'Bummer,' I look at her in dismay. 'I really need to get hold of …'

'But hey,' she rattles on, 'you never said you were re-applying for next year, you dark horse. *Can* you go, then?' her dark eyes are shining with joy for me. 'I mean, your dad … is it sorted?'

I stop, deflated at her news that there's no mileage in continuing up this way. I'm going to have to go back the way I

60

came, there's nothing for it. I shake my head at her abruptly. It isn't sorted. Nothing is sorted. I haven't even got proof of an offer.

'I'm mad, aren't I? Here I am, prepared to go over to the bloody Macraes who bear us nothing but ill-will, in *horrible* weather conditions all in the forlorn hope that they'll let me have the letter, all assuming it's the one I'm longing for and … and what for?'

'What do you mean, *what for?*' She turns to frown at me now. 'You know what for.' She grips tighter onto my arm as I nearly go down on a large icy patch.

'You've got a vision in your head, haven't you?' she turns to laugh at me suddenly. 'Of a tall, handsome guy who's punting down the river Cam on a wooden boat. It's a sunny day in spring and all the bluebells are out under the trees and everything's fresh and new. He catches the eye of a seventeen-year-old interviewee who's sitting on the river bank and he smiles and winks at her and that's it - she's smitten forever.'

For goodness' sake. I can't believe she still remembers me telling her that. I give her a rueful grin. Shona knows me too well. We were best friends, once – from our first meeting at Merry Ditton infants all the way up to secondary school when I passed for the Grammar and she didn't. Leaving her behind then was one of the first real shocks of my life…

'That was over a year ago,' I flush. Shona smiles.

'You want Downing College because it fits your idea of somewhere safe and it's the place where you're going to find your prince. And why shouldn't you dream of it?'

'Because - I'm probably never going to get out of here, Shona. You've just said it yourself. My dad needs me here. And *he* certainly wouldn't want to go anywhere. He would see us moving out as some sort of victory for the Macraes - and that's how they'd see it too.'

'Look. The Macraes cheated your dad of his land, everyone knows that.' She stops in the middle of the icy path and turns to me suddenly. 'Afterwards, he got hurt while on their property.

Coincidence? The Macraes say it was nothing to do with them,' she gives a half-glance backwards, then turns to me again. 'You believe otherwise, and you already know how much everyone in Merry Ditton was divided on it at the time. Nothing was ever proved either way, Rose. If you stay or you go ... nothing's ever going to bring your dad back to full health now.'

'On the other hand,' she adds when I don't reply. 'It's not so bad this place, is it? I know at one time you kept moaning that everyone had left but ... I'm still here, aren't I?'

'You are,' I pat her hand.

'And personally, I don't know why anyone would *want* to leave this village.' She's got her head down now, taking great care where she puts her feet in the snow. 'We've got everything here that we need.'

'I guess,' I mutter quietly.

'I mean, *I* found a job and a boyfriend. You could have those too you know.'

I look at her in surprise. Here? A job ... what, in the hairdressers? That's where Shona works and I know she loves it but it'd kill me. She's left out the baby, she's expecting. I don't want one of those, either. She's only eighteen but she'll be getting married in the spring.

'Maybe in a bank somewhere locally?' she's saying now. 'You'd make manager in no time at all, with your brains.'

I shrug. The image of an entire lifetime spent living and working around Merry Ditton has just reminded me of why I was so desperate to get up that hill.

As for the kind of boyfriend I'd attract around here ... we both glance back towards her dad who's still half-supporting, half-carrying my tormentor.

'On the other hand - if you really think you need to stay here - all you've got to do is make sure you stay well enough away from the Macraes.' The solution seems simple enough to Shona. 'Don't go walking on their land and they won't bother you, will they?'

'That's what I've spent the last five years doing!' I turn and pull out of her linked arm. 'But I'm tired of living in a place where I have to be careful to avoid my neighbours all the time I don't *want* to do that.'

'So you run away from them instead?' she asks innocently.

'No, that's not it. It's precisely because I won't spend my life running away from people like them that I want to study Law. You may think that Mum had all these mysterious and wonderful powers but none of that's any good in the real world, is it? None of that's ever going to give Dad back the peace of mind he lost the night he was attacked. He still wakes in the night, you know. He still wakes up at times calling out for me, worried to death I'll be the next victim because his own experience was so senseless and unprovoked he's become frightened of the whole world. And I won't be that, Shona.'

'I'm so sorry, Rose ...' she's looking at me now with quiet admiration in her eyes.

'I have to go away if I'm going to prove to him that I can stand on my own two feet. And that the world still makes sense out there. I just don't know how else I can ever make things better - for him or for me.'

'I know you have to go,' she says quietly now. 'I was only kidding about the bank. You're like that blue butterfly we once found on the school wall, remember? It kept trying to fly off but it ...' It couldn't fly. I kept trying to pick it up, I remember. I wanted to help it on its way. *I'm not like that butterfly, though, I think suddenly. Because I am going to get out of here ...*

'Hey,' I give her a gentle shove. 'It's not that I want to leave you behind, you know that don't you?' Right now she's about the only friend I have left here.

'I'm *glad* you're still thinking of going, Rose. Glad for you. I think ...' she stops as we reach the juncture of the path with the hill. 'This is where we part?'

I guess I'd better head back home too. All this talk of marvellous dreams but where's the opportunity to make any of them come true? In my pocket I can feel my phone buzzing, reminding me that Mrs P has already tried to get hold of me a couple of times.

As I round in on Clare Farm ten minutes later, something looks different. Something *feels* different. I hope everything's all right? But out front, the crisp white snow shows evidence of several visitors having arrived. Three separate sets of footprints are etched into the drive; they've come up round the bottom of the ugly fire-escape my uncle Ty had put in as an emergency exit from Dad's bedroom when he first became disabled. I quicken my pace.

Nothing bad could have actually happened in the forty minutes or so that I've been away, could it?

Lawrence

I watch Dougie as he stands up behind his desk and the
wad of papers I've just brought him from Lestat on Sunny's behalf
slide untidily onto the floor. I resist the urge to pick them up,
glancing at my watch. If the surgeon is going to alter how they
operate on Sunny, then I promised the Registrar I'd get back to
him by 12.30. We're getting on for noon already and I've not yet
made any progress with my boss. Right now it looks as if he might
be about to dismiss me without giving me any further chance to
speak. I'm feeling frustrated. At the same time I can't help feeling
bad for Dougie, that I've put him in this difficult position. He
doesn't want to fire me, I know that. I haven't left him any other
option. He's the guy who took me under his wing when I first
came here, taught me the right way to use the mosquito net,
warned me what a military plane sounds like when it's still over a
minute away, pointed out which of the local 'delicacies' might kill
me if they weren't prepared properly ...

He hoists himself over to the tent entrance, solid and
imposing and just - steady, and it dawns on me that Dougie's a
huge part of the reason why I've stayed on here so long. I never
knew that till this moment. Whatever happens now, I'm really
going to miss him. I want to say something to him. I don't know
what, though. And I don't know how. Whatever it is, it just stays
stuck in my throat, unspoken.

'I want you to go home, lad.' He turns to me at the edge of

his tent. 'I want to put you on the next available flight back to the UK. I'll say you were due home leave and that's true. Once you're out of their reach ...'

He wants me to go home. I don't even register what the thought of that does to me inside. I've got other, more important, things to deal with right now.

'What about Sunny?' I bend gingerly to pick up Lestat's wad of papers. 'Can we get him on that Aid Abroad list?' My boss just stares at me open-mouthed as if I'm some kind of idiot. Don't I see what level of personal danger I'm in? I see him swallow, then, his face softening as it might for a well-meaning but misled infant.

'Not a chance.'

I get up and join him at the tent entrance.

'In that case, Dougie,' the words come out before I even get a chance to think them through. 'I'm not going anywhere. Tell that guy who rang you just now that you have me in your custody. Tell him he can send over some military police to pick me up right now.'

'You're crazy,' Dougie's face darkens again, and I know this is not just him being angry at me for being stubborn. He's *scared*. 'Do you really know what you're saying? Do you?' He turns and I can sense all eighteen stone of him quivering now. He wants to help me. He needs to act fast and all I'm doing is standing in his way.

'I think I have a fair idea.'

'I've only ever had one member of staff end up in jail in this province and believe me, you do not want to go there.'

'You're right I don't ...' My God, he's no idea of the lengths I've already gone to, to avoid just that.

'Then *why the hell* won't you accept the Get Out Of Jail Free card that I'm offering you? You do realise if I get you out of here it's not going to go down so easy on me, yes? There's bound to be consequences at this end. Questions asked. I may go down on a disciplinary myself ...'

'I know.' I bow my head, feeling humble beside him because

66

Dougie really is a good man. 'But I can't abandon Sunny.'

'You can't help him, you young idiot! No matter what you do you're not in a position to help him. All you can do now is save yourself. Don't throw your life away, Lawrence. You could rot in jail for years here and nobody would ever come along to save you. This way, you could be home free by Christmas Eve ...'

Home free? I don't think so. Something in my face must warn him, and Dougie gives me a long penetrating look now as if something of the truth about me is trickling through at last.

'If you let me get you home you'll be free to go on and help *others* like Sunny,' he breathes now. 'Take my offer, it's the best you're going to get, believe me.' I can almost feel him itching to get out of the tent. He wants to go and organise that flight for me. 'Lad, understand this; we haven't much time.'

'If I go back to the UK,' I say slowly now, 'If I take that flight back home like you want me to - I could find Sunny some sponsors there.' I hear his gasp of exasperation. 'Dougie, I swear I could. All I need is for you to rubber-stamp all these forms for me. And use some of that same leverage you're going to need to use to get me out of here ...'

'I should let you rot in jail.' He snatches the forms right out of my hand and goes over and flings them down on his desk. 'Do you know that? I'm sure Lestat already *told* you what all this would entail. It can't be done. I'd need ... I'd need signatures from a willing sponsor. Someone of the right standing. I'd need medical teams available to oversee his recovery.'

'You'll have that. All of it.'

He closes his eyes for a minute, as if it is too much, having to deal with a crazy, delusional young man like me.

'I'll have that?'

'Sure. I'll fax it out to you. Whatever you need. You do your bit at this end, that's all I ask.'

'You'll have everything signed and agreed before 31st December when the Aid Abroad flight leaves?' It's a rhetorical question but I answer it.

'Yes.'

'No!' he says now. 'You won't. You can't do, know why? Because it's impossible to get people together that quickly, that's why. Why can't you just leave this Sunny to his fate, Lawrence?'

'I can't,' I tell him softly now. 'I can't, and you already know why. It's the same reason that you won't hand me over to the military police. Instead you're willing to put your own position at risk to get me out of here.'

My boss stares at me, dumbfounded for a moment.

'And why is that, Lawrence?'

'Because after all we've been through together, you *care*. If I get hurt, that's going to hurt you too. I'm not going to lie to you, I don't want to go back home. I won't be welcome there when I do go back. I might well be arrested for something I did a long time ago and end up in jail anyway.' I hear his sharp intake of breath but I carry on –

'I know I can't undo what I did, Dougie. I can't change what's still waiting for me back there but when I look at that kid with all the tragedy and the disability that's dogging him now, I see a version of myself in him, I can't help it …'

'Listen. What was the very first thing I ever taught you when you came out here?'

'Don't make it personal,' I intone.

'That's it. Take my advice now, I'm begging you. Just leave it be.'

'I see a kid who was once gonna grow up so tall he was gonna knock that football moon right out of the sky. I see a kid who was deeply loved and who's lost everyone who ever loved him. I see … a kid who's still fighting for himself, Dougie, despite all the wounds he's sustained and *I want him to make it*.'

When he turns away, I catch a glimpse of the despair on his own face and I remember that he's had his fair share of hard times in the world. Dougie's been an unfailing tower of strength to me while I've been here. It's easy to forget sometimes that he has his own vulnerabilities. He leans heavily on his desk, not saying anything for a moment. When he turns back to me now, his face grey with worry, he seems to have made up his mind on something.

'If I agree to try to save this lad for you - *try*, I say, you know there's no guarantee here - you'll get your things and take the jeep that leaves for the airport in the next half hour? With the checkpoints, it'll take you over an hour to get there but you'll easily get on the evening service down to Colombo. Then you'll take the flight to Heathrow. I'll organise it from this end. Just get out of here. You'll do this - no quibbles?' *He wants me on the jeep that leaves in the next half hour?* I swallow.

'I'll be on it, sir. I'll go straight away.'

And that's it. I see Dougie draw in a breath. He looks at me, and his eyes are hooded but so sad I can't bear to even look at him. If I don't move now I'll never give him the hug I so totally out of the blue want to give him. I won't tell him what a great guy he's been and to 'have a good one' or any of that crap. I've only got half an hour to get my shit together and I know the minutes are ticking down.

'I guess this is goodbye then, sir?'

'I guess it is.' He gives a sad little smile. 'And lad - when you go back home and do your Knight on the White Charger thing to save that kid …?'

He leans forward and clasps my hand warmly, hugs me close to his chest in a bear hug and for one small moment of joy and pain I know exactly how much I'm going to miss this dude.

'You do it for me, too. Agreed?'

'Definitely.'

Outside, it's begun raining again. The fine, incessant see-through rain that's been a constant over the last few months.

'*Two hundred rupees, sir?*' The flier-pasting guy is like a pesky bluebottle zuzzing around again, sniffing out my desperation and I wave him away impatiently. Goddammit, I can barely even see where I'm going right now; this rain, why does this blasted rain have to keep on falling all the time like this place can't stop crying?

69

It's only when I'm racing across the muddy track to tell the Registrar we've got the go-ahead for the new op that it dawns on me what we just said about this being Goodbye.

I really am never going to see Dougie again, am I?

Rose

I must be mistaken. Clare Farm is the last place on earth my family would turn up to on Christmas Eve. And yet … in the hallway there's a pile of wet coats and melting boots by the front door - one's a man's big overcoat and the other two are dainty women's ones. There's also the welcoming aroma of fresh coffee brewing and I can't remember the last time someone wiped the cobwebs off our coffee maker.

What's going on?

'But Mrs P - even if the car can't be fixed … Mummy said we could take the *train* to Guiliana's. We could, couldn't we?'

That's my cousin Samantha's voice I swear it! Only it can't be, because they always spend Christmas in Rome with my aunt Carlotta's family and then push off for the skiing somewhere …?

What the heck are the family doing here?

I should be pleased. I feel a pang of guilt that I am not, a momentary shot of panic at the unexpectedness of their arrival, because all I really wanted, coming home, was to spend a little time on my own, regrouping. Guilt that my first thought is; *why did they have to turn up now, just as I've come in all white-faced and wobbly because of that nasty encounter with my pervy neighbour?* I rub my face with my hands, trying to bring a bit of warmth back into both. I didn't realise that Pilgrim had affected me so much. While I was with Shona, I could put Pilgrim out of my mind easily enough but the minute we went our separate ways it struck me how much getting caught by him had shocked me. Frightened me. As I walked back down the lane, I could feel my legs shaking. Now I'm feeling sick. Those Macraes. Why does that same family always have to be the bane of our lives? I take my jacket off and throw it in the corner because that creep touched it. I am never going to wear it again. Not even if it's been washed.

There's no way Dad's getting wind of what just happened, either. I know what it would do to him.

I swallow, catching sight of the note I left for Mrs P. It's still where I left it, on the mat. Didn't she see it? Now the family are here - heaven knows why, but they are here - and everyone will be wondering where I got to, wanting explanations, no doubt, and I bet I look a mess. I go over and scan my face quickly in the hallway mirror, smooth down my hair a bit. It could be worse. Nothing actually happened, did it? I'm fine. I'll tell them I went out to try and get my letter and I got caught out by the sudden turn in the weather.

'Rose, you're back! Wherever did you get to?' My uncle Ty appears from the kitchen now looking tall and still handsome and so much like my dad did ten years ago that he makes my heart lurch.

'I ...um.' I blink.

Never mind where I just got to ... what the heck are you lot doing here? I look at him, wide-eyed.

'The Bentley broke down.' He squeezes past the coats to give me a hug that's both warm and distracted at the same time.

'The Bentley?' The penny drops. Uncle Ty must be the 'posh guy' Shona and her dad were up here to get the spanner for?

'We were on the M20.' He leans back to look at my face a little better and I get this sudden panicky thought that he'll be able to do what my dad always did - read me like a book, know that something's up; I'm hiding something, and he'll be able to coax it out of me, 'It so happened Merry Ditton was the nearest place for us to come to,' he says, more slowly now.

'Wow,' I say.

72

'I know - it must come as a bit of a shock to find you've suddenly got three unexpected guests on your doorstep.' He gives an apologetic laugh. 'Hopefully we won't be detaining you for too long …'

'I'm not detained,' I say stupidly, suddenly feeling a huge rush of relief just to have him here. 'I mean, it's *great* to see you!' Suddenly, it really does feel great, the thought of having company. I only wish they could stay. If only they would, then me and Dad wouldn't have to be alone over the whole of this holiday. We'd have people to talk to, *family* to be with.

'Dad was just saying the other day - it's been years since the family got together for Christmas …' I stop, in case he thinks there's any reproach in that. There's not, but his eyes look sad.

'I wish we could stay,' he says, and I believe him. His comment makes it perfectly clear, however that they will not. I bend to pull off my Wellies, first one, and then the other, prop them up carefully against the hall radiator.

'You'd be very welcome to stay on. If the car couldn't get fixed in time …' I look at Ty wistfully as he bends to pick up the jacket I've just discarded on the floor and hangs it carefully over the radiator.

'We've taken up all your space on the coat rack,' he apologises.

'No, not at all. I'm just …' I put my hand over my heart, aware that out of the blue and to my horror, I'm suddenly welling up. 'I'm really glad to see you, that's all.'

I wipe my face with the back of my sleeve surreptitiously. I don't want to blub in front of my uncle, this is terrible. I turn away from him but there's no way in this tiny hallway to avoid my uncle noticing.

'Rosie, what's wrong?' The kindness in his voice only makes the pain in my chest feel worse. I'd rather *not* experience any of his kindness and concern. I'm okay now, anyway. I'm home and I'm safe and far away from the nasty Macraes. Better, by far, if we could gloss this over and carry on and drink some of that hot coffee they've got brewing in the kitchen.

'I'm fine.'

'Darling,' my uncle takes hold of my shoulders, turns me gently to face him. Damn it, he looks so much like my dad used to do, he's got the same eyes, his voice *sounds* the same. 'What's wrong? Is it *your dad?*'

I gulp. My dad. Of course, that's what they'd all think; that Dad's having troubles and I've been soldiering on and not said anything to anyone. If Ty thinks that, it gets me off having to confess I've just been a massive idiot and gone trespassing in the worst place possible and got caught. I nod my head now, sinking my face into my uncle's soft jumper. I'm going to get his jumper wet with my tears, I think. It'll get wet and it's probably one of those dry-clean only jobs and it'll be ruined. There's a strange satisfaction in the thought that my feelings are worth ruining his expensive jumper for. That I matter that much.

'Rose.' Uncle Ty lifts my face to see my eyes now. 'Tell me what the trouble is?' His voice is soft and cajoling. 'Come on. What's all this about? I know we've turned up out of the blue but … your Mrs P seemed to be a bit put out when she couldn't find you,' he admits. 'She didn't seem to know where you'd gone. There hasn't been any trouble?' His fingers under my chin are firm, don't let me turn away … 'An argument, maybe?'

'No!' I shake my head fiercely. 'Who on earth would I be arguing with?'

He sighs, shakes his head.

'I have no idea. Samantha argues with her mother all the time. She's taken to walking out.'

'Sam is four years younger than me. I have to look after my dad,' I remind him. 'I don't *walk out*. I went to … to fetch a letter that had been mis-delivered, but …' my voice betrays me and I stutter into silence before I end up saying anymore. I look down.

'A letter?' he prompts.

'I thought it might be my Uni offer letter,' I admit quietly.

'You've re-applied?' The significance of that filters through to him slowly. 'And Jack?' His brother needs me here to look after him. Yes, I know.

I give a small shrug. I don't know how I'm going to fix that bit of the equation. I live in hope. I've been hoping he would help me. I shoot him a painful look but I can't quite bring myself to say the words. He's only just arrived. This feels like something I should be working my way up to and I haven't got there yet. What if I ask him and the answer's '*I wish I could help*' delivered in the exact same regretful tone in which he just told me they won't be sticking around for Christmas?

'I take this as a good sign,' he says cautiously. 'We've only been here twenty minutes - you've probably guessed,' he makes a small joke, touching his own cold cheeks. 'I've barely defrosted yet. But from what I've seen so far, Jack seems ... well, better than I've seen him in a long time. Years, in fact. He told us he's been put on some new form of medication ...?'

'He has.'

'Successfully, I take it?' His eyebrows lift slightly.

'So far, uncle.'

'But - *what?*' He sucks in his bottom lip, frowning. 'There's a problem with it?'

'It's not that.' I shake my head. I want to tell him. Standing here safe in the hallway of my own home I want to tell him everything; the whole story about where my missing letter has got to and how I don't know what to do to get it back and how Pilgrim just accosted me. I want there to be someone on my team who's strong and capable and brave enough to help me face our bullying neighbours and help me get back what's rightfully mine.

But if I tell Ty ...

I pull away from my uncle now because he isn't my dad and I can't expect him to fill that gap. No; Ty isn't the one who's going to make things all right for me. I have to do that myself, now. I draw in a breath.

'The new meds are working wonders,' I tell him. 'They can't cure Dad but they help control his symptoms just great. It's not

75

the same as being *well*, though, is it? Seeing you out of the blue just now - you reminded me so much of what Dad used to look like - it brought it all back to me, that's all.'

'Oh, Rose.' His voice is heavy with sympathy. 'I'm so sorry. It's a lot to put on you, isn't it? You've always coped so well and we all know how much my brother values his independence. You *do* know that if there's anything you ever need ...' He rubs the side of my shoulder consolingly. 'All you have to do is say the word.'

Is that really all I have to do? I shoot him a glance. I've never asked them for anything, that's part of the trouble. Maybe they really do have no idea how much I need their help now?

'There *is* something I need.' I catch my breath now, surprised at how quickly that came out. Shall I just say it?

I'll say it. Tell him that I want the family to help me if that offer does come through. I'll do it. I pause for a moment, gathering the courage while the words catch and gather in my throat, reluctant as some heavy pebbles rolled along a slow river bed.

'The thing is, uncle ...'

A renewed blast of fresh-coffee aroma and the fragrance of warmed mince pies accompanied by a gale of laughter turns our heads towards the kitchen as my aunt Carlotta and cousin Sam look as if they're about to come out into the hall.

'I want ...' my fingers grip tight around his elbow suddenly, calling his attention back to me and he turns to look at me in surprise.

'I *need* you to help me out with Dad.' My words come tumbling out all high-pitched and fizzy like the pop of the cork on a champagne bottle. '... Uncle Ty, even if I'm made an offer, I won't be able to go unless you can agree to help.' I watch his eyes dart over to his wife and daughter who have seen us, who are walking right up to us, but I have to get this all out before his attention slips away. His dark eyes are on me again, sympathetic.

'Dad can't live here without assistance. In fact, he'd be loath to leave, but maybe if you could take your brother into your own home …?' Ty's eyes open wider in surprise – shock, even? He wasn't expecting that, obviously. When he said he could offer help he probably meant money. Or advice?

He clears his throat and when I remove my fingers from his arm he gives me the faintest of nods, acknowledging my words but little else and then;

'She's back!'

Any other words I was going to say to him die in my throat.

'Rose. We missed you. Where were you?' My cousin grins. I smile faintly at her and when she comes over to hug me I get a whiff of her heady signature perfume, a quick shot of her clothes, which are exquisitely-tailored and expensive, matching her mother's, a whole picture that says they're on their way somewhere else, somewhere exciting and fabulous and this unexpected blip of a stop-over at Clare Farm is a minor inconvenience. I swallow, taking it all in. Is uncle Ty really going to let himself be affected by what I've just told him? Their lives are so busy, *so full*. Full of their own desires and wants and pleasures. They haven't got room for an ageing, disabled, needy relative have they? Room in their house, maybe - but in their hearts? I bite my lip. Our situation here is nothing to them. They've never really concerned themselves with it too much, have always just assumed me and Dad would cope just fine.

'Darling it's been *ages*,' Carlotta smiles at me a little sympathetically and I imagine she's thinking I could do with a better hair-cut, maybe some high-lights …

'Where did you get to? Your home-help thought you might have gone to fetch some logs. We noticed the fire was burning a bit low …'

'No.' I stick my hands in my pockets, shrugging off her question. When I glance behind me I can see my uncle. He's a step or two behind us, letting us get on with all the 'female relatives greeting each other' thing but I can feel his pensiveness from here. What I've just said to him has really affected him, I can sense it. His women-folk seem oblivious to any of that, though.

'If you're cold I can always put some more wood on the fire?' I offer.

I shoot my uncle a glance, give a little shake of my head so he knows I'm not going to bring the topic up again now, in front of his two women, this question of what's going to happen to Dad. I get the impression if there's to be any chance of this happening at all - Dad going to live with them - then it's all going to have to be broached very delicately and sensitively with all parties concerned.

'Coffee?' Sam offers brightly, holding up her cup. I take my cousin in with a teensy pang of envy. At just fourteen she already looks suave and sophisticated and has the air about her of being generally well-kept. I wish I could be *well-kept*. I push my hair back self-consciously and my shabby, faded jeans that I've worn for ages are suddenly embarrassing in a way that I'd never even noticed before.

'Sure,' I say, 'I'd love a cup,' and my voice sounds over-grateful, as if it weren't my own coffee, in my own home, that is being offered. 'How long do you think you'll be here for?'

'Not long,' my aunt says quickly. Too quickly. When she glances a little coyly at her husband I get the impression that this is a rehearsed line; something they've already talked about on their way up here. *We won't stay, okay? We'll tell them we're only stopping over briefly, that we have to be on our way.*

'But ... if it takes a while to fix the car you may be here for Christmas after all?'

This time Carlotta's smile is a little more strained.

'We're not planning on that happening, Rose.' As we move into the living room she goes over and pulls back the curtains, immediately frowning at the sheet-snow that's coming down thick and fast. '*Bloody hell!*' I hear the annoyance surface in her voice at the sheer scale of it. I can well recognise the feeling of frustration.

'We've got somewhere else that we need to be, Rose.'

Snap, I think. I do too. My uncle's forefinger and thumb,

squeezing gently on my elbow says a whole host of things that I can only guess at: *well done for not letting the cat out of the bag; we'll talk about this a little later; I'm on your side.* I imagine it means all of those things.

Right now I can only hope.

Rose

'South East trains have all just been cancelled,' Mrs P mutters as she joins me at the kitchen sink an hour later. 'Mr P is walking up to fetch me - should be along any minute - but Rose, I think you'd better start planning how you're going to put this lot up?'

'*All* cancelled, you sure?' I'm placing the coffee cups carefully one by one on the draining board and she's picking them up and slowly wiping them dry. No trains. I've had the growing sense in the last hour since the family arrived that they weren't getting away and this confirms it. I feel a sense of satisfaction flood through me at the news, a quiet excitement. It means I'll get a proper chance to talk to Ty about what we opened up before. We might actually be able to rough out some kind of plan, agree something in principle. I hope it'll also mean Dad can get some quality time with his brother, something I know he's yearned for.

'It's going to be a big let-down for them, Rose,' Mrs P warns. I see her give a swift glance over her shoulder. 'At least they'll have a roof over their heads.' She shakes her head reprovingly and I know that a comment Carlotta made earlier is still rankling with her; something about how she's not sure Dad and I are coping with everything and how this place is 'looking a bit run down'. I'm washing up quicker than she's drying. I tap the draining board with my fingers and she wakes up again.

'It means we'll have to clear out the living room,' Mrs P thinks out loud. 'We'll put the sofa bed to one side and pump up an air mattress for Samantha. Do we know where the air pump is?' The air pump? I have no idea what she is on about.

'What's wrong with Samantha kipping in a sleeping bag on the carpet?'

'Hah!' is all she answers. She gives me a knowing look. Then she runs on; '… the other thing is, I only bought you and Jack a crown of turkey breast for your Christmas dinner.' The implications of having an extra three people stay are spreading through her mind as quick as wild-fire. 'You'll have to give them large portions of roast potatoes tomorrow, Rose. Don't forget the sprouts and the carrots and parsnips. Mind that you peel enough …'

'I'll peel a hundred,' I assure her. 'I'll peel a thousand.'

'Don't do that!' She says in alarm. 'There's Boxing Day to think of, too. And maybe even the day after that. I'm not back till the New Year don't forget. I'll have to get the emergency loo roll down from the loft.'

'You keep some in the loft?' I look at her in surprise.

'For emergencies,' she nods. And there is clearly an emergency looming in her book. Or there will be in a few days when we run out of potatoes and loo roll …

'Do you really think the trains will be out for as long as that?' I look at her dubiously. 'The family could be here for days!' She nods dolefully but I can see the possibilities opening up here. We'll all get a chance to catch up, properly catch up. There are so many things I don't really know about their lives. It's … exciting, that's what it is.

And I'll get plenty of time to put my case to Uncle Ty.

'The air mattress must be up there as well,' Mrs P is thinking out loud. 'I don't know where else I could have put it. There's scarcely room to swing a cat in this joint. If we could only open up your mum's old room…'

I turn sharply from the kitchen cupboard where I've just put away the dried cups.

'You know we don't use that room, Mrs P.'

81

'Not normally, no.' She's drying her hands thoughtfully on her wet tea-towel.

'Not *ever*, Mrs P.' Her pale blue eyes come up to meet mine for an instant, but whatever she's thinking, she keeps it firmly to herself. I want the family here. I'm happy that they're here. But I don't want them poking around in Mum's room, moving her things about, disturbing stuff. That room is out of bounds. Mrs P gives a small 'humph' like she does on the very odd occasion when I ever have to cross her. We get along very well, but at the end of the day, she doesn't have the final say in things.

'Opening that room would just … spook Carlotta out,' I remind her kindly. 'Remember the time when Mum was sick and they came by?' It wasn't long after Mrs P had started with us but I know she hasn't forgotten. That day Ty had dropped by with his wife, knowing Mum was ill, to 'see if they could do anything to help'. The whole visit had been made awkward and painful by Carlotta's obvious discomfort at catching sight of some of Mum's things in her room as they'd walked past it in the hall. I think she saw the crystal ball or some such thing, some tall candles that had been left burning in the darkened room, anyway, she freaked out; she made the unfortunate comment that she thought 'all that kind of thing' was the work of the devil. They hadn't stayed for very long.

'She won't *want* to stay in there, Mrs P.'

'Well, I don't honestly know where else you think you'd have the space to put them up.'

I shrug. 'The adults can have my room and I'll kip out in the sitting room with Sam. It'll be *fun*.'

She looks a little dubious. 'As long as you don't forget all the usual routines, with all the fun. Your dad's meds ...'

His meds. The minute she mentions them a memory breaks through from earlier, something I meant to bring up before but we've been so preoccupied …

'Mrs P - did you pick up the tablets?'

I think she realises even before I mention it; the fact that we're out of the red ones. She cups her hand over her mouth in horror. The dispensary's on the way to her mid-week job and she always picks them up for me.

'You *didn't?*' Oh, shit. I look at my watch. The dispensary will have closed by now – even assuming anyone could get there in this weather to pick them up. This is not good. Not good at all. Mrs P looks mortified.

'I am so *sorry* Rose.'

We've got to figure this out. I have to get hold of those meds because Dad can't be without them over the whole of Christmas. He wouldn't die - but they help control his symptoms, headaches and so forth. They make life a lot more comfortable for him. I really didn't need this. Especially not right now when we have the rest of the Clares staying over and Carlotta on the look-out for every little slip up that we make. She already believes we're 'not coping' doesn't she? If that belief made her more inclined to give a helping hand then it wouldn't be a bad thing. It's more likely to lead to her looking up local homes that might be suitable for Dad.

And he's not going into Forsythes!

'You'll have to ring the locum,' Mrs P is saying. 'Ask him what they can do about it. Perhaps he'll be able to arrange a delivery out to you, himself?'

'It's unlikely,' I say in a muted voice. Damn it, if only I'd remembered this before there would have been time to have *done* something about it.

'Rose, Mrs P.' Carlotta is suddenly at the kitchen door, looking fed-up and exhausted. *Crap. Did she hear anything?* It doesn't look like it.

'Ty's just been on the phone to eight local taxi firms and not one of them is offering any service right now.' She spreads her beautifully-manicured hands in a 'this is ridiculous' gesture.

'Maybe you know of someone – an unemployed man, perhaps, who'd be grateful of the chance to earn something?'

Mrs P gives me a quick roll of her eyes.

'That chap who gave us a lift up to the village - the one who's fixing the car, maybe?'

'If the taxis aren't running then that's a good indication that you won't find anyone, Mrs Clare.'

'There must be *someone?*' Carlotta insists. 'We have to get to Guiliana's, Mrs P.' I almost feel sorry for my aunt she looks so desperate. Whatever Guiliana's is, it must be somewhere pretty glamorous, I'm thinking wistfully. It must be somewhere pretty damn amazing. I bet the people who go to Guiliana's don't have to worry about seeing to their parent's medication or about on which part of the floor they are going to put up unexpected guests ...

'We were just talking about how we were going to put you up here,' I step in consolingly. 'Given that it looks like you're not going anywhere.'

There's a small silence in the kitchen as Sam joins us, just in time to hear the bad news. The coffee machine makes the spluttering sound I remember it making when it had run out of beans and there's a definite sense that the *joie de vivre* they've been displaying ever since they got here has also run its course ...

'We don't want to put you out, Rose,' Carlotta says, quietly hurt, as though, just by saying the words, I have manifested some dreadful truth that did not exist before.

'We'd love you to stay, though.' I can feel the enthusiasm I'm radiating bouncing back off them and returning to me empty and hollow. They do not want to stay. 'It won't be as exciting as Guiliana's,' I rush on, even though I clearly have no idea what Guiliana's is - 'But it'll be nice for *us* to have you.'

'I'm sure it will. But, you see, Guiliana's is something I've waited a very long time to get an invite to. It's ... *exclusive.* You understand me, don't you, Rose?' I understand her, but I don't see what any of us could be expected to do about it.

'Well. It *might* settle down,' Mrs P takes a peek through the kitchen blinds which we've closed to help keep the heat in. 'You might make it ... tomorrow?' She says it in a tone which implies there is as much chance of that as there is we'll be sitting out on the lawn tomorrow sunning ourselves. 'Would you like me to take a look in the airing cupboard for you Rose? Sort out some bedding for them for later on?'

Sam pulls a sudden moue, and I see she's not looking so cheerful anymore. Neither is her mother.

'For God's sake, what possessed Jack to buy a house in such a God-forsaken out-of-the-way, back-woods location as this?' Carlotta is muttering to herself as she's suddenly on the phone frenetically texting someone.

'My mother did,' I tell her and she stares at me. I stare back at her.

'Now,' Carlotta murmurs, her voice, I feel, quite deliberately provocative. 'Why am I not surprised?'

There's a brief moment where I can feel both our hackles rising. Mrs P gives me a tiny warning shake of the head and I shift my gaze away from my aunt. She doesn't look best pleased.

'Look. Let's not go there, Rose. I have no quarrel with you, you know that.'

No; only with my mum, I can't stop myself thinking. Because she was different. Because she never subscribed to all the things that keep *you* happy and sane and safe in the world; because she did her own thing.

'I'm sorry you can't go to Guiliana's,' I tell my aunt, and she lowers her gaze, looks away. 'But we really were very happy to see you all just now. We don't have much but … we'd be honoured if you'd like to share whatever we have over the holidays.'

'Thank you,' she says stiffly. 'Jack's always been most hospitable to us and I know you take after your father.'

Mum was hospitable to you too, I think crossly. I know she was. I bite my tongue but the words come out anyway.

'Let's agree not to bring my mum into any of it,' I manage to say evenly, 'and I'm sure we'll all get along just fine …'

'Well, *really!*'

'Darling,' my uncle pops his head round the kitchen door and we all look up expectantly. Right now I'm almost hoping he's

85

going to tell us he's found some way to get them out of here. That they're going to go.

'Nothing doing, I'm afraid.' His voice sounds strange, a little strangled. Am I imagining that he's looking at me rather darkly? Has he just heard our uncomfortable exchange? He shakes his head at my aunt, and she raises her chin, flashes her pretty green eyes and puts on an obvious 'brave face'.

'It's what we expected,' she says. He squeezes her hand.

'Um, Rose,' he beckons me with his head now towards the hall. *A quiet word*, his whole demeanour seems to say. He wants us out of earshot of the others. 'Perhaps you'd come and … give me a hand bringing in a few fresh logs for the fire?'

Mrs P bustles about, suddenly busy showing Carlotta where everything is in the kitchen, opening all the cupboards and drawers as my aunt looks on unenthusiastically.

'If it's about what my aunt and I were just talking about in the kitchen …' I take in a breath, as me and Ty reach the hall, 'well, I was a bit upset, that's all. I'd prefer it if she didn't bring up my mother.'

'Oh.' He looks immediately apologetic. And surprised. 'What did she say?'

'I can't remember the actual words that were used. I think …' I mumble, 'I was a little sharp myself. We did both apologise.' I look up at him through my fringe. 'If that's what this is all about …?'

'It isn't.'

Oh. I feel my shoulders stiffening.

'It's about what you were proposing before; my brother …' He's got that apologetic look on again and my heart sinks right down to the damp Wellington boots which I'm now slipping back onto my feet. We're going out to the log shed so he can talk to me in private but it's going to be bloody cold out there.

If he's going to say he can't help, then he might as well just say it here and now …

86

Lawrence

'They'll be asking to see our passports and security clearance in a short while, Lawrence.' Dougie's batman Arjuna nudges me gently and I open my eyes for a fraction of a second.

'We are still in the militarised zone. They may enquire about your purpose of travel …'

My purpose of travel … I turn my back to him, away from the too-bright sunshine pouring through the window of the jeep. I know what my purpose is. But I was asleep, such restless sleep. Perhaps it is the rows of all the bombed-out houses that we've passed along the way that's stirred this up? All chunks of concrete and bits of mangled metal. I've seen the damage bits of falling masonry like that can inflict on anyone who's trapped underneath. The smell of the plaster stays in your nostrils for days after; the dust and the cold and damp, they clog up your insides till you think you'll never be free of it, but the worst thing of all, perhaps, is the hours that must be spent alone inside the prison under the masonry, waiting for release.

Such a thing I could not endure again, I know this. I know what I would do to avoid it. I close my eyes and once more the old memories from England are there, hovering like flies inside my churning mind:

Was he dead?
I bent over double, meaning to catch my breath but all I did

was throw up over the wet bark of the silver birch in front of me, heaving the empty contents of my guts till my stomach felt turned inside out. I couldn't run anymore, I couldn't stay away, and yet I couldn't go back either ...

When I glanced over my shoulder the last golden sliver of the sun was just disappearing through the forest canopy. Soon it would be dark. I leaned against the tree trunk and contemplated that fact without relish. I didn't want to spend another night alone in this place. I didn't want to be in the dark. I'd already used the last of my matches and tonight there would be no moon, it would be black as hell.

And I was already in hell.

So far, forty-eight hours had elapsed since ... since it happened. I could have used that time to put a hundred miles between me and here but all the while I'd been going round in circles, something keeping me tied to this place as surely as a predator remains tied to its prey. Partly, I suspected, it was because I hadn't hung around to discover how much damage I'd done.

And I had to know.

I sucked at the back of my hand which was scratched and bleeding where the hawthorns had torn at me as I'd run. I felt as if my legs were going to give way beneath me any minute. Where to go now? Who to turn to? But if I carried on a little further - just a little way up from here, I might find shelter for the night at the old ruin. If I was lucky I'd have some tins and packets still stashed away up there from all the other times I'd needed to get away. I might even still have a candle or two, an old lighter to give me light. It'd been a year or so since I'd last had to do this but there might still be some provisions left up there.

I spun round, hyper-alert then as a pin-prick of light caught my eye, advancing towards me through the trees. They were still out looking for me, damn it. I'd made sure to stay out of sight for the first twenty-four hours. On the first night, I stayed immersed in the river for three hours, till I was frozen so bad I thought my bollocks would drop off, till they led the dogs away. I have no idea how they *didn't manage to find me.*

When they didn't, I made a decision after that, that I wasn't going to be caught. If I could survive that, if I could make it through that stormy, fuck-scared August night, then I could survive anything. I could go on and live a life, a good life, if I chose to. I wouldn't have to spend God-knows-how-many years rotting in a jail cell.

But now they were back. I turned to run but my ankle twisted against a jutting-out root and I went down, face-first, into the mud. The pain seared through me like a lighted brand and I couldn't get up. For the first few minutes I couldn't even think about getting up, and by the time I could, my pursuer was on me.

'Lozza!' WTF?

'Marco … what are you doing here?' I could make out Marco's worried face in the gathering dark. His round arc-shaped eyebrows, his high forehead covered by his jet-black hair.

'I've been looking for you for hours - for days.' I thought; I've never heard his voice sound so high-pitched. He wasn't scared of me was he?

'What are you looking at me like that, for?' Marco knew me well enough. He'd worked for my father for years. What I did the other night … he must have known I'd never meant it to go so far. He must have known why I did what I did.

'Don't you know, man?' He stopped, looking at me remorsefully and his reaction to me freaked me out, because it could only mean that things were worse than I yet knew. That I had done much more damage than I'd ever intended to. I looked him straight in the eye and asked him the one thing it scared the life out of me to ask and yet I had to know:

'Is he dead?'

'Lawrence,' Arjuna's voice is more urgent now. 'Come on, sir.' I open one eye, groggy, and my travelling companion is tugging at my sleeve. The jeep has already drawn to a halt. Ahead of us, at the military checkpoint, two bus-loads of passengers still have to be sorted through but for some reason we're the ones who've been flagged to the side.

'Have your luggage out please sir, and ready for inspection.' The young guard who unsmilingly glances through our papers hands them back now through the window.

'They've taken the couple who were sat in front of us for a body search,' Arjuna notes uneasily.

'Not a problem,' I force my thoughts back into the present and my mouth tastes acid. 'They won't find anything on me.'

Not unless they plant it, his strained silence seems to imply. Have they recognised my name, is that it? I wipe the sheen of sweat off my face and Arjuna hands me the water bottle.

'How much further?' I sort out the passports I've just been given and pass him back his. We've been travelling along this bumpy, hot and humid road for nearly forty minutes now. By my reckoning we can't be that far away from the tin-roofed shelter at … I scrabble in my pocket for the slip of paper Dougie wrote the destination on - Hospital Road. That's where we're due to pick up the shuttle that'll take us to the air base at Palali.

'Not far. Another two kilometres maybe …' Arjuna's distracted, fretting about what the military might want next, so I leave him be, peering through the dusty window instead. To the far left of us I can see the remains of yet another bombed-out house along the roadway. Some of the tourists from the bus up front have come out of their vehicle and are taking snapshots.

When you see these bombed houses from the outside it hardly seems possible anyone could survive. But I know Sunny was trapped in a pitch-black pocket underneath the beams for some four days and nights. No food, no water. All he had was the dust-saturated air. By the time they'd brought him to me he'd been shrunken with dehydration, covered from head to toe in blood and dust and he'd got the bewildered, wide-eyed look of the newborn on his face – that look that said '*Oh, here I am. I'm here, then.*' I remember the first thing he'd said to me, quite calmly and in his halting English was that he'd known all along someone would be coming for him; that he would be saved.

Something about that simple faith of his touched me deeply. I've never worked out quite why but I know it gave me a deep sense that here was someone it would be worth going the extra mile for; someone worth saving.

'You are with an *International Aid Agency*,' Arjuna stresses once the guard is out of earshot. 'When they ask - you are returning to your family for the holidays.'

'I know, Arjuna.' He doesn't need to read me my lines. I feel an unexpected flash of affection towards my companion, nonetheless; Dougie's tasked him with making sure I get safely out of Colombo and he means to see that I do. Because of the urgency of it and with me not speaking the lingo, Arjuna's accompanying me all the way down.

'I'm gonna be all right, okay?' I've got to keep a low profile, I know. I just need to get out of this country. But because right now I'm on a mission on Sunny's behalf, and because I know Sunny is somehow blessed, I'm convinced I'm going to be helped.

'Remember to smile.' Arjuna isn't smiling. He hands me a *dosa* - a paper-thin rice and lentil pancake he bought at the roadside at the last checkpoint where we were stopped for a while with nobody checking anything. 'Eat this. Guilty men can't swallow. It'll help keep you looking - innocent.'

'*I am innocent*,' I protest. I pat my passport which I've kept in easy reach on my lap, all the documentation to show who I am, where I'm coming from and why I'm going home. In my backpack I've got the names and numbers Dougie's given me for people to contact regarding Sunny's medical care once he arrives in the UK. There are at least two charitable agencies who support international efforts in cases like Sunny's and I have details of the back-route, short cut movers and shakers who, once they make their mind up to help, can get things going. Almost miraculously, Dougie has already spoken to one of them, and he's promised to speak to the second person too, an old-time friend of his, in advance of my arrival in the UK.

This part of it I know is Sunny's grace; all the difficult,

impossible-to-solve parts of this puzzle seem to be melting away before my very eyes. It's the seemingly easy bit that I'm really worried about.

'A man in a hurry always attracts attention in these parts. You are no VIP, Lawrence, and no other UK aid worker gets the star treatment,' Arjuna notes. 'The flight from Palali to Colombo - nearly seven hundred rupees. *Plus* my fare. Everyone else gets the bus. So - until I set you on that plane back to the UK I'm on tenterhooks. *Innocent or not.*'

I know he is referring to the Sri Lankan who I decked a few nights ago. I know that's why Dougie has gone to all this trouble to get me out of here but right now that isn't what's preying most heavily on my mind. Arjuna's dark eyes take me in penetratingly and for one moment I fear he can see right into the shadows, into all the murkiness and the memories I've spent the last five years hiding from.

'Is he dead?'

'He isn't dead, Lozza. Just … what did you do it for, man?'

I'd looked at Marco painfully, leaning my body weight against the tree behind us. My father wasn't dead then. The thin hysterical sound of laughter that came out of my lips didn't sound like me at all; it sounded like someone else. If he wasn't dead then I wasn't a murderer. It also meant that I would never again in my life know what it meant to be free; to be safe. When he caught up with me, my father would crush me like a beetle underfoot, that's what would happen. 'What in heaven's name possessed you?'

I looked at Marco suspiciously for a moment. Was he alone? Was he there to take me in, there was some reward attached to my capture - was that what this was about? I managed what must have passed for a thin smile.

'What possessed me? You have to ask?'

Even from where I stood I could see that he was trembling. He looked fuck-awful. Like he hadn't slept any more than I had. Had he really been out looking for me all this time?

'I always knew ...' I watched him take a packet of cigarettes out of his jacket pocket and he offered me one. I didn't smoke. He knew this. Perhaps he felt this'd be a good time for me to start?

'I always knew you were one edgy guy, Lozza. But even I never figured you'd take things this far. Why, man?' he shook his head, clearly distressed.

But we'd already covered that one.

'Who's been helping you? You can't have avoided the fuzz this long without help.'

I shook my head. I had avoided them. There'd been no one to help. Marco looked perplexed.

'They'll be out to get you, you know that. You ... you can hide out here a couple of days - a week, at the most, but they'll still get you in the end.'

'They won't catch me.' I didn't know what was making me say it, but right at that moment I got a shot of clarity brighter than I'd ever had in my life. The police weren't going to catch me. I knew it, deep in my bones, even if it defied logic to explain why.

Marco didn't know that, yet, though. He didn't have the clarity that I had.

'They'll catch up with you, Lozza. Bound to. It's not the sort of minor misdemeanour they're likely to let slip now, is it?'

'He isn't dead,' I said, and I felt a kind of wonder at it. I never went in there intending to kill him and yet ... after what happened, the hope that I might have finished him seemed my only salvation; it would have meant that I hadn't thrown away my own life for nothing.

'That's amazing.'

Marco's eyes narrowed as he took a drag on his wet ciggie before throwing it into the undergrowth. I folded my arms and let him run on with what he'd got to say. He seemed determined to say it, anyway.

'Why don't you just ... face it, man?' He stuck out his chin at me.

'I can't.'

'You can't, you can't?' He kicked at the undergrowth and I could see my apparent calmness was upsetting him.

'No. They'll put me in jail.'

He shrugged his shoulders, simultaneously opening out his arms. He didn't get it, that was the thing. I could face a pit full of venomous snakes sooner than I'd face being banged up. I could face an eternity and a half in hell.

'You've never been in the clink,' he soothed. 'Not as bad as you think. Specially not for one as young as you.' No, he didn't understand.

'I can't.'

'If you leave now you're never coming back, Loz. Ever in your life. Think about it.' He was doing his best to persuade me, to keep the logic and the good sound common sense coming but I could tell from his voice he knew he wasn't getting through.

'I know. My father must have the luck of the devil though, I swear. I thought I'd killed him, Marco.'

'Your father …?'

Marco made a strange sound in his throat then, leaned forward. For a moment I thought he was going to punch me out. He could do it. He was three types of karate expert and it wouldn't cause him too much strain. Maybe he was thinking, as my friend, he'd got to turn me in because that's what would be best for me. That I'd see the sense and thank him for it eventually.

'He deserves nothing less,' he said at last. 'I know what you've had to suffer, believe me. But Lozza - that man you hurt two nights ago …' He pulled me in towards him, and for one long moment hugged me close instead, whispered into my ear;

'That man wasn't your father.'

I don't know who he was: I never found out what happened to him in the end. I bite into the *dosa* Arjuna bought me as the checkpoint guard decides to wave us on after all and my companion heaves a quiet sigh of relief. He won't relax till he sees me out of the country, I know. He thinks that then I'll be safe. But getting on the plane back to England holds no such promise for me.

By the time my international flight - transiting Abu Dhabi - touches down on a snow-sprinkled runway at Heathrow I realise I have been travelling a good fourteen hours since we parted company. Due to the time-difference it is still mid-morning though - it is nudging 10.30 am on a dank winter's morning in England, and it is already the following day; Christmas Eve.

As I step out of the terminal, hoping to hitch myself a ride that will take me into Kent, that man - that nameless man, who wasn't my father – he comes back into my mind once more, and the memory makes me cringe. It isn't just what I did to him that troubles me. It was five years ago, but I must surely still be wanted in Merry Ditton because of it? I'll need to keep my head low, keep out of sight while I'm there. I don't want to get arrested, but ... I can't help the feeling that, by returning to Kent - even after all this time - I am somehow sealing my own fate.

Rose

'I want to help you, Rose.' The light in the woodshed is dim. A mean, forty-watt bulb hangs naked from the ceiling and I can't properly see my uncle's face. I'm standing stock still. Having tentatively reprised the topic of what happens to Dad if I go to Uni, I'm watching Ty fill up the wicker basket with logs waiting for his answer.

'I do want to help you but I need to be certain of the best way to do that before I jump to any conclusions …'

What conclusions? I feel my heart sink. I only want him to tell me if they will help me or not. Everything rides on his answer. *Everything*.

'What do you mean?' I drop a handful of smaller bits of wood into the wicker basket at my feet, keeping it casual but right now my stomach is one tight knot.

'I *mean*, I'd need to know about the level of commitment I'd be getting the family into,' he says candidly, 'And how best to execute that. You wouldn't want me to promise something I couldn't deliver, would you?'

'Well, no,' I swallow.

'All I'm saying is, if we're to get involved in his care I'd need my brother's case to be reviewed by a specialist team.'

'Why?' I look at him painfully.

'… people who might be able to give us a better prognosis than he's had up till now.'

I sigh quietly. He thinks we haven't been through all these medical hoops and obstacles already? I know where he's coming from but he's wasting his time. This'll just mean more tests, more hours for Dad spent being hooked up to scanners, more interminable waits in consultants' waiting rooms.

'What would be the point?' I ask my uncle. Is he thinking medical science might have moved on, that there might be more options available now than there were five years ago? It's possible, of course, but I can't help noticing that Ty still hasn't answered my question. If Dad's prognosis were to remain exactly as it is - would the rest of the Clares be willing to help us out?

'When was Jack's last review done?' Ty insists and I see him let out a long, mist-filled breath.

'Dad gets seen regularly,' I stall. I don't remember when the last actual review was.

'I'd still like to get an independent review done for him. With your permission?'

'You'll need *his* permission,' I point out.

'Naturally.'

He won't want to give it, I don't bother to add. Dad's sick to the back teeth with hospitals, but it looks as if Ty's not committing himself till he knows quite a bit more about his brother's condition. Fair dos.

'That's settled then. We'll talk about this more later, I promise, Rose.'

No! I think, a feeling of panic rising up in my chest now, galvanising me into action. I step in front of him by the open door, blocking his way and he looks at me in surprise. It isn't settled. Nothing is settled. Only that he'd like Dad to be seen by more specialists; that's it. But it's not enough. *What does all that mean for me? What does it mean for all my hopes and dreams?* I need more of an answer than that ...

'If you don't help me,' I blurt out suddenly, 'I'm never, ever going to get away from here. You know that, don't you?'

'That isn't one hundred per cent true ...' Ty has stopped in his tracks, is looking at me intently. He's standing beside me at the open door now, ready to go. All around him a thin settlement of snow and ice are lining the door lintel; at his feet, our boot-tracks, made so recently, have frozen into solid ice. I think; he's already made up his mind, hasn't he?

'You still have choices, Rose.'

'What choices?' I mutter. Ty looks at the ground now, choosing his words carefully as if he's well aware that what he's about to say next won't go down well.

'Jack may actually be better off living in nursing accommodation than in a family home. Have you ever thought of that?'

'*No.*' I frown.

'I'm not saying that it's so,' he says gently. 'I'm just saying that I need to be sure and if that is the case …'

I kick at the door of the log shed as we go through it, mad at him, frustrated that he won't just say yes, yes I'll take my brother in and make sure that he's cared for and looked after properly. I wanted him to say that. I needed him to say it. The fact that he won't makes me feel heartsick. Trapped. Angry.

I don't want to talk about the possibility that 'Dad's interests might best be served in a home'. They won't. I know him better than anyone so I think I'd know that much. I'm not even going to go there.

'I am looking out for my brother's best interests,' Ty pulls at the sleeve of my coat before I can walk on out onto the snow-lined path ahead of him. 'You have to believe that.'

'Sure,' I dredge out. I keep my head down not wanting to even look at him as I answer. Right now I'm just desperate to hide my feelings. He's clearly reluctant to get too involved but he's still the best bet I've got right now.

'We'd better get back with the wood,' I say.

'Yes.' He hesitates, 'Look … thanks for not bringing up this subject in front of the others. I'll broach it with Carlotta later but she's upset enough about things at the minute - now wouldn't have been a good time, you understand?'

'That's okay,' I say sadly.

'Rose ... I want to look out for you, too,' he swallows. 'I've got to do my best by everyone concerned. You understand that, don't you?' The tone of his voice makes me turn round.

'Of course,' I say, watching his eyes carefully. He does *care*, I can see that. He's just got a lot of difficult balancing to do when it comes to the people he cares about in his life. His own family take precedence, naturally. I just don't know if me and Dad are going to weigh heavily enough in his concern for him to want to make any difference to us.

I was hoping he'd have some kind of answer for me; that he'd asked me out here so he could throw some kind of life-line to me but I'm still none the wiser and the heaviness I feel inside has not been lifted.

'You might want to lock up the log shed before you go,' my uncle turns and indicates the door behind him as we step out into the snow. 'We heard on the radio coming up here, that the police are looking for someone.'

'Oh?'

'They were warning people to check that their sheds and outbuildings are kept locked. Just a precaution. Samantha was laughing about it on the way up but now we're stuck here - well ...' he looks at me sheepishly.

'I don't think we need worry *too* much,' I say dully. We're pretty remote up here. I can't see anyone would bother to trek up this far unless they had a purpose to. I go back and click the shed lock in place though, just to please him.

'Thanks Rose. There's one other thing.' He hesitates, 'I know it's a lot to ask, and it wasn't something I wanted to bring up in front of the others ...'

My eyes open slightly; what now?

'Given that we're marooned, at least for the night - would you have any objection if we took over the spare downstairs room for our own use? Just until the weather breaks?'

No. *No;* that room isn't a spare room. He knows that.

'Why do you even ask me?' I say painfully. 'Carlotta won't want to sleep in there anyway. It's full of Mum's things,' I remind him.

'We'll help you move them. It's just … three extra people in a two-bed farmhouse is going to be a tight squeeze if we don't use every available bit of space,' he warns.

I don't want to move all Mum's things. I don't want Carlotta sleeping in that room. We wouldn't be able to shift everything out of there and I know even though she'll be scared Carlotta is the curious type; she won't be able to resist poking about in every drawer and then coming out later with passing comments on whatever she finds.

And yet - it seems such a very small thing for him to request, in view of what I'm asking them to do for me. I'm going to have to give in on this one. He's right; it's a huge thing to ask me, but I don't want to antagonise them so I can't be rigid about it.

'We'll have to consult Dad,' I say cautiously.

'I asked him earlier,' he confesses. 'He's okay with it.' He hangs his head a little to one side. 'But … I wanted to make sure you were, too?'

Dad's okay with it, is he? I feel a small stab of betrayal that Dad told his brother it was okay without consulting me. He *should* have run it past me first.

'That's all right then,' I say with a false cheerfulness I do not feel. They are going to go in and use Mum's room. The space that was hers, that's been closed up for so long … It's stupid, I know, but for such a long time I've been consoled by the thought that the air in there will have been last breathed in and out by her; the surfaces, last touched by her fingers. I had this silly idea that if it stayed unused then something small might still be retained of her, in there; some part of her that we could keep, even though all the rest had gone.

Only she hadn't been in there when I went in to make that spell yesterday, had she? The room had been musty and stale, fair

100

enough, but there'd been no sense of *her*. Still …

I take in a deep breath.

'As long as … As long as everyone's careful with all of Mum's stuff.'

'Naturally, we will be.'

'It's just that … I've never had time to go through all Mum's belongings yet.' I pause. Five years is a long time. He's never going to buy that one. And Mrs P has offered a dozen times to give me a hand if I ever wanted to go through Mum's things. 'I mean, I've never really felt up to it, Uncle Ty.'

'We're in your debt, Rose.' He rubs the side of my wet coat consolingly, appreciatively, and I get a momentary reprise of all the feelings I was experiencing before when I was blubbing against his expensive jumper; that it's okay to feel sad that they're opening up Mum's room; that it's okay to admit that I've avoided going through her all her belongings this long because part of me couldn't bear it. But he knows all this. I can see it in the way his eyes are crinkling up at the sides in compassion and kindness. He looks … he looks so much like my dad that he makes my heart ache, because I've lost my dad too, in so many senses of the word. I've lost the one person I had left who was still looking out for me.

Who still *could*.

'We'll help you with packing it all up,' my uncle Ty is saying 'My girls are very good at that - organising things …'

I smile at him, suddenly full of gratitude.

'I need help,' I get out, my voice all croaky because it's something that I wouldn't normally say. We've reached the front door of the house but something makes me hesitate, pushing the key into the front door. I turn to him.

'I'd appreciate that, if you could all help me … I mean, make some decisions about what to keep and what to give away. Every time I've ever thought about it it's all felt so overwhelming, like I was … I was chucking bits of her away, like I was rejecting something when really all that's left in there are her *things*.' Suddenly, unexpectedly, I feel a little liberated though, at the thought. That it might actually be possible to open up that room, let some new air come rushing into it, not to have to worry so much about losing anything precious that might have been left over in there from before, to just … let it all go.

I'm pushing the front door open, relishing the rush of comfortable heat from the house, full of a lovely warm feeling of being included; of being supported, *that I don't have to do it all on my own*, when I stop.

I'm suddenly aware that something's wrong.

Something is not the way it should be; like a bone pulled out of its socket, like a note in a beautiful song that is being sung slightly out-of-key; *something's wrong.*

From here I can see that the door to Mum's room is already ajar, that's what it is. How could it be open? I can feel my heart hammering faster in my chest. *Who* could have opened it? Standing there, rooted to the spot I slowly become aware that I can hear voices coming from within, women's voices. It's Carlotta and Sam, I know it is. What is going on here?

I didn't … I look at my uncle in panic. I didn't mean for anyone to go in and start barging around and interfering in there without me being present.

'What are they doing in there?' I grab at my uncle's arm and the distress fluttering in my stomach feels like the half dozen pigeons I once surprised up in our loft, scattered and aimless and shocked. They shouldn't be in there. We've only just spoken about this. Nobody gave them any permission yet …

'Oh!' he says, surprised, as his wife comes out holding a can of furniture spray aloft. She's got a bandanna of some sort wrapped around her head.

'What are they doing?' I look at my uncle accusingly. 'What on earth do you think you two are doing?' I swallow, squaring up to my aunt angrily.

'It's quite all right, Rose,' Carlotta misunderstands the shocked look on my face. 'Your Mrs P had to go. But we're not above getting down and doing a little bit of dirty work ourselves

…'

When I push past her and look inside, there's already one black bin bag propped up against the wall beside the door, jammed so full that its contents are half spilling out. Samantha looks up guiltily, about to cram in Mum's *besom* - which she's just snapped in two, to make it fit inside the bin bag. I walk over slowly, my legs feeling strangely heavy. I pick up one end of the black bag and give it a little shake so I can see what else they've dumped. The sight makes my eyes water. All Mum's beautiful candles have been tipped in there, too. Her books. Her crystals. Her incense sticks, *everything* …

'I thought it was quite obvious that this is where you'd have to put us up,' Carlotta pushes her bandanna back a little and a coiffeured curl falls forward. 'So I thought I'd better make a start.'

A painful lump arises in my throat and for the moment I can't speak. I can't even say a word. Even from here I can see another cardboard box full of broken bits, those look like Mum's porcelain animals, so many of her things, the very things he just promised me they'd be careful with.

'You weren't supposed to do this,' I put my hand over my mouth. '… come in here without me. You weren't supposed to chuck anything away. *These are Mum's things.*'

'Rose?' Carlotta looks a little bemused at how upset I am. 'Well. We haven't actually chucked anything out. We used the black bags because we didn't have anywhere else to put them but … most of those animals had little chips in them. Everyone knows chips breed germs …'

Right now I've got the same searing feeling in my belly as if I'd walked in to find burglars had turned the place upside down. The room has been tarnished, somehow, invaded. They didn't have any right to come in here and just fumigate the place for their own use; how could they?

'Quite unhygienic, to be honest.' Carlotta looks down at the brush and dustpan in her other hand. She looks a little cowed. 'I thought we'd be doing you a favour, Rose.'

'This room is never opened,' I get out. 'We keep it closed, we keep it … special, to her memory.'

Carlotta exchanges a defensive look with my uncle.

'Your Mrs P told us this place had been closed up since your mother passed away?'

'That's right.'

'*Someone* has been in here, though. There were dust trails all over the table. New ones,' she turns to Uncle Ty. 'Someone's been in here recently.'

I don't answer that.

'I thought maybe … it would be easier for you if someone else did all the clearing-out work in here. You could give this room a whole fresh start. Unless, of course,' she looks up at me through her mascara-thickened lashes and, even though her tone is neutral, almost contrite, there's the tiniest spark of challenge in her eyes, 'you're already using it yourself from time to time?' I can almost feel my uncle's intake of breath behind me at that.

Using it for Wicca, she means, even though she hasn't said that. It's what they're all thinking.

'You're not, are you, Rose?' Ty has taken my arm and turned me to look at him and in the panic and distress in his eyes I see a whole host of unsaid, unsayable fears rise up to the surface like bubbles in a tall-stemmed glass. It is as if he fears, for one split second, that all the secret worries the Clare family harbour about me, Isla's daughter, might have some foundation after all.

But they needn't worry about that.

I shake his hand off my arm. There are other things they should be worrying about. Like preserving other people's dignity, like being careful with other people's memories, which is what my uncle promised me they would be if I let them use the room.

But they aren't careful people, are they? They won't be careful with our hearts, with what Mum's belongings mean to us. And they won't - I run up the stairs, so they can't see the stupid tears of disappointment that have sprung into my eyes - they won't be careful with my dad either, if ever they're left to be in

104

charge of him.

I need to be honest with myself about that much.

Rose

Christmas Day

'Pass the gravy boat, will you Isla dear?' The second time Dad says it I almost choke on my over-cooked turkey. Carlotta puts the gravy boat down and looks over at me with a tight little smile.

'I don't really look like your mum, do I?'

'Of course you don't,' Ty rallies round. 'It was a mistake, darling. He's probably reminiscing on Christmases past, eh Jack?'

'Here you go, Dad.' I snatch up the gravy boat and pour it for him myself, acutely conscious of the fact that his hands are trembling. I saw it when he raised his wine glass earlier. I'm pretty sure Ty noticed it too, even though he hasn't said anything.

'I'll have a bit more too. It's delicious, Carlotta,' I make a point of commenting. 'You've done a great job with the meal.' Carlotta adjusts her orange paper hat and acknowledges the compliment with a small nod. The fact is, she *has* done a great job. Okay, so some of the vegetables got burned to a crisp, and two of dad's special wine glasses got smashed when they were taking them out of the cupboard earlier. She's still managed to pull off a feast.

'This *is* almost like the old days,' I agree with Ty, getting caught up in a sudden shot of nostalgia. 'When we used to have a proper Christmas. When Mum was still with us.' When I look around the table, everything looks so festive and special. I showed Sam earlier how we used to adorn the table with berries and white paper flowers and I have to admit - even with the limited resources we had available - we've all done a pretty good job. I made a point when I got up this morning of putting Mum's room right out of my mind. What's done is done and I need to move on past all that now. Seeing all Mum's things in bin bags yesterday was hurtful, yes, but I have to believe they didn't mean any harm. Dad smiles at his brother suddenly, reading out a really corny joke from one of the Christmas crackers and they both laugh loudly. I tuck in, enjoying the meal. It's *good* to have the family round, I think. If only this kind of get-together could happen more often ...

'So. Did you use to celebrate Christmas like this before then - with all the trimmings?' Carlotta queries innocently now. 'With Isla being a pagan, I mean?'

I look up at her in surprise.

'Course they did, Carlotta. Jack's not pagan and neither is Rose,' Ty reminds her. She already knows this.

'You've always sent us Christmas cards, haven't you?' I lean over and adjust Dad's plate now so it's a bit nearer to the edge of the table. He's un-coordinated today, seems to be having a bit of trouble with his knife. I see from my aunt's expression that this hasn't missed her scrutiny, either. She doesn't comment, though.

'Well yes,' Carlotta wipes delicately around her mouth with a napkin. 'I thought it best to err on the side of caution.'

'And you *do* know Christmas is based on an old pagan festival anyway, Mum,' Sam pipes up. Carlotta gives her daughter a withering look.

'You don't normally put so much salt in it though, dear.' Dad pulls a sudden face as he tastes the gravy. He puts his fork abruptly back down on his plate and Ty leans in towards me a little, muttering in my ear now.

'He *is* all right, isn't he?'

'Sure.' We both know that Dad has never tasted Carlotta's gravy before and this is another reference to Isla.

'It's just that Jack seems a little more distracted today than I remember seeing him before.'

'You don't see him all that often,' I counteract. Ty shrugs, acknowledging that, and moves back towards his own seat. It's only been forty-eight hours since Dad took his last red tablet, I think uneasily. Despite my protestation, Ty is right. Dad isn't quite himself today. It can't be *that*, can it? The more I dwell on it, the more the thought grows worryingly large in my mind. If it's lack of medication that is causing this, then things are only going to get worse and every single time I look at Carlotta, her eyes are always on my dad. She's going to notice something's up. They're already noticing.

It's gone uncomfortably quiet at the dinner table suddenly. Then I add; 'I guess we're not much used to having company anymore. It's all a bit overwhelming, that's all.'

'I imagine it must be,' Carlotta muses. She's sounding faintly hurt. 'We're not where *we* expected to be, either, Rose.' She makes a sudden move to start clearing some of the finished plates away.

'I'll get those in a minute. You've done quite enough already and we do appreciate it,' I soothe. 'I can imagine it would have been an easier Christmas for you if you'd made it to Guiliana's ...' My aunt sighs quietly, and I'm reminded that for all the show they're putting on, spending Christmas stuck out here in the sticks with me and Dad was never their first option. It never will be. 'Maybe next year, eh?'

'I haven't quite given all hopes up for this year *yet*, Rose.' I don't answer her. If she hasn't looked out of the window so far this morning then I won't burst her bubble. Maybe Guiliana's is a several-day long event? 'On the other hand, I can't help but feel it's not an entirely bad thing that we've been diverted up here?' she adds unexpectedly. I see my cousin's eyes open wide in surprise.

'Not at all,' I agree heartily. I spear the last roast potato on my plate.

'I'll be honest, Rose,' she looks at me candidly. 'It's been in my mind for quite a while now that we Clares should be taking a keener interest in yours and Jack's affairs.' My uncle shifts uncomfortably in his seat and my stomach does a sudden flip. I swallow the potato in my mouth down in one go. Has he told her about our conversation in the log shed yesterday, or hasn't he? I can't believe they'd have had much chance to discuss it yet, even if he'd brought it up. From the discomfort on his face, I'd say he has not.

'Hear, hear,' Ty says. He holds his wine glass aloft suddenly, as if keen to cut across whatever it is he fears she might be coming to. 'Salut, everyone! And you're right, Lottie. Now that we're all spending this happy time together, I intend for us to keep up the momentum in the New Year.'

'Salut!' we all chime. Dad's drink wobbles so much in its glass as he raises it, I'm amazed there isn't a third wine glass mishap. Ty takes his wrist and helps his brother place the glass safely back on the table.

'Exactly,' she agrees. 'And if Jack's condition is deteriorating then it's important we all keep abreast of it.' Ty shoots her a warning look, but Dad seems oblivious. He's back shuffling through the jokes again, he's got a little pile in front of him that he's gathered from the rest of the table.

'He's not deteriorating,' I say in a quiet voice. Something about their demeanour seems to have knocked all the stuffing out of me. I stand up now, and start to collect the plates. Dad clearly isn't keen on eating any more of his *with all that salty gravy*. If we can only get Christmas pud over and done with, without any more 'Isla' comments, I think with a sudden urgency, then I'll get him in front of the telly with a glass of port. With any luck he'll doze off this afternoon before we can have any more gaffes. It's not his fault, of course. It is mine. I'm the one who should have remembered the tablets and I didn't. Now I just have to live with the consequences. I'm not too sure about Carlotta's sudden interest in our affairs, either. If she were a different person, I might be welcoming her concern. Even Ty knows she's not going to take too kindly to the suggestion I put to him yesterday. That's why

109

he's got to wait for the right moment to bring it up, I'm guessing. Dad's odd behaviour today isn't helping our cause, either.

By the time I get round to Carlotta's side of the table I've already made the decision that it's best to come clean with them. It's only fair I should let them know that Dad isn't always this discombobulated.

'He's not deteriorating.' I repeat, as I come up alongside my aunt. 'What you're picking up on is because he's missing one of his medications, today. The doctor warned me they'd go straight out of his bloodstream if he didn't take them,' I blurt out. 'They help with his mood and his co-ordination and a few other things.'

'But - how could that have happened?' Carlotta comes straight out and asks. 'What do you mean he's *missing* them?' For a moment I just stand there, feeling caught out. I can feel the plates piled high wobbling in my arms.

'We've run out of them,' I admit. I make to move on with the plates but her next words, addressed as much to my uncle as to me, stop me in my tracks.

'How, though? Didn't they have any at the pharmacy?' She looks deeply concerned at the thought.

'No, they *had* them.' I feel my face going a little pink. I know where this is going. Mrs P already told me she overheard Carlotta hinting yesterday that the place was looking run-down and we weren't 'coping' didn't she? 'We just - somehow - never picked them up.'

There's a stunned silence while she and my uncle take in this piece of information.

'Has this ever happened before, Rose?'

'No, of course not ...' I begin. 'I know I haven't had my eye on the ball as much as usual. I've just had the most stressful week ever waiting for my Uni offer letter and Mrs P's daughter is about to have her first baby which is probably why *she* forgot ...'

'She forgot.' Carlotta nods, her face very serious. 'And you didn't remember either? And now we're looking at going through the whole Christmas period with poor Jack not able to access the medicines he needs?'

'I've done what I can to put it right,' I assure her and Ty. 'I spoke to the locum and he's opening the dispensary specially. He's agreed to take the tablets to a half-way point where I can collect them.'

'You are, Rose?' She pulls a surprised face. 'How? Who's going to drive you?'

'No one.'

'You won't be able to get there then, will you?'

'Actually I was planning on …'

'It's perfectly all right, Rose, you don't have to explain.' My aunt's eyes are suddenly open, earnest, trying to persuade my uncle of something it now seems obvious they must have been speaking about earlier. 'It's too much to expect a girl of her age to be on top of all of this, Ty. Even with that home-help of theirs …'

'I'm sure they do their best,' he says quietly. He folds his napkin neatly on the table in front of him, smoothing it over with his long fingers and it's clear he's not comfortable. But Carlotta is muttering louder than she thinks about how Jack really needs 'responsible adult' supervision, and how forgetting his medicine 'is not an option.' I can't hear what Ty's murmuring in reply. She takes in a deep breath suddenly.

'I think you need to be *realistic*, Rose,' my aunt tackles me now, a sudden purpose in her voice.

'What do you mean, 'realistic'?' I look towards my uncle for support but he is focused on his wife, he doesn't look at me. From the glance they exchange now I get the feeling this conversation has suddenly turned in a different direction altogether. The plates that I'm holding are starting to feel heavy. I shift the weight of them in my arms.

'Your uncle already mentioned to me last night about your hopes to go off and study for a career.' Carlotta's finger is stroking the top of her wine glass now, going round and round in circles. For some reason, I can't take my eyes off it. She's been burning to bring this up with me ever since she got up, I think. I get the impression we are suddenly onto the real topic that has been eating away at her all morning, the reason why her mind was so distracted she burned the vegetables, maybe?

'Ty and I spoke about it at length last night.'

'Oh yes …?' If they've come to any conclusions after talking at such length they certainly haven't mentioned anything to me about it this morning. Not a good sign. When I glance towards the place at the table where Dad is sitting I see he has suddenly decided to have forty winks. It's as if he's opted out of this conversation. I feel a pang of regret wash over me, because here we are, all the family he's got left, about to discuss him and his fate and he is fast asleep. If only I had remembered those tablets. They would have made all the difference to how he's coped with lunch today. I know they would have.

'If you're serious about wanting that career then you'll have to be realistic about what's achievable and what isn't,' Carlotta is saying, her voice deadly quiet all of a sudden. She looks - stressed and put out and as if everything in her life is all too much. I can't even begin to imagine why. She doesn't work, as far as I know. They have no money worries. They seem to spend a lot of time away on fabulous holidays but here she is - *stressed*.

'I'm not sure what you mean, exactly,' I mumble.

And then she says it. 'A few years ago, Rose, your mum could have saved a lot of strain on the family if she'd just gone into care when things went downhill for her.' The family. Me and Dad, she means. They certainly never got involved so I can't see what business it is of hers.

'Dad doesn't need to go into care,' I flush. And why did she need to bring *Mum* into the conversation here? 'Uncle Ty?' I turn to him for support but he seems divided. He picks up his glass and swallows down some wine.

'We need to look at what's going to be best for Jack,' he says, infuriatingly non-committal. What happened to all that business of getting Dad looked at by more specialists?

'You've already made up your minds then?' I accuse.

'No,' he says.

'A loving daughter would be prepared to let her father have the very best care and be *honest* about things if she wasn't the one who could provide it.' My aunt looks at me solicitously and I find myself putting the plates back down on the table, an uncomfortable warmth spreading across my face. My cousin Sam busies herself scraping the last of the sprouts into a smaller bowl and then emptying the peas into the same container. She's got enough collected to go into the kitchen but I suspect she doesn't want to miss out on the outcome here.

'A loving daughter ...?' I say, and my throat suddenly feels raw and dry. *You're the selfish ones,* I think. *You're the ones who won't even entertain the idea of helping Dad out and you'd sooner put him in a stuffy old people's home rather than take him into your own lovely one.* I swallow those thoughts down, though. Saying them out loud won't help.

'You need to make sure you don't end up acting in a selfish way, too, Rose,' Carlotta adds. I blink. Selfish *too?* she just said. Like who ... my mum?

Not only can she not leave Mum alone, it sounds as if she - and maybe Uncle Ty? - have already made up their minds I am not doing a good enough job of looking after Dad. Even if I stay on here, doing the very best I can do for him, I would be being selfish, *like my mother.*

Round and round her finger goes on that glass, it is like her argument, held in a loop with no way to break into it. Oh, the truth is, she is upset because their Christmas has been ruined, because they've had to sleep somewhere she hates; there isn't enough festive food and drink here and my dad is behaving unusually which has spooked her and maybe she senses her whole life is suddenly being threatened by the burden of caring for one of her husband's relatives. I can understand that.

'I am not selfish, even though it may appear that way to you. I've even come to terms with you taking over Mum's room for your own use. Just please, Carlotta, don't *ever* imply my mum was selfish because she didn't go into a hospice, ever again.'

Her eyes open wider and Ty splutters out a cough.

'Rose!' Dad admonishes, coming in at the end of the conversation. *Fine time to come back to your senses now, Dad!* He brings his fist down somewhat mildly on the dining table but it is enough to make the wine glasses wobble. A little splash of wine jumps out onto the tablecloth and they all stare at it in shock.

'Rose, apologise to your aunt at once…'

'I'm not apologising.'

'I was only speaking the truth,' Carlotta says, her head suddenly bowed.

'*Your truth*,' I say, my face burning. 'Not ours.' What is there to say after that? I leave them there, aware that the atmosphere at the lunch table has been utterly ruined and Dad has just woken up and has no clue why.

'She misses her mum,' I hear him making excuses for me as I leave them all and go up to my room. Great, that's great. Now *he's* making excuses for *me*. About half an hour later, I hear Sam sheepishly knocking on my bedroom door. If she imagines she's going to find me in here weeping and embarrassed she's got another think coming. Actually I feel mad as hell. She comes in and sits on the edge of my bed tentatively, watching me shove a few undies and some toiletries into my backpack. Without even looking at her, I can hear in her voice she's feeling mortified for me.

'It's Christmas Day. It's snowing. The local news agencies are warning there's a fugitive on the loose and you're going … *where?*'

I can't believe I'm actually doing this, being this pathetic and childish. Twenty-four hours with the family and I am going mad. I'm not thinking straight. I know I am not but right now I can't seem to stop myself. I'm not really looking at what I'm packing. I'm not even *thinking* about what I'm doing I'm just shoving any old thing in, making a big show of it so Sam can be left in no doubt about my intentions …

'I am going to the crossroads post-box where - as you know, I arranged with the locum over the phone this morning - I can pick up the meds Dad should have had yesterday.'

'If you're only going out to pick up your dad's medicines then what do you need to pack up your *clothes* for?' Sam insists.

The truth is, I don't. All I'm really planning is to pick up the meds and then come back here. I look at my cousin.

'I am packing up my clothes in case … in case the locum didn't make it this morning. Then I might just spend the night with my friend Shona who lives on the other side of the hill. If the tablets aren't there ... I assume they will be by tomorrow.'

'*Why?*' She gives me a pained look. 'Why not come back here?' I arch my eyebrows at her. 'I mean, we're here,' she continues. 'We hardly ever see you and it's going to be so boring if you're not here ...' but I'm not in the mood to be cajoled. I shove a box of chocolates into my backpack, so it looks as if I might be taking a gift for someone. I might as well go on to Shona's for all the good anyone seems to think I'm doing here.

'I'm sorry about your mother's room.' Sam glances at the black bags which I salvaged from the hall last night, now piled high at the bottom of my bed and she cringes. 'And - what Mum said, But …' she touches my arm lightly, 'What about your dad? You can't go and leave him on Christmas Day, surely?'

'I'm not *leaving* him. I'm going to fetch his meds. I'll only go to Shona's if the meds aren't there. He seems happy enough with his long-lost brother to talk to and my aunt seems to have taken over the whole household, so I'm sure Dad will be fed and watered.'

'That isn't the point. It's Christmas. Everyone will expect you to be here.'

'Which I *will* be - if Dad's meds are in that box. Otherwise - don't wait up for me.'

'Rose.' She stands up as I pull my socks on determinedly. 'This is ridiculous. You can't go out in this. At least wait and Dad will go with you. I'm going to tell my parents …'

115

'I don't want to wait. You don't really think I want anyone's company right now, do you?' Sam takes my point. I have temporarily reverted to reacting like an eight-year-old in a huff and I know it.

'Rose ... don't go,' my cousin sucks in her bottom lip. 'There's a man on the loose,' she reminds me fretfully. 'They'll go spare if they know I saw you go out and I didn't say anything.'

A man, huh!

'He's not going to be roaming around up here in the snow like Magwitch in the marshes is he?' I give her a dismissive look. 'Besides, how else are we going to get hold of Dad's meds?' I warn her as I shove my phone into my bag. 'If you stop me now then you'll be stopping your Uncle Jack from getting his tablets.'

That seems to give her pause for thought.

As I step out into the whirling snow and trudge down the lane it doesn't take me all that long to realise I have probably made a big mistake. A bloody-minded stubborn streak makes me keep going instead of turning back and waiting for someone to come with me, though. I can do this by myself. I'll show them.

Rose

Damn, it's dark. I need to concentrate. Did I pack a torch when I was throwing all those things into my backpack earlier? It takes me a good five minutes to pull everything out of my bag and check and even in those few minutes it gets noticeably darker still. I didn't pack one, but there is the tiniest of torches hanging on the end of my key-ring. It's not much, but it's better than nothing. I switch it on and the faintest pin-prick of light picks out a patch of ground at my feet. The ground is glistening and hard with the ice under the tracks I've just made coming up.

I expected to have reached the post-box by now. Maybe I would have if I'd used the road but it's too icy, I've had to trek up the grassy embankment which is now covered in snow. I stop and take my bearings for a bit. About two hundred metres further up, at the top of the hill I can spy the outer bailey walls of the old castle ruins. The ruin looks eerie in the half-light, strangely beckoning. They say there's a chapel at the north end that's still fairly intact, but the rest is just a series of roofless walls all at various stages of crumbling away. I screw up my eyes, squinting over at it curiously but I'm not tempted to go over there.

This whole site is surrounded by Topwoods, which was once part of my dad's holdings; the part Macrae stole on the pretext of doing his restoration project. I used to come up here with my friends as a kid, playing hide and seek in the dense undergrowth but we never played amongst the ruins ...

All I want to do right now is find that post-box and go straight home. I only brought this backpack to shake Sam up. I wouldn't really have gone on to Shona's, no matter what. I was angry with all of them but Dad needs his meds. I look around warily. Only half a mile to the west there's a place the kids dubbed Dead Men's Copse which was a favoured spot at one time for people who wanted to end it all. This place is too lonely and isolated. I don't mean to stay long.

A bit further up the icy hill and my perseverance pays off. At the crossroads, I find the post-box. I lift the catch on it and sure enough, there is the blister pack of Dad's meds, safely deposited by the locum and awaiting collection as promised. I let out a triumphant whoop of relief but my voice only echoes in a strange, spooky way, taking the wind out of my sails.

Suddenly, it seems even darker than it was a few moments ago. I take in a deep breath, as it dawns on me that getting up here has taken me that much longer than I planned.

Still, I've got Dad's tablets and now I'm going to take it slowly and carefully on the way down. Even if it takes me an hour. I'm going to get back in one piece and everything is going to be … I take another breath in because I can't afford to go to pieces yet - everything is going to be *fine*.

It feels like it's got colder, even in the last half hour, and now, in the faint beam cutting through the darkness in front of me, I can see the snow has started coming down again. I turn my face upwards and I can feel the sting of little snow drops landing on my skin. It's coming down quite fast.

Maybe that's why I decide I'd better pick up the pace and abandon my plan to take it slow and steady. Maybe it's the strangest sense I've been getting, ever since I called out a few minutes ago, that I'm not alone; that somebody is watching me?

I mustn't panic.

It's important I keep my wits about me, concentrate on where I'm putting my feet, focus on the direction I'm going in but I can't shake a growing sense that somehow I've lost my bearings. Without a path to follow, everything looks the same. I look backwards over my shoulder but that's no help. This place looks so different with the sun gone down.

I keep thinking, *the last thing I want to do right now is fall over in this. Whatever I do I mustn't fall over.* The more I think about it, the more the idea takes hold. I'm taking so much care and then … I don't know how it happens but suddenly my feet slip out from under me and … *wallop*, there's a sickening sensation of pain as the back of my head hits the frozen ground but it doesn't stop there. The ground just beneath the surface must be sheet ice because suddenly I am sliding, half-plummeting, arms flailing out in an attempt to grab at something - anything - to stop myself but there's nothing but chunks of snow and ice, nothing I can get hold of. I just keep going and going and for a few terrible moments that feel more like hours the only thing I know for certain is the only way this is going to end is in a painful crash at the bottom.

Even as I'm falling, an even scarier thought is occurring to me; no one is going to know I'm here. Nobody will come and rescue me because if I don't go back home they'll assume I went on to Shona's. Just like I said I would. By the time I stop, heart thudding with fear and shock, the only vague thought I can get my head around is that my backpack fell off my shoulders somewhere near the top. My backpack has my phone in it. My phone is my only hope of summoning help. I don't think I can move, let alone crawl back up to retrieve it. Even if I *could* find it in the dark.

When I try calling out once or twice my whimpers echo into the muffled stillness on the hill because there is nobody here to hear me, nobody there to see me. It seems a strange thing, in this world that's so full of people, that anybody could fall in the snow and nobody ever find out till it's too late. Is that what's going to happen to me, now?

I cannot move.

I wonder how long it'll take before the family realise that

I'm not at Shona's. Will they ring her maybe, just to make sure I got there okay? Maybe nobody will think to wonder what's happened to me at all until morning?

Shit. By then I'll be a frozen corpse. The thought dawns on me with an unshakeable certainty now. I made such a show to Sam about packing up the bag. They won't know I'm here at all and by the time they *do* ... The news teams will make their way up here and they'll find the area cordoned off with that yellow police tape that they have while they search for evidence of foul play. I bet they'll all jump to the conclusion I've been murdered by that guy that's on the run because that'll make the most exciting news story. Everyone will be riveted to the box over the Christmas period eating their cold turkey sandwiches while the commissioner of police comes out and says they are looking into every avenue. *Crap*. I don't want to be a tragic Christmas news story. This is so unfair! I've got things to do yet. Whether or not I've got that Downing College offer I wanted I've still got a whole life to live and I've still got to get those medicines back to my dad ...

After a while, I calm down, though. All those thoughts, they seem muted, less important. Vaguely, I'm aware of a searing pain in my right thigh that happened somewhere along the way down but even that isn't worrying me too much. Slowly, I am getting this strange, overwhelming urge coming over me to just close my eyes for a bit and rest.

I mustn't. I know this. Part of my brain is warning - *in these temperatures if you lose consciousness now you may never wake up again*. It is so cold, though. It would be so *comfortable* to sleep, block out the cold that way, and the pain ...

Rose - her voice in my head sounds just like it always did - *don't sleep, Rose. Help is coming. Don't sleep!* And now, instead of the comfortable numbing I was starting to feel, I get a prickle of extra cold like the trickle of frozen water down my back, on my face and arms, forcing me back into alertness. And I hear Mum's voice again; kind and loving just like she used to be before everything changed ...

Help is coming, Rosie-Red. It's coming soon. Don't sleep, not yet!

Lawrence

Man, this place is cold.

In a moment I'll go out and drag in some more of that firewood I found stacked outside when I arrived here yesterday. That'll be Marco's stash, no doubt – he's had my father's permission to fell these trees for use in his solid-fuel burner for years. He won't miss a few odd logs. I'll do it before the light goes. I open up my rucksack which I've placed on the stone floor and peer at my stash of food. I purchased it yesterday when the HGV driver who I thumbed a lift from near Heathrow stopped for petrol. He took pity on me, gifted me the duffle coat his last hitch-hiker left behind in his cab before the weather turned, and I'm grateful for that. There were gloves still left in the pocket, a scarf tucked under the collar. I only wish I'd procured a bit more food now. The snow hasn't stopped since I got here. If I can't make contact with my mother as soon as I'd like it isn't going to be easy to get hold of more. Still - at least this place seems secure enough. I swing my torch round, peering into the darkness of the chapel ruin. It's all … pretty much as I left it. There's a small pile of rubble at one end where part of the internal masonry from some botched repairs has fallen down, but that's pretty much it. The small workmen's hut erected to the side of the chapel indicates there might have been intentions of having some work done up here at some point but it doesn't look like much ever got done. Neither are there any broken bottles or fag ends or any indication that anyone's been hanging out here. The old church pew is still there. It's shoved up against the chapel wall, right where I left it.

I go and run my finger along the length of the wooden back-rest. The wood is damp, cold to my touch but it's still intact. Still good to sit on. I let myself sit down.

I'm back, then. Really back, and that feels odd. I never thought I'd come here again. This old place - when I draw in a long, cold, lungful, it smells just the same. Musty, like old Roman baths in a museum. It smells safe. Nobody ever used to come and trouble me up here, did they? They won't now. This is Macrae land. Nobody trespasses. Nobody comes here unless they have a legitimate reason to. Like me.

That's why I'll be safe. I won't be disturbed.

In a moment I'll go and look out over the edge of the castle ruins beyond the chapel and check on the state of play at Macrae Farm. It's visible enough from here. I'll see if the lights are still on in my father's study or if he's gone out, yet. With any luck, there'll be no sign of him. He's got to leave soon. He goes to visit his father every Christmas.

Normally he'd have gone by now. From the fact that his jeep was still on the drive when I looked earlier, he hadn't left yet, though. I frown. He *should* be gone already. Why isn't he gone?

I get up, feeling a sudden urge to be on the move, to pace the floor or take some action even though right now the only thing I've got to do is be patient. That's all I need to do. Bide my time until my father's out of the way and then I can go down and get my mother's signature for Sunny. I'd never leave him with them at Macrae Farm, I only want her signature. She'll be surprised to see me. Shocked, maybe. I'll have to deal with it. But right now I can't think of that. I need to keep focused. So few days left … I look at my watch, which I've been checking obsessively ever since I arrived here yesterday. Today is the 25th December. The last Aid Abroad flight leaves at the end of the year. Dougie said they'll need all the paperwork signed and delivered by the 28th at the latest. Today is Christmas Day.

I let that sink in, then I quicken my pace to the door of the chapel. I want to go and check out the farm again. I don't want to spend Christmas with the family, whatever Arjuna and Dougie imagine. I just want to look at Macrae Farm and remember that I came from somewhere, once, even if that place is somewhere I have chosen to leave behind. I push the door open and the snow flakes that are drifting down in huge chunks remind me of the carols they used to sing at school about Good King Wenceslas. It reminds me that I'm all alone without even a beggar to keep me company.

Truth is, if a beggar walked by outside now I'd have to mind my own business.

I can't afford to be discovered. I've got to do what I came to do. That's all. Up here, it shouldn't be so hard to keep my head down. I'll need warmth to get me through the night. I have a little food. That's all I'll need.

I drag in the logs, and shake the snow off them, tearing off the brown, drier undergrowth for use as kindling as I learned to do long ago. My fingers are already numb with the cold and the sensation is an old one, the contrast with the place where I have been, striking. Only a few nights ago I was sweating under a mosquito net. I woke to the sound of the rain pattering down against the forest and when I put my head out of my tent in the morning a haze of heat was already rising up from the muddy ground, people were about their business everywhere, hundreds of people.

Today I woke to an icy morning in winter and I am completely and utterly alone.

As I work with the branches now, it dawns on me that I had forgotten the depth of the silence up here. How it can be deafening. How the mind rushes to fill it in with something, *anything*. The comforting creak of the wooden pew as I sit on it. The squeak as I pull the leaves off the logs I've dragged in. The sound of my own footsteps echoing against the stone floor.

When I hear the sound of that girl's scream, long and terrified, ringing out into the dusk I tell myself she'll be somewhere with her friends down in the valley, larking about in the snow. The sound has travelled up here unusually clearly because of the snowfall. That is all. Whoever she is, she won't have been alone. It's Christmas Day, and nobody is alone. But then without wanting to, I find myself straining to hear the reassuring sound of her calling out again, perhaps laughing this time, the sound of everything being okay, of things being as they should be.

And I remember that, even if they are not, it is not my business.

Rose

'Hello?' Through a foggy distance in my mind I can hear a man's voice. A young man. I must be dreaming because he doesn't seem fazed at finding me here. He sounds exactly like an ambulance man would sound only he can't be *that*.

Can he?

'Hello Miss. Can you open your eyes for me, please?' I would, too. I like his voice, it is steady and kind. I want to open my eyes but right now they seem to be glued tight shut. He pats my hand reassuringly when I whimper at that. *Why can't I open my eyes?*

'Do you think you could tell me your name?'

'Rose,' I get out. That takes some doing, and the effort of it somehow makes me more conscious of the bruising all the way down my side, of the sharp stinging pain in my thigh. *Ow.*

'That's great. Thank you, Rose. Do you remember if you hit your head on the way down at all, Rose?'

I hit my head, yes. I think I hit my head, but right now it's my leg that's really bothering me.

'Rose?' I can feel him gently rubbing the back of my hand but there's an unmistakeable urgency to his voice. 'Stay awake for me, Rose.' I'm trying, but right now that feels incredibly hard to do.

He crouches down until I can feel his face very near to my own. He is so near that I swear amongst the cold drops of ice that

126

are still falling on my face I can feel the heat coming off of his skin. I can hear his breath close to my ear and his voice, when he whispers the next word is almost hoarse; '*Please?*'

There is something almost deeply shocking in that and it does the trick. My eyes snap open and he moves back immediately. I blink. In the light from the torch he's wedged into the snow beside me I can see his face and he looks concerned, attentive. Perhaps a little relieved? My rescuer is handsome, too. Dark, short hair, not much older than me I'd guess. I realise, with something of a shock, *boy, is he handsome.*

'Do you remember if you hit your head?' he's asking again softly. My head. *Maybe I did and I'm hallucinating you*, I think. Right now I am looking at the cutest guy I ever laid eyes on in my life.

And here am I, flat on my back like an up-ended tortoise gaping like a star-struck fool. I can't shake the feeling that there is something familiar about him.

'I want to sit up,' I say with an effort of will that surprises even me. I can't know him. If I'd met him before I'd have remembered it, I know that I would.

'Do you think you might be able to do that?'

I have got to at least try. He wants me to stay awake for him doesn't he? He just said so. It's better than becoming a frozen corpse. It hurts when I try and sit. He helps me by putting his arm behind my shoulder, supporting me on the way up. I wince.

'Sore?' he says. 'How's your head?'

Gingerly, I move my head from side to side. When I put my hand to the back of my skull there's no blood. Nothing is cracked.

'My head is fine,' I croak at last. My voice seems to be coming from somewhere else; as if I left it parked at the top of hill when I fell and my *bum* is real sore. I can't mention that to this guy, though. 'My leg hurts.' He nods, but he doesn't seem too bothered about that.

'All the way up?' he urges now. I hook my fingers into the crook of his arm and let him lift me into a standing position. I

127

stand there, swaying for a bit and he doesn't let me go. Where to from here? I look at him questioningly. Where's the ambulance?

Because there must be one. Maybe I'm confused about timings because he couldn't have materialised out of nowhere could he? He stands back a bit, still holding onto me but assessing the situation for a moment before he concludes;

'You're not going to be able to walk anywhere are you?'

My voice has deserted me again. Now my leg *really* hurts. I feel about four years old, in the hands of someone else who's going to have to make the decisions, guard my life for me. I shake my head at him. He's right. I'm not going to be able to walk anywhere. I feel too shocked .My body feels battered and bruised.

'I'm going to have to carry you myself then. Is that all right, Rose?'

He's going to carry me. I nod. I should be feeling mortified but the strange dislocation from reality that I was feeling before has set in again. Waves of sleep are threatening to wash over me. When he lifts me off my feet my head falls comfortably against his chest and I'd be happy to nod off, right here, but he keeps talking to me all the time, asking me questions. So many questions; w*here do you go to school, Rose? What's your favourite TV soap? Do you have any pets?* I notice he doesn't ask me what I'm doing up here all alone on this abandoned site so late on Christmas Day. He doesn't ask me if there's anyone I'd like him to try and contact for me, anyone at all?

In the back of my mind, there is my lost backpack, Dad's tablets, I know I should ask him to go look but he keeps asking questions. *What music do I like? What am I hoping to do next year …?* He even cracks the odd joke or two. I know he's trying to keep me conscious, not to let me drift off and he's given me the job of holding the torch for him now, *keep it pointed forward, Rose, so we can both see where I'm going.* We seem to be going straight upwards, from what I can make out, directly towards the old ruin. I play along with him, answering in monosyllables but the crunch of his footsteps against the snow is mesmerising. The sound reminds me of when I was a kid and I'd crack the ice on the duck-pond at Shona's then shatter it like a window-pane of ice against the yard floor. It'd splinter into a thousand shards, but that sound of the ice cracking … it's the sound of danger being near but in a place where you know that you're safe.

How do you know that you're safe, Rose? The sensible part of my mind is asking. The part that speaks in Carlotta's voice. *Why isn't he heading down the hill, taking you back to the place where you've come from? Who even knows who this guy is, or where he's from?* These are questions I can't answer but I know, somehow, that this man is safe. *He could be the fugitive guy that the cops are after,* Carlotta's voice is saying but I put her on mute. My foggy brain just can't take in anything else at the moment. I'm going to have to trust him.

Then I get a light-bulb moment. Of course! He must be the locum - on his way home from delivering Dad's meds to the post-box. The realisation sends immediate relief flooding through me. He's got to be the locum, hasn't he? How else would he know to ask all those health-professional sounding questions? Maybe the way down via the other side of the hill is clearer than the one I've just come up? 'I dropped the medicines,' I confess to him. 'They were in my backpack. Did you see it on your way down?'

I see him blink, taking this in.

'I'll look for it in a minute,' he says.

We've got up as far as we can go. Beyond the entrance ramparts the inner bailey walls are much lower than I'd always imagined them, the half-broken arches end suddenly, desolately, in the air. All is still and dark, the hill-top remains surrounded by fog and all the while the snow keeps on falling. I blink, forcing my eyes to keep open, look at him curiously. His dark duffle coat is wet. The light from the torch he's given me to carry shines momentarily on his damp hair, picks out the concern in his eyes as he looks down at me.

'Thank you,' I tell him and it's heartfelt. 'You're the locum, right? Can we get to the village if we go down this side?' I see him suck in his bottom lip. His shoulders rise in what appears to be a sigh. He gives the smallest shake of his head.

'That way will be blocked by now. I'm sorry, but there's no way we're getting to the village in this.'

'No?'

'I'm afraid we're going to need to shelter in here for a bit, Rose.' His voice is measured and reassuring as he bends down to turn the metal handle of the chapel door. The wooden door creaks open - strangely, it opens outwards, like a shed door - and when he takes the torch and trains the beam on the inner walls it's immediately apparent that the rumours about the chapel being the only stone structure still standing intact around here, are true.

He puts me down on a wooden pew near the entrance, while we both take the measure of our surroundings. My immediate response is to recoil; it's damp and as cold as you'd expect and it smells musty. *Ugh*. When he says we have to stay here for a bit I hope he doesn't mean a very long bit. I mean, I hope it's not going to be for more than a couple of hours. I rub my hands together in my gloves and I can barely feel them. I'm not feeling too good right now. I watch as he flickers the torch over the walls so we can take in the shape of the chapel; it's maybe twenty feet across, fashioned in a roughly-hewed semi-circle, with a step up towards what might once have been the altar at the North end. He shines the torch upwards and high up on the walls some narrow stained glass windows are admitting a meagre amount of muted moonlight from outside.

'I'm going to fetch that backpack of yours now, Rose.' He smiles softly and as I watch him disappear through the door I think - I don't *want* to stay here overnight. Even with this doctor who's got the looks of some kind of soulful film star, and who's so attentive and kind and ... everything you might imagine or want a guy to be if you were going to be stuck in an abandoned ruin for several hours. I remind myself there are girls from my old sixth form who would die for an experience like this; on paper, anyway.

In reality it doesn't feel so good. I don't want to be here.

I'm frozen and everything hurts and *it's Christmas Day* and Dad needs his medicines …

'Oh, *thank you*.' I look up as he comes back holding my backpack aloft a few minutes later. 'You found it easily then?'

'I picked out the dark straps as I trained my torch over the snow. I was lucky.' He places it in my lap and I double-check that everything's still in there, that the tablets and my phone at least haven't fallen out. When I look up he's watching me curiously. I zip up the bag and put it to one side, a little self-conscious.

'Will we be stopping here for long, do you think?' He looks surprised. 'Before … you can take me home, I mean?'

'I don't know how aware you were of those weather conditions out there Rose, but I wouldn't suggest either of us has much chance of making it out of here tonight.'

'*Tonight*?' He's kidding me. We're going to be stuck in this dismal place *the whole night*? I cover my face with my hands and inwardly groan.

'You're saying there's really no way we're getting home?'

'We won't, Rose.' He's taken off his coat and he's shaking the snow off it. 'There's no electricity but there are plenty of logs from the felled trees stacked up outside. No reason why we shouldn't have some warmth and some good light. Then I'll take a look at that injury on your leg, if that's all right with you?'

'What injury?' It was hurting before but my leg's feeling pretty numb now.

'You're bleeding,' he points out. 'There, see.' He indicates my thigh. 'Right now what you need is some medical attention before you worry about anything else,' he says firmly.

'I've got my bag in here, somewhere. Some medical supplies …' The muffled echo of his footsteps against the flagstones reminds me of the sound of being inside a cave. 'I can probably deal with the injury to your leg myself,' he's saying. *He's going to do what …?*

My leg is bleeding. I didn't notice that before. Yuck. Now he's pointed it out, I can't stop shivering. I feel so strange and numb and disconnected. As if all this were a dream and nothing more.

'You've gone into shock, Rose.'

In an almost tender gesture he drapes the coat he's just taken off and shaken out around my shoulders and I am brought spinning right back down to earth.

'If I'm going to need to treat you then I guess I'd better tell you my name, too.' He bends down and the unexpected warmth of his hand on my shoulder sends a shudder of happiness right through me. I feel my face growing hot because *he really is too cute* but this is no time to be coy.

'I'm Lawrence,' he says.

Lawrence

I don't need this right now.

She's a pretty girl. Under any other circumstances she might have been good company. But she's injured - I glance up at her from where I've been hard at work getting the fire going - she's possibly concussed and she's almost certainly in shock. She needs medical attention and I … I need any sort of attention right now about as much as I need a hole in the head. I can't believe I just told her my name.

The fire I made earlier in the day has gone out. The wood I picked up yesterday will do for the moment but I'm mindful that we'll soon need more fuel. I strike a match and hold it gingerly up against the tinder I've just shoved in under the metal brazier the workmen left behind. A few pieces of an old copy of 'The Mail' flare up bright orange and then shrivel into black curls in an instant.

The news from Sri Lanka when I spoke to Arjuna this morning was cautiously optimistic. They tell me right now Sunny is recovering well from the operation, and that's good. They need the ward bed back though, ASAP. That is not so good.

Arjuna seemed stressed when we spoke earlier but then, Arjuna is always stressed. I'd have preferred to speak to Dougie - but for some reason Arjuna didn't explain, Dougie couldn't come to the phone. That didn't bode well. There have been some developments even in the few hours since I left Jaffna. Some of the contact names I came away with have had to drop out. My boss was supposed to be bringing me up to speed with the director of the medical charity that'll most likely be helping Sunny out - one Herr Lober. Dougie was going to book me a telephone appointment with the man's secretary. I need to know how I'm going to proceed once I've got my mum on board with her sponsorship signature. I know the fact it's Christmas will have made it that much more difficult to reach people.

I strike another match and set fire to the tinder in several different places at once in order to give the fire the best chance of taking.

'You're very good at that,' my companion observes.

'Thank you. I've had enough practice at getting fires going from damp wood in my time.' *Most of them up here, as it happens.*

'Are we really going to have to stay here overnight?' There's resignation in her voice because she already knows the answer to that one. I glance up at her and she's still shivering. Ideally, I'd have liked to have got her back down the hill tonight if possible but with the weather like this it isn't going to happen.

'I'm sorry, Rose.' Is she regretting it now, I wonder? Running away from home or wherever it was that she ran from? I've spent enough time going AWOL myself to know a runaway when I see one. She's scared and she's got that unmistakeable air of desperation about her. Apart from that, I picked up her backpack a few minutes ago. I don't know what she's got in there but it's more than just a bottle of water and her mobile phone that's for sure. This girl wasn't just planning a bracing walk up to the post-box to get some medicines was she? I keep my head down, concentrating on my task.

'Do you need to phone anyone?' I ask her at last.

I know *I* want to phone someone. I really, really want to phone Dougie right now. Jaffna is five and half hours ahead of us - over there it'll be coming up to 10 pm his time - but I'm also acutely aware of the fact that on the journey down to Colombo I agreed with Arjuna that we'd stick to specific times. For one,

Dougie could make sure he was in a safe place to talk that way. Secondly, I should ideally keep my phone switched off as much as I can. I've got no way of recharging the battery up here and I can't risk missing an all-important call just because my phone's gone dead at the eleventh hour ...

The best thing I can do for the moment is put Sri Lanka right out of my mind. I glance up at the girl now.

'Anyone who might need to know that you're somewhere safe?' The tinder in the brazier is obligingly glowing bright orange. Some little flames are beginning to lick hungrily around the smaller sticks. My companion doesn't answer me. She's looking very sad.

While the going's good, I feed in some small chunks of rotting wood I've hacked with my pen-knife out of one of the felled trees I found stacked in the courtyard. The decaying wood burns fast, pretty soon increasing the heat enough for me to start feeding in some small sticks. The growing warmth which spreads through my hands as I slowly build the fire is a comforting relief.

'I'd better text my cousin,' she answers eventually and her voice sounds slightly strangled. Not too keen to make contact with her folks, by the sounds of it. The truth is, I'm not ecstatic about her telling people that she's up here. Inevitably it's going to draw attention to me, too.

And why her cousin?

Where are your parents, Rose? I'm surprised they even let you out in these weather conditions. Not my business, I know but ... do they even know you're out?

I feed another two slender branches of wood into the burning heap. Then several more. Without making it obvious, I watch her as she rummages for her mobile.

'You going to mention that you're up here?' I ask casually.

'Better not,' she shakes her head curtly. 'There's nothing anyone can do tonight and they'd only worry. They'll assume I've gone on to my friend Shona's house. I said I'd do that if the medicines hadn't been left in the post-box ...' she stops abruptly as I straighten and I see her typing in a brief text.

The fire is at a stage where it needs to be left for a few minutes to take before I can feed in some of the larger pieces of wood that'll take us into the night. For the moment, we have some warmth at least, a fair amount of light.

'Go on.' I pick up my paramedic bag and come over and kneel down beside her.

"The medicines …?' I prompt. I saw her checking for them, earlier. Is that really what she was doing up here? Picking up something from the crossroads post-box? It's possible. It's a tradition as old as these hills round these parts. I set my bag down on the floor beside her and I see her steeling herself.

'Important medicines, right? To come out of the house on a day like this…' She looks pretty choked up, when I ask that. She nods.

'For you?' She doesn't answer. 'Come on now, Rose, You've been doing great up to now. Don't disappear on me again will you?' I pick up her hand and her palm feels too cool for my liking. I feel her forehead.

'Still woozy? Any pain to the back of the head or neck? Any tingling sensations, numbness?' She's shaking her head to all my questions. 'Okay. Everything feeling pretty normal then, apart from the soreness where you've bruised yourself?' I unzip my paramedic bag and in the orange firelight I see her large eyes open slightly wider.

'Everything's okay.'

'I'm still a little concerned about your leg, though. Will you allow me to have a look at it?'

'I'm *fine*,' she tells me.

'You're bleeding,' I point out. 'There, see.' I point at her thigh and even in the half-light, the darker patch where the blood from the wound has soaked through is worryingly more visible to me than it was before. 'Do you have any idea how that might have happened? Did you see what you might have snagged yourself on, on the way down?'

She shakes her head. Right now she's looking very close to tears but I can see she's battling like mad not to show that.

'I noticed there's quite a lot of bits of old rusty wire up here, that's all. Can you tell me if you're up to date with your tetanus jabs, Rose?'

'I think so. I had one last summer when I scratched my arm on the farm gate.'

'That'll do. I'd still like to look at your leg. You'll need a dressing on that. Maybe one or two stitches ...'

'Stitches? Oh. *If I need stitches*, then who's going to do them?' She swallows nervously. I spread my arms, trying my best to make her feel at ease. There's nobody else here to do it.

'I'm medically qualified to do it, I've done dozens before,' I promise her. 'I know it's a little uncomfortable but you'd be better off having the suture done promptly if it's needed. It might not even be needed. Shall I just take a look?'

She hesitates.

'I can't roll these jeans up that far,' she says after a slight pause. 'Am I going to need to take them *off*?'

I appreciate this is awkward for her.

'I'm really sorry. There's no way I can check it out for you otherwise. Do you need any help in taking ...?'

'*No!*' she says.

'Look, I'll go back and tend the fire for a bit. You take as long as you need. Feel free to cover yourself with my coat and let me know when you're ready.'

'Fine.'

As I go and kneel down to tend to the fire, I can hear her struggling with her jeans.

'There's a *lot* of rusty wire around these parts,' she's suddenly talking rapidly. It's the nerves, I know. 'Our horrid neighbours seem to think it's necessary to put it up all along their boundary walls. It's pointless,' she says feelingly. 'Wild animals get hurt on it all the time. It's not as if it would deter anybody who really *wanted* to get into the property anyway.'

137

'I don't suppose it would,' I tell her softly. Barbed wire doesn't seem to be much of a bar to people who want to get out of a place, either. For a minute the memory of the camp at Jaffna looms large in my mind, surrounded as it is by rusty barbed wire. I loathe the stuff with a vengeance. Over the last year I've administered more tetanus jabs, sewn up more jagged tears on the skin than I care to remember, mainly to children, because of it. The proximity of so many people and animals and the constant damp and mud is a perfect breeding ground for bugs.

I feed a medium-sized log into the brazier now and it catches immediately.

This is the entire reason why I'm even here, the thought intrudes. So Sunny can recover under hygienic conditions. But he's doing all right, I remind myself. He's still got that bed in the field hospital and Arjuna has promised it's his till the end of the year. I need to put Sri Lanka out of my mind. I need to focus on what I have to do right here.

Behind me, she coughs slightly now and I turn. She's covered up the top of her legs with my coat but there's a nasty-looking jagged cut on her right thigh. That's going to need stitches all right but it's not too bad - only a couple of inches or so. There's blood all over the thigh which I need to clean up for her but all around the wound it's already congealing nicely. Three or four stitches will do it and I travel with the equipment I need as standard in my bag. I almost didn't bring my paramedic bag. When it came to it though, I couldn't bear to leave it behind and Arjuna agreed it would help my cover story in getting out of the country.

'Is this going to hurt?' her voice sounds nervous as I go and kneel back down beside her.

'The anaesthetics will sting a little bit when I put them in around the wound but after that you won't feel me stitching, I promise.' I take the torch and place it where the light can fall best for me to see what I'm doing. 'Not ideal conditions, eh, Rose? But you'll be fine.' I look up and smile into her eyes for a few seconds. Her eyes are shiny, wide open, scared.

'You trust me, don't you?'

She nods. Poor girl, she has no option, does she? Best to keep her mind off things, keep talking to her so she doesn't have time to worry about the fact that she's stuck in a ruin with a complete stranger. A stranger who's about to sew up a wound and she's sitting here frozen and hurt and with no jeans on …

'Okay, Rose? Just a little sharp jab as the anaesthetics go in.'
'*Ouch.*'

'Sorry.' Her face puckers up a bit. I know it hurts but I've got a hunch there's a lot more going on for this girl right now than just the discomfort - and indignity - of having me stitch up her wound. I'd better keep her talking, I guess.

'So - those medicines you mentioned you came up here to pick up, were they for *you*, Rose?' I glance at her to see how she's doing and she's staring hard at the fire, avoiding looking down at her leg at all. Avoiding looking at me.

It's none of my business, I know. If she came up here because she was running away from home for whatever reason she's not likely to tell me the truth of it now, is she? If she is on some sort of medication it might be important that I know it, however. I would have ascertained that earlier, if I'd been thinking straight. She doesn't answer, just glances down at her leg and then rapidly away again. I've got a squeamish one here, all right.

'I'll do a neat job for you, I promise,' I tell her softly. 'I'm pretty good at sewing, Rose. Quite handy for a boy.' That elicits a small smile and she looks up at me for a split second, her pretty eyes meeting mine. Are they green, I wonder? Maybe blue?

'Were the meds for you?' I persist gently.

'The meds were for my dad,' she looks puzzled now. 'You brought them up here, didn't you? We spoke, on the phone, remember? This morning.'

'We've never spoken before, Rose.'

'Oh.' She looks confused. 'I thought you were the … Well,' she shrugs, 'I spoke to the locum. I thought he said he was the one who'd be dropping them off himself?' Her eyes narrow curiously now. 'Who are you - some sort of paramedic then?'

I nod.

'And I guess you got the short straw and - they sent you instead?' She glances at me, wincing. She seems convinced *I'm* up here on a legitimate mission anyway - I'm the one who dropped off her dad's tablets for her. Apparently.

'How much longer?' she asks through gritted teeth.

'The anaesthetics are all in now.' I'm pretty pleased with myself, at how it's going. A few minutes ago my hands were trembling, they were so cold when I was making up that fire but now that I'm working my hands are steady as a rock. Her leg will be numb soon. She'll only feel a little tugging on her skin as I pull the thread up.

'So these meds,' I press. 'A matter of life …?'

She pulls a face at that, realising that I'm chiding her gently for coming up here. If they weren't urgent, she shouldn't be here and she knows that.

'It's just that I couldn't help notice you've packed quite a bit of stuff in your backpack. Were you planning on going straight home?'

'Um…' she looks at me sheepishly. 'I know I packed up some clothes and all but that was just for show. I wasn't really going to go on to Shona's.' She's sounding a little embarrassed. 'There was a … a bit of a family argument over something. When I left the house I was feeling mad at everyone.'

'You just wanted the family to think you were staying away tonight?' I hide the smile in my voice, concentrate on my task. *Families at Christmas, eh…?*

'I *was* going to go back home, Lawrence,' she assures me. 'Once I'd got the medicines and I'd calmed down. Family can make you feel so mad sometimes, can't they?' She turns to me now entreatingly. 'I can take the flak from more distant relatives like my aunt Carlotta,' she adds unexpectedly, 'but my dad - you'd think he'd know me better, wouldn't you?'

'One would hope so,' I pull at the first stitch and snip off the thread. One down.

'I get all the responsibility for doing everything at home, you know?' She draws in her shoulders despondently and I discreetly concentrate on my task. Injured people often open up to you when you're ministering to them. It doesn't do to pay them too much mind. I'm sure half the time they don't even realise they're doing it, it's just a reaction to the shock. Whatever was on their mind before the accident, it all comes spilling out. The second stitch is in now. Even in this light, I have to say, I'm pleased at how this is going.

'My dad relies on me a lot. All the time in fact,' my companion continues. 'The rest of the family are never even around. And then when they do come along, my aunt feels it's acceptable to have pop at Mum. So I had a go back.'

'Fair do's' I murmur.

'But that isn't the worst bit,' she splutters. 'The worst bit is that my dad defended her. He knew she was in the wrong. I could see it on his face. So why did he side with Carlotta?'

Why indeed?

'He probably felt he had to,' I console. 'Generational thing, isn't it? They side with each other.' I give her a conspiratorial grin.

She frowns as I tug at the second stitch, finishing it off, pulling the skin together neatly. This is going to heal up beautifully in time. She's got her hands under her knees and her fists clenched.

'Well it maddens me that he won't defend Mum more than he does. When they come up with those mean-spirited comments then he should.'

'Mum not around to defend herself?' I offer gently. I see these kind of family dynamics all the time.

'Mum's dead,' she says in a dead pan tone. 'She died when I was thirteen.'

'I'm sorry, Rose.' I really am sorry. Rose has been coping so beautifully all this time and now there are these huge tears welling in her eyes. I think, even with her best effort of will, she's not going to be able to stop them.

141

'You miss your mum?' I put in the third stitch. My patient has a stoic look on her face now.

'The truth is ...' she says quietly, 'I both miss her and sometimes ... I feel mad at her at the same time.'

'Feelings are complicated things, eh?' I give her a wry grin.

'I feel mad at her because I find myself having to defend her all the time.' Rose has started picking at the fluff on her jumper sleeve. I recognise the signs. She's just fiercely wiped the tears off her face and they've dried up immediately. I'm impressed. I adjust the torch a little, settle a bit closer in to my work.

'Defend her for...?'

'For being who she was. For having the beliefs that she did. My mum was a pagan, Lawrence.' Rose gives me a little sideways glance here, checking out my reaction. 'A hedgewitch, if you like; she could be a bit of an eco-warrior, too. Not everyone in my family went along with that.'

'No?' I say neutrally. There used to be a whole campful of New Age types living in the area at one time, I recall. It takes all sorts ...

'No. Especially when she went off and spent months living in an underground burrow under the Topwoods. We *all* objected to that. But whatever anyone's beliefs, it really bugs me when they make comments. Because she was a good person. However she chose to live her life – that was her business and ours. Not theirs. Why should they judge her?'

I catch Rose's eye but she looks away from me quickly.

'I'm sorry, Lawrence,' she gives an apologetic little laugh. 'We've only just met and here I am, unburdening my whole life story onto you. I didn't mean to. In fact,' she sounds embarrassed. 'I can't believe I said all that. It's not stuff I'd normally...'

'People often become talkative when they've experienced a trauma,' I tell her. 'Even the quiet ones.'

'Do they?' She sighs. 'I suppose you're used to it then.'

'It pays to develop a professional amnesia,' I wink at her. 'I promise you by tomorrow I won't recall a word of what you're telling me ...'

'It's just been a bit of a crap Christmas Day, you know? *Everything* has gone wrong.'

'Not everything,' I remind her. 'I found you. You could still be out there in the snow right now, freezing to death.'

'Except for that,' she concedes. 'I'm sorry. I didn't mean to sound ungrateful. You've ... you've really been my guardian angel, haven't you?'

I flash her a small smile and she looks away, shy.

'All part of the service,' I say softly. I swab at the skin around the wound with some antiseptic cotton balls now. The blood comes off cleanly and evenly.

'I miss my mum too,' I confide before I can stop myself. 'I haven't seen her in a very long while. Only - my mum isn't dead.'

'Oh.' She looks at me as if that surprises her. 'Well you should put that right, Lawrence.'

'I should.'

I snip off the last stitch, carefully place a padded dressing over the suture. Then I stand up. 'We're done with these, I think. That didn't hurt, did it?' I know it didn't hurt. *There's something else that's hurting you far more than the wound in your leg right now isn't there, girl?*

Then I add something that I normally wouldn't.

'Rose, this pickle that you're in ...' I keep my eyes carefully on my bag, putting away my bits and pieces, while she pulls on some trackie bottoms she's retrieved from her backpack. 'Does it involve a member of the opposite sex, by any chance?' I might be reaching, here, but I've been around long enough to recognise most scenarios. *Is this really all about her mum? There's been an argument at home. She's upset and she's sad and she's desperate enough to have packed up a bag to leave home. I'm thinking, if she's pregnant, that'd make a lot of sense, join up a lot of dots. Could it really be the morning-after pill she's risked coming up all this way to fetch, not something for her dad, after all?*

Rose quietens for a bit, looks at me wonderingly; whether

143

that's because I've just stumbled on her secret or not, I don't know, but then she laughs.

'Chance would be a fine thing,' she says. 'But since you're asking ... no.'

'It's just that ...' I hesitate, aware that I'm on precarious ground. 'If you were in a ... in a difficult situation, so to speak, you might want to try talking it over with someone before you ...'

'No!' she comes back stronger. 'No, Lawrence. I'm sorry, but you're making assumptions and you shouldn't.'

'I'm sorry,' I say quickly. 'It's none of my business, is it?' It isn't. I don't know if I believe her *'chance would be a fine thing'* story. A girl like her wouldn't lack the chance, would she? Maybe she doesn't want to go there and fair enough, I shouldn't have asked her.

'You shouldn't,' she repeats in a hoarse whisper, 'even if we *have* only just met and you've already seen me in my knickers ...'

'I didn't see your knickers,' I remind her. 'I lent you my coat, remember?' She looks away, arms crossed over her stomach and I could kick myself for asking her that. Damn you, Lawrence, when are you going to learn? You've got enough troubles of your own to be worrying about.

Her phone is buzzing now, a text no doubt, replying to her own recent one and as I watch her answer I am sorely tempted to check my own phone, find out if there have been any developments at the Jaffna end.

That is, after all, what my being up here is all about.

According to Arjuna, Dougie expected to hear from Herr Lober today. There might be news. I need to know if this is happening. I should wait, I know, think of the phone battery. I'm not going to be able to take any further action till tomorrow in any event. But, like an addict unable to stay away from the thing, I pull my phone slowly out of my pocket. I switch it on. While I wait for it to connect, the task that's looming up ahead of me comes forcibly back into my thoughts.

Jeez. I've still got to get my mum on board with this, haven't

I? In my mind, that was always going to be the trickiest bit. I haven't seen my mum in five years. I haven't contacted her. Not a phone call, not a postcard, not an email. *Nothing*. What Rose has just said about her own mum has brought it all back; the love that's mixed with the frustration. Loving someone who isn't the way you want them to be, who can't be how you need them to be.

After I left home myself, not making contact with Mum was hard. How would I know if she was all right? How would I ever know if she needed me? I wouldn't know, and I couldn't do anything to help her even if I did, so I put her right out of my mind, it was the only way to survive.

That cost me but Mum won't know that. She'll be hurt and mad as hell at me, she's bound to be because I cut her out of my life, didn't I? In the end, that was a matter in which I didn't have any choice.

If all goes according to plan, she'll see me soon enough, though. As soon as my father's Cherokee is no longer parked in his space out on the drive I'll go in to her. The thought of going back into the house where I grew up sets the muscle in my jaw pulsing. But I don't want to think about it too much, I can't afford to.

'It's all right,' Rose says softly through my thoughts now. 'I shouldn't have come back like that. You've been so kind and I *was* the one who started telling you all my woes …'

'No, honestly, Rose, don't tell me.' I don't want her to, I shake my head at her, watching her put her phone away.

And right now my own phone has connected. I get a small shock as I see straight off there's a message flashing from Arjuna:

Small problem with H.Lober and D. will again not be available 2 ring u tmrw - I will ring u at agreed time instead. Do not worry. Λ

Do not worry? Shit. What's that supposed to mean? I look at Rose ruefully, careful to hide my thoughts from her but I can't help heaving a huge inner sigh. Man, this is going to be one hell of a long night, it really is.

Rose

Snow not letting up tonight, Sam's just texted me. *So it's fine with P's if you stay at Shona's. Thought plan was to return here if you had the meds, though?*

Shona's is nearer and the way is all snowed up. I text back.

Okay then, she comes back immediately. *Uncle Jack says he's feeling a bit worse for wear without tablets. Fingers x'd predicted rain will come tmrw and we'll all get out of here soon. S xx*

If it's raining tomorrow that'll mean I can get back to Dad, thank God. She says he's already feeling a bit worse for wear and that's not good...

'Everything okay?' My rescuer must have just seen the look on my face. 'Good news?'

'It should be raining by tomorrow, apparently.' I close down my phone. 'I'm sure we'll make it out of here okay if it rains. Once we can see where we're going, that is ...'

'Ah.' He comes over and sits down beside me on the pew. 'Rose. I need to apologise for what I said to you before about ...' He checks himself. 'You were right. I shouldn't have made any assumptions about you.'

I lean back a little, considering him carefully.

'That's okay,' I say. 'You must have been wondering 'What is this stupid girl doing wandering round up here' anyway?'

He shakes his head vehemently.

'Whatever other assumptions I made, you never for one moment struck me as *stupid,* Rose. Anything but.'

I smile at him and for the first time I notice he's got a backpack of his own with him, too. It's one of those big affairs with a rolled-up sleeping bag on the top. I eye it enviously. The fire he's built is great but we're both going to need a sleeping bag tonight. He must be following my train of thought;

'We're going to need to pool our resources, aren't we? I don't suppose you packed any food in there along with those clothes?'

I suck in my bottom lip. I don't have much.

'Not food as such. Except if you count the box of chocolate liqueurs I put in there for Shona. And there might be one or two polo mints rolling around the bottom ...'

'We might need all of those,' he advises, 'if it *doesn't* rain and it turns out we're still stuck in here by tomorrow.'

'You think?' The idea that we wouldn't be able to progress out of here once it's broad daylight hadn't occurred to me. 'You think that could happen?'

He spreads his hands.

'They might be predicting rain but ... I don't know. While I was out there getting your bag it was really chucking it down. You haven't seen it since you came in, have you? If we are going to be delayed here, we're best to be prepared for it.'

'Damn,' I mutter. This has got to be the worst timing ever. And what does he mean 'we need to be prepared for it'. How can we be prepared for it? We're not!

'So: what I can bring to the feast is; two tins of tuna, one packet of cream crackers and six assorted sachets of cup-a-soup.' He sits beside me, pulling the items out of his bag, places them between us on the wooden seat.

I take in the very un-Christmassy selection of food items in front of us and a thought occurs to me now; it's uncommonly lucky for us that he's got anything to eat in there at all ...

'How come you've even got that backpack with you, Lawrence?' I wonder. 'I mean, if you only came up here to deliver those meds?'

'I never said I had.' He looks at me candidly. 'It must have been the locum you spoke to who left the medication for you. I *am* a paramedic, as you assumed, but that's just turned out fortunate for you. I'm here for my own reasons, Rose.'

'Oh?' That's a bit of a shock. He's not who I took him to be, then? What is this guy even doing up here? I look at him curiously.

'I've only arrived in the UK from Colombo very recently hence the backpack. I'm on a ... a mercy mission, if you like. In a nutshell - I need a sponsor's signature that will allow a young Sri Lankan lad access to humanitarian support here in the UK.'

Sri Lankan humanitarian mercy mission ... his voice bounces over me like a child's balloon on a breezy summer lawn. All I can take in is that he *really* isn't what I took him to be, at all, is he?

'You're saying that you've just come in from *Sri Lanka*?' That explains his tan, at least.

He nods.

'Then – when I assumed earlier that you'd taken the locum's place why didn't you ...?'

'Why didn't I put you right? It's the first rule of engagement I learned, Rose; don't unnecessarily alarm a patient who you're about to perform a procedure on. You made the assumption that I was the locum, and you seemed comfortable with it. Now I've done the stitches, you can know why I'm really here.' He reaches into his wallet and pulls out a photo of a group of children standing in a huddle on what appears to be deluged ground.

'Refugees,' he tells me. 'That one there is Sunny.' He leans in towards me to point him out better. He seems oblivious to the effect his moving closer has on me. I move out of range the tiniest bit. Boy, I need to get out more. When I get to Uni I'm not going to let myself be bowled over by the first cute guy I see, am I? *Concentrate, Rose – he's telling you why he's here ...*

'This little lad with the plaster cast?'

'He's the one I'm here for. If I can't sort out all the paper-work for him in the next few days, chances are he's going to need a major operation if he stays where he is.'

This lad Sunny matters to Lawrence, I can see that. He *really* matters. I take the picture and stare at the kid for a few minutes. He looks just like any ordinary kid, really. But one who's living in horrific circumstances. And his plight has inspired Lawrence to come back all this way … it kind of puts my few poxy stitches into perspective, too. I hand the photo back to Lawrence.

'A *lot* of paperwork?' I pick up the unexpressed suggestion that this might not be an easy task.

'My boss Dougie thinks I haven't a hope in hell, actually. I still have to try.' This unexpected confession takes me a little by surprise. I smile.

'You have a compassionate heart,' I tell him. Now for the first time, something I've said seems to have an effect on him. Lawrence turns away, stores the photo back in his wallet hastily.

'Just doing my job.'

'So you're saying …' I'm trying to get my head around what he's just told me, 'You've come all the way to Merry Ditton to reach your sponsor. Is that right?' Surely there are people in the capital who would see to this sort of thing? Who could there be in this little village that has connections with international humanitarian efforts?

His eyes look strained now. He looks … *tired*.

'Maybe I'm asking too many questions?' I offer when he doesn't seem to want to answer that one.

'It's all right, Rose. Maybe I've just been on the go for too many hours now. I need to hit the sack. Literally, in my case. I found some discarded animal feed sacks in the workmen's shed out there when I went looking for your gear. I'll sleep on those and use them as a cover. You can have my sleeping bag. I insist,' he adds as I'm about to half-heartedly protest.

'I know it's not late, but maybe we could both do with an

early night. I hope you ate a good Christmas lunch?'

I pull a face. Right now I couldn't stomach a morsel, which is probably a good thing.

'The workmen left some of their brew behind in the wooden shack. I think it might have been a good while since they were last around. There was some solidified sugar in there too,' he laughs. 'It'll do. I'll melt some snow in that old stainless steel bucket for water and you can have a hot drink of tea before you rest. It'll do you some good.'

'You're pretty resourceful aren't you Lawrence?' I concede my admiration at last.

'My life has provided me with many opportunities to become that way, Rose.' His gaze locks on mine for a good few seconds longer than he needs to. *I know you Lawrence, I swear I know you from somewhere ...* Then he smiles softly. It's me who has to look away first.

Why does he do that? Doesn't he know he gets right under my skin every time he holds my gaze in that beguiling way? Doesn't he know how he sets my pulse racing so hard I can't concentrate, can't even look at him, let alone answer him when he does that?

I suspect he does.

Rose

I sleep for a bit but I wake up when I turn round because the flagstone floor beneath the sleeping bag Lawrence gave me, feels way too cold.

My head hurts, my leg hurts and my heart aches. I need to get back to Dad. And I want my mum. *Where's Mum?* All my befuddled brain can remember is that she hasn't been around for a long time, has she?

The encampment at Topwoods was taking over Mum's whole life. We visited in the autumn, me and Dad. She'd asked for blankets to be brought, though it was clear she didn't really want us there. We were an embarrassment to her, I imagined. We stood out like sore thumbs with our drab jeans and jumpers, stood out for our ordinariness amongst that eclectic group. They weren't all pagans, dedicated to saving the woods because of spiritual reasons; some of them were eco-warriors and some of them were rebels who'd join any cause and others, I suspected, just had nowhere else to go. Autumn arrived with a flurry of huge gusty winds and rain that year. As the trees grew naked outside, the burrows beneath the woodland floor got flooded with rainwater making living conditions very uncomfortable and insanitary. Many of the activists left but the die-harders – including Mum – refused to give up. She was so near home – and yet we barely saw her!

'*Isla cares more about those blinking trees than she cares* about us' - I remember Dad saying bitterly but we both knew once Mum had made her mind up about something there was precious little that could budge her. That Saturday in October, I remember the rain had made a cess-pit of the mud around the camp, the whole place smelled earthy but in an unwholesome way. Dad had spent the whole of Friday washing and drying those blankets for her. He took her some bright red ones that he knew she liked, even put fabric conditioner in to make them nice for her, but she put them on a rock as soon as we arrived, she hardly noticed. By the time we left they'd fallen to the floor and were as muddy and wet as everything else around there. I saw the tears in his eyes when he noticed that. I have never forgotten them.

He wasn't a demonstrative man, my dad, but I saw him go back and plead with her that afternoon like a child. She was suffering from depression, he told her. She wasn't herself. If she would only come home and see sense ... but she laughed him off.

I can still see his face to this day, pinched and sad and confused. He loved her. If he didn't have her, then what did he have? He came to me begging me to try and persuade her; promised me that place on the school skiing trip he knew I'd been asking after, if I could get her out of the woods, promised me the moon on a plate. 'Rose - you can have anything you want for your birthday, anything - if you can only persuade your Mum to come home.'

I didn't need bribing. Dad had indulged her passion for the woodland because he thought it'd bring some meaning back into her life; she was never cut out for domestic routines or even a career that involved her having to commit too strongly to anything. She'd been working as a ceramics designer when Dad had met her, hand-painting pots. Apparently she'd been brilliant, her work much in demand, but Mum never liked having too many demands made on her. She'd wanted her freedom, so she'd given up her cottage industry. She wanted her freedom still, to do what she wanted to do now, which was to save those woodlands. But it was obvious to both me and Dad that things had gone too far. The trouble was, Mum couldn't see it. All she kept saying was that the woodland was cen-

turies old and that, once lost, it would never be replaced. It was important, and somebody had to stand up for it.

I agreed to stay over with her that weekend, to try and persuade her we needed her home. But after Dad drove off, miserable and lonely, I remember being mad at her that she made him sad, irritated that she didn't seem to care anymore about normal everyday things like cleanliness and keeping her hair brushed and ... and us. Had she really just been pretending to care about us all my life? Did her old life no longer matter to her at all or had she just given up?

By the end of the weekend I was stiff and damp and miserable and I knew I'd got not one jot nearer to persuading Mum to come home. I knew Dad was going to be devastated.

Right now though, my thoughts drift back to my present predicament. Dad's going to be gutted that I didn't make it home tonight. I roll over again, facing the fire. He needs those meds I went to fetch him. And he needs me at home. I should not be here and I do not like this place.

It is dark, but not completely and utterly dark because Lawrence is keeping the fire well tended-to. I watched him in the early hours, bending down and patiently feeding more wood into the brazier. He's focused, patient. He knows what he's doing and I like that. I like the way he carried out those stitches on my leg earlier with the minimum of fuss and how calm and kind he was about everything. I like Lawrence, my tired brain acknowledges, but right now where I need to be is back home. My eyes close as sleep washes over me.

Dad needed Mum back home too. I remember that now. How was I going to get her back? I had to get her back. She didn't want to come and I didn't know how that was going to happen but then ...

Hadn't she spent years drumming it into me - that was the beauty of magic? You didn't have to map out the path to your goal. You simply had to set your intention, do your ritual and the way would magically become clear.

Lawrence

I had to push with all my strength to get the chapel door open even a chink this morning. The snowdrifts had piled up so high during the course of the night, I had to dig the wooden door open, bit by bit, from the inside. All I had to work with was that workmen's shovel with a broken handle that I managed to pick up last night, but it did the trick.

It's 7 am - barely light, but I've been awake for hours already. I couldn't sleep. It wasn't the cold; the heat coming off the brazier was comfortable enough. I was so dog-tired last night that even the hard flagstones wouldn't have kept me awake. My own restless mind did that, fretting over what Arjuna could have meant by his last text. *A problem with Herr Lober,* he said - one that could scupper the whole plan? I have to believe not. I still have to keep to my part at this end, dangerous as it is for me personally, and with no sure outcome in sight. Damn the man. If there's a problem why couldn't he just say what it was? There's a few hours left before I need to switch the phone back on to receive his call.

Meanwhile, I'm out shovelling snow. It's a freezing, dull morning, uncannily still with a pea-souper of a fog on the hills. No faraway sounds of cars or animals or people. No wind. No birds. I'd forgotten how quiet it can get up here. I'd forgotten how the whole site is so cut off from the rest of the world, once you're up here it's easy to pretend you no longer have to be part of it. Right now, that might be a relief but I've got to keep on working.

I plan to hack out a pathway up the front so the minute there's a change in the weather we can make a break for it. The snowdrift was a good three foot high outside the chapel door this morning. Every foot of snow I clear gets me closer to my goal. We have to be ready.

As I work, I can feel the dull ache in my arms and shoulder muscles. I can feel the sweat beginning to drip down my back but the hard exercise is good for me. It helps keep my mind focused. It stops me thinking about Dougie and why it might be that he's failed to keep his telephone appointments with me so far. It keeps my mind off the fact that by the time I've dug to the edge of the ruin I'll be able to see out over the hill. Chances are, what I'm going to see when I get there is that nothing much has changed since yesterday. I've got a bad feeling that my father won't have gone out, that his car will still be there. That the diggers and the tractors won't have been out yet, clearing the roads. It's what I'm dreading. According to my intelligence, he should be gone already but if we're stuck here, then maybe so is he? I curse under my breath at that because I had planned for him to be gone. I *need* for him to be gone. Without that there is no way I can go in to her.

I plunge the shovel deeper into the snow at my feet and the loud crunching sound as it makes contact is strangely satisfying. I lift the shovel, my arms aching with the weight on the end of it, and hurl the snow over to one side. There are some areas in my life where I can make a difference. Some obstacles I can remove. Others will not be so easy.

Rose sleeps still. I'm glad of that. Glad she didn't see how the chapel door was virtually wedged shut this morning by the weight pushing in from the outside. That would freak out most girls I know. They'd get panicky. I wonder if she would? She's a strange little thing. I watched her after she went back to sleep so easily in the middle of the night. I was up and restless, counting the hours till dawn. I melted some snow in one of the old metal buckets that had been left to catch the rain dripping in from the roof and sat there drinking tea, watching her, envying her the release of sleep. I wondered where she went to in her dreams, she looked so peaceful. Somewhere far away, I thought. Maybe somewhere where only people with a clear conscience are allowed to go?

At one point, while she was dreaming, her eyes fluttered, her lips parted in a smile. Such a radiant smile! Even asleep, she enticed me, drew me in. *Who were you smiling at, Rose? Was it your boyfriend?* In the dark orange shadows cast by the fire I found myself watching her curiously for a very long time, unable to drag my gaze away, wondering about her, who she was, what she was really doing up here; if she wasn't pregnant, then what was the real reason for the desperation I've sensed in her from the beginning?

At one point she looked as if she were about to say something. I strained forward to catch her words but like water streaming through a stand-pipe into a child's open hands I could catch almost nothing. Mutterings and mumblings, there was nothing I could grasp. Her words weren't meant for me. She wasn't *my* girlfriend, was she? She wasn't ever going to be.

I'd never leave her in that sad and lonely place she finds herself in now, that's for sure.

Then she spoke my name. I swear, she said my name out loud and I felt like a voyeur in her dream-time. I told myself, it's got to be some other guy called Lawrence who she knows, she's talking to him in her dreams but part of me knew full well that she wasn't. She was talking to me. For some reason that made me feel a connection to the girl which I haven't felt towards a woman in a long time. '*Lawrence …*' What did she want from me? At that moment I'd have given anything to know, to have been party to her thoughts. She piques me, this girl, arouses my curiosity. If I'm honest, arouses me in more ways than one.

But everything is intensified in this place. It's an unnatural situation to be in, and I know this is what happens. I've been in war zones often enough to know that - when you think your life may be at risk - how the very same nurse you've worked alongside for months without a second glance, suddenly seems eminently kissable. Don't know what principle is at work there. It's nature's way of perpetuating the gene pool, maybe, who knows?

I keep shovelling snow. The exertion helps dull down the ricochet of thoughts churning in my mind. It doesn't silence them completely though; *what happens if the old man's still there tomorrow? The day after that?* It's not something I've addressed yet. How I'm going to deal with that. I didn't think it would be a problem - he's always gone away over Christmas, every year for as long as I can remember. It was the only thing that ever made Christmas worth anticipating for me; we never had much in the way of festivities in our house, but his absence for a few days as he went to pay his respects to his old man, *that* was worth waiting for …

Has the weather this year really put him off?

I'm going to need a back-up plan, aren't I? I didn't want to do this but if push comes to shove, I may have to ask Marco for help after all. He won't want to, I know that. He's not the sort of guy who likes to get involved, he keeps himself to himself, always has done, but we were mates once. He's the one person I rang before I left Sri Lanka. Waiting for the connection from Colombo to Heathrow, I phoned him from a call box inside the airport. I needed to know what the situation was like at home, was my father expecting to go away like he always did? Marco seemed to think so and I reckoned he should know. He was freaking out big time to hear my voice though, I could tell that even over the phone.

When I rang him from Colombo that day, he was clearly edgy, *why had I rung him*, he kept on asking me? He kept saying he couldn't speak, he shouldn't be speaking to me, I'd get him into trouble. It was awkward for him. I can see that. But if things don't lighten up here, weather-wise, I'm going to have to contact him again. Asking him if he'll be my back-up help now isn't going to be easy either, given his reluctance, but I can't afford to hang onto my pride.

I keep shovelling the snow, clearing another two foot of

path before I stop to peel off my coat, then my jumper. I'm down to my short-sleeved T-shirt now but still I'm feeling like I'm burning up from the inside. At last, I peel off my T-shirt as well and fling that on top of the coat. It's a strange feeling, an almost enjoyable sensation, as the morning air freezes the skin on my arms, my chest, my cheeks. A day or so ago I was in a country where I was so hot all the time I couldn't remember what snow felt like anymore, what it smelt like. I couldn't remember what it felt like to be in temperatures this low. But I am back.

I am back, and he is still here, my father. He hasn't gone anywhere. He is so near. *I* am so near to him - and yet he does not know it. This whole thing is surreal, that's what it is.

I wipe the sweat off my forehead with the back of my hand, a slight panic rising at the thought of how *near* my father is. But I won't give up on Sunny. Fuck that. I'll find a way.

'Good morning, Lawrence.' Rose shocks me now, her voice coming out of the deep silence. I didn't know she was there, watching me. I turn around to look at her standing by the door. Her face is sleepy and rumpled but she's more alert this morning, steadier on her feet, I can see it.

'Good morning.' I smile.

She steps properly out into the uncovered area of the ruin now, joining me. We both stand there, looking at each other and eventually she laughs. How pretty she is. Pretty and fragile like ... like a bunch of white lilies I saw clustered in a pond soon after I arrived in Colombo. Like them, she feels somehow very strong, full of a beautiful dignity.

'What?' she spreads her arms. *What are you looking at?*

'You remind me of ...' I try and think of the right words - 'A snow angel.'

'A *snow* angel?' She brushes the white flakes out of her eyes, her hair. She laughs again, this time intrigued.

'There used to be two little angels, up there.' I point to a place just above the jagged edge of one of the broken castle walls. Every time I used to run up here as a kid I'd see them. I used to

159

think of them as two guardians, protectors, waiting for me. They stood up there through rain and snow for centuries until one day my father came with his diggers …

'When it got really cold up here they'd get covered in frost. If you shone a torch at them their robes would glitter like fairies on a Christmas tree,' I tell her now. 'You remind me of them.'

'Do I?' she smiles shyly. 'You've been up this way before then?' she breathes. Too late, I realise that was something I had not meant to reveal.

'Many times,' I say, knowing that this will open up the way for her to ask when and why, but I am not going to deny it.

'Oh,' she nods her head; *I see.* She doesn't pursue it. But then, I'm sensing now that she's distracted by my nakedness. Her eyes take in my discarded jumper, the coat I threw on the jagged wall. She's looking at my bare arms, my chest, drinking me in. Is she wondering why it is that in these sub-zero temperatures I'm naked from the waist up?

'I was digging. I got hot,' I tell her. She must realise she's staring because she looks away, suddenly self-conscious.

'I heard the sound of shovelling outside,' she says breathlessly. She's studiously looking at the ground now, the path I've just made with the snow piled up on both sides, carefully not looking at me, looking at her feet which she's stamping rhythmically into the ground. 'You were up so early. Couldn't you sleep?'

'I had a job to do,' I shrug. 'I have to keep a path clear so as soon as it's safe, we exit.' Then I look at her more closely. 'How's the leg holding up this morning?'

'Great.' She smiles suddenly. 'I'm a lot better than I thought I'd feel. I think I could make it down there today.' I stare at her for a moment. My clearing efforts have given her a false picture, obviously.

'Take a look.' I step back and beckon her forward. She moves past me, goes and looks out over the edge of the ruins to see how much more of it has fallen in the night. She gives a quiet gasp when she sees how bad it is. Right now the landscape is complete-

ly obliterated; the hills and the valleys and the trees and houses …
everything is hidden under one soft, uneven, undulating layer of
white. Everything is *gone*.

'It's … it's so quiet.' She frowns, and I sense the return of yesterday's unhappiness, her restlessness to be out of here. 'I thought
maybe …' she breaks off. 'Looks like we're not getting out of here
today, after all?'

I join her and I see what I've been avoiding looking at all the
while that I've been digging - that my father's jeep is still there. It's
covered in snow, but I can still tell it's his from the size and shape
of it. Damn him. *He's still there.*

'Not unless the forecast works out and it starts to rain.' It
isn't raining, though. It's snowing, and copiously now. It floats
down in large lazy white flakes and lands gently on her uncovered head.

'You should go in,'

'I thought you might want to come back in out of the snow
with me.' We speak at exactly the same time and we both laugh.

'You're going to get wet,' I say, lifting my eyes to the sky.

'You already are,' she points out.

'Then I've nothing to lose.' I watch her smile shyly again,
pushing back her hair. She's happy to stay out here with me, clearly. Maybe she was lonely in there, she wants the company? I bend
to retrieve a little brass-coloured object she's just dropped in the
snow.

'What's this?' I turn it over in my palm curiously.

'Oh *that!*' She feels for it unconsciously in her hair. 'That's
my giraffe pin. I just found it again in my backpack. It's a … a sort
of lucky charm.' She looks a little abashed.

'Is it?'

'Look.' She comes a little closer, her head bowed and I can
see every breath as it leaves her mouth. She's so close to me that in
a minute I am going to be breathing in the same breath as she did.
Just like we'd do if we were kissing, I think.

'See the way he's holding up his arms and he's smiling … you

161

can turn him upside down and then his arms become his legs and he looks like he's frowning.'

'Clever.' I hand it back to her, suck in my lips. 'A lucky charm. Does it work?'

She shrugs, a little embarrassed as she pushes it back into her hair now.

'I'm not sure. I'll keep him pointed upright so he's smiling; just in case.'

'A wise precaution.'

She turns her head away now, a little embarrassed maybe at confessing to being so superstitious?

'You'd better go in, Rose,' I suggest. 'You could boil up some snow in that larger metal bucket for us. Keep the smaller one for boiling drinking water, yes? We can take it in turns to wash. I'll carry on out here for a bit and then we'll share some breakfast.'

She doesn't make a move to go, takes in my intention to keep clearing snow when she knows there's no way I can clear the whole path down. She looks pensive.

'That child you told me about yesterday,' she says. 'What will happen … if you don't get to his sponsor in time?'

I look away from her. The adrenalin that was pumping through my muscles earlier is still circulating. I'm itching to carry on digging. I've got every reason to.

'Then - Sunny will most likely have his foot amputated,' I tell her. She doesn't move.

'It's a war zone, isn't it – the place you were at?'

A war zone. The story of my life.

'It has been, for a long time. The war is over now but casualties keep on coming.'

'And you've been there - how long?' She steps a little closer.

'Roughly twelve months.'

'You must have seen many amputations then?'

'Too many. I've seen too many, Rose!' I fling the shovel down at that, harder than I meant to and there's a crunching sound as it slices through the snow. She flinches but she doesn't

162

move away as I turn to face her full on.

'I don't want it to happen to him, that's all. Sometimes you get to a point where you've got to say - *no more.* I have to save Sunny. You understand that?'

'Of course,' she says softly. 'I need to get out of here too.' I see her bite her lip. 'But - the snow ... there's so much of it. I've never seen so much. We're never going to get out are we?'

'Not yet.' I hold her gaze for a few seconds, fathoming her out. Then I add the obvious. 'Not unless one of us rings for help.' I see her gaze drop away.

'Maybe ... we shouldn't though,' she falters. 'Not yet. I mean, the emergency services are bound to be stretched to the limit right now and ... and we're okay for a bit, aren't we?'

I see that she - for her own reasons - is reluctant to alert anyone and I am careful to disguise my own relief.

'We are, Rose.' I lean forward and pat her shoulder encouragingly. 'I'm going to help you get out of here and ... I promise you, we are.'

She nods, slowly.

'I already melted some snow in the metal bucket like you did last night. I did it while you were digging. I hope you've got some dry clothes in that backpack of yours. You need to come in and change now or you're going to catch your death.' She turns and her small fingers reach out, brush the snow fleetingly, unexpectedly, from my shoulders and then, more hesitantly from the tops of my arms and my chest. Her eyes, though full of compassion, don't quite meet mine.

I glance down towards the valley. That is so much truer than you realise, Rose.

Up here, I think, I probably will.

Rose

'Tell me a little about your life, Rose,' he says. We're sitting on the canvas sacks by the fire, eating breakfast. Tuna fish on crackers has never tasted quite so good. Neither has sugared tea without milk. We're eating our breakfast slowly, taking little bites and savouring each tiny morsel to make it last.

'What's to tell?' He's the guy who's been off doing heroic things in foreign lands. Before he was in Sri Lanka he did a stint in South Africa, he told me. Just before that he'd spent a couple of weeks helping trawl through the rubble after an earthquake in China. What could I possibly say that he'd find interesting?

'Anything. Anything at all.' At least he's got his clothes on again. He put on a T-shirt and a black sweater when he came back in, dry ones out of his backpack. I gave an inner sigh of relief when he got dressed. Having him walk around here half-naked was a bit disconcerting. Okay it was *nice* - but disconcerting. He's got a very nice body and I didn't know where to look so as not to make it seem like I was looking at him.

Especially as I really wanted to look at him.

'None of my life is interesting,' I protest. 'I lead the most boring life imaginable.' *Getting holed up here with you is probably the most exciting thing that has happened to me in a long time …*

'You do not know how *good* boring sounds right now.' As he says that he looks wistful, sad even. In the morning light filtering through the chapel windows I can see the little tired lines in the

164

corners of his eyes, as if his life has been too eventful, too busy, for way too long. I'm glad he let me persuade him to leave the path-clearing for now. He wants it clear, and for a good reason. He's one driven guy, I can see that. But sometimes you've just got to give up and wait.

'Boring sounds good?' I ask softly. In the echoey silence where every tiny sound bounces off the chapel walls, a splash of water drips from the ceiling onto the flagstones, hisses into the fire, startling us both. His eyes come back to meet mine, smiling.

'Boring sounds good to me. Boring means that you are living a normal life,' he explains. 'One where you need not live in fear of what each day might bring; of what you might have left, at the end of it. Each day is … dependable, solid. It's full of reliable breaks and beginnings and finite endings.' Is he talking about his *job*, I wonder now, or is he talking about himself, and is there really such a strong line demarking them both?

He makes it sound as if he's been living on hyper-alert for a very long time. Perhaps he has. Perhaps that's why he was aware enough of his surroundings to realise I was in trouble yesterday, to come and find me. He saved my life, I have no doubt of that. What I'm still not so clear about is - what was he, really, even doing wandering around up here, himself? He's on his way to get some sort of sponsor on board, he tells me. It's urgent. It's all come at the last minute. Okay, I don't know how things work in war zones. When it comes to international humanitarian aid efforts, maybe sometimes it is all last-minute cobbled together life and death scenarios, who knows? Whatever the case, I'm still a little fuzzy about what this guy is actually doing *up here*. Why didn't he go directly to the person he needed to see? I know we both got trapped yesterday by the weather. But unless you were headed for Macrae Farm I don't know why anyone would come by this way if they wanted to visit someone in the village? And - ha! - Macrae Farm is surely the last place on earth you'd go to find humanitarian aid. He must have lost his way.

'Sounds like you might need to go on some sort of sabbatical,' I offer. My tummy rumbles because I'm working hard on making my breakfast last. What wouldn't I give for a nice piece of fruit right now? Or a slice of that luscious iced cake Mrs P left unopened for us on the sideboard yesterday … We've been sharing the tuna crackers off one plate. We've only got one mug, too, and they both came out of his backpack. The workmen who left us the tea bags weren't considerate enough to leave us behind any mugs so we're taking it in turns to drink our tea. I'm going first. I don't normally take sugar in mine but I am today because I am ravenous. I don't know if he is - after all that hard slog outside he has refused to eat a single bite more than me even though I told him that was grossly unfair, and he should. He doesn't seem to mind.

I watch him curiously. I figure he's used to putting up with a bit more hardship than I am, that's what it is. I wonder if he does ever get any time off? And if he does - where does he go to, how does he spend it? Even today - the day after Christmas Day, he seems to be on a mission of some sort, working.

'Maybe I do,' he agrees eventually. 'I want to hear about you, though. Remind me how normal people live.' He says it like he really wants to hear.

'I'm not sure my life is entirely normal,' I fence. God, do I really want to go into all of …

'Come on, surely you can tell me something. One little thing about you?' he cajoles.

'Like …?'

'Okay; tell me about your family, then,' he presses when I don't immediately continue. 'You told me yesterday that your mum was a hedgewitch?'

'That isn't exactly normal, is it?' I mutter. I shouldn't have told him about that bit should I? It always leads to more questions. I wasn't thinking straight yesterday. 'Besides, that wasn't her job description. She used to help with the school dinners at the local primary.'

'And Dad?' Here we are on slightly safer ground.

'He … well, when he was working, he was a loss adjustor for

an insurance company, specialising in maritime claims, tankers, liners and so forth.'

'Interesting combination.' He raises his eyebrows a fraction.

'You're wondering how such an unlikely couple came to be together in the first place, right?' He shakes his head slowly but there's a twinkle in the corner of his eyes.

'It's what everyone wonders. That's why I said the background I come from isn't entirely normal. Dad's as strait-laced as they come, academic, middle-class. Mum was ...' I stop for a minute, wondering how to really describe her when she was always so difficult to pin down, a free spirit, an elemental.

'She was a total bohemian. Maybe it's because she was an only child and her parents emigrated without her when she was still in her teens, left her with a friend. She never had any contact with them. It's certainly something Dad's family have never ceased to wonder; what was it that bonded them? They never got over him marrying my mother.' *Christ, why am I even telling him this*? I don't know why, but my mouth seems to be blabbing on all by itself, I can't seem to stop.

'She was probably a babe,' he mutters.

I shrug. 'He left his first wife for Isla. He left his lucrative job in his wife's family firm and as a result relations with his own people have been strained ever since. I don't think they've ever quite forgiven him.'

'Difficult situation.' He looks at me curiously now. 'What *did* draw two such different people together, do you suppose?'

'They fell hopelessly in love ... or so they told me.' I manage a laugh.

'Romantic.' He smiles.

'You think?' Maybe he's a romantic too? 'Falling in love with the wrong person can make life very difficult, you know. They may have loved each other but their life together was by no means an easy one.'

'Nor yours?' he offers softly, but I've said enough.

'Your turn.' I shake my head. I take a sip of my tea, relishing the sweetness of the sugar. 'You were saying you might be taking a sabbatical?'

'After this job, I think I'll have no option,' he says mysteriously. Lawrence has brought a tattered pack of cards out of his pocket, secured with a rubber band. He's put them on the sacking we're using for a mat. Is he going to suggest we play rummy or something in a minute?

'So - you're not planning on going back to Sri Lanka?' The thought makes me feel ridiculously happy. 'Will you stay on in the UK, maybe?' I say it casually, like his answer is of no possible interest to me whatsoever. Like I'm not wishing fervently, *say that you will, say that you're staying in the UK and staying somewhere near enough that we'll maybe see each other again ...*

'I'd love to stay in the UK.'

My heart sinks. He says it like he can't. *Damn.* Why can't you though, Lawrence? I'm getting the picture that there's a lot more to this guy than meets the eye, a lot more than he's letting on about ... about *everything*.

'Well. Will you?' I insist. I rinse out my drink, plucking another tea bag out of the box and fill the metal cup up to the top with boiling water for him. With all that snow outside the door, one thing at least we won't be going without, is enough water.

'I don't know,' he says infuriatingly. 'Right now I can't see that far ahead. I wish I could.' He gives me a sudden smile and all my faint misgivings about him vanish into the air. If there was one thing Mum always drummed into me it was to trust my own judgement about people. And Lawrence - he's a good person, I believe that. Right now there are a whole load of things I don't know about him or don't understand but there is something bugging him - I feel it - more than just his concern for that boy Sunny, that he isn't letting on about. Call it intuition.

'So - if your mum was hedgewitch - did she ever read people's fortunes, Rose?'

I laugh, at that. She used to read the tea leaves for people, if they asked her. Sometimes she'd look at her tarot cards and at other times she'd just pluck random information for them out of the air. She was spot on with it, most times. But you never really know how people are going to react if you admit to stuff like that.

'Sometimes,' I fence.

'Did she ever do yours?' Ah. I was right that he's worried about something. He wants his fortune done. I glance at him a little anxiously. I hope I'm not about to learn he's got *girlfriend troubles*. If he has a girlfriend then he's forbidden territory. I really hope it isn't that. I dab at the last few crumbs of tuna on my side of the plate. When it is completely and utterly clean, I admit;

'No. Mum didn't.' I never let her, that's why. I already had a pretty good idea what she would say and I didn't want to hear it.

'Have *you* ever done it?' He sits up, suddenly, crossing his legs in front of him. I glance at his tattered pack of playing cards - is that what they're for?

I shake my head, smiling. Mum said I'd be a dab hand at reading cards if I ever took it up but of course I didn't. That was all I needed, wasn't it, on top of everything else, people round here calling me '*Gypsy Rose*'!

'Scared, Rose?' he teases gently now.

'Scared of what?' I mutter in a low voice.

'Scared of being wrong?' He's shuffling the cards in front of him expertly. 'Scared of being *right*?'

'I'm not scared by what my mum used to do.' That isn't entirely true. I lean forward on my arms now, peering into the tea cup. As I stare into it the dark water swirls and shimmers in the fire light. She taught me how to scry in the water, too; how to see images on the surface where the shimmering light flickers into your mind. *It's all about knowing how to look, she'd say*. Right now I can see the wind bending back some tall trees. Just there, on the surface of his cup, a bright day scattered with clouds; rain. The dark shadow of a man, running; the same man I've seen before. But I don't want to see him again. I let out a breath, pull back. Lawrence thinks it's all some kind of joke all this stuff; magic, predictions.

It's not.

When I look up at him his eyes are riveted to mine, amused, interested, but he shouldn't be.

'Do you like your tea weak or strong?' I ask now.

'I like it however you want to give it to me, Rose,' he says in a low voice.

Man, I wish he wouldn't do that. All that double-entendre; though he's delivered it with a poker-straight face, I can feel the colour creeping into mine.

'I'll let it brew a moment then.' The bags must be yonks old, because this one's split at the bottom. 'Careful, there'll be the dregs of tea at the bottom of that cup.' I stir the bag round to hurry the brewing on a bit.

'So … you need your fortune telling, Lawrence?' I can't resist asking, even though I'm not going to offer to do the honours.

'Do you think that would be a good idea?'

This isn't about what I think, I frown slightly at him; it's about *what you want?* He's not opening up on that though, is he? Mum always said that ninety per cent of people who came to her for a reading wanted to know about their relationships. Do I *really* want to hear about the girlfriend? It's bound to be a woman isn't it? What else would make a sensitive guy like him feel so cut up and unsure about what he should be doing next? I sigh.

'It depends. People always want their fortunes read when they feel there's most at stake. When they're feeling most vulnerable.' I cut him a sideways glance but his face remains inscrutable. He isn't giving me any indication if this is the case. 'However, Mum used to say that can be the most fruitful time. When we're at a crossroads, all possibilities open up. We have to make a decision what path to take.'

'What if I've already made my decision, though?' He looks right at me and I know, for all the things in his future he seems so unsure about - right now, he's set on a course from which he won't be deterred. 'What if all I need to know is if it's all going to work out all right?' To look at him, he seems so quietly still, so centred, and yet out of the corner of my eye I can see he's drumming his fingers against his thigh.

You've made your decision to do what? I wonder curiously. If he doesn't want to tell me it seems impolite to press it.

'Mum used to say; it's *our choice* that's the thing that counts. Not the outcome.'

'Most people would say it's the outcome,' he notes.

'They would. That's because we all want things, don't we? It's easy to forget that it's how we get there that counts.' I stop short, because it's all very well to quote Mum's view about 'our journey being the most important thing' when *I* haven't been able to journey anywhere for a very long time.

Maybe that's what I get for violating one of the first rules of Wicca.

Shit. I feel a rush of heaviness to my chest and I push it away immediately; just like I always do. For heaven's sake. All I ever wanted was to be normal. Lead a normal life ...

'So - what do *you* want, Rose?' He pulls my thoughts back to him.

'I want to go out and experience everything that the world has to offer, that's what I want to do right now, not stop at home wondering what it all means ...' He laughs, taking in my ambivalence.

'So; if I could find some way to grant you your Christmas wish.' Lawrence leans in a little closer as if he's hanging on my every word. 'What would it be?'

My Christmas wish? Wow. It's been such a long while since anyone asked me something like that.

My Christmas wish.

'I want ...' *I want someone like you*, I think before I can stop myself. I know we only met less than twenty-four hours ago but ... I want to know what it would be like to be with someone who makes me feel the way you make me feel. I want to sit over there where you are, lean my head so close to your chest that I can hear your heart. I want to feel your strong arms around me like I did

171

yesterday only not because you're *rescuing* me, but because you want to hold me, and to know that you're someone who'll *be* there for me, through thick and thin.

It's a nice fantasy, so I continue it.

I want to hear that you too, are really interested in me and I'm not just imagining it. I want to know that there isn't any girlfriend waiting in the wings and that you'll still somehow be around in the coming weeks, the coming months …

It's still a fantasy, of course. This guy is way out of my league. His eyes open slightly wider and I catch his vague amusement at my confusion.

'What do I want?' I stutter. He's just asked me a question and all I've done is stare at him, open-mouthed. I feel caught out, as if he might somehow be reading my thoughts in my expression. This is … this is unbelievably embarrassing. Is this what it's like to feel like you might be falling in love? Hell, it can't be, surely? I'm not ready for this. All these feelings swirling up from deep inside of me. How can you know if you're falling in love if you've never felt it before? Like your world is about to spin out of control because you're entering new and unchartered territory and yet something still feels so very, deeply right about it that you know there's a danger you just might sacrifice everything, *anything* to keep on feeling it …?

I pick up the spoon and lift the tea bag out of his cup. I ladle a couple of spoons of sugar in and hand it to him.

What do I want?

'I want to get out of Merry Ditton.' I manage after a while. Before I met Lawrence yesterday, getting out of Merry Ditton was the most pressing thing in my life. Hell, it still is the most important thing in my life. Who am I kidding?

'You say that like it's something real important,' he observes.

'It is,' I admit. 'It's not just the snow that's got me stuck here, Lawrence. My whole life has been stuck for quite a while.' I pause, wondering how far I should go with this. I'm not about to pile on the details about Dad. I know from past experience that the min-

172

ute I mention it, people make all sorts of assumptions about me. Either they get bored immediately or they go into that poor-little-you routine and I hate that because it's self-pitying and helpless. It's also not very sexy. I'm sure the fact that I'm a Carer has been one thing that puts boys off me big-time.

'I want to go to Uni,' I share with him now. 'I've had one or two set-backs but ... I'm expecting my Uni offer letter will turn up any day now,' I say assuredly. Just to make sure he knows I *have* got plans. 'In fact,' I add for good measure. 'I think my letter may have turned up already but it's gone to the neighbours by mistake.'

He nods sympathetically but I can't read him, I don't know what he's thinking. I don't know what he's got into his head about me but now I think of it, me being up here must have seemed pretty odd to him too, I realise. He must have wondered what I was really doing wandering around up here all packed up like I was desperate to *get* somewhere on a day when we were all supposed to stay indoors. Sure, I told him about the medicines, I told him about the argument I had with the family, about how I packed up all that stuff just for show but he might not believe that. He might still think I'm some sort of ... runaway? Well I'm not. No matter the circumstances I've found myself in, he needn't think I'm just a small-town girl with no aspirations of my own.

'... which is a real bummer,' I add, 'because I need to reply to that letter urgently if it is what I think it is.'

'You'll get there.' He says it with such an air of quiet authority that I believe him for a moment. 'You want it bad enough and you will.' He picks up the mug of tea I've just made him and takes a sip. 'But you, Rose ... it's not just going to Uni, for you, is it? You're determined you're going to get away from here, aren't you?'

'Is it that obvious?' I pull a wry grin.

'It's a feeling I recognise myself, that's all.'

He's felt like it too? He hangs his head a little now, picks two cards out of his deck and leans them up against one another like he's going to build a house with them. I watch him, intent at his task, lining up a stack of foundation cards but the canvas sacking

173

beneath is uneven. They're going to fall over before he even gets to the second layer ...

What place did *you* need to get away from? I wonder curiously now. *Lawrence who so far has no second name,* I suddenly think; *handsome Lawrence who just dropped out of the sky to spend Christmas with me and make me get all flustered over him.*

'You know the feeling?' I prompt.

'Like you've come to the point where things in your life are never going to progress unless you leave? Oh, yes.'

'What is it you're going to study?' He gets that in before I can ask him where it was he wanted to get away from and I have to bite my tongue because ... oh, because it seems all too soon to push confidences if he isn't ready to share them. He reminds me of a silver fish darting tantalisingly in and out of the water in front of me, playing *now you see me, now you don't.*

'I want to read Law.' I kindly hand him two more cards from his pack.

'Law?' He's intent on his task again, building his house but something inside of him seems to have gone very quiet and very still. 'Any particular reason you chose that?'

'I guess ... I just need to prove to myself that there's still some justice to be found out there.'

'Some justice,' he says softly. 'Because ... life has showed you different, Rose?' Oh, Lawrence. Don't do this. Don't probe right into the very depths of what makes me tick like it really matters to you when I know that I can't possibly matter that much. Not yet. Not like *you're* starting to matter to *me.* I shoot him a painful glance.

'Because life has shown me ...' I go down on my elbows on the canvas sacking beside him, 'That it's only too easy to lose things that are important to you if you don't have a leg to stand on in this world.'

'If you don't have any power, you mean?' He flicks one of his cards high into the air and it lands right in the centre of the fire, curling up and shrivelling into black ash in a second. He looks at

174

me, and I shrug, because he's getting too close to the mark and I'm not sure I want to go there. I *don't* have any power, do I? I'm just a teenage Carer who everyone probably expects will go into her middle age looking after her ailing Dad, but a guy like Lawrence would never fall for a girl like that. He'd go for a girl who had dreams and ambitions, someone like the girl I am on the inside.

'This Uni offer letter,' he says after a bit. 'You'll be able to get hold of it as soon as the weather calms down, right?'

'If they haven't already thrown it away,' I mutter. 'If I can manage to get far enough past their dogs to enquire about it ...' He seems surprised that retrieving the letter won't all be plain sailing.

'Guard dogs?' he asks. It's farming territory. Enough people have working dogs around here. I nod.

'Ferocious ones,' I say.

'No one who can go with you, Rose?' I shake my head. Shona's dad Matt Dougal, might help. But then he's always been a bit ambivalent about aligning himself with us Clares because he gets a lot of work come his way from Rob Macrae.

'I could go with you,' he offers after a while. 'I'm good with dogs ...'

I smile, taking in the fact that he's just alluded to a future beyond this place, beyond today, when he and I will still have a reason to be in contact with each other. Does he want us to stay in touch?

'You'll get there, Rose, to that University and ... everything else you've been waiting for. You just mustn't be afraid.'

Afraid? I shrug my shoulders as if that is the very last thing I am but deep down inside I know it is true.

Afraid of what?

Afraid of staying on here with my father getting frailer, my own chances slipping by year on year and me just getting older. Afraid of going away because it will mean huge change and I've already had such a lot of unwelcome change thrust into my life there's a part of me that longs to cling to the familiar. Even when

175

it's horribly uncomfortable. Afraid of never having any power in the world. Afraid of my mum's powers that I've quashed, pushed down so deep into the shadows but which threaten to jump up every so often and overwhelm me.

Afraid of being alone.

And afraid - I glance at handsome Lawrence as he sits back on his heels and surveys his house of cards, three storeys high, crooked as hell but still, miraculously, standing - afraid, most of all afraid, of falling in love.

Rose

'Whatever scares you, owns you.' Mum's sitting cross-legged on her straw mat in our garden, her eyes closed, like she might just be making an observation to herself but I know she's talking to me. I must be coming up to my birthday because the crocuses are just pushing up in their little nooks and crannies all around the farm, promising spring, but it is still cold.

'Let's talk about what scares you,' I shoot back. Her hair is so straggly, it irritates me. Brush it, I think, tie it back with a comb or a band like you used to. Her mane is still dark but the long silver threads laced here and there within it, tell a tale of someone who has got suddenly much older, someone who cares a lot less than she used to and it pains me to see it.

'Going for some medical treatments, for one. That scares, you right?'

A small smile plays on her lips at my childish haranguing. As if she is so far away and at peace within herself that nothing can touch her. That's what too much meditation does for you, I think. Too much communing with nature; it makes you float away like a puffball on the wind and then nobody can get hold of you. She calls it being serene.

'So - I've told you about me.' I look up as Lawrence has just deliberately flicked a card right into the middle of his edifice making it collapse and bringing me back to earth with it.

'How about you?'

'What about me?' Oh, he's a cagey one, isn't he?

'Tell me a bit about yourself. Your family?'

'My family.' Lawrence swoops in with his arms, gathering up all his cards. 'I'm not close to them. As I told you, I haven't been, in years. Otherwise …' He makes a gesture with his arms that includes both him and me. 'Most people wouldn't be wandering around in a snowstorm on Christmas Day, would they?'

Even if they had to save a little Sri Lankan boy, that's true.

'Was it always like that?' I ask softly. When he spoke yesterday about not having seen his mum for a long while, I thought he mentioned it with regret.

'I was close to my brother, once upon a time. When we were kids, I used to look out for him, you know …'

'Younger brother?'

'Younger, yeah.' He gives a shy laugh. 'I remember when he was born, how pleased and proud I was to have a brother. I was four and a half years older than him, not all that old myself but I never knew that at the time. I thought four was big, almost grown-up.' He almost visibly puffs out his chest. 'He was the baby,' he continues. 'I was the one who had to keep an eye on him. I always did.'

'I never had any siblings.' I say a little enviously. 'What was he like?' I ask. 'Your brother?' He puts the cup he's been drinking from down onto the canvas sacking.

'Trouble!' he remembers, but there is a pained amusement in his voice. 'He used to hide all over the place when he was just a toddler. I had a job keeping a look out on where he was - Mum used to dress him in bright colours so you could spot him a mile off wherever he was on the farm, but I'd walk deliberately past him, scratching my head and saying loudly *where can he be?*'

I laugh, imagining Lawrence as a six-year-old, a seven-year -old, playing the grown-up with his little brother.

'He had a laugh …' he smiles back at me, 'that reminded me

of ... of chocolate coins at Christmas.'

'Chocolate coins?' I look at him, amused.

'I used to think that. It was special and bright, full of something sweet and good ... can you imagine that?'

'It sounds like a beautiful laugh.'

'It was.'

I lean in a little closer. 'Tell me more about him.'

'Man, he was trouble, Rose. He was always getting into places he shouldn't have. One day my attention must have wandered, I got distracted by something and he disappeared. He'd have been about five years old. It had snowed - like this - and he wanted to go out and play. Mum said no, so he went to his bedroom window and he jumped.'

'*Serious*?' I pull a disbelieving face.

'She went mental, looking for him. Called the police over and everything.' His voice suddenly gets slower, changes. 'Not something she'd do lightly. My father wasn't too fond of ...' Lawrence's eyes glaze over a little at the memory. 'She was sure someone must have come in and taken him but he'd fallen head-first into a snow-drift. I was the one who found him.'

'Conscious?'

He shakes his head slightly.

'Not breathing.' When I pulled him out by his boots he was as limp as a rag doll. I watched one of the coppers do CPR on him for over fifteen minutes. He kept going, long after everyone else had given up hope. I've never forgotten that ...' His voice catches a bit. 'How that guy brought him back from the dead. A miracle. It was what first got me interested in all this ...

'That's amazing. So if it weren't for your little brother jumping out of the window maybe you wouldn't be here right now?'

He smiles slightly. 'True.'

'How about now? You don't see him?' The smile fades a little.

'I left home when he was just twelve, Rose. By then he was already becoming someone else. He liked to take my gear; my watch, my bike. If it was mine, he wanted it …'

'Little brother rivalry?'

'Maybe.' He's digging his thumbs into the sides of his temples now, as if his head is sore. 'Maybe he just had the makings of a thief,' he mutters. 'I'd hoped to take him with me when I left, Rose. I'd hoped …' his voice falters, cuts out.

'Are you okay?'

'I'm sorry, Rose. I'm just a little tired.'

Maybe he has overdone it? He was doing all that digging before, I don't think he slept well. Or maybe - it's time to change the subject? I lift myself up and shuffle over to sit a bit nearer to him.

'So; how about if I could grant *your* Christmas wish, Lawrence. What would it be?'

'I'd like a little peace,' he comes back immediately, sinks his head into his hands for a moment.

'I've wanted peace for a long time,' his muffled voice comes through his spread fingers. His voice sounds unbelievably weary all of a sudden.

'Christmas is a good time to find peace,' I say gently.

'Is it, Rose?'

'It says it on all the Christmas cards, doesn't it? *Peace and Goodwill to all men?*' I rush on, wanting to make things okay again. 'Up here is a good place to find peace.' No telly and no computers and no music and no Internet and no news of any kind, our mobiles switched off to save the batteries. Up here we only have us. I lean forward, and then, after just a moment's hesitation, begin rubbing at the back of his neck with my fingers, gently, slowly, easing away the tension as if we had known each other for months or even years, rather than just hours. It doesn't feel strange to do it, and if he thinks it's over-familiar, he doesn't object.

Is this what it might be like to have a boyfriend, it occurs to me? I like the feel of the muscles of his shoulders and neck beneath my fingers. I like the way the little short hairs on the back

180

of his neck feel so soft. I like the warmth of his skin. After a while, still slightly marvelling at my own bravery, I realise reluctantly that my legs have gone numb from sitting in the same position and I have to get up, picking up the mug as I go. He lies down now, pulling the fire-warmed sacking right over him and I wish … I wish I could lie down and curl up beside him.

'I'm expecting a call. If I sleep, will you wake me up in a couple of hours?'

'I'll wake you up,' I promise. There's a little bit of tea left in the bottom of the mug, l notice. I swirl the liquid by rocking it between my hands gently. It's a thin metal mug painted white on the outside, blue on the inside and at the bottom there are the dregs of the leaves from the tea he just drank. Mum would have looked at them, seen the pictures they formed in her mind, and teased out the meaning. Maybe if I looked into the tea leaves I could learn something of the truth about you, Lawrence?

Why did you ask about getting your fortune told just now? Why did you get so upset when we started talking about your brother? You left home so young and you seem so driven … I want to know more about you. I'm itching to look at those tea leaves and yet something is telling me no; this isn't the way to find out what you want to know about him, Rose. It isn't *your* way. I hesitate.

I don't look.

Instead, I dunk the cup straight into the melted-snow bucket to wash up.

Lawrence

Strange girl. Strange little girl, get out of my mind. Why did you even come up here? You shouldn't be here. I should be up here by myself like I planned. This place is my hideout. I needed to be here alone so I could think, so I could focus. What I've got to do next, it's not going to be easy. It's going to take all my courage and all my attention. I'm only going to have a small window of opportunity to get this right and I need to be ready. I need to be strong.

I don't need to be hindered and you, Rose, you hinder me. I pull up my rolled-up T-shirt that's serving as a pillow tucked under my neck, I'm trying to make myself more comfortable but it is not comfortable no matter which way I turn. I've got my back to her. She's rinsing out some clothes - maybe those sodden jeans from yesterday? I can hear her, dunking them in and out of the washing up bucket, then the sound of the water splashing as she wrings them out. As she works, she is singing faintly under her breath. Her voice is sweet. It's some sort of child's bed-time ballad, I think. A lullaby.

I am not used to companionship. My fingers go up to close around my shoulders, the place where she was massaging me before. There is not usually someone there to say; *you need to go back inside, you'll catch your death*. There is not usually someone there to trouble about how I take my tea. No one to rub my sore neck. Her little fingers on my aching neck muscles were surprisingly effective, gentle, not painful but warm and supple, just right.

But also, I know, all wrong.

All wrong, Rose. She knows it, as well as I do. She wonders what I'm really doing here, I can see it in her eyes. I've shown her the pictures of Sunny and she's gone along with that and yet she's too intelligent not to be asking herself all the other questions. *Why is he here? Why not stay over with that sponsor he speaks of, whoever they are?* It's a logical question. We haven't come to it yet but I know that we will. Then she has that secret of her own that she's nurturing close to her heart, doesn't she? I still don't know …

But I don't want to know! Don't tell me, for God's sake, Rose. Don't tell me anymore about yourself. Don't pull me in. I can't be involved with you. I can't accept any more of your kindness, either, it's way too painful for me, can't you see that? Your kindness is like … it's like the cutting edge of a fisherman's knife opening up a sea clam. Your kindness will make me weak. I can't accept it, I don't want it. I have to remain strong.

I've got to rest now, Rose. I've got to stop struggling with it all and let it go because I am so dog-tired and now at last … *at last,* the hardness that is the flagstone floor beneath me is melting into my bones. Joaquin is here. He's telling me that I'm late, he seems to be angry that I didn't turn up. My mouth is so dry. Did no one tell him I was coming away to England? Joaquin fades. I want to find Dougie. I'm walking down the muddy main road at West Camp, it's early morning and the sun is beaming through the mist and I'm trying to find the place where Dougie is and I can't find him. In my heart, I already know I'm not going to find him, that he's nowhere to be found. I'm frustrated, thwarted. Then I remember I'm supposed to make a phone call to him, that's the way to get to him, but I can't recall the number.

A loud spit from the fire half-awakens me now. I turn, look up and the white plaster patch where the repairs were once so badly done on the chapel ceiling, beams down at me. I have sunk so far into the stupor of sleep I barely know the time, the date. I know where I am, though. I have lain beneath this chapel roof so many times before. The fierce, one-directional heat from the fire, the familiar scent of pine cones burning, the cool damp smell of the centuries-old chapel walls mean I could only be in one place; my sanctuary. And if I am here - my thoughts swim through the sea of fog in my brain - that means that I am hiding out again.

I don't know what happened this time. I don't remember. But I am here, playing cat and mouse once more, vying for survival. When my father blows a fuse, it is the only way to come out of it intact. I have had black eyes from him in the past; a little finger bent back so far I'll never properly straighten it again, broken ribs. Now I don't wait around. I run. I come up here and I stay out of sight because Rob Macrae is like a weather vane. Wait long enough, and the storm blows over. He forgets he was ever raging. He goes back to being simply unpleasant. After a while, it's as if *he* goes into hiding. Then I can come out. I can creep back down to my bedroom at Macrae Farm, where I'll listen out for a bit, hyper alert to any tiny signs or sounds of disturbance. If there are none, I will hear them talking, my mum and my dad, like nothing, like nothing's ever happened. They paper it all over, do the content couple bit. She's relieved and she likes to forget. For a while, things might be calm because that's how it always goes but you know the calm won't last. It'll never last. And I can never forget.

I pull up my legs beneath the sacking, trying to calm myself, trying to quieten the rate of my own breathing. *It's gone, it's all gone Lawrence*, I tell myself but the memories are so powerful, they live on still inside of me. I can't forget. I hate my father with every breath, with every bone in my body, with every waking thought. I hate his great red ex-boxer's fists and his snarling teeth and his big barrelled chest that's so filled up to the brim with blackness and temper and his need to destroy anything or anyone who ever gets in his way.

I groan out loud and the singing I have been hearing on the edge of my mind stops in an instant. There is a taut silence, but the silence is in the chapel and I am not there, I am somewhere far away, remembering all the things that hurt me. I can't get them out of my mind. How he used to pummel my mother into the ground. She was so weak. She was nothing, a wisp, a feather in the wind, but one small word from her was enough to send him into a frenzy.

I used to lie awake in my bed at night and dream of how I would stop him. I used to think; if I can only find some way to stop him, our misery will all be over. I used to lie there tying myself into knots at my own inaction, hating myself for hearing her cry and doing nothing but hating equally the thought of what I'd have to do to bring her misery to an end. And then ... in the end, hating her too because she didn't have the strength to leave him.

She *wouldn't* leave him.

I turn around now on the canvas sacking, my shoulders aching, the skin on my face exposed to the full warmth from the fire and the girl has started singing again, hesitantly, quietly, almost beneath her breath but I strain to listen to her. Such a sweet voice. She sings first in some ancient tongue - Celtic, Gaelic, I don't know. Then in English. It tells the story of some warrior who's been fighting in the wars far away and when he gets back he's scared it's all going to be gone, everything he left behind but it's not; his sweetheart is still waiting for him.

Do things ever really work out like that in the real world, Rose? My eyes flicker open for a few seconds and the sight of her makes me happy. She tucked me in just now. I shouldn't care, but I do. She opens up a ray of sunshine in my heart, makes me believe, just for a fraction of a moment, that things could ever be different.

I believed that once before, though, didn't I? There was a time we were all going to have a fresh start, away from him. All we had to do was bide our time and be patient. All Mum had to do was save up for a bit, help me get the money together so we could take ourselves and Pilgrim to some other place that was far enough away from here. I thought she'd do it, help save us. I thought she'd have the courage.

In the end, she didn't though.

185

I close my eyes and Rose … Rose fades as I dip back into a deep, forgetful sleep. Right now I know that is the only place where I will find any peace.

Rose

According to my phone, it's now nearly midday. Lawrence has fallen asleep again by the fire. It seems a good time to try phoning home for a brief check-in. Find out if Dad's okay. By now he must have had his breakfast and the first tablets of the day. Even if he hasn't got the ones I went to fetch, he still needs to take the other ones. As I wait for the call to connect, I wonder if he's remembered to tell the family about the cocktail of tablets he takes or if they've realised about it themselves? The call fails and I ring again. I'm not getting enough of a signal in here, that's the trouble. I hold the phone up towards the light from the fire; no, not enough bars to signify there's any signal in here. I'm going to have to go outside, darn it. And it's so *bloody cold* out there.

Once I'm muffled up, I push the chapel door open again, peeking outside to see if anything has changed in the last hour or so. The door sticks and jams at first, with the ice underneath it. I push it slowly so it won't make a dragging sound and disturb Lawrence. Outside, the path he cleared so recently has already got a covering of snow lying softly over the top of it. But at least out here I am getting one bar of signal, two bars …

'Hello. *Hello*?' I say as Dad picks up his mobile but he can't hear me. I need to move a little further away out into the open.

'Hello Dad, it's Rose. *Rose!*' I say again, louder. I move a little further down into the courtyard.

'Rose,' Dad says. His voice sounds croaky and confused to

me - but maybe that's just the bad connection? 'Where are you?' He sounds sad.

'Safe and sound,' I reassure. 'I've got your tablets, too. I just can't get to you yet. I'm stuck.'

'Rose is stuck,' I hear him saying to someone at the other end. 'She's safe and sound, though.'

Of course she is, I can hear a female voice saying to him, *she's at Shona's remember, we told you?* Oh dear, my little white lie, I think. Fingers crossed they don't think to ring me at Shona's at any point.

'How are you holding up, Dad?' There's a long pause while he seems to take his time configuring what I'm saying. My heart sinks a little, recognising that already he's slower, he's taking longer to process things; I know this is because of the missing tablets.

'I'm having a good time,' he says after a bit. 'Catching up with Ty.' Well if that's true then it's a result. If Uncle Ty is actually being forced to spend time with his brother maybe he'll come to see how things really are with Dad. And Dad will be getting the time that he needs with his family instead of them shooting off to do *more important things* like they usually do.

'I hope they're looking after you well, Dad?'

'Oh, yes.' His voice sounds distracted and far away. I feel a tug of worry at the thought that Dad's got people there with him, sure, but they aren't people who know anything about him and his needs. They won't know that he forgets to mention when he gets cold. You have to put a rug over his knees if he looks like he needs it. He doesn't feel thirsty so you have to make sure he gets a drink. He doesn't like water, though, he likes tea. I wonder if anyone's remembered that the soya milk that's in the fridge is what I have to put in his tea because he can't tolerate dairy ...

'I miss you, Rose.'

'I'm sorry I left the way I did, yesterday, Dad,' I rush out. 'I'm sorry I can't be there right now.' This is the first Christmas he'll have been on his own without either me or Mum there, the thought dawns. This emptiness, this loneliness I hear in his voice

- it's going to be like this for him when I leave, isn't it? I bite my lip.

'Dad, are you sure you're okay? I'll be back as soon as the weather lets up. As soon as I can.' As I speak to him, I make my way carefully over the cleared path to look out over the valley for the second time this morning.

And for the second time, it really takes my breath away. It's like everything has just … gone. My house is gone. The hill down to the rest of the village is gone. The neat row of bungalows by the infant school is gone and the school is pretty much gone too *and* the shop-cum-post office. I can see the spire on top of the church steeple but only just. Even the tall trees surrounding Topfields are so laden with snow you can barely make out any of the branches underneath. A solitary crow flies off to the West, disappearing into a blur behind the back of some trees. Apart from that bird, there is nothing to focus your view on, nothing but a fragile stillness that is so large and so quiet that it feels like the whole world's been enclosed in icy bubble-wrap. Out here, the signal is at least a little clearer.

'I'm okay,' Dad says, but his voice sounds so strange, so distant as if he's not really talking to me at all, as if his attention's been taken up by something on the telly or something else going on in the room. I don't know if he really is okay.

When I leave home, it's going to be the same. I stare out over the battlements, the strange glary whiteness I see in front of me seems to fill up the whole earth and the entire sky and pretty much everything else in the middle. It looks, I think, like a blank page. It's the unknown; it's what's going to happen to Dad once I leave here and it's my future. It could be anything - everything or nothing. As I stand there, looking at it, the cold seeps in under my coat and onto my chest so all my muscles start juddering. My leg starts to ache, now, the stitches feeling pulled tight as my skin contracts with the cold and yet stubbornly, I want to see how long I can withstand being out in it. I have to imagine tolerating it, because sometime in the next day or so, it dawns on me, we are going to have to. Two tins of tuna and some packet soups aren't going to last forever, are they?

There's the sound of the handset being handed over to someone else now and Sam comes on the line.

'Rose,' she says solicitously. 'Everything all right?' She sounds as if her teeth are chattering - haven't they even got the fire lit at home?

'I'm all right,' I defend. 'You?' Then; 'You sound cold, Sam.' She shouldn't be cold, she's at my house.

'Dad's out back getting some more logs in. These solid fuel fires are a bit pesky aren't they?' she complains. 'The one in the living room keeps going out and the central heating doesn't work very well here does it?'

'It's temperamental,' I admit. As long as they're keeping Dad warm. 'Listen, my dad, is he…?'

'He's fine,' she comes back immediately, a little impatiently, even. 'We found the box with the medicines in. We gave him his morning ones. He says he feels a little bit wobbly today because he doesn't have those other ones - the ones you went to fetch. But given the weather conditions don't come rushing back till it's safe. Dad says he'd rather you wait till he can fetch you, now, or till Shona's dad can bring you back.'

Shona's dad? My heart sinks a little as I remember. They've actually got a reason to be in contact with him, haven't they? As soon as he gets onto fixing the car again, Uncle Ty and the rest of them will realise I'm not at Shona's. I *haven't* been at Shona's. Bugger. Still, I've only told them a lie to save them worrying, not for any other reason.

'Once this clears I'll make my own way back, honestly …'

'No, you won't,' Sam warns. 'Dad wants you to keep safe. You *have* seen the news, I take it?'

'Of course,' I fib. 'Weather warnings etc …' As I talk, I make my way back towards the chapel entrance, stamping my feet as I go.

'Not that,' she says impatiently. 'The *other* local news. You

190

know - that man the police want to question - he's still on the loose. Somewhere around Merry Ditton, they have reason to believe. He's a violent criminal ...'

'And no one must approach him,' I say wearily. Okay this is just using up my phone battery uselessly now. 'I won't approach anyone, I promise. I can't. I'm stuck indoors like everyone else, aren't I?'

Do they think I am a complete moron?

Before I even reach the chapel door, I can clearly see that it's open. I frown. I'm sure I closed it. I was thinking about conserving heat, I remember that. Has Lawrence woken up, gone out and I didn't notice? Almost involuntarily, I slow my footsteps right down, treading softly as I come up to the door, Sam's recent dire warnings about 'a man on the run' still ringing loudly in my head. But Lawrence hasn't gone anywhere. When I peer cautiously inside I can see that he is still there. Only now he's sitting, for some reason, by the open door, and he's being very, very still.

What's he doing?

He isn't meditating or doing some kind of yoga, which was my first thought. I can tell, even from here. Something about the way he's holding his whole body so tautly, tense as a spring, tells me that much. His face is at a slightly uplifted angle, facing the light. My God. He looks - he looks so very sad that just to see him brings a lump to my throat.

I halt. I don't know what to do. It doesn't feel right to go in and disturb him but I don't want to stay out here in the cold, either. I'd hoped, secretly, that he might be awake by the time I got in. I've got so many things I want to ask him. Whether he thinks we'd be justified calling out the emergency services because we've been trapped or whether we should just weather it out, leave them to deal with the real, genuine emergencies? I wanted to ask him if he thought there was any chance at all we'd make it out tomorrow. I wanted him to open up and to tell me more about his protégé back in Jaffna, Sunny.

Is it … maybe because of Sunny that Lawrence is feeling so upset right now? A whole host of scenarios run through my mind; he's heard that Sunny's taken sick; he's learned that he can't bring Sunny over for some diplomatic reasons and they've decided to amputate …?

Is that why - even though there are no tears running down his face - he looks as if he might be crying? It must be something like that, something bad, because in the short time I've known him he's only ever come across as resilient and strong; the sort of guy who'd take all of life's troubles on the chin. He's a coper. I don't think he'd want me to see him so vulnerable and so raw, but - if there was any way I could help …?

God, what best to do?

I've never seen a boy cry before. *I've never seen a lot of things,* the thought echoes straight back, like a ball lobbed over a net, *I've never seen a boy naked before either. I've never let a boy see me.* The thought embarrasses me, because I don't know the guy, I shouldn't be thinking like this. He'd think that too; that I've walked in on a very private, guarded moment. He wouldn't want me to catch him like this, I know.

I clear my throat a little and his eyes flicker open instantly. He looks straight at my phone and I see him register that I must have been calling home. With his eyes open, his expression is drawn and spooked. He doesn't look like the catnap he just had has done him very much good.

'Hey,' I say. 'You okay?' Then, when he doesn't immediately respond. 'You're sitting by the open door,' I offer. 'You're not cold?'

'I wanted to sit by the light,' he says.

'By the light?' He watches me as I come in and push the door closed behind me. Now there will be no more daylight coming in. Nothing except the thin morning beams which are filtering through the high windows at the sides, and the light from the fire. 'I'm sorry,' I remind him. 'We've got to conserve the heat.' He nods, rubs his face with his hands.

'Bad dreams?' I ask.

'Bad dreams,' he agrees. He wanted to sit by the light, he said. I glance at him sympathetically. He must *really* hate the dark if he's prepared to put up with these temperatures so as to get a little bit of light. It isn't just that, though is it? I wonder what his dreams were that they have made him go like this, his shoulders so hunched, his head bowed but he must sense my interest. He clears his throat now, changing gear.

'Family all okay?' He indicates my phone.

'They're as okay as they could be,' I tell him cautiously. I'm burning to ask if everything is all right *with him*. 'My uncle and aunt and my cousin are only staying over because the weather hi-jacked them - a bit like us staying up here, I guess. Anyway, they haven't quite got the hang of how to use the wood fire and they're cold. And Dad … he could still do with his meds which I was supposed to bring him, of course.' I'm rambling, I know I am, talking about any old thing that rolls off my tongue when I wish, *I just wish* I could ask him what the matter is?

'They're okay with you being away, though? With where you are, right now?'

'They're okay with where they *think* I am,' I remind him. He nods, acknowledging what I've just said. I could be mistaken, but I think I saw a flash of relief on his face at that. Now he looks as if he really badly wants to ask me something but he won't. Maybe it's the dreams he was having, still bothering him? After a while;

'You just asked me if I was having bad dreams.' He looks a little abashed. 'Did I … was I calling out in my sleep, Rose?'

'A little.' I switch my phone off to save the battery, and he watches while I put it away safely in my pocket.

'I'm sorry. I do that sometimes, call out in my sleep. I hope I didn't scare you?'

'Nope.'

'Did I say anything intelligible?' he asks in a croaky voice.

'Like what?' This is important to him, I realise. But it's a delicate situation. If I show too much interest he's going to scuttle away like a startled deer in the forest. I've got to make like I didn't see that look I saw on his face when I came through the door. I go over and check the jeans I rinsed out earlier, see if they're getting any drier, hanging over the back of the pew which we've pulled closer to the fire.

'Like … *anything*.'

I smile at him. 'Nothing important except … you called out where you had hidden the treasure map, I'm afraid. And I now know that X marks the spot.'

'Ah. You see now why I don't have a girlfriend.' He makes an attempt at returning my joke but he's still looking anxious. 'They value their beauty sleep too much.'

'I wouldn't worry. That calling out in your sleep thing - I'm used to it,' I admit. 'My dad's been doing that for years.'

'He has?' Lawrence settles down by the warmth of the brazier, stretches out his fingertips.

'Sometimes Dad calls out in his sleep as if … as if the very hounds of hell are after him. The nurse who used to visit told me that it's a common occurrence after people have suffered from some sort of trauma. They dream, and in those dreams revisit whatever's terrified them and often they call out. Half the time they don't even know they're doing it.'

I shoot Lawrence a sideways glance, 'You knew you were calling out though, didn't you?' I wait to see if he'll elaborate on his own situation but he doesn't seem inclined to.

'When Dad calls out in his sleep, I sing to him, sometimes.' The jeans are drying beautifully in the heat from the brazier. I turn them round to even out the process, giving my exaggerated attention to my task as I speak.

'Does it make it any better,' he asks softly now. 'When you sing?'

'I don't know if it makes it any better.' I look up from flattening the damp jeans with my hands. 'I don't know if anything can, to be honest. I know it quietens Dad. It soothes him when I sing, that's all.'

'You sang to me too, just now, didn't you?'

194

I nod, feeling immediately and chronically embarrassed. Hell, I didn't realise he was actually *listening* to me. Earlier, I sang Lawrence the song Mum used to sing to me when I was very young and couldn't sleep.

It seemed to calm him down. He opened his eyes and looked at me at one point when I went over and put the sleeping bag over his shoulders. I sat there with him for a little while. I don't know how long. I remember I put my hand out tentatively when he began to whimper. I rubbed the top of his shoulders again, very gently, very softly as if I could soothe all his worries away as easily as rubbing chalk off a blackboard.

'Thank you for that. I guess I've got too many memories that I don't want. I've got no place to put them because I don't want them ...' he says cryptically.

'From the war, you mean?' *Damn*, If he realised I was singing, I think uncomfortably now, did he also know I was rubbing his shoulders while he lay there, too? *I thought he was asleep!*

'You've seen too many things and now you can't forget?' I prompt. He seems to be shivering and yet his face looks very hot, a fine sheen of sweat glimmering on his skin in the firelight, his short hair plastered all over his forehead. Poor Lawrence, my heart goes out to him. What can he have been through in all those troubled places he's mentioned that causes him so much distress? He doesn't say much but I'm picking up he might have seen some pretty gruesome things ...

'Not from the war,' he surprises me. 'It's this place.' What on earth can he mean, *this place*? It reminds him of somewhere else, that's what he must mean, but;

'Don't ask. You don't want to know about me, Rose,' he looks at me candidly.

I do, though. I come and sit down tentatively beside him.

'You don't.' He grabs hold of the ends of my fingers suddenly as if to emphasise his point. 'You really don't. I've seen the way you look at me, and ...' I make to protest but he doesn't let me out of it, presses my fingers a little tighter. 'And - I'm not what you

195

see on the surface. You need to know it. That person who you've already made up your mind I am - I'm not him.'

'I don't care who you are.' I don't know what makes me say it but the moment the words are out, I know it to be true.

'A girl like you ...?' He turns his face away, cut up by his own thoughts.

'Believe me, you would care.'

Rose

'Maybe I care about *you*, Lawrence?' I breathe softly, daringly.

'That would be a mistake,' he begins but I pick up the struggle in his eyes and I persist.

'Tell me. What is it that makes you call out in your sleep like that?'

'It's this place,' he repeats after a while, his voice barely audible. 'This place brings back a lot of memories ...'

'Oh?' I move in a scooch closer, waiting for him to explain. In the long silence that follows a cascade of uncomfortable thoughts crash through my mind. How could this place - *this ruin* - be the source of so many unhappy memories for him? He already hinted earlier that he's familiar with the area - he mentioned those stone angels, didn't he? But what reason could he have had before to come up here and do anything other than sight-see? And even *that* he'd have had to have done with caution. It's on Macrae land, isn't it, and they don't like people wandering around on their territory.

'What kind of memories?' I urge, though I've got a pressing feeling that maybe I should be leaving well alone. I've never liked this place. As I wait for Lawrence, clearly struggling to come up with some sort of a reply, it dawns on me that it really is rather dark in here. I hadn't noticed before just *how* dark. It's the kind of closed, stagnant darkness I remember from that time Shona

197

and I missed the last bus home and took the shortcut over the old disused cemetery. I feel a small shudder go right up my back.

'I had a - *mishap*,' he says the word carefully, feeling the sound of it in his mouth, trying out the taste of it as he comes back to me at last, and I get the sense he has not shared this with many people.

I brace myself.

'I was running away from someone, and I came up here. I'd come here many times previously ...' He looks around him as he speaks and I get a sense of his familiarity with the place. This is not the first time the chapel has been his sanctuary, is it? I didn't realise he was local. I feel a small knot of unhappiness in my stomach at the thought.

'Running away from *whom*?' Why would a guy like Lawrence have to run away from anyone?

'My father.' He says the word 'father' like it's something out of a foreign language. A word he doesn't in the least like the sound or meaning of. A word he's not comfortable using.

'You were running away from your father,' I say. Is he going to tell me *why*?

He doesn't.

I'm putting two and two together. He fell out with his father. Is this the reason why he hasn't seen his mother in a very long time, like he told me before? The reason he left home so early, too, I'm guessing.

'You came up here and you had a mishap, you say? Something *bad* happened?'

He takes in a deep breath and I get the sense that there is more to come.

'See that big plaster patch up there?' I follow his gaze.

'That was where the chapel ceiling had to be fixed after a huge chunk of it came down during a storm. The whole place had been weakened because of the digging works ...' he trails off.

'You know this place well, then?' He's *definitely* local ...

'Better than I should, Rose.' His voice goes very quiet now.

'One time I got trapped up here. They'd brought the bull-dozers in to tear down some work that was never going to be completed.'

'The Macraes, you mean?' I look at him disbelievingly. That must have been back when they recanted on their promise to re-store the castle.

'But what were you even …?'

'They didn't know I was in here,' he continues. 'Nobody knew I was here. I shouldn't have been. When the walls first start-ed caving down on me I was asleep. By the time I realised what was happening it was too late to get out. Can you imagine that? The noise … cutting through my sleep, the impact as the stone and timber structures they'd erected started falling all around me, it was like - it was like the end of days.' He bites at his short, short fingernails as he says this and for the first time I see that he's al-ready bitten them down to the nub.

'You must have thought ... you were going to *die*?' I look at him, stricken.

'I thought I'd be buried alive.'

I hear myself gasp.

'Is that what the bad dreams are about? You're re-living the memories?' My hand goes to my throat.

'I don't remember a lot of it. The truth is, I don't want to remember. In the end, I was trapped under the fallen masonry for three days. If it hadn't been for my dog going berserk …' He shakes his head. 'He knew I was in here. One of the workmen got me out in the end.'

Christ. I can't take this all in. He just said three days … *has he really just told me he was once stuck under the rubble up here for three days?* That's horrific, really horrible. If it's true, how come I never heard about that - surely the village would have been buzz-ing with it, if a local boy had disappeared for that long?

'You were … hurt?' I venture at last.

He shoots me a wry grin. 'Physically, no. Scratches, that's all. Those little angels must have been looking out for me, Rose.'

'Thank God.' I'm still trying to work this out. He wasn't injured, he says, but there are mental scars. There must be. He was trapped for three days. Under the rubble. Alone, and in the dark. Is that why he's so unhappy in the dark? I shoot him a compassionate look.

'Thank God that your dog knew you were in here and led them to you. But ... how *old* would you have been, Lawrence?' I'm still grappling a little with the discovery that he's a local boy. I used to commute to the nearest all-girl's Grammar so we'd have been at separate secondary schools. He's older than me, too. I don't know him. And yet ... a faint memory edges to the front of my mind as I watch his face now. I thought I recognised him when I first laid eyes on him, didn't I? I thought then that I had seen him somewhere before ...

'Fifteen, going on sixteen.'

'Lawrence ... are you seriously saying that no one had missed you at home?' I look at him disbelievingly but he just gives a small laugh.

'Let's just say - they were used to me disappearing when I felt like it. Nobody would have raised any questions.'

Nobody to look out for you, Lawrence? I lower my eyes to the floor.

'Heard enough?' he says. Not nearly enough. I know he's just told me something *huge*. He's hinted at a past, precarious and ensnaring as a spider's web, teetering out in all directions around him; the place he ran from, the place he's run to, all dangerous places, no safety and no respite in any of them. Some of the things he told me earlier this morning, when I thought he was talking about his job, filter back to me now; *boring means that you are living a normal life*, he said; *one where you need not fear what each day might bring, what you might have left at the end of it.* I suspect I know more about this man right at this moment than many might who have known him a lot longer. He's opened up, told me things he'd normally keep hidden.

And yet ... he feels more of a stranger to me now than he did a moment ago. All the things I had assumed about his past - a

200

stable home, a loving family - they shrivel up and disappear. He's someone else after all, isn't he, just like he said? A small shudder goes through me, I should leave this alone, leave well alone, something inside me says and yet ... an insatiable desire to learn more is there, too. Even though I know I should be afraid to learn more. Something tells me nobody goes through the kind of trauma he's just hinted at and comes out unscathed. I shake my head a fraction, *no, I haven't heard enough*, but whatever *I* want, he clearly feels he's said enough.

'Tell me,' he says after a while, 'Do you believe in Fate?'

'*Fate*?' I frown, shake my head a little. What does he mean?

'Do you believe in Fate, little Rose?' he asks again. 'Kismet?'

'I'm not sure,' I say at last. His question has made me remember where it is I thought I knew him from. He's put me in mind of the day Mum took me up to Topfields and we picked all those cowslips along the verge, *Titsy-totsy, tell me true* ... I take in Lawrence a little more closely and suddenly, it's like a burst of sunlight beaming down through a break in the clouds and I can feel all my limbs trembling with a certain recognition. Dear God, it's him, isn't it? The man I saw that day in my mind's eye, running through the woods, towards Dead Men's Copse. I *think* it's him.

Titsy-totsy, tell me true
Who will I be married to?

This man is the same man I saw that day when I was twelve and Mum promised to show me my soul-mate. But we can't be together. From what I felt that day on Topfields with Mum, we won't be.

Only it *can't* be him.

I frown, rubbing at my face because this has all begun to feel too surreal. It's the lack of sleep and the strange place, the terrible things he's just told me and being in here under circumstances of duress; I'm imagining things.

What I saw that day up on Topfields - that was all just the

over-active imagination of an adolescent, being encouraged by a mum who should have known better. I don't want to remember it and I don't want to believe it.

'Do you think we can ever avert our fate?' he says quietly, urgently, and the nudge of his fingers contacting mine sends a tingle right into my hand, right the way up my arm.

The answer seems really important to him, but the truth is, I don't have any answers. I don't have any words in my mouth right now, even if I did have an answer. He gazes quietly at me for a little bit and the early afternoon light coming in through the high-up chapel windows seems to brighten for a moment. I take in the gentle features of his face, the slightly blunt brow of his nose, his short hair that curls softly at the nape of his neck and I see how easily it might be possible for me to love a man like this. How it might be possible for him to love me.

'I hope we might avert it if it's not a good fate,' I say at last. 'I hope so, Lawrence. Why?'

He shrugs, 'I'm back here now because I have to be. But I've always felt ...' he looks around him warily. 'This place could be the death of me.'

'If you felt that,' I look at him seriously, 'and you've already had one very bad experience up here ... maybe you should never have come back?'

He offers me the ghost of a smile.

'Then I never would have met you, would I?' He puts his hand on my knee now, just for a fraction of a second and something in his expression makes me long to ask; *would that have been a cause for regret, Lawrence?*

But I don't ask.

I'm about to lean towards him, take his hand, say something, anything that will keep him here, capture us together in this moment where we've shared so many things, private things.

But then he stands up. I know he just wants to stop this thing that seems to be going on between us. He knows that I'm falling for him ... *I've seen the way you look at me* ... have I made it that pathetically obvious? I turn away, my heart aching because there is nothing I can do about how I feel and the worse thing is, up here, nowhere that I can go to hide it.

I have to look on the bright side. At least now I know for sure that he doesn't have a girlfriend. Trouble is, I think I just caught a glimpse as to what might be the reasons why.

While he goes off to have a wash, I line up the damper pieces of kindling wood that we dragged in before breakfast, push them up near the brazier so they have a chance to dry out before we need to use them later. I have to break some of the branches down into smaller pieces like he showed me. It's a tedious job but I'm glad of something to do to distract me because my mind's racing now, deeply troubled by some of the things he's just revealed; his father who he ran away from, how he nearly got buried alive, how nobody even came looking. And does he really believe what he just told me about this place being the death of him?

I feel sick with worry at the thought of it. I really hope he didn't mean that. I don't like to believe that things in our life can be set in stone, that there are some things we have no way of avoiding. I like to believe we can make a difference. That it's worth trying to. Mum believed in Fate though, didn't she? After a lifetime of spouting all that stuff about 'choices', when push came to shove, she was as fatalistic as they come ...

'You could go and see the doctor like Dad keeps asking you to. Ever since you've come back from that camp you haven't been right. What if it's something that wild marshmallow roots aren't going to fix like you think?'

With her eyes closed Mum couldn't see me kicking the gold and royal blue clump of crocuses behind her with my foot. She couldn't see that I was kicking the petal heads off them, sending them spinning wastefully to the ground. There, that's what you get if you go round living too much with your eyes closed.

'Going to see a proper doctor you could ... you could maybe prolong your life.'

203

'To everything its season,' she quoted infuriatingly. She'd been home for three months now. I don't think Dad really had a clue about how bad things had got with her. She wouldn't see a doctor so he wasn't about to find out either. But I suspected, and I was pretty sure she did too. She maddened me, and that was the truth. She was all too quick to accept it. Too quick to say 'it was how it was meant to be', be at peace with it and all that crap.

'Talking of seasons, I know what you're after for your birthday, my love. I've spoken to Dad and it's all been arranged.'

It had?

She said it as if what I'd wanted for my birthday even mattered anymore. She was dying. Me wanting to go on that school trip only seemed selfish now. It was true I'd longed to go on that skiing trip. And yet … all I ever really wanted from Mum was that she would try and be a little more normal. I'd wanted that trip because everyone else was going. I'd wanted it because it was what other people did with their holidays - not squat out in the mud. I'd looked at Mum painfully. Now all that I longed for was that she might be well again, but it seemed all too late for that.

'It's all arranged?' Could my parents really have gone to all the trouble of organising it so I could go on that skiing trip after all? And kept it quiet from me, too? It would have been a miracle if they had. Since she'd come back from the camp, pale as a woodland mushroom, sick as a dog, things hadn't been going too smoothly at my house and her increasingly poor health had been the focus of all our thoughts.

'People aren't just like … like pots of yoghurt waiting in the fridge with a sell-by date, Mum. We have moved past the Middle Ages you know. You could prolong your season, if you chose.'

'I can't.' She didn't even open her eyes; I can still remember how that made me feel. She was way too happy sitting there in her bubble of light, basking in … whatever she basked in.

'I can't prolong the season, Rose. I know that you want me to.' Mum's voice floats back to me now, wavering like the heat floating up from the brazier. 'I know that you've done your best my

204

love. You've tried. But I can't change the way things are going to be.'
Damn it, after what I had risked to get her back.
Didn't she know ... didn't she know what I had risked?

Lawrence

'I just *heard* something out there!'

I look up and Rose's face looks white and pinched as she scuttles back through the door. She plonks herself down beside me, her eyes as wide as saucers. 'It was something big,' she adds. 'Not just a bird or anything like that. I think ...' she lowers her voice to a hiss '... *there is somebody out there.*'

'It won't be a person.' I'm whittling down some branches I've hacked off the underskirts of a nearby conifer, keeping myself occupied. We've been keeping ourselves occupied, one way or another, ever since that conversation earlier where we both said things I don't think either of us meant to say.

'It won't be, Rose.' I hide the smile in my voice because I know she'd get mad if I suggested as much but let's face it - she just went out to answer a call of nature and when you're out in what feels like the silent wilderness with your pants down, it can be very easy to get spooked. Any little noise can sound like a monster coming to get you ...

She hesitates. She's been a bit quiet ever since I opened up earlier and told her all those things about my past. I get the feeling she might be wishing now she'd never pressed me to tell her. Maybe that's the thing that's really making her uneasy? My story discomforted her, as well it might. And she doesn't even know the half of it.

I'm already regretting now that I told her as much as I did.

She's a sweet girl. I like her. I really like her. I could go for her big time but it wouldn't be fair. I don't want her getting hurt, that's all. She's falling for me, that's obvious. I know the signs. I've seen it happen often enough. I'm not convincing myself it's because I'm an irresistible bloke. Women just tend to fall very easily for the men who rescue them. It happens all the time. It's nature, I think. Only, you don't usually get to see them for longer than an hour or so after the event and by the time they realise how irresistible they think you are, you've buggered off to do the next job and their nearest and dearest have come round and they remember they've got another life.

Rose hasn't had a chance to reconnect with her real life yet, that's all that's happened. That's why it's been a little difficult here this afternoon. She's been quiet, wrapped in her own thoughts, mulling around on what I told her but it's important now that we get our focus back onto the matter of how we survive up here till the weather breaks.

I look towards the dwindling log pile and then take in the fading light behind her.

'You left the door open,' I point out but she doesn't make any move to get up and close it. I know she thinks I should be taking her concerns more seriously.

'We're going to need to get some more wood in. The logs I brought in yesterday will last till this evening if we're lucky. They won't take us through the night,' I put it to Rose, making idle conversation, but;

'I *heard something out there*,' she says again. 'You're not paying attention, Lawrence.'

'You might have,' I point out reasonably. 'But if you're being logical about it, what would it likely be?' She shudders slightly, looks down into her lap.

'I still need to go out there,' she says in a small voice. 'But I won't go out again, not on my own. I can't.' Rose looks up at me shyly. 'I need for you ...' she takes in a deep breath, 'I need for you to come out with me.'

'You want me to come out there with you and … hold your hand?'

'Just be there.' There's a reluctant pleading in her voice. 'Look the other way, of course. You don't have to be too near me. In fact,' she reconsiders. 'You don't have to be anywhere near me at all. You just have to be there.'

Jesus wept.

'I'm expecting that phone call from Arjuna, don't forget.' I hope Arjuna hasn't forgotten either. It's way past two o'clock already. That'll make it gone seven-thirty in Jaffna. He was supposed to ring at seven and I switched the phone on half an hour ago hoping for some news. It's not a good sign that he didn't make any progress yesterday. It's already the 26th.

'I haven't forgotten,' Rose says now. It's costing her to ask me this, I realise. I shouldn't make her beg. It's dull out there and maybe a little spooky and she'll be imagining she can hear things … but there won't be anything there.

The truth is, right now I've got more urgent matters on my mind. While I've been sitting here ripping up the branches for tinder I've been working out the logistics of how I'm going to approach my mother as soon as the coast is clear; how I'm going to put it to her, bring her on board with it. She won't be able to breathe a word to him indoors which I know she'll find hard. She doesn't like keeping secrets from my father. Does she?

'Fine,' I relent. 'I'll come and stand guard.' I remove a lighted brand from the fire, brandishing it about like a sword the minute we come outside, onto the path I cleared earlier.

'This'll scare off any spooks and ghoulies that might be hanging around out here …'

'Very funny.' Rose pulls a face at me and we both look around as the firebrand throws long dark shadows against the decaying walls. The sky is so overcast, it's darker than I thought. It's stopped snowing for the moment but you can feel more is on its way, as if the sky has just taken a breath. The silence is so profound it's unnerving.

'See what I mean?' she says. 'You can't *imagine* you hear something when …when there is nothing else at all to hear.'

She's got a point, but … we both stand stock still for a minute, just listening. Nothing.

'There isn't anything out there, Rose. Most likely, it was the snow falling off some branches you heard, further down the valley.'

'It wasn't snow falling,' she says quietly. 'It sounded like a living thing. That doesn't sound the same as snow falling.'

To reassure her, I walk right out into the ruin, casting the torchlight all around me but there are no traces of any footprints other than our own ones from before. There is nothing. I was right, she was imagining it, yet a strange sense of discomfort is flooding through me, too. I have been up here so many times and yet this afternoon the landscape feels unfamiliar. Alien. I don't recognise anything and nothing feels the same.

'*What if it's him?*' she says in a small voice behind me now.

'Him who?' I spin round to look at her and she pulls a discomfited face. Who is she talking about?

'That guy who the police are looking for,' she says under her breath. 'That guy on the news.'

I walk back to stand beside her, bend my face down so I can see her eyes properly. I take in a breath.

'Who are the police looking for, Rose? I didn't know the police were looking for anyone.' Rose has been in contact with her cousin, though, hasn't she? She'll know what the local buzz is, even if I don't. I lift her chin up with my fingers.

'Who are they looking for?'

'I don't know who he is.' She looks around as if worried that he might be here with us, as if he might jump out from behind one of the broken walls any minute. Then she looks at me, and her eyes are still wary, hooded and I can feel my pulse quickening.

Is she wondering if I might be that guy, now? I hold up my hands self-effacingly, give a little laugh and she smiles back at me, a small smile because she is still afraid.

'I'm going to go round the corner now, okay?' she says. 'Just there. Will you wait for me?'

I wedge the fireband in the snow and open up my arms; what am I doing out here, otherwise?

'At your service, my lady. If you hear me talking to someone,' I remind her as she disappears around the corner. 'That'll be Arjuna.' She doesn't reply. On the outside, I am affecting calm, but on the inside I can't keep my heart from thudding. Unlikely that it's me they are after, I know, *I know this*, but the fear of discovery is always on the horizon. I shouldn't have come back here, that's the thing. Even coming up here, even risking getting this close, it was always going to be like walking into the lion's den with the lion still in there.

'If there's anyone else,' I yell into the echoing courtyard. 'I'll just … deal with them for you, okay?' She's gone. It's 2.30 pm. It's getting darker already, and cold, so cold I feel my lips will freeze on my face just standing here. I bash my hands together, button up my coat, and peer into the lowering sky. When I screw up my eyes hard enough, the clouds appear to be moving. Perhaps they *are* moving away? Could we possibly have seen the last of the snow for now? When I walk over to the edge of the battlements all the lights are on at Macrae Farm, the half-hidden shape of my father's jeep is still on the drive. If it doesn't snow tomorrow perhaps he'll get the tractor out and carve a route for himself through the lanes and onto the main roads. Those must surely be getting cleared by now. Perhaps he'll just … go? He must, I tell myself. If it stops snowing and he goes, I'll get a chance to go in to Mum.

It also means the police will start taking a closer look at outlying areas they haven't been able to reach up to now. Dad always had good links with the police force around these parts didn't he? If they know something, maybe he knows it too? Even if it's not me they're after - *of course it won't be me, nobody knows I'm here* - it'll still raise awkward questions if I'm discovered up here. I mustn't be found. I've got to do what I came to do and then go.

Marco wouldn't have said anything to anyone, would he? The

210

thought is like a little needle of ice hitting my chest. He wouldn't. He's the only one who knew I was coming and he wouldn't betray me, no way. It must be someone else they're looking for, but still …

The sharp pain in my chest grows deeper and wider. For a minute I wonder if this is what a heart attack does to you. Or what a panic attack feels like. But it's just the cold hitting my lungs. *Hurry up Rose.* I want to get out of here. I don't want to stay out here too long. I'm going to have to come out here in a bit to take that call from Jaffna though, aren't I? Arjuna had better have some news for me now I've waited all this time. He'd better have been pro-active, not sitting on his dumb arse waiting for 'other people' to get back to him.

2.35 pm. That'll be gone 8 o'clock Jaffna time. Damn it. He isn't going to phone. He's forgotten. He's gone off duty and got too busy with domestic things. He hasn't heard from anyone. I cover my watch with the top of my gloves to stop myself looking at it anymore. It's getting too late. I stamp my feet to keep the circulation going, keep moving, keep pushing that news Rose has just given me that the police are looking for someone, out of my head. *Think*. Lawrence, keep your mind on what you need to get out of this phone call, don't let yourself get distracted.

I should have a pen to hand, I'm thinking. I dig into my duffle coat for a biro. I'll have to write down any details he provides on my hands. Flight times and meeting times and names and numbers. If I can still move my hands by then, that is. Sod it. He'll just have to text me.

What was it Rose just said she heard?

I stiffen, willing myself to be quiet, not move a muscle, not even take a breath, and I can't hear a single thing. Nothing at all. There is no one coming up here to find you, Lawrence. It was crazy even to think it, I know. As I go to dig in the log pile for some more bits of wood we can use later, I take my phone out of my pocket, on the alert for it to ring. When it goes off, it's going to sound very loud up here, I think. In the silence the sudden noise will rip through me. I set the ring tone to buzz. Even the noise of the buzzer can sometimes be too much. It shimmers in my hand like a tazer without the pain but my brain fills in all the gaps.

I clench my jaw.

I've got to think of Sunny, the reason why I'm here. Remember how important this mission is for him. Remember what impact this sacrifice is going to make on the rest of his life and *you're the only one who can do it, Lawrence. The only guy who can make it happen for him.* You will, too. As long as you don't get caught before you can sort it all. You've got to breathe. Deeply and evenly. Don't let yourself remember anything that you don't want to remember and everything will go according to plan.

So I think of Sunny, waiting for me to make it all right like I promised. In Jaffna the rains will still be torrenting down. At night it'll be hot; the mosquitoes, big as houses, will be circling round the net and he won't dare put his foot out from under it. I let myself remember the heat, the uncomfortable itchiness of sweat on my skin because I was so hot and nothing could alleviate that, but nothing ever really bothered me out there. I knew I was safe, I suppose that was it. I didn't feel like I feel here. Raw, turned inside out, as if I am waiting for the axe to fall even though we are alone up here, Rose and I.

No one to harm us.

I look around me warily. No. There is no one else up here. Except - I know that sometimes the worst blows come when you are least expecting them. Just when you think you might at last be home free and things might be about to go your way; they come when you let your guard down …

'No sign of him yet?'

'No sign of who?' It's Sunday, my one day off in the week and I've been out searching the lanes, putting up posters. Kahn's been missing for five days now. He's a huge dog. If some motorist had hit him there's no way they would have missed it. There's been no sign of any injured animals taken into the vets, I phoned them days ago,

left them my number. I stop as I come in through the kitchen door, take in properly what my Dad's just asked me.

'Who are you talking about?'

'Your Kahn, of course.' He used his name. As if he'd concern himself with anything so trivial as my dog going missing. The significance of him asking me this trickles through to my brain. He hates Kahn. He only tolerates him because he likes having animals everyone else is scared of, on the property.

'No sign.' I mutter, pulling my muddied Wellington boots off, affecting nonchalance, but the feeling of unease that's been growing all morning; the fear that something bad has happened to my friend, it won't go away.

'I can help you look, if you like.'

The band of iron that's been forming around my chest pulls a little tighter. My father said something similar when I was on my way out to work two days ago I recall now. But I was late; I didn't have time to take it on board, the fact that he was offering. I dismissed him at once, didn't want his help anyway. I missed the important bit which was that Rob Macrae doesn't offer to help his family out in domestic matters. He's not that kind of man.

What's his game?

'Look where?' I watch his eyes uneasily. 'I've already looked everywhere.'

'Not everywhere,' he puts to me reasonably. 'Since you haven't found him yet,' He knows something. Fuck. A sorrow and a rage are suddenly surging inside me like the swell of some deep underground river, threatening any moment now to break its banks.

No. Not my Kahn. My only friend in the world.

'What have you done with him?' I say slowly. My father looks deeply injured at the suggestion.

'If that's your tack son, let's just forget it.' I swallow, battening down my pride because my father knows where Kahn is, I'd swear it.

'No. I'm sorry. I shouldn't have said that.' I think my voice is going to crack but I say the next words anyway. 'I want - your help.'

213

'I offered you my help Wednesday, as I recall.'

'Yes. I'm sorry. I had to work. I thought he'd come back of his own accord.'

'He didn't though, did he?' he says in a strange voice.' I saw Summerson in Maidstone yesterday,' he brings up now. My boss at the kennels? I shift uncomfortably in my chair.

'And?'

'And he's got to let you go, he says.'

My eyes widen. Summerson never said anything about that to me.

'Why would he do that? He told me I'm the best employee he's ever had.'

'Mebbe because he believes you should be putting those skills to use in your father's employ?' Fuck.

Is that what this was really all about? My defying him and taking my labour elsewhere for the summer? Is that why Kahn has gone missing all of a sudden?

'I'll work for you,' I say slowly. 'I just need you to … help me find him.' The words rankle more than I'd ever care to admit.

'That's more like it.' My father turns to look at me and in an instant the reasonable face he's been wearing all week is replaced by a nasty smile of triumph.

'Thought you'd see reason. I need you here. You should have asked me earlier, son.' As he picks up his coat and car keys, motioning for me to put my boots back on quickly, he adds, his eyes narrowing significantly; 'I'm good at getting things back, see.'

When I look out over the battlements now, I see that the lights in my father's study are all turned off, but his car is still there on the drive. I remember the reason why it is I don't let my guard down too often.

Even so, when the sharp, icy blow comes to the back of my head it is shockingly painful. More so because I wasn't expecting it. I didn't hear it coming.

I didn't suspect a thing.

Rose

Okay I'm an idiot and I shouldn't have made Lawrence come out here to wait for me. It's got to be pushing minus four. Now that I'm out here again it's so deathly quiet I can see why he'd think I was making a fuss over nothing. Round the corner - well out of sight of him - I wriggle my jogging bottoms down. As I wait for nature to take its course I go over this crazy situation again in my mind.

I only met Lawrence a bare twenty-four hours ago. Yesterday was Christmas Day and we have known each other for ONE day that is all. That alone seems impossible; how can so much have happened in such a short space of time? How can I have developed such strong feelings towards someone who I barely even know? And I don't know him. He was at pains to point that out, earlier. He as good as warned me off him, didn't he? My stomach feels queasy with the emotions churning inside of me every time I think of what he said; and worse, what he left unsaid.

Oh Lawrence, what have you done? Why are you really up here?

I've seen the way you look at me, he said. *You don't want to know about me. I'm not the person you think I am.* His words have been going round and round in my head since then, trapped like a shoal of silver fish in a trawler's net with nowhere to go because after he said all that, after he hinted that, whatever it was he'd done, it would matter to me - 'a girl like you would care' - he refused to say any more. I got the impression he regretted saying even as much as he did. But what is it I'd care so much about if only I knew it? How could he be so cruel as to leave so much to my imagination? It isn't fair. I feel torn apart with it. Madly, stupidly, because this is all too quick to be feeling such strong emotions towards someone, I know it. I just can't help it, that's all. I've never before in my life felt anything like what I feel towards this man.

And he doesn't want me to feel it. He doesn't, he says. But then he looks at me with such tenderness, with such attentive loving care. He held the ends of my fingers before and just that one small touch sent a spark of electricity up through my arm, it was a feeling so strong I thought it would set light to my whole body. That's how out of control it is. He cares about me, I know he does, though he tries to hide it. Even if it's just a tiny bit, nothing like the extent of what I'm feeling for him I'm sure, but he does care.

I have proof. He confided in me about what happened to him up here didn't he? Even though he was so reluctant to go there. He still told me. That means, even to some small degree, he must trust me. He must want me to know these things about him, to learn about where he's come from. He wants to let me in.

I believe what he told me about Sunny, too. If he were lying about that I'd know it, I'd see it in his eyes. But I see it's the truth every time he talks about the boy; how much he cares. So; he's come back here because he wants to help out Sunny. I know that much. I don't think he's actually told me any lies. He's just *left out* a whole load of stuff.

He didn't much like the news that the local police had been warning people off approaching strangers, did he? That doesn't inevitably mean he's the guy they're after. There could be a very good explanation for his reaction. He might just feel that we two would be vulnerable, stuck up here on our own, if this violent guy came sniffing around. Lawrence could just have been concerned about our welfare.

It's not as if we haven't got enough to worry about up here.

Lack of food, for one. I'm starving. Lawrence has suggested that - to eke rations out - we should only have two meals a day. We'll have some more crackers and tuna and a cup of soup this evening. Ha - maybe that's what the queasy feeling in my stomach is all about and it's not the pangs of unrequited love and the worry over Lawrence that I'm taking it to be? And I'm not even letting myself *think* about how Dad's getting on.

I'm done here. Thank God for the miniature tissues in my coat pocket ... never thought I'd ever be so happy to find some of those!

I pull my jogging bottoms up, put my gloves back on and pray that it's not going to take too long to find some of those smaller pieces of wood to burn. I hope he doesn't say I told you so when he sees me now. He was right about there not being anyone else up here but he could have been wrong. I bet he'd have had a big surprise if he had heard something while he was waiting for me. That Dead Men's Copse isn't so far away, and I know there's a bit of a stir every so often when some fool decides to go and hang themselves from one of the trees up there. They're supposed to come haunting up here. That's what people say, anyway. So he shouldn't poke fun, even if I was being a bit edgy, earlier.

Lawrence needs teaching a lesson, really.

I grin to myself, stooping to pick up a mound of soft, fresh snow and forming it into a large snowball in my hands as I make my way back to the courtyard. I'll get him back for making out I was imagining 'spooks and ghoulies'. He looks ridiculous, too. I lent him my hat earlier, and it's not as if you can take anyone that seriously when they're wearing a girlie pink beanie hat with long plaited earmuffs, I think wickedly. When I offered it to him - because my coat has a hood and his one doesn't - he put it on quite unself-consciously and I had to stifle a laugh. Admittedly, it also made him look cute. Like a little Dutch girl. Only a six-foot-something gorgeous male version of a little Dutch girl.

I round the corner, snowball in hand and I see that while he's been waiting for me he's been busy. There are three perfect-sized logs waiting on the side to be taken in. He doesn't see me. He's standing there right now completely wrapped in thought. What are you thinking so hard about, Lawrence? Could it be me?

He doesn't even hear me coming. I slow my steps down, realising that I have the advantage of him. Some fine look-out you turned out to be! I raise the snowball, aim it directly towards the back of his head. Spooks and ghoulies, eh, Lawrence?

I'll show you.

'*Argh!*'

Oh. Shit.

For a good minute, he doesn't even move. I hear him gasp and then ... he's just standing there, looking at me as if seeing me in a totally new light. I've got his attention now, all right.

'You just surprised the hell out of me there, Rose. I had no idea you were such a good aim.'

'That was a mistake,' I begin, but there's no mistaking the look on his face which has shifted rapidly from shock to something akin to *two can play at that game* ... and there is no going back now. He glances warningly at the glistening snow at his feet. It seems I may have declared open war.

'And mistakes ... must be paid for, no?'

Oh well. Here goes nothing. I aim a second shot before he can get one in himself, only this one is a little *too* well-aimed - just like the first.

The snow splatters onto his forehead and I watch in equal horror and mirth - it seems to take an age - as it slithers down his face, past the bridge of his nose and when the ice gets to his mouth at last, he puts out his tongue, tasting it.

'Oh, Rose,' he grins.

There's nothing for it, is there? I swoop down for more ammunition and he abandons the log-gathering in a trice. He's spotted the latest snowball I've made and he's on me in an instant, wrestling it off me.

'Hey - make your own!' I protest, but he just laughs. '*Thief!*' Right now he's got my arms pinned in front of me, he's pressing gently on my wrists to make me drop it but I won't. *I won't, but the sight of him standing there wearing my girlie hat cracks me up* … I bend over double, laughing at him and that's when he gets the advantage of me. The snowball drops to the ground, he yells out in triumph.

I don't know why I even started this. I am going to get plastered. I am going to get soaked to the skin and with my jeans still wet the only thing I'll have left to wear are my PJ bottoms but it is way, way too late for that.

He's picked up the snowball I just dropped.

'Do you yield?' he says.

I'm not sure what yielding will mean. I get the feeling I am going to get clobbered with that snowball whatever I say.

'You win,' I concede, wondering if I could wriggle past him, get away round the corner …

'And thank you for not putting that snowball down my neck.' I read the intention in his eyes as he moves in closer, grinning. I've got so cold now that my teeth are chattering and he takes pity, stops just short of doing it.

'I win?' He's taken off my hat. His hair is covered in drops of snow, his cheeks and his nose are very red but he still, *damn it*, looks irresistibly gorgeous. I nod, slowly. *You win.* 'You sure?'

'I'm sure.' He's so close right now I can feel the heat of his breath on my face. He stands there for a moment looking at me in a way no boy has ever yet looked at me in my life and I get a sudden realisation; o*migod; it is going to happen, isn't it?*

He is going to kiss me.

Isn't he?

'Rose.' He's put his hand to my cheek now. I stop breathing, tilt my head back slightly waiting to feel his lips on mine, waiting for the moment to come while all the world fades to white, everything that mattered to me has ceased to matter, all the people and events from the past, present and future rolled into one all don't matter anymore because there's only one thing that matters right now and the miracle of it is, I know he's feeling it too.

He's smiling, now, so softly, gently, leaning his forehead closer in to mine. *I could stay here forever, I think, joyously. Just like this, so close to him.* God, he smells good. He feels warm. He knows he's got me where he wants me, I can see it in his face. I can see it in the shimmer of laughter in his eyes, feel it in the slow movement of his hand up my back towards the nape of my neck but then, then … I sense - just one second too late - what's coming next …

'You … you complete and utter *sod!*'

His turn to shake with silent laughter now as I scoop the rapidly-melting ice away from the back of my neck. My surprise turns rapidly to disappointment.

'You *absolute* …' I have no words to aptly describe what I want to call him right now. Oh, God! Did he ever really mean to kiss me at all? He's backing away, his face filled with delighted mischief. He knows I'm going to get him again and my aim is good!

Okay, touché, then. I asked for that, I know I did. But he hasn't given up on getting his own back, yet. He's already standing in front of me with a snowball in his hand that is somehow three times the size of my last one. I see his arm go back, taking aim. Not content with shoving my own snowball down my neck he's going to clobber me with another one!

I shake my head, backing away.

'Don't,' I warn. 'Don't!'

He stops, and I see him sucking in his lower lip. Does he accept that I've yielded or is he thinking of where to aim his next shot? I decide to strike first. I swoop down to gather up some more snow before he gets a chance to think. My aim is true, but this time he is ready. He ducks it and my snowball glances by the side of his head. There is clearly nothing else for it now but to run. Run where? I back away, laughing.

'*Rose*, be careful …'

Ignoring him, I scramble, breathless, striking out blindly till I come to hide behind one of the old castle walls on the west side where the snow's nowhere near so deep. It only takes a few minutes to bend down and build up some ammunition, prepare for his onslaught. It's gone all quiet now around the corner but I know he's got to be coming after me, he won't let me get away so easily and all the time I'm nearly choking with laughter remembering the surprise on his face when I aimed that first snowball, remembering how close he just came to my lips - how *he nearly kissed me* - and my heart is thudding *boom, boom, boom*, with the thrill of the chase.

While I wait, I allow my mind to roll back to the sweetness of the moment we just shared. He'd made fun of me because of the noise I heard, but he'd been gallant enough to come out and wait for me, anyway. I like that in Lawrence; his protective instincts. I like that he was prepared to humour me. I recall the sound of his voice;

'*I win?*' he'd said, standing so still and so close to me that I'd hardly dared to move, I hadn't wanted to move when he'd demanded that I concede the game. I'd done so willingly, I remember now, happy enough for him to win and take his prize. I'd *wanted* him to kiss me, I realise with a trickle of disappointment, I thought he'd wanted it too; just then, just at that moment, he could have done. But he hadn't.

I wait.

It's all gone very quiet. Where is he?

I can't hear him coming. There is no noise at all coming from round the corner. He *will* be coming, though. And I am ready for him. This is a game, right? A game of cat and mouse. We're waiting to see who moves first. I stifle the laughter that bubbles up in my throat at the thought of him waiting there, poised with a snowball to get me. I'm not going to be the one to come looking first. As I wait, my breath slows down though I can still feel my heart thudding. The snow flakes, which had stopped, have started coming down again. They come straight down, falling in perfect geometric lines as I stand there. There is no wind, no movement in the air. The sky is so white and the light so dull I can barely see a thing when I stop to look behind me. I wait for the slow crunch of his feet, the faintest sound that tells me he must be on his way but there is nothing. Nothing, and after a while my excitement starts to fade to disappointment.

Maybe even a little bit of worry?

Is this really all part of the game? A test of patience, as I thought? He wants me to come round the corner so he can deck me with the mother of all snowballs, right? Or is that not it? After six or seven minutes have gone by, I begin to wonder if maybe he's gone back inside? Maybe he isn't coming after all?

'Lawrence?' I call out his name and my voice feels chopped up into little cold pieces by the snowflakes. '*Lawrence?*' My disappointment sinks to the ground like little chunks of ice.

Are you there? Too much time has gone by now, I realise. Only minutes, I know, but in these temperatures even minutes feel like time spent in a freezer.

Why isn't he coming? I clap my hands together, forcing the frozen blood round my veins and the truth of the situation dawns slowly and painfully. I've been deluding myself here, haven't I? The real reason he hasn't come tearing round that corner after me is because he doesn't want to come playing chase with me. He's … he's a professional who happens to have got stuck up here by pure chance at the same time as me. He's a guy who already leads an exciting and useful life in the world out there - somewhere far away from here - and no matter what he said to me before about not going back there I think I know that he will. He won't stay here, in any event. Not even for me. Why should I have allowed myself to imagine that he would?

The skin on my face has got so cold I can't even feel the snow falling on it anymore. This is just me, isn't it? Me being naïve and inexperienced and just … plain stupid and desperate. I feel a pang in my chest, letting myself remember his voice when he spoke my name just now. How it had sounded to me so intimate and low, the way you would pronounce a cherished name, the name of someone who mattered. Someone you meant to draw towards you. But was all that just me hoping too hard, my imagination, that I thought it was so? I let myself hear so many things in that one word, my name; an unexpressed longing, a desire, a wish that in time we would come to know each other better.

Did you not mean for me to hear any of those things, Lawrence? I'm aware of a heaviness and a pain in my chest, now, though whether it is the cold or the weight of an unexpected sadness settling on me I cannot tell. Sadness that he did not come looking for me; that he didn't want to; '*Don't ask, you don't want to know about me, Rose*,' he told me before. Sadness that I could have read his signals all so badly wrong.

When am I ever going to learn? My hands inside my knitted gloves are feeling numb now, the ice ball in my palms leaking through the knitted fingers and onto my skin and I remember; sometimes the longer you wait for something, the more you just know that when it finally arrives it won't be the thing you were after. It'll either be too late, you don't want it, or it won't be what you expected …

I guess maybe I put too much expectation into my thirteenth birthday. It was a useful distraction. It stopped me having to worry about Mum or let myself be reminded of the painful truth of what was happening to her. What else could I do? Sink into a deep depression and despair over my mother's complete and utter refusal to take a stand for her own life? I couldn't understand it and I couldn't bear it so I did the only thing I could do; I packaged it. I didn't think about it. I turned my mind to other things …

As the last few weeks before the big day kicked in, I told all my friends I'd landed the jackpot of all birthday presents; my parents had finally agreed to allow me to go on the school skiing trip to Austria at Easter.

Never mind what it cost, and the fact that they really couldn't afford it because Dad had needed to take so much time off work this year. Never mind that every day Mum was looking greyer and more listless; that every time I hugged her these days I couldn't be

223

careful enough, she felt as if she were made of paper, made of the dried up wings of the dead butterfly I once tried to help escape off the schoolyard wall, ready to crumble the minute I put my excited fingers around it.

My dad was distracted and distraught and my mum was dying but I could push all that to one side with the beautiful knowledge that at Easter I'd be in Oberlangau, with all my other lucky classmates. I would be doing something normal. Some of them had older siblings who'd been before, who knew what went on. We were longing to learn what après-ski really meant. Leigh Mallone was planning to smuggle a bottle of sauterne in her luggage inside a hot water bottle. I didn't know what sauterne was. The fact alone that it must be smuggled in was enough to make it desirable. We went round each other's houses and stayed till late discussing plans about what we'd do if there should be any lads from a boys' school staying at a nearby chalet at the same time as us, and if any of them came over to speak to us, how we'd play it, essential things like that.

The other girls seemed to have a pretty good idea of what they needed to bring. It became obvious, listening to them, that I was going to need a whole new wardrobe to go to Oberlangau with. I hinted as much to Dad, but he just looked at me blankly, as if he didn't have a clue what I was talking about – all part of the cunning plan to keep the surprise, I thought.

The fact that nobody at home seemed in the remotest bit interested in that side of things didn't put me off dreaming.

Nothing would do that. I dreamed big-time, conjuring it up just as Mum always taught me, visualising it just as I wanted it to be. I had to. If I didn't do that I'd have to let myself see what was happening at home right in front of my nose. I'd have to acknowledge that the time was coming soon when I'd need to say goodbye to her.

Instead, I had my dreams. Me; sporting the cutest, designer ski-wear that had miraculously been acquired from somewhere (Carlotta, maybe?). Me; gliding effortlessly down a steep mountain slope that had been covered just that morning in the fresh powdering of gleaming white snow. The sky above me would be the deepest cerulean blue. The sun would be so bright I'd get a lovely tan while I was out there skiing and much to everyone's surprise, I'd be a natural at it. Later on, in the evening, we'd put on music by the 'charming log fire' and dance the night away after eating 'schnitzel and strudels made by Gretel your inspired chalet cook' and much later, when none of the teachers were about, no doubt, we would drink the smuggled sauterne.

And all this was going to happen because Mum had guessed how much it mattered. She wanted me to have something precious and special -'a wonderful memory to take your first steps into adult life, with'. That was what she'd told me, wasn't it? She couldn't mean anything else. There wasn't anything else.

The only trouble was, they were leaving it all a bit late to tell me about it. I knew it was meant to be a surprise, but all my other friends would virtually have their suitcases packed before my birthday came along. I hoped my parents weren't going to wait until the actual day itself, because there was no way that'd leave me with enough time to get everything together.

But I didn't like to say anything. She was so ill, I didn't want to ruin the surprise they'd planned for me. So I waited. I waited and I said nothing. All Mrs P had to offer - when I tried to wheedle something out of her - was that 'Patience is a virtue, and all good things come to those who wait; you'll get there, Rose.'

I drop the snowball I have made onto the ground.

Lawrence isn't coming, is he? He was never going to kiss me, either. He did that just to tease me because he suspects that I like him. Not to be cruel, but because that's a boy's sense of humour. He was getting his own back for a face-full of snow - that was all. I feel the familiar sense of crushing disappointment that I got my hopes up way too high.

He doesn't fancy me at all.

It all matters to me way too much and things aren't going to head the way I was hoping, that much is pretty clear. When it comes to all the things I've really, desperately wanted in my life, they don't seem to.

I move further round the corner and now I can see him. Lawrence is there, glued to his mobile phone after all that. I stare at him. He's … *he's on the phone!* I forgot. He was waiting for a call from someone. How could I not have heard it ring? How could I not have guessed? Whatever or whoever's at the end of that phone is the thing that's really important to him in his life right now. It isn't me. It never will be me, he's been honest about that much. I feel the old familiar mantle of let-down as it settles about my shoulders.

Why, why do I keep on getting my hopes up over impossible things?

I shouldn't.

Still, he could at least have told me that he was taking a phone call, not kept me waiting like some dummy with a snowball after he pretended he wanted to kiss me and … and instead he seems to have forgotten all about me! That's how totally unimportant I am to him. By the time I get back to my own life he'll have forgotten that he ever met me. What am I even doing, weaving so many fantasies around a bloke who's gone out of his way to warn me off him? He's giving mixed signals, yes, but that doesn't mean I need to get mixed up in my own mind.

I turn and make my way carefully back over the path he cleared this morning. I'm going to look out over the battlements because my pride won't let me walk past him right now. *He'll see.* He'll *know* how mortified I feel. Besides, I tell myself, I want to see if there is any conceivable way I could get out of here today. I can't stay here anymore! I don't want to, I feel so … so crushed because he'll be well aware I was waiting for him. I must look so stupid in his eyes.

But there is no chance in hell anyone's making it out of here this afternoon. All that lies before me right now is a whole wide hinterland of pure uninterrupted snow.

I cross my arms in front of my chest, hurting, remembering; it is snow like the snow in the Austrian mountains I was once going to come hurtling down, isn't it? Snow just like I'd imagined on that wonderful holiday that was supposed to have marked my transition into adulthood ...

The brightly wrapped parcel perched on top of Mum's duvet had got to be some item of clothing, that much was obvious. Maybe a ski-jacket and some salopettes? It was the contents of the envelope - surely more than just a card? - that interested me more, though. I tore it open, all fingers and thumbs.

'Happy Birthday Darling!' Somewhere in the far distance my parents were smiling in unison, but there had to be some mistake ... Where was my ticket to Oberlangau? The itinerary, all the details that my friends had already been poring over for a few days. I wanted to know what group I was in, who I was sharing a dorm with; all these things I had waited patiently to find out, and it was clear my parents were taking this whole 'delayed gratification thing' a little too far.

I tore off the shiny wrapping paper, but inside, instead of the ski-wear I expected, there was the faux fur jacket I'd spied in a catalogue months ago and hinted to Mum that I fancied. That was way before the ski trip was even mooted. Where was all my other stuff? I'd looked at Mum and Dad, not yet crestfallen because I simply didn't believe that that could be it. No. It could not. There had to be something else, surely? Maybe the ticket was in the jacket pocket?

I jumped on the smaller packet still lurking on the table. It looked like it might be a photo-frame. It wasn't. It was a butterfly! Just like the one that had landed on the wall between me and Shona that day so many years before. Dad beamed at me expectantly.

'Mum said you were keen on them,' he explained shyly and I realised that he must have gone out of his way to find a specimen of the exact same species ... only - this one was dead. It was mounted in a frame. It didn't have quite the same appeal.

I swallowed down my disappointment at that, but then ...

'Try the jacket on, then!' Dad rallied round and I let him help

227

me on with it. When I surreptitiously felt in my pockets, feeling certain that this must be where they'd hidden the real prize ... the ticket wasn't in there either.

There wasn't any ticket!

'Thanks.' I'm sure they took my choked-up voice to be a sign of amazed gratitude at their thoughtfulness, instead of extreme disappointment. I don't think either of them had a clue how much I hated that jacket. Nobody noticed that I never got round to wearing it.

They didn't notice I'd chucked the framed dead butterfly into the back of my wardrobe and that never saw the light of day, either. Of course they didn't. After that, things got a lot worse at home. Mum didn't last for much longer after my birthday. She died in the spring.

Why the spring? Just when every other living thing on earth was pushing out in all directions, finding a foothold on life, she gave up on hers. And her dying was such a monumental thing, such a huge thing to hit Dad and me that suddenly the whole fanciful business of dreaming of school skiing trips seemed frivolous and wasteful. The jacket - the last thing she bought for me - remained enshrined in its tissue paper, my resentment of it merely a reminder of my ingratitude. By dying - by choosing to die when she did - she had the last word, and her last word pinioned me like a butterfly to a mounting board. I felt ... I felt as if I would never fly free again.

I turn back to look towards the chapel door, heartsick, hoping that Lawrence will have moved on by now so I can go back in. I need to go back in. I have to stop this; all this unrequited longing for things that I will never have. I have to get real, concentrate on what's coming up for me when I do arrive back home.

I'll have enough trouble to sort out then. They'll all find out I wasn't at Shona's and I'll be called to account for that. If they find out I was hanging out in the ruins with a stranger - after all those warnings - they'll go ballistic! And I still have the other problem of getting my letter back.

Maybe that's just another of my unrealistic expectations,

too, the thought pops up out of nowhere.

I'm probably not going to get into Downing College, either, am I?

Realistically, in the cold light of day, I am chasing after rainbows. Chasing after a guy like Lawrence will turn out to be exactly the same thing.

Lawrence

When the mobile went off just now I almost didn't hear it; I was too busy gathering snowballs, chasing after Rose when I should have been concentrating. I fumble for the phone like a madman, pulling off my gloves because my fingers have gone so stiff, so frozen up I can hardly move them.

'Hey,' I say, hoping against hope that it'll be Dougie's voice back on the end of the line, someone who I know will have got on with it …

'Good afternoon, Lawrence.' It's Arjuna. *Afternoon, I think, it feels more like the middle of the fucking freezing night, here.*

'How's Sunny doing?' There's a long moment of static and I take the firebrand I plucked earlier and move out as far as I can along the courtyard, wedge it into a snowdrift further down. The last time I was standing right at this spot Rose came up and dusted the snow from my shoulders, I remember suddenly. I remember her little fingers, fluttering as soft as butterflies over my chest.

A few minutes ago, I nearly kissed her.

I didn't mean to do that. That was madness. She threw that snowball at me, shocked the hell out of me even though she hadn't meant to, clearly only wanted to play. I chased after her and when I caught up with her, the rest … the rest was just instinct.

An instinct I haven't felt in a while, and this isn't the time or place to feel it. I need to be more careful.

'Hello, Lawrence?' Arjuna's polite voice is back on the line.

I pick up his upbeat tone in an instant, different from yesterday. Good news, perhaps?

'Good evening, Arjuna. How's the little guy doing?'

'Excellent. If it weren't for the fact that they keep threatening to turf him out of his bed, I'd say, couldn't be better. Yourself? I take it you've had a chance to catch up with your family?' Pause.

'Everything is in hand, Arjuna.' I'm not going to give him any excuse to slack off at his end. 'Everything's going as planned,' I breeze. 'You have any news for me?'

'Good news on one front. Your manager is due back tomorrow.'

Hallelujah! 'He'll be back?' The relief in his voice is echoed in my own. Okay. Arjuna's not going to volunteer where Dougie got to, clearly.

'So,' I prompt. 'You have some news for me from Herr Lober …?'

'Not yet.' *Not yet?* I bite my tongue. I knew this was coming. He's wasted a whole day, that's what he's just done. But no matter, Dougie will be back on board tomorrow. The 27th. That's cutting it a bit fine for my liking, but …

'There is another matter that's arisen here, though,' Arjuna cuts through my thoughts now. 'To do with Sunny.'

'Yes?'

'Questions are being asked about the wisdom of removing him from here. We've been thinking - if someone from his own family could be located …' *We've been thinking*, he says. Who's *we*? I wonder irritably.

'I tried that,' I explain patiently. I already tried all that, what do they think? 'Everyone's dead, Arjuna.'

'Perhaps you didn't try every avenue, though? No offence intended,' he hastens to add. 'But, coming from outside, not speaking our language, you may not have been in as good a position to search. I've been looking into it all day.'

'You've been spending the whole day trying to locate Sunny's people?' I stare at the phone in dismay. 'Instead of chasing up

231

the contacts that Dougie left us like I need you to?'

'Only while I was waiting for Herr Lober to get back,' Arjuna sounds faintly hurt. 'I didn't think he would, by the way, after all it is Boxing Day for most people in Europe.'

Boxing Day. *I want to box your ears, that's what I want to do.*

I swallow, battening down my disappointment at the man because I've suspected all along that he'd be no ball of fire.

'Look. I really need to speak to Dougie. Where is he? I can't afford to wait, Arjuna.'

'We can't afford to do anything else.'

'Will you stop being so damn mysterious?' I blast him now. 'At least tell me what's happened to Dougie. Where's he been? Why hasn't he been able to answer his own phone?'

'He just hasn't, Lawrence.'

'Tell me why.' There's a pause and I can feel the man's reluctance trickling down the line. Slowly. Bit by bit.

'He can't because he's been taken for questioning by the Sri Lankan Military Police. For aiding the flight of a suspected criminal from the country.' *Fuck.* I hit my closed fist against the unyielding stone wall to the left of me.

'He's in prison ... because of me?'

'They're releasing him tomorrow,' he assures me but my mind's going ten to the dozen; *what if they don't? What if they do what they so often do and promise one thing but actually deliver another? Dougie's screwed. Sunny's screwed.*

'In the meantime, he told me to tell you to carry on as if he were still in charge of everything. I'm doing what I can, Lawrence.'

'I know you are, Arjuna.' It's not good enough, is it? It isn't even in the slightest bit good enough.

'You carry on as you were,' he says blithely. 'Enjoy time with your mother, have a good Christmas. Tell your family all the good things you've been doing in my country. They'll be proud of you, Lawrence. We all are.'

'Thank you,' I try to keep my voice neutral. *Nobody here is proud of me. Nobody ever will be.*

'One of us will make contact with you at the agreed time tomorrow,' he says. 'And, Lawrence?'

'Yes?'

'You mustn't mind me looking to see if I can find any of Sunny's people over here.'

'I don't mind.' You just won't get anywhere, I think. I've already been through all of that.

'He's missing them, Lawrence. He's been crying for them. It's his family he wants. This dream of taking him to the UK is all very well but at the end of the day he's still going to miss his people.'

'*Miss who?*' I point out. 'They're all *gone,* Arjuna.' He doesn't get it, does he?

'Ah, but I have discovered about fifty new people came into East Camp about a week ago,' he's saying brightly. I groan, inwardly. *I went there,* I think. *I'm way ahead of you.* I put my hand over my eyes. I don't say anything more because there isn't any point.

Frustrating as it is for me, he's doing what he can. He's not Dougie, that's all. He can't work miracles. I just have to be a little patient. I click the phone off. When I look down the path I cleared earlier to the chapel door, Rose is standing there looking awkward. She must be waiting to help me gather the logs we're taking in for the night.

I pull the firebrand up and go to hand it to her. She takes it without a word. She doesn't give me any eye contact.

In the short time we have been out here it has already gone quite dark, but the firebrand casts out long streams of light. The ice crystals in the snowdrift behind her glitter and shimmer, lighting up her face in the most interesting way. She's pretty, is Rose. I remember that before, I nearly kissed her. She nearly let me. If I hadn't caught myself in time who knows what it might have come to.

'Your call came through then?' She tilts her chin and her voice is as chilly as the air with more snow on the way. I suddenly remember that she must have been waiting for me, round the corner, probably with baited breath and a snowball in her hand all this time while I took Arjuna's call.

Damn.

'Has anyone ever told you ... how incredibly beautiful you look when you're cross?'

Rose throws me a scornful look.

'Don't even go there, Lawrence. That is the ... the corniest line I've ever heard. You're not good boyfriend material, remember?'

'I'm not known for being the best advice-giver,' I say helplessly, but she's not going to be so easily persuaded out of her sulk. She turns to me the minute we're inside, pulling off her damp gloves and scarf and putting them to dry over the back of the pew.

'I want to go home,' she announces. 'Dad needs me and ... and I shouldn't be here.' Does she honestly think either of us have any choice?

'We can't get out, Rose. You've seen the ...'

'I don't care!' She pulls a tortured face and I see a new determination in her eyes. I imagine it must have been something like that which propelled her up here in the first place. I also glimpse the same profound sadness that I spotted before.

I've let her down, somehow, haven't I?

'I'm going to make a break for it out of here tomorrow, whether you want to help me or not and whether it snows again or not. I'm leaving here. I'll ring the emergency services if I have to. I've got ... I've got people at home who are waiting for me. I'm not staying here a moment longer after it gets daylight. Do you understand?'

'Rose ...' I cajole, but she's turned away from me, her face looking hurt and stiff.

She's angry at me.

I pull off my sodden gloves, lay them beside hers on the back of the pew and she moves away from me abruptly. Is it because I nearly kissed her, before? Is it because I didn't? Women are

234

complicated creatures, that's for sure.

She'll be missing home, that's what it is. Like Sunny, it's her family that she wants.

I remember what that feels like. Being up here, so close, it brings it all back to me; what it's like to have people you care deeply about, things from home that you love.

I did once, too.

We took the jeep down the narrow lane past the lower back fields, my father driving crazy fast like a man does who is very sure of his destination. He never spoke a word and I didn't dare to. Clearly he knew where Kahn was. All the way I could feel the growing despair and fear in the pit of my belly, not knowing what he could have done to my dog, not daring to let myself know the reason why.

He couldn't have discovered our plan to leave, could he? He couldn't! There was no way the bastard could have found out, only Mum and I knew of it. I'd spoken to no one and I knew she wouldn't have, either. But my father could have sniffed our intention in the air, that's the kind of man he was. He could have sensed something amiss in the lightness in my step in the morning, in the easy lifting of the burden from about my shoulders.

The jeep drew to a sickeningly abrupt halt, right in the middle of the abandoned country lane. I heard the crunch as he pulled up the handbrake, pulled it hard right up to the top like he always did as if he feared if might make off of its own volition if he left anything to chance. Like us?

He switched the engine off. Folded his arms.

'You'd better tell me everything.'

'What do you mean?' I took one look at his face and my worst fears were confirmed; he knew. At the very least, he suspected, or we wouldn't be sitting here right now, would we?

'You know exactly what I mean.'

I think I shook my head. I don't remember. I couldn't tell you if the day outside was rainy or blue. I couldn't tell you if it were winter or autumn or spring. All that got stuck in my mind from that moment was the smell of his aftershave; the bitter spicy smell of that got up somehow with the taste of terror in my mouth, the sudden splitting pain in my head. He knew about our plans. Somehow, without us leaving the slightest, faintest clue, he knew.

Why do you say that? I kept repeating, over and over in my mind. I wanted to speak the words out loud but they wouldn't come out. No denial would come out, either.

'You want to see that dog of yours again, right?'

I nodded my head, watching in fascinated horror as he flicked at his macabre skeleton key ring with his thumb. It was still hanging off the ignition. Every time it swung back towards him he'd flick it away with his thumb again, the ugly thing jiggling and shivering its bones with every pass. He was always amused by that thing, said it had been carved out of a real man's bones, it still had traces of blood on it. I believed him. Right now he looked like he was going to smash it to pieces.

'Where is it,' he said, his voice deliberately slow, 'that you were planning on going?'

I shook my head. We didn't have anywhere to go. We were just planning on making a run for it. I told her; don't make any reservations, don't pay for any tickets with cards that can be traced, don't make any phone calls, don't speak to anyone about anything. The day we leave, we'll just leave, take the money we put aside and go wherever the wind blows us.

'Nowhere,' I got out. 'We weren't planning on going anywhere.'

'Who's we?' My father's eyebrows shot up. 'I asked where you were planning on going.'

'It's just me,' I said quickly. 'Nobody else is involved.' Too late, I saw he'd trapped me. He saw it too.

'Did you think you would get away from me, son? Planning on taking your ma and brother too?' He hit the dashboard with extreme force, then. Hit it so hard I was surprised it didn't splinter into a thousand shards of plastic. 'Well. You're the real big man now aren't you? Aren't you, you pathetic, worthless excuse for a son of

236

mine ...?'

How would I ever have dared to answer him? I didn't. I didn't utter a word. His face was going the strangest shade of mottled pink. I thought it was possible he might be about to strangle me, right there, right then. He had the largest hands, my dad, hands that I'd seen wield a meat cleaver many a time when he slaughtered the pigs.

It flashed through my mind then, what might be the quickest way to die but I had defied him and it wasn't going to be that easy. He hadn't finished with me yet.

'Understand this. You're never getting away. Not you. Not her. Not him. None of you, ever. Because I'll hunt you to the ends of the earth, that's why. I'll hunt you to hell and back because you're all mine, all of you and in the end I have to win. Even if it means finishing the lot of you that's how it'll be but, I'll win ...' *He leaned over me then in one sudden movement and I shrank back but all he did was open the jeep door on my side.* 'Now. Get out.'

'Pilgrim didn't know anything about it, Dad ...' *He was twelve. Only twelve, my little brother for Pete's sake.*

Before I'd even properly got out he'd already turned on the ignition again, slammed the car into reverse and was backing off down the narrow lane. I picked myself up, from where the sudden movement had thrown me off balance. He'd left me intact, but - where was he going in such a hurry? I dusted myself down, still shaking; to see where Mum was, no doubt. And Pilgrim.

But why had he even brought me here? Why here?

My dog must be here, somewhere. The realisation hit me suddenly. He'd got to be. Dad was bringing me here to taunt me with it, use that as a carrot to get the info he wanted out of me and then I'd get Kahn back. I had an uncomfortable feeling he'd just got more information than he'd bargained for. He hadn't suspected that Mum might be involved too, had he? Was he going back to see to her, now?

He might have been, but I knew that by the time he got back she'd most likely already have gone out. She liked to visit church on Sundays. She'd be safe, for now. I had to find Kahn.

237

I didn't have to look for too long. A few hundred metres along the lane petered out onto the back of an overgrown field surrounded - like the rest of my dad's property - with periodically-broken barbed wire. Something attracted me towards a clump of trees at the far end. Dead Men's Copse, the locals called it. I didn't go there much. Why would anyone want to? But on this particular day, something drew me towards it. It must have been very hot when I think back now, due a storm; I remember the thunder bugs that appeared out of nowhere, small black things crawling all over my T-shirt, hovering around my head. I kept calling out his name, again and again, but there was nothing. As I entered the cooler shaded area of the copse I imagined I could feel Kahn, though. I knew he was there, even if he was making no sound.

I kept walking. My heart was aching like crazy all the time because I couldn't stop thinking; all week I've been at work instead of being out looking for him, getting him back. I should have come looking much sooner. Yeah, I kept on walking and as I came to the final tree there he was, my dear old fella, my true friend. He'd been tethered by his neck to the trunk with the shortest rope; so short he wouldn't have been able to reach his nose to the ground, that's how short, no chance left that he'd have been able to turn back on himself and chew right through it; by the weals on his neck he'd clearly tried.

In death, he looked no more fierce than a new-born pup. I think I fell to my knees. I must have put my arms around his neck, stroking back his fur away from his beautiful proud face, those lifeless eyes. When I touched his fur, the body underneath didn't even feel all that cold. He might have been dead a few short hours, no more.

If I had only come before, if I had got up earlier, if only I had come looking yesterday … A hundred thousand 'if's' flew up out of my soul, cut off from ever becoming possibilities like some treacherous path you run up that only leads to a dangling cliff-top, nowhere to go, because all those 'if's' - they all belonged to yesterday. Yesterday, when he might still have been alive, when it might still have been possible to keep him that way.

238

My only friend. You were coming with me. I promised you that much, I told you, you were coming with me, dear God …

But I'd let my father get hold of him, taken my eye off the ball. I'd been so taken up with my new-found work at the breeders, my plans to get out of here, that I hadn't paid attention to my dearest friend.

I stayed with him for a long, long time, stroking his fur, brushing away the burrs and the dust that had gathered on his coat in those cruel hours while he must have been waiting for me to come for him. I cleaned his paws with the edge of my T-shirt. I untied the rope and freed him, my brave heart. Then I used my bare hands to dig him a grave. Right there, at the tree where he died. I had to do it because I couldn't carry him back all that way and I wouldn't leave him so I dug him a resting place, pulling out clumps of soft wet earth and bits of flint and rock with my bare hands till my fingernails were caked with soil and my palms were bleeding, my face all streaked with mud and tears.

When I pulled him at last into the shallow grave, what hurt the most was that he was so much lighter than he should have been; I could feel his skin and bones beneath his fur and I knew that all that he was, everything I'd loved, had shrunk away to nothing, his life had been stolen from him, from me. And I knew this was my father's version of a warning shot, of telling the family that we'd have to keep enduring whatever he wanted to dish out to us for as long as we lived because we were never going to be allowed to get away from him.

And then I realised that it wouldn't matter if Mum had gone to church or even if she'd walked on her bare knees all the way to heaven, he'd still have found some way to drag her out and make her pay for ever daring to think that we could be free.

No. I knew there was only one way now that was ever going to happen.

'I'm sorry about before,' I say to Rose's stiff back at last. As the day outside has grown darker, the stillness in the chapel between us has become almost unbearable. She's carefully avoided any direct contact with me for the last few hours and I don't know what to say, what to do, to make it better. I was careless with her feelings, I see that now. I was focused on my task, thinking about Jaffna and all the people I left behind there.

I push the plate with her supper on it near to her head so she will see it, smell it. I know she must be hungry. It will make her mouth water.

'I'm tired,' she says in a small voice. 'I'm not feeling well.' But she doesn't push the plate away. She's lying face down on the canvas sacking and now that I am near to her I see that she's been taking care to cry very quietly, her face turned away from me so I wouldn't know she was doing it. I want to reach out and touch her; say, *it's okay, please don't cry, don't cry, Rose* but I know that will only fuel the longing that she's still feeling inside.

She wants me, and I ... I am a man, not something made of wood. She is a beautiful girl. I thought it the first time I saw her. I think she has no real idea how beautiful she is. I think maybe she has never really had anyone there to tell her. And she is sensitive, clever and funny. And daring. And brave. When I've caught her looking at me a few times, the look I've seen in her eyes has threatened to draw me in, make me involved in her life, bind me to her in the most intimate way that a man and a woman can be bound.

She wants this. I am not immune but - I am not the right man for her. I told her this. I told her everything I dared to.

Why won't she just believe me?

240

Rose

When I wake suddenly at 2 am it seems to me I can again hear the sound of footsteps outside; soft, like someone is treading carefully, but footsteps no less. I open my eyes and lie there for a long time, listening, staring into the darkness in the apse by the chapel door. Once I am fully awake, alert to what might come next, the noise stops. Should I get up and go and have a look outside? I don't want to. It is cold. Besides, if there is anything out there it won't be that man on the run, I tell myself. It will be some animal moving around. I push my head right down under the sleeping bag and *will* myself to go back to sleep, because I find I don't like being awake in this place in the dead of night. It gives me a raw and uncomfortable feeling in my stomach.

But I can't go back to sleep. It is too dark, it is too quiet and I can't stop thinking about things I really don't want to think about, recalling things that I would rather forget.

For a while, no more sounds come from outside. Did I dream it? Did I dream the whole thing? When I turn to make sure Lawrence is there, still asleep just beside me, his face is turned away. I stare at his back for a few minutes, trying to work out if he is really asleep or if he is listening to the noises like me. He lies there very still. So still that there is no way I can even tell if he is breathing or not. The thought sends a small shot of irrational panic through my chest.

It reminds me that soon he will not be in my life anymore,

and how that is going to hurt. I wasn't very fair to him yester-day, was I? I sulked a good part of the evening after he came off the phone and I regret that now. It's not his fault my life's in the mess it is. It's not his fault my mum died when she did and Dad got injured with all of the devastating consequences that's had for me. None of that is Lawrence's fault. I wanted to get a chance to talk to him but I ran out of time. We had our meagre suppers early because we were both so hungry and I know for a while he was trying to coax me to talk to him but my pride got in the way. My hurt feelings. Even though I knew that was stupid because … why should I feel this boy owed me anything at all? Okay, so we'd been playing in the snow and his phone call came through. He didn't chase after me; I got hold of the wrong end of the stick and I ended up so *disappointed*.

He won't know the real reason why. He doesn't have a clue. What he means to me. How I am going to miss having him around; having someone there to say *it's going to be okay, you'll get through this, you'll make it; you just don't have to be afraid*. How I'm going to miss the way he makes me feel every time he at looks me; as if he sees the person that I am inside. The me that nobody else ever gets to see.

The me that feels that it is all too much to cope with, some-times. The me who worries about all the things out there that I don't understand. The me who worries - still worries - about all the things Mum used to do in that room of hers downstairs, when Dad and I were in the other room watching the TV. Oh, she never did anyone harm, I know that, that was her mantra - *Harm no one*; she might have been Marie Curie, working away with all that deadly and powerful radiation, in an effort to help other people but there was always the worry that some of it - whatever it really was, *magic* - might seep out under the door and affect us.

All those energies she was always summoning, working with, she was always telling me how *powerful* they were, wasn't she? Emphasising how they mustn't be toyed with …

I wonder if she ever knew?

I turn my face away from Lawrence now, disconsolate, recognising that it's a pattern with me. That I can't have what I want. I feel a deep heaviness in my throat and chest at the thought; that I will never, *can never*, have what I want. Is that my fault? Is it because of what I did? I press my hands into my chest, not wanting to think like that, not wanting to have these thoughts but they won't go away. I don't want to be alone right now, not here, in the dead hours in this chapel but I won't wake him. I lie still for ages, listening to the hiss and splutter of the water-drops that drip down from the crack along the ceiling into the fire. It's only a small sound but it is amplified a hundred-fold by the acoustics in the chapel, by the fact that everything else is so completely and utterly still. And every time a drop hits the fire it's like a thought hitting a nerve in the most sensitive part of my mind.

She warned me, didn't she?

She warned me not to meddle.

Oh, God! I feel so alone. I feel so *cold*. When I push my nose out from under the cover, the fire is burning low again. I should go over and shove another piece of wood into the middle of the brazier. The minutes tick by. The damp wood crackles and spits. The water drips down unceasingly from the ceiling, trying to put our fire out. Now that I'm wide awake, I think, trying to chivvy myself, I could put some ice in the pan to melt for water, I could make some tea. But the truth is I don't want any tea. I don't want any anything, other than some comfort, some company.

But I cannot have what I want. That thought goes round and round in my head, like a serpent chomping on its own tail. Is it because of what I did?

I remember a time once before that was like this time. When it felt as if the very fabric of my life had been rent asunder. Mum was sick. We were waiting for her to die, there's no other way to put it. She was going to go and we were desperate for her not to, but until she did, everything went into a strange sort of limbo. Minutes, hours, whole days, all merged into one and there was no rhythm or order to it, nothing I could do that would let me escape

243

from it. I remember hovering by her bedside, wanting her to tell me that it was okay, that everything was all right. I needed her to speak, God, how I needed her to, but she never said a word.

It wasn't just that she was dying and leaving us. It wasn't just that. I wanted her to say she forgave me; that she understood why I did what I did, but the words that could have come to my rescue, been the healing salve between us, they somehow never got spoken …

My eyes close now, heavy suddenly. I turn around and pull Lawrence's sleeping bag right up to my nose but the emptiness of the dark night is like a vacuum, sucking up all the discarded thoughts and memories from the dusty corners of my mind, bringing them right back up to the surface ...

'Will she get what she wants now?'
'She should.'
How old would I have been the day I saw how it could be done? Eight, nine, maybe? I didn't often go in to look at Mum working but Dad must have been out that day and Shona and I had argued - I hadn't seen my best friend for a week - so Mum had invited me to come in. Her friend Beth's cat had been missing for days and she'd asked Mum to do a recalling spell. We were in Mum's downstairs room, I remember. She was clearing away the paraphernalia of her spell-making; the candles and the incense, opening up the heavy curtains onto a sparkling day outside.

I'd picked up the photo of Beth's cat. The one who Mum had now - somehow - presumably recalled, wondering at it all. How it could work, this magic of hers? I already knew it did. Wondering too if I dared ask her the question that was burning on the tip of my tongue?

'If you can make Beth's cat come home … then, does that mean you could make humans do the things you wanted, as well?' Could she make Shona stop sulking and come and play with me, I was thinking?

'Can you control people?'

244

'Never!' There was an edge of warning to Mum's normally soft voice that startled me, a sharpness I didn't associate with her and I'd looked up in alarm. 'We never, ever, try to force another's will by using Wicca. Do you understand? Never.'

'You could, though?' I'd persisted. She scared me when she was like this, but a contrary part of me still wanted to know.

'It might be done.' She'd frowned, her dark eyebrows looking fierce, angry even. 'But it would be very wrong. A person's free will is their birth-right Rose, understand this. It is sacred and to interfere with it would - I fear - not go unpunished.'

It's 4.15 am before the noise comes again. This time I sit up, alert. Quietly, so as not to disturb Lawrence, I pull on my coat and then my gloves which are crispy-dry in some places and uncomfortably cold and wet in others where the fingers weren't pulled out flat.

Away from the immediate light of the fire, the chapel is very dark, almost pitch black. I have to grope my way inch by inch to the door, not wanting to take a lighted brand from the fire because that might disturb him, but once outside, under the rays of a cold white moon, it is brighter. It's also colder - it hits my chest the minute I walk out so I have to stifle a gasp as I open the door. It's not just the noise I want to investigate. I need to know if it's snowed anymore. Could it even have rained, maybe? I need to know if anything's changed because today I mean to go home, don't I? That's what I told him.

Once I go home, I won't see Lawrence again. I'll have to learn to stop wanting to.

The sight that greets me outside the door is beyond my wildest imagination. It has snowed again. A billion, trillion tonnes of snow have fallen in the night. In a slightly different direction this time, or I couldn't have pushed open the door, but there's no mistaking I'll be in an even worse position to try and make a move out of here today than I was yesterday. Crap! Wasn't it supposed to have rained? *Why couldn't it have just rained?*

I feel a crushing sense of disappointment in my chest at a hope that I didn't even know I'd been harbouring. If only it had rained, I could have coped with it all. The adventure here would have been at an end. I would have been on my way home. But being forced to stay on in this place with him, it's going to be unbearable. Every time I look at him, he will surely start to see all the things I don't want him to see. He'll see that I still want him. He'll see how much he matters.

'Rosie. What are you doing out here?' He's shuffled on his still-damp coat and got up out of his canvas sacking to come after me. *I thought I'd been so careful to be quiet ...*

'You okay, Rose?'

I turn my face away from him, so he won't see my relief that he's awake again. I indicate the blotted-out valley below.

'I'm sorry,' he says, and his voice is full of sleep. I *love* his voice, I think mournfully. I wish I could wake up to hear that voice every day of my life for the rest of my life. But I won't. 'I know you were hoping to get back to your family today. I know you wanted to, but ...'

'But I should just stop wanting, right?' The words come out jagged and shaky, not how I mean them to, at all. I can feel his surprise, but I keep on going. 'It's the best cure for disappointment, I hear. Stop wanting. If you don't want anything, if you don't hope for anything ... you'll never be disappointed.' I bite my lip, horrified that my feelings have somehow worked their way so perilously close to the surface.

'Don't stop wanting.' He's at my elbow now. Not touching me, but close enough to. Close enough that I can feel him, every inch of him, behind me and I long to turn round, to be as close to him as we nearly were yesterday but a stubborn streak - a self-protective streak? - won't let me.

'Rose?' he persists when I don't answer him, won't look at him. I can feel him, hesitantly now, touching the hair at the back of my neck.

'Leave me alone, Lawrence.' *For pity's sake, leave me alone!*

There's a silence behind me, as I feel him taking stock. He'll imagine I'm still in a huff, pushing him away after yesterday. He'll imagine I'm being impossibly touchy and unreasonable and any minute now he'll take a step back or two when he realises how chippy I'm being ...

But he doesn't. He puts his arms out, turns me about to face him, instead.

'Do you really want me to leave you alone?' His eyes are sad. 'Is that what you want?'

I don't answer. I can't. It doesn't matter *what I want* anyway ...

'You're disappointed that it's snowed again, I can see that. You're sad that you can't go home to your dad, you can't go and fetch your letter ... but, you'll get there, Rose. You've had some set-backs, that's all.' His voice sounds weary this morning. He's used to more than *set-backs* in his life, I remember. He's used to dealing with crises on a day to day basis. He copes with things like war and horrific injuries and tragic tales and here I am - a girl who's lost a letter, a girl who's stuck in a make-shift shelter for a couple of days, that's all he'll see ...

'I know that's what you think,' I say in a small strangled voice. 'But the truth is, Lawrence you have no idea of anything about me. No idea of my life. No idea of my dreams. No idea of why I'm not going to achieve any of them ...' I swallow down the rest of my words shakily.

Christ, I didn't mean to say any of that. Where did they all come from, these words, where did they all spill out from?

'Tell me then.' I can feel him shivering. He could go back in, leave me to the cold morning and enjoy a bit of warmth by the fire but he doesn't do that. When I look at him properly I can see the bristles of his three-day beard, so much more pronounced than yesterday, looking stark against his cold pinched face in the moonlight.

'Why?' I ask. Why do you even ask me these things, Lawrence? Is it so I come again to believe that you really care when we both know that you don't. I don't matter to you, do I? Not enough.

'Tell me all the things about you that I don't yet know,' he says softly. *Tell me all the things …* I look at him painfully.

'Do you really want to know?' I can feel his eyes on me, drinking me in, compassionate because I am hurting and only a little curious about what it is I have to say. I don't even, really, know why I have to say it.

'Tell me,' he nods.

Shall I tell him? The thought takes root, sends out little tendrils in every direction so I can taste the flavour of what it might be like to share this place with someone; gauge what his reaction might be. I never talk about Mum with other people. I never talk about how she died. I take in a little shuddering breath; *I never talk about magic.*

The moonlight is so bright, the dark sky so still, so closed. The snow muffles all sounds for miles around, feeling like a protective blanket, cocooning us in here so I get the feeling that it will be okay for me to speak. Nothing I say will ever go any further, and maybe - he will even understand?

'The reason I got so upset with you yesterday,' I gulp. 'It wasn't entirely to do with you. Oh, I wanted you to kiss me, yes.' I glance up at him nervously but there's a certain freedom in having made the decision to be honest with him, and he nods, acknowledging my words, unsurprised by them.

'But I guess the thing that really hit me hard yesterday was realising that every single time in my life when I've really wanted something - *really wanted it, more than anything* – something bad has happened.'

'Every time?'

'Every time that matters. Every time I can remember. I've been going over it all in my mind, all night. What I said to you just now about the best course for me being to just not desire anything, to stop wanting - I really meant it.'

He considers this for a while.

'And right now ...' he says slowly, 'you want *me*?'

I blush fiercely.

'And you're afraid that, if you keep on wanting me ...' He lifts an eyebrow, 'Something bad will happen?'

My teeth have begun to chatter. I don't know what we're doing, standing out here having this conversation. I don't know why I even started it. I can't finish it. I just stare at him.

'Is it because of what I said yesterday?' he asks unexpectedly now. His eyes look sad. 'About me not being the person you think I am?'

'No,' I croak. 'It's because of *me* not being who *you* think I am ...'

'Have we both been leading each other on, then?' He looks pensive.

'Perhaps.' I lift my chin a fraction. 'You think that I'm ... innocent and sweet and good, don't you?' A small smile creeps into his eyes now. I see him lick his lips.

'The thing is ...' I clear my throat. 'I haven't always followed an honourable course.' His eyebrows raise slightly.

'You, Rose?' He looks as if he finds that hard to believe.

'I haven't.' I look at the ground which is a strange blue-grey by the light of the moon. 'Did you know Wiccans believe that whatever intent you put out to others, it'll always come back to you three-fold?'

He doesn't respond. Of course he doesn't. What am I expecting him to say to a statement like that, anyway? He's got a hundred other more urgent things on his mind. The snow. The lack of food up here. Sunny. Lawrence looks up at me now, full of feelings but whatever he's thinking he's keeping his counsel to himself.

'It is one of the first rules of Wicca,' I say to him in a small, strange voice, now. 'That you must never seek to impose your will on another. Did you know that?'

'I am not familiar with the rules of Wicca,' he says at last. 'Your mother was a witch.' He hesitates for just the briefest second before asking; 'Are you telling me now that you are too?'

'No! No ...' I take in a deep breath. 'I am not a witch.' I feel like I'm readying myself to jump into the deep end of a very cold pool and the shock of the water when I hit it - I know it's going to hurt. 'I'm no witch. But I've always known how to do what she did. I learned it at her knee. I've known for a long time how to use her powers ...'

'You used them, Rose?' He's standing very still. Oh, what is he thinking? I wish I could read his voice. I wish I had some way of gauging his reaction but I have none. I give a small nod.

'What did you do?' he says at long last. A tranche of snow to the right of us breaks off under its own weight. It slides off down the broken edge of the wall and plumps down into the snow, startling us both.

'I brought Mum home,' I say in a small voice.

'You brought her home.' The word 'home' hangs uncomfortably in the air between us for a good few minutes. I cannot imagine the reason why.

'I missed her. Dad wanted her back, but she wouldn't come home. It's *all my fault* that she's gone.'

'Whoa, whoa ...' Lawrence gives me a puzzled look and I know I'm not making any sense to him at all. I'm going way too fast. 'Just ... what did you do?'

'I brought Mum home,' I say again. 'I didn't mean for her to die ...'

Rose

She didn't want to come back to us; no, I knew Mum had made up her mind she was happier where she was, she was never coming back.

'I wanted her back. So I set up a magic circle.' I glance fleetingly at Lawrence to see if I've lost him but his eyes are riveted to mine, intent. 'I knew to do it properly it had to be nine feet in diameter.' My head is suddenly full of irrelevant details;

'I marked it out from the centre using a string that was four-foot-six.' I glance at him uneasily. 'I used a length of old knitting wool. Bright blue. I took it out of Mrs P's knitting bag while she was out. I used the sitting room because it was the only room big enough.' I stop, aware that I am shoring up the pain of my confession by swamping it in facts and figures. But nothing can stop the fact that my nose is running; my lungs are feeling very short of breath. Lawrence is shaking his head;

'You didn't *do* anything, Rose.'

'I *did* do something though. I did. I cast a spell to bring her back.' Is this what it feels like to confess to a crime? I wonder now. All the details and particulars of what I did, they stand out in bright shapes and colours in my memory. They stand out like separate objects, apart from me. I remember I sprinkled salt around the perimeter to seal it. The salt was coarse and granular. I spilled some of it. I took her besom and swept the circle, brushing away the excess and clearing the energy like I'd seen her do before. I

251

took some strands of her hair - off a brush I'd used on her myself just days earlier - put them in a muslin pouch with her name on it, attached to the end of a silken cord. I lit four candles, one for each of the four directions of the compass, asking in my mind as I did so that she might be pulled back to us, from whatever direction it was that she wanted to go.

'To make her come back to us. To *force* her to come back. I knew that was wrong; that you should never compel anyone. I knew that.' I made up some words, too. Any words would do, though rhyming words seemed to be the best;

> *By the rule of One, You home shall come,*
> *By the rule of Two, I call to You,*
> *By the rule of Three, Your home you seek,*
> *By the rule of Four, You'll be at the door.*

'I knew by the fourth day she'd be back,' I breathe. 'I knew it just as sure as you're standing there in front of me.'

He blows on his cupped hands now. I realise I have kept him standing out here for a long time. The light from the firebrand he brought with him is flickering fiercely. It's almost gone out.

'And was she? On the fourth day?'

'Oh, yes. She was. After refusing for months to leave that place - she suddenly took sick and she had no choice but to leave the camp.'

'She took sick?' I see a glimmer of understanding dawning now in his eyes. 'Don't do this to yourself, Rose. You never asked for her to get sick.'

But I've hit the cold, dark water in the pool of my deepest shame. *Smack*, and I'm in, head reeling, all my muscles juddering, gasping for breath and all I can feel right now is the shock-waves of an unspeakable, terrible remorse.

'That's how magic works though, Lawrence.' My words all come out in one breath. 'Magic shifts the energy around us, moves mountains, even, but it doesn't trouble about who'll get crushed

252

underneath.' I should have known, *as her daughter, I should have known ...*

'That's what happens if you don't do it properly; if you're uninitiated and don't know what you're doing or you're careless, and that's what I was, all of those things ...' I'm shaking, shuddering now, as a draft of pure cold goes right through me, right through the centre of me.

I should never have meddled ...

'You say she'd been living in the woodland camp,' he considers slowly. 'You don't think - living in those damp underground burrows had anything to do with making her sick?' Oh, that's what anyone would say but I need him to understand the true significance of what I did ...

'It was four days precisely, after I cast that spell, that she turned up at our door. Do you really think that was a *coincidence?*'

'I think ...' He gives me a long, hard look. 'You wished for her to come home. You hoped for it. I don't believe in spells.'

He's wrong. I frown stubbornly.

'Why did she get sick then?'

'Who knows? Who knows how long that sickness might have been dormant in her?'

'They never got to the bottom of that. She refused any treatment for it ...' My voice is shaking and he puts his hands over mine now.

'*Rose,*' he says. I can feel, first, his hand creeping tentatively into my hand, then his arm comforting behind my back, rubbing my shoulders lovingly, saying this is okay, whatever it is, it's okay because you aren't in it alone. 'Are you saying that your dad didn't insist she went for any treatment?'

'Dad?' I look up at him, puzzled. Then I shrug. 'He tried, Lawrence. But she could be stubborn. She didn't want to know.'

'Whatever it was she wanted, it looks as if she chose her *own* path, Rose.'

'What do you mean?' I say, unsurely. 'I cast that spell. Don't you understand? I made her sick.'

253

'You never *made her sick*. All you did was love her, Rose. You loved her and you wanted her back - what child wouldn't? In the end, she never let you choose for her, did she? She wasn't compelled by anyone, magic spell or no.'

You loved her and you wanted her back ... His hand is around my shoulders still, rubbing my back consolingly, comfortingly.

'She came back in four days, just as the spell had intended her to.' I look at him wildly.

'No.' He shakes his head at me. 'She came back in her own good time, Rose. It sounds as if she'd have taken longer than four days to get as sick as you describe. She chose to respond to it, how and when she did.'

Christ, I look at him shakily, *she did, didn't she?*

I wipe at my eyes fiercely because it seems an obvious thing now that he says it but it has never occurred to me before. I'd *begged* her to go into hospital, hadn't I? Nothing I'd said or done could shift her, though.

'She ... she could have gone for treatment, you're saying?'

'That's exactly what I'm saying. Who knows what the outcome would have been? From the sounds of it she didn't even give it a try.'

No, she didn't, because she'd already made up her mind.

The image of that butterfly on its mounting board comes sharply into my mind now. *I never made up her mind for her*. The pain between my brows lessens a little bit. The thought eases itself into my mind. *Maybe I didn't make her sick. I didn't make her stay sick ...?*

The butterfly in my mind opens its wings out suddenly, a flash of sapphire-blue in my memory. In a moment, it is going to soar off, just like I always wished it could do. It's going to fly away, free. Could it be true what he's saying? I didn't do that bad thing ... I didn't make her die?

'It wasn't me, was it?'

'No. It wasn't you.'

'But ... why did Mum want to do that, Lawrence?' I look at

254

him painfully now. 'Refuse all treatment so that she would leave us the way she did?'

He bites his lip.

'Sometimes ... people have just got to leave, Rose. Trust me. It doesn't mean they don't love the people they've left behind.'

'Those last few days before she passed away ... I was so *mad* at her, you know that?' My words rush out now as if a floodgate has been opened; a floodgate on a lot of things that make me sound callous, bad things that I never wanted to say.

'I was mad at her for going away and mad at her for getting sick and mad at her for ... for everything. She embarrassed me.' I say in a small voice now. I've never admitted as much to anyone but it's true. 'All those flowing robes and incense sticks and ... and everything that went with it. Do you know she used to turn up at parent-teacher evenings looking like something out of the sixties? Didn't she see what they were all thinking about her - *about me* - what they were all saying after she'd left ...?' I shake my head helplessly. 'Oh, I always defend her memory to the hilt with the likes of Carlotta but the truth is I've spent a long time distancing myself from Mum, making sure everyone knows I'm not like her.'

'You don't have to be like her,' he says quietly. 'She was always going to love you, anyway. No matter how you turned out. From the first time I saw you, I knew - you were a girl who'd been very loved, Rose.'

Oh, and now there is a pain working its way up from my belly, up into my throat like a thousand razors, it hurts, *it hurts*, but whatever it is, it's coming out of me now, easing itself up and away in the long, keening sound that's coming out of my mouth ... and I am mourning her at last. All those hot salty tears I never cried the morning I took up her last cup of tea and found that she'd left us in the night; all those cold, hurtful tears I didn't shed the day we sprinkled her ashes over the side of that boat and into the choppy sea. All these tears, hiccupping and crashing right through me like white water on a frenzied, swollen river ... where the hell have they all come from, where could I have been storing

255

them all this time?

'What do you mean by that?' I say at last.

'Your parents loved you.' His hands slide gently over mine. 'I know this because it shines out in everything you are and everything you do, all the time. You've been loved. Once you've been loved, that's something that stays with you a lifetime. It's like a stamp on your soul. It's like a very powerful light, attracting other people to love you, too.'

Other people? I look at him, gulping down my next thought. *But not people like you?*

'She died before I had a chance to tell her …' I look away. 'I didn't get a chance to tell her that I loved her.'

'I'm sure she knew.'

I miss her. He asked me that the first time he met me, didn't he? I denied the extent of it then. I've been denying it for a long time. '*I miss her* …' I wail. He pulls me to him, rocking me like a child. I'd forgotten what it was like to feel this open and vulnerable and raw. I'd forgotten what it felt like to hurt this bad and to feel so bewildered and helpless and new.

'I know,' he says.

I pull away from his warm shoulder now, wiping my face, my grotty nose, on my sleeve.

'You're not shocked?' My eyes search deep into his, but I see that he isn't. Not at all. 'Why aren't you shocked?'

'Maybe I'm more difficult to shock than you think I am?' He smiles, then. A smile that could melt this mountain of snow-fall into a summer river, a smile that starts to melt the glacier around my heart. And then I feel him nudge my arm.

'I think I've discovered what's responsible for those noises you keep hearing. *Look*.' He indicates with his head towards the snowy slope beneath, and there, barely even visible in the moonlight, is a completely white fox. I gasp. The creature doesn't move. He just stands there, looking up at us for a good few minutes, all round shiny eyes and pink nose and not much else visible at all. Is this the animal responsible for the footsteps I heard outside earlier? Not an intruder, not the fugitive, nor some roaming spirit, all the scary things my restless mind came up with in the early hours when I was so alone? I feel an instant flood of relief. I imagine the weather has forced it out further from its usual hunting grounds, searching for food.

'My God. It's an albino. I've never seen one of those before. Have you?' My crushed mood has lifted in an instant. I feel light, and somehow clean and whole inside, as if things make sense again. 'Have you ever seen anything quite so beautiful?'

'I don't believe I have,' Lawrence says and his voice sounds sad. When I turn back to look at him in wonder, he isn't looking at the fox, though.

He's looking at me.

Rose

'You don't have to say kind things to me, Lawrence,' I take him in hesitantly. A moment ago, I would have added; *don't, because this isn't going to go anywhere and you being kind is only going to make things harder for me.* But since then, when I told him everything I did, things have changed dramatically between us, I feel it.

'I wasn't being kind.' He looks at me helplessly. 'I know what it is you want, Rose.' I want to turn away from him now, save what's left of my dignity because he finds it all too easy to read the naked longing in my eyes, but I can't.

'*Rose.*' He rubs his hands up and down my arms now. 'My life's not … not in the right place for me to have a relationship with anyone. You need to know that. I can't stay. When I finish what I've come to do here, I won't have a job anymore. I don't even know where I'm headed next.'

'I understand,' I say, even though I don't, and my voice feels thick in my throat.

'If things were different, believe me, I wouldn't be saying this. I'd be saying something else. I don't want to see you waste your life away with wanting, that's all. It's just … I'm not…' He kicks at the snow on the ground disconsolately with the tip of his boot. He chuffs it up into a big messy pile. The snow looks blue-grey by the light of the moon. 'You think you know me but … you really don't. You don't know me, Rose.'

'Tell me, then,' I say hoarsely. *I just told you all about me.* 'Tell me what it is about you that I need to know before you'll accept that I … I care for you.' Oh God, I said those words out loud. I said them, even though I never meant to. Maddeningly, he shakes his head.

'Is it - someone else? A girlfriend?' He said before he didn't have one, but still … my heart is thudding, my head giddy with his touch but he's already moving away. He shakes his head again slightly.

'I haven't got a girlfriend, Rose.'

'A *boyfriend*, then?' He smiles slightly.

He blows on his hands, sticks them back inside his pockets as if he's scared of what he might do with them otherwise. 'I've been on the go for a long time now,' he adds as he sees that I'm waiting for more. 'Never stayed stuck in one place for too long. That's made having relationships a mite tricky.' *Why have you never stayed in one place for long enough,* that's the question?

I see him bite his lower lip, look down. When he looks up at me again, I think maybe he's going to answer me at last but instead there's a curiosity burning on his face that wasn't there before.

'Do you?' he asks.

'Do I what?'

'Do you have a boyfriend?'

I swallow, taken aback by his interest. Does he even *care*?

'No,' I say and then, without meaning to, I add. 'I saw my soul-mate once, though.'

'You *saw* him? You know him, then?' He sounds a little disappointed by that but I shake my head.

'I saw him in my mind's eye.' I pick my words carefully.

'Oh?'

'More *felt* him than saw him. But I knew that it was him and I knew …' my throat threatens to close up but Lawrence nudges me, makes me say the words.

'I knew that he and I could never be together in this life.'

259

'Oh, Rose,' he breaks into a sad smile. *Superstitious girl*, the expression on his face says. Because of what I've just told him about that spell I believed I'd cast, and my mum, no doubt. He might be right about that one, but this is one thing I know I *am* right about. 'How can you even say that?'

'I say it because I know it to be true.'

'You'd never be together?' he says softly.

'We couldn't. It wouldn't be allowed.' Saying the words out loud has made me feel sad, as I knew it would. I have never told that to anyone. Not even Mum. Lawrence's hand has somehow slipped into my hand. He lifts my gloved fingers to his lips. He has no real idea what that does to me inside, does he?

'Don't let that make you afraid to love someone, Rose.'

No idea at all.

He steps in closer to me and the movement is as natural as breathing. Beside me, his face just nuzzling mine, that's where he should be. It's where, no matter what I've just said about all my disappointments and my hopes and my fears, I want him to be.

'You *are* beautiful,' he says thickly. His hand reaches up, tentatively, just touching my cheek and my whole face feels as if it is burning at his touch. 'You are beautiful and you deserve to have someone special who loves you, never doubt that.'

And now at last, he leans forward and kisses me softly. His kiss is as warm and as light as a breath against my mouth. And just for this moment, as short as a heartbeat, as long as an entire lifetime, there is nothing else. Every other single thing in my entire life melts away. Even me. I don't know where I've gone right now. I'm a soft, downy white feather floating on a warm summer's breeze. I'm the ripples in the pond the first time I ever skimmed a pebble right to the centre. There is only his kiss, his lips sweet as wine on my mouth, and a slow spreading joy rising up from my belly like the bubbles in a champagne glass.

If only it could have gone on for longer, that kiss - forever, maybe. *I would have been happy to have stayed like that forever*, I think deliriously, *for us to be like two little figures locked together in a Christmas snow globe for all eternity ...*

Even as he pulls his head back a little, tentative, observing me, all I can feel is bereft that his lips are no longer on my own; at the same time both intoxicated with joy and flooded with sadness because instinctively I know that, without him, I will never be as much again

'I wasn't expecting that,' I murmur. *God, he is beautiful*! I can't believe he thinks that I am, too. That kiss, I'm thinking ... it must have been a consolation kiss, because he can't have a relationship with me. Because he isn't in the right place in his life right now - whatever else it was that he just said - I don't know, I can't remember. He said lots of things just now, didn't he? Lots of words about ... how he's been on the go for such a long time and stuff, how I don't really know him, *how I am beautiful and I deserve to have someone special to love me.*

You, Lawrence. I look at him helplessly. I want to have *you* to love me. Now that I have felt your lips on my own, no other man is ever going to do.

Something out of my control makes me move a little nearer to him now, my fingers pulling at the buttons of his damp dufflecoat, holding him there close to me. Behind him, I imagine I see the dawn just beginning to break, a faint brightness permeating the sky above the trees to the east. The jagged dark line where he said the little angels used to keep guard above the battlements stands out proud. Another day is coming. A day I suddenly feel fearful of, a day that I wish with all my heart would not come so soon. *I wish I could stay here with you forever, that's what I wish. I wish we didn't have to go back to the real world, our real lives.* As we stand there, the flashing orange tail-light of a plane appears over the horizon and I see that it is not daybreak as I thought, not dawn yet. But I know that it is coming. That it has to come. With the back of his hand, Lawrence is stroking my hair away from my face, so gently, so lovingly, it's as if he too, understands that these few moments we have together here are precious. They will not come again.

261

'I didn't expect it.' When I look up at him his eyes are bright, shining with something lovely, something beautiful, and I know he feels as happy as I do at this moment.

'Or *this*?' His next kiss is deeper, lasts for longer. When I pull his head down to me, drawing him hungrily towards my own lips for a third time, I hear him give out a gasp of desire, and the sound stirs something in me, too. Something that I'd buried so deep I didn't even remember it was part of me anymore.

'*Rose,*' he's saying, 'Rose ... I didn't mean for us to do this,' but his voice as he says my name is coming from somewhere deep within his throat and I know that it's too late: it doesn't matter what he intended because a deeper, more animal volition has taken over, a physical hunger that will not be so easily subdued. Slowly, we've moved back up against the snow-covered wall. He's pulled off his gloves. He's unbuttoning my wet jacket. My eyes open wider, slightly disbelieving because out here we are so exposed to the elements but he seems oblivious to that. Now that he has started I do not want him to stop. The air that leaves our mouths turns to icy mist, and I see his breath is coming harder, faster. Despite his impatience his hands must be frozen and the buttons take an age to undo. By the time he's done and he looks up at me something makes him suddenly laugh out loud.

'What?' The sound of his laughter catches in my own throat. 'What's so funny?'

'Your nose.' He leans forward, nuzzling it gently with his own. 'Is bright red! I've let you get too cold, *Madame.*'

'What do you suggest?' I let out a long, icy breath as the words leave my lips and he covers my mouth with his own again. I'm aware that every part of me is suddenly trembling.

'I imagine we'll think of something.' His hand on the small of my back presses me in close to him now, so that I feel him, right along the length of my body, every part of him, lean and muscular and - *hard.* I groan. I'm glad it is dark still, so he can't see the blush that rises to my face. He can't see the confusion and the hesitancy mixed in with my desire. I'm not all that experienced at this. Not like he'd expect someone of my age to be and there is a kind of shame in that. It isn't the sort of thing you want broadcast to the world. Lawrence is going to find out soon enough, though, isn't he?

Oh God, what am I doing?

I hardly know Lawrence really, do I? He's a stranger I've met in a snowstorm. He's a kind, sweet, gorgeous stranger who's warned me since we met - a very short time ago - that I mustn't do this, fall for him, want him - *expect anything from him?*

'Come.' He motions with his head for us both to go back inside. We are both shivering, frozen to the core but I instinctively know as soon as I follow him inside that what's going to happen next is something there will be no going back from.

Lawrence

Is this what it feels like to be happy?

I had forgotten.

I lean forward, propped up on my elbows to watch the gentle rise and fall of her breathing. Rose went to sleep nestled in my arms. After a while, cramping, I had to lay her down. I slept for an hour or so myself but awoke suddenly and now I am too acutely aware of the fact that she is still naked under the cover of my sleeping bag. Just there, just inches away from me, her breasts and her stomach and all the other places I have touched tonight, they are still unbearably, intoxicatingly, close. And it has been so long since I have been with a woman.

I would have her again but I would not for all the world wake her. She looks so peaceful right now. As I cannot touch her, all I want to do is watch her. The soft glow from the brazier is flickering pinks and marmalade orange hues all over her skin, burnishing the darker strands of her hair to a tawny gold. She does not seem cold. She looks, if possible, only more beautiful than she looked to me before.

Surprising then, that she was at first so coy when we came in here, when we first undressed. She seemed embarrassed to even let me see her, I think. Not like other girls I have known, who've made the most of their assets, who knew all the tricks, how to make a man beg. Not Rose. She made a joke that she was glad of the dark, even if I did not like it. She said she felt more

264

comfortable that way. I was so fired up, so hungry that I hardly noticed that she came to me blindly, unsure, not knowing where to put her hands at first, a little surprised at where I put mine. She didn't know some things that I had assumed all girls must know. I guessed, because of her circumstances, that she'd be a little inexperienced but I never knew - never even suspected the truth. Not till the moment she cried out when I entered her.

I saw her eyes close for a moment in pain. I'd been careful not to touch the wound on her leg, it couldn't have been that. Her cry made me stop what I was doing, shocked, when I realised what it was. *Why hadn't she said*? If I'd known it was her first time I'd have gone easier on her, been more careful ... but when she opened her eyes a second later, Rose was smiling. She looked ... triumphant. Like she'd just passed some milestone in her life; one which was well overdue for passing. She pulled me down towards her, her mouth locking on mine and it was clear that she wanted me to continue. I hadn't needed much encouragement. Afterwards, quiet, sated, in the glow of the firelight, she'd turned her head, smiling, mouthed something at me. I couldn't quite make out what. I leaned my ear in a little closer to her mouth, unable to resist tracing the line of her neck, her beautiful, perfect shoulders, along the way.

'Thank you,' she breathed, and the scent of her skin so close up reminded me of honey on fresh bread, reminded me of the mornings in springtime when I was a lad, the time before I came to be who I am now.

'No, my Rose,' I said to her. I held her fingers in my hand and kissed them, unable to say any more because she couldn't know what she had restored to me, after so long in exile; my dignity, my manhood. The hope that I might ever be truly loved by someone;

'Thank *you*.'

I watch Rose now as she shakes the snow off the leafy ends of one of the branches I've brought in, uses it as a broom to sweep away the ashes that have accumulated around the fire. She's shy this morning, smiling, but she feels an ease around me that was not there before. She wants to keep busy. She's keeping the place tidy at least and, stark and cold as it is, homely. I had to go out digging in the log pile again this morning. Each time I have to dig deeper to get out enough small pieces, but now we've got a row of logs lined up in front of the fire. There is also an assortment of wet clothing hanging off the back of the wooden pew and a collection of small animals Rose constructed out of the silver foil from the chocolate liqueurs which we ate for breakfast. This is beginning to look like some sort of domestic arrangement, I think. It reminds me of the tent I shared with Joaquin back in Jaffna. I have never shared a living space with a woman before but I see now that it's better.

I see that one day I might want to.

When I woke this morning I felt in a different place and I knew that must be because of her; because I was not alone. Not scared. Not hunted or cold. I remembered that my life hasn't always been bleak. In the few hours when I slept last night, I had peaceful dreams. I can recall snippets and glimpses of them; me and Kahn, taking the woodland route to school in the morning when the air was warm and full of birdsong, the green moss springy and damp beneath our feet. He was a young dog again, brown-coated, bright-eyed, maybe a year old, sniffing at every rabbit-hole, padding past clumps of lilac harebells, obedient, alert, happy to be at my side. He made me feel like a king.

Like she does.

'So.' Rose settles at last, flops down onto the canvas sacking. She looks pensive, her fingers picking hesitantly at the edges of the sacking. She's got something on her mind, hasn't she?

'When you ran up here,' she asks at last. 'That time you got trapped.' She takes in a breath and then she plunges straight on. 'What were you really running from, Lawrence?'

Ah.

I feel my shoulders involuntarily tense up even though I

have known that we must return to this. After what she shared with me before, it was inevitable she would want to know more about me. And Rose and I - we've moved a step closer to each other now. We've shared each other's bodies - would it be such a bad thing to share some of my truth with her, too?

'I was running from my father,' I tell her eventually. She tilts her head to one side, inviting more. She knows, I can see it in her eyes, that I do not want to speak of this, that it will be painful for me. I think maybe she wants me to share some of that pain with her but honestly, *I* don't. I want something else. I lean in to her. I kiss her, hard, on the lips and I hear her gasp in surprise at my renewed hunger. My hands go up to cup around her breasts, testing out the waters, seeing if she will lie with me again and I think for a moment that she will, but she only smiles softly, grasps hold of my hand, wriggles away.

'Tell me,' she breathes. 'Why you had to run away from your father?' I sigh. In her world I imagine, a father is a person you run *to*, not from.

'Getting trapped under that rubble - that wasn't the first time I'd ever experienced anything like that. Being closed in, I mean, in the dark. Entombed.' I feel her shudder as I say the word but it is too late to go back now. I grasp her hand tighter, not letting her go. She asked. She wanted to know and now she *will* know.

'We used to have an old World War Two shelter out back. If my father ever felt me or my brother were out of order in any way he'd take his belt to whichever one of us it was - usually me - and then fling us down there for a night and a day. Solitary confinement, he called it.' I pause, aware of her breath catching, acutely aware of her inching closer to me. She cannot know how I have longed for the comfort of human companionship. She cannot know how the endless silence, the darkness, engulfs you after a time. The mind starts playing tricks. You come to think that maybe you aren't really there anymore; that maybe you're dead and already buried.

The water drops down from the ceiling into the brazier and the hiss makes us both jump. 'Down there, there was nothing; no food, not the slightest ray of light. I'd hear him draw the bolt across on the outside and I'd know that I wouldn't see daylight again till several eternities had passed. There was nothing to drink. Sometimes I'd lick the cold stone walls in the hope that some moisture would have condensed on them ...'

She lets out a strange noise but now I have started.

'There wasn't much room to move about, Rose. And once I was in there - it was like the whole world forgot about me.' I feel a strange hurting in my chest, recalling it. 'My dog Kahn ... he knew though. He knew I was in there. I used to hear him, scuffing at the door outside, whimpering. He'd wait for *hours* ...'

'Stop.' She puts her hand on my arm. 'That's so cruel. You didn't have to open up and tell me any of this. I'm so sorry, Lawrence. I'm sorry I insisted.' She bows her head. 'I see now why you ran. Of *course* you had to run from that.'

'It's not something I feel proud of. Where I've come from; what it was like. It's not the sort of thing you want to tell people about yourself.' It feels strange, this. Sitting here with this ... this beautiful, kind, sensitive girl who let me love her last night; allowing myself to accept her sympathy and understanding. She hasn't - as I feared - jumped up in horror when she's learned the shame of it. She hasn't moved away from me.

'Now you know why I left that day,' I say gruffly after a bit. 'I had to leave. I was only young and I had to make some tough choices but I had to keep believing I could make things better, that things *would* get better.' I look away from her, aware that I've left out a whole chunk of what happened. The day I got trapped up here under the rubble was only one of the days I ran off from home. It wasn't the day I left home for good. But I can't tell her about *that*.

She nods, taking all this in, intensely interested. She's drinking in all the details about my life as if she could never get enough.

'So - you left. But you went on to study for a career ... things must have got better for you?'

'Yes. When I left home I went up to Bradford,' I tell her. We're on safer ground now. She lifts her eyebrows questioningly and I confess with a little smile;

'Bradford was as far away as I could hitch a lift. I thought it'd be far away enough. No one would know me. I struck it lucky, to be honest. After a few weeks of sleeping rough, I begged work from an elderly Asian couple. They had a corner shop but the long hours were getting to them. They were also getting a bit of flak from some local yobbos. I promised them I could help them out.'

'They agreed?' Rose smiles. She likes this part of the story, I can tell. It's the bit where hope comes in, help arrives.

'They took me in. Took pity on me, I think,' I tell her as she seems to be waiting for more. 'Their only son lived abroad and they still missed him, never saw the grandkids either. I became a surrogate one of theirs. They even put me into a local school. I worked the evenings for them. I finished school. Eventually, I went on to do the paramedic training.' She nods, her eyes shining. I know I've made it all sound simple. At the time it was anything but.

'They sound like a *wonderful* couple.'

'The first time I went in and asked for work off Mr Patel he chased me out with a broomstick,' I tell her ruefully and she gives a short laugh.

'But why train in that particular area, though? You especially attracted to blood and guts?' She gives a small smile.

'Not really. I'd just spent sixteen years in the presence of a man who was very fond of hurting people.'

She winces.

'I wanted to make sure I only ever did the opposite.' I look away from her, because it's the truth, but it's not the whole story as I know.

'I'm sorry, Lawrence.' Rose hangs her head.

'If that makes me sound like some sort of angel, I promise

269

you I'm not,' I add, wanting to be truthful. 'Things didn't always go too well for the Patels. There were some pretty nasty thugs in their area.' I paint her just enough of the picture. 'I did what I could to protect them. I was pretty well-built for my age. I could kick a bit of ass if I was around when the lads came harassing but … I wasn't always around.'

'Your friends were being bothered?' Her eyes looked pained. Bothered, yeah. I rub at my eyes, not wanting to remember that. I came to love that couple like I really was the grandkid we all used to pretend I was. Then one day, they stopped pretending.

'In the end, they went away to live near their son in India. They said they'd have a better life. I've lost touch …' I look down, filled with remorse that I didn't try harder to keep up with them, remembering that at the time I was too mad at them for leaving me, to want to. I was learning, though. Learning not to put too much store by people, not to expect too much. That's why what Rose said before hit a chord with me. *I should just stop wanting*, she said. That's what I've done pretty much. For some reason, when she said it, I didn't want her to feel that way though. I *want* her to keep dreaming, to keep wanting. It's what I want for Sunny, too. They're important. They've got to know that.

'After they left - I managed to get a grant to complete the first part of my paramedic training.' I clear my throat because my voice has somehow gone hoarse. 'Then as soon as the opportunity came, I took off abroad myself.'

'You never thought of coming back …?' She looks about her, at the place that surrounds us. She doesn't quite say the word *Home*.

'I never thought of coming back,' I say. That comes out more sharply than I intend and her eyes widen. 'I'm sorry, Rose.' I've told her some of it and she can guess at the cruelty but she's not to know everything. 'There are some places you don't want to re-visit in your life, right? Besides, I told you, I'm no angel. I've got involved in some things I regret, too. I can't tell you how much I regret …' I look at her searchingly.

'Rose …' If I could only tell her and she'd understand. The thought lands heavy as a bird on my shoulders. If I could only tell *someone*, what a burden it is to me to have to carry the knowledge of what I did, carry it all alone with no other person beside me to share it with. But I can't. I mustn't.

I can't let everything unravel now, not now when there's still so much at stake.

'There are some things I left behind that I didn't want to be reminded of, Rose. I know - you won't believe it, but I've got a temper. There have been times when it's had the better of me.'

She doesn't say anything, just keeps on waiting for me to fill in the rest. But I'm not going to give her all the rest! She doesn't need to know it. I don't need her to know it. It serves no purpose other than to open up old wounds and that's not what I'm here to do. I stitch wounds up and I put plasters on them and I let them be, that's what I do with wounds.

I move over to the brazier, push the end of another log onto the fire and wait patiently while it catches light. It's damp and it takes a long time, burning only reluctantly, slowly. I get the feeling any moment now it's going to go out altogether.

'And … your father,' she says after a while. He's still on her mind. 'What happened to him?'

I look at her in surprise. 'What happened? Nothing. He's still there. I haven't been home since. There have been times in my life when I thought maybe I should go back and face him again but I've never been able to bring myself to do it …'

'You shouldn't have to,' she says quietly. 'Someone else should do that for you. The police, maybe? He should be made to pay for what he did to you and your brother, Lawrence. People shouldn't be allowed to hurt other people and get away with it.' Her eyes are shiny, suddenly. I see they are full of tears. For me?

'No,' I agree, my voice gruff. 'They shouldn't.'

'I'm sorry,' she gives an apologetic little laugh. 'You'll think I'm silly, crying like this.'

'No need to apologise, Rose.'

271

'It just makes me feel so *sad* ...'

I pull her in towards me suddenly, fiercely, protectively. Gently, I kiss the top of her head. I kiss her face. Then her mouth. 'It's over now. Long past, and I'm a big boy as you can see. I can look after myself now. Hey - *don't cry*!' With my thumb I wipe away the tears from her cheeks. 'I made the decision to lead a different life. I had to leave home to do that. You know about that, don't you?'

'I can't lead a different life,' she says softly now, so quietly that I can barely hear her. 'It's different for me.'

'It's never easy for anyone to fly the nest,' I murmur. 'If you've had a loving family, a good home, it's even harder I'm guessing.' But she's already told me about all her plans and dreams. How she wants to leave Merry Ditton. How she plans to go to Uni. She's dying to get out of here and make her mark on the world; I could tell that from the way she spoke yesterday.

She's positioned herself so that she's leaning back onto my chest, this beautiful girl. I'm cradling her in my arms. Oh, what would I not give to have her stay here? For us to be together. I had not thought such a thing would ever be possible; that any girl would make me feel like this, make me *want* this. But Rose makes me feel ... human again. I'm like a small boy who's been trying to stretch his fingertips up high enough to touch the sky, like Sunny reaching for the moon. She's come along and lowered my hands down, pushed them into the crumbling brown earth; reminded me of what is real. She seems sad, though.

'You're going to be *fine*, Rose.'

She doesn't immediately answer and I pull her in safe, close to me. She feels warm in my arms, delicate as a bird that I long to protect and I recall that last night I dreamed of Sunny, too. I saw him walking - *walking* - on a sunlit pavement on the opposite side of the road to me, moving along in the crowd. He looked a little older than he is now and he had other young people his age with him. He was laughing and talking. I called out, but he didn't hear me. It was as if I weren't there, he couldn't see me but it didn't matter; he didn't need me anymore. I felt a deep relief and gladness at that. I felt *peace*.

When I kiss her once more, I feel it again.

'Things are ... a little more complicated at home than I've let you know,' she says. I feel her gaze settle on me now. I recall her mentioning that her father is not a well man, how she was concerned about him. She came up here to fetch some medication for him and I know they've had phone contact but she hasn't really said much about him, has she?

'Dad's poorly,' she confirms now. 'I'd have to get his family to agree to help out with his care before I could leave myself. Right now the chances of that happening ...' She looks at me ruefully. 'They seem a little slim.'

'Have faith, Rose.' I give her a little shake. 'Things can change! Everything can change and even when you think there's no way things can ever get better something good can come along - something joyful and wonderful just like ... like you coming into my life right now.' Her face lights up in a smile when I say that.

'For you,' she says and she presents me with a tin-foil giraffe she's managed to fashion out of three bits of bright silver foil paper.

'Thank you.' I take it from her, twirling it between my fingers. We both stare at it as it catches the light, shimmering and proud; it seems suddenly like a very precious thing. In this quiet, peaceful moment, devoid of all other distractions, it takes on the importance of a masterpiece in an art gallery.

'Why a giraffe?' I ask. 'Have I been a pain in the neck?' The sudden laugh coming from her throat is full of an unspoilt joy, and I think; *I would do anything to capture this moment*.

'No. Because it's so tall it can see what's coming up next,' she says immediately.

'Like me?' I lean in close to her, kissing her nose.

'Like you're going to need to be,' she says without thinking. Then she blushes, lowers her eyes. 'Sorry,' she says. 'I wasn't trying to be Mystic Meg or anything. That just came out.'

Out from where, I wonder?

'I guess I do need to have more faith,' she runs on, clearly keen to cover up her last statement. 'It's just - you know how it is. Sometimes it's difficult to see your way out of a rut.'

'You really think the family *wouldn't* be willing to step in and help you?' I take her in curiously now. 'How poorly is he? Is it a progressive illness?'

'Not an illness, as such.' She shifts in my arms, looks at me from under her long lashes and I sense she doesn't like to talk about this.

'You don't have to tell me if you don't ...' I begin, but she puts her hand on my arm, stopping me.

'Of course I'll tell you,' she says softly. 'After all the other things we've told each other over the last few hours, I hardly think you'll be shocked.' She pauses for a bit.

'My dad was *injured*,' she comes back eventually. 'It happened five years ago - not long after my mum passed away.'

'I'm sorry, Rose.' She blinks and I know that this is something else that must have hurt her deeply, a double blow coming in so short a space of time.

'How did it happen?' I ask because it seems to be important to her to talk about it. For myself, I don't need to know, I am not curious. Her father was injured and I feel sorry. The world is full of people who are hurt and who are hurting, and I have been one of them myself for so long ...

'Someone hurt him,' she says now, and I feel a flash of anger on her behalf. Whoever hurt him, hurt *her*, too. If I had been there, I could have helped them, protected her, maybe, but then - five years ago I was a desperate kid myself, running from my own troubles.

'He'd gone over to try and reason with our neighbour.' Her eyes are hardened to pin-points of pain. 'But something went wrong. *Badly* wrong.' Her fingers are smoothing over and over another little foil wrapper left from this morning. She's smoothed it out so insistently it's begun to curl back on itself like a fish-tail.

274

Their neighbour. Someone close by, then? Someone not too far away and maybe even someone I know? Her tragedy shifts a little closer to the circle of my own life. Her words sink down like little lazy chunks of ice, drifting slowly into my space but I can't feel the import of them yet. Not quite yet.

'Five years,' I say, stroking her hair. 'That's a long time.' It's felt like a lifetime to me, hasn't it? The little piece of foil paper which she's been smoothing in her hand tears suddenly and she stops and stares at it.

'Dad had gone over to try and resolve an issue over some property,' her voice sounds very disjointed. She doesn't talk about this, I think. Ever. I recognise the signs. 'But it was dark. He went over very late and they'd untied the dogs. He had to go into their barn to get away from them. He never meant to go in there.'

'They'd untied the dogs ...?' A spark jumps up out of the fire, a damp patch of wood sizzling, and there's a faint smell of burning on the sacking now. Something catches in my throat. Some old memory. Of the sound of the dogs barking, of how they were always let loose to roam around the farmyard once dusk fell. But a lot of people have dogs around here don't they?

A lot of people have guard dogs. I swallow.

'He didn't intend to go into that barn,' she says. Her fingers pull at the little bits of foil and then suddenly she lets them all go, all the little scraps of bright paper, they come fluttering down like a meteor shower across the Milky Way and under my breath, I make a sudden fervent wish. A silent wish, because there are many barns around here. There are many dogs that roam loose after sunset. Rose sits up. She turns to look back at me and her face is a perfect heart-shape, her mouth the perfect mouth. I wait.

'Someone attacked my dad, Lawrence. He left him really hurt. We never found out who. Our neighbour Rob Macrae denied all knowledge and nobody was ever brought to book for it.' As she says my father's name I can feel the edges of my mouth trembling. *We* ... are her neighbours?

I feel a sudden lurch, like a mule kicking me right in the

stomach.

'I thought your dad was sick,' I say stupidly. 'You never mentioned before that he was injured, Rose, that *anyone beat him up*.' I stare at her and she looks at me strangely.

'They did,' she swallows. 'He wasn't expecting any trouble but ... what happened that night changed his life. He was attacked, brutally, and without warning, *for no reason*, Lawrence.'

I have no breath at all in my lungs right now. I double over, holding the pain in my stomach inside, trying for her not to see. I have no words in my mouth. I edge myself back a little, make like I'm adjusting my position because I can't sit here and hold her anymore. She sees my eyes open wider, feels my shock. Maybe she assumes it's because of what she's telling me?

It is, but not for the reason that she thinks.

Somehow I get to my feet. My stomach is cramping though there's precious little in it other than bile. I feel shocked right now, dazed and confused.

That man I attacked the night I left Macrae Farm, that man I thought was my father ... she cannot be his daughter. Not Rose.

Not Rose!

'Hey,' she calls out, alarmed, scrambling up even as I do. 'You okay, Lawrence?'

'I've got to be ... sick.' My throat is full of bile, my mouth and eyes acid, as I stagger outside. She follows me, her eyes large and concerned and I hear her taking in deep breaths, suddenly distressed, not knowing what to say, only watching me, and then I am sick all over the soft white snow.

Lawrence

'*Lawrence*,' Rose says. I can feel her, wringing her hands. She's stopped some way behind me, out on the path. Somehow I have staggered to the end of the wall. I cannot be with her now. I cannot be with anyone. I lift my eyes up. Morning has broken. A red streak lies flat on the distant horizon, an old wound spreading out over the day. The man I injured the night I ran from this place - he was her father.

He was Rose's father.

I put my hands out on the icy wall to steady myself and my hands feel like someone else's hands this morning. The wall looks like a different wall. I brace myself against it, for a while gulping down pure cold air in the hope that something inside me will stutter to life again; in the hope that I can reconnect with some kind of reality that makes sense to me.

I can still feel her, hesitating some way behind me, I can feel her distress. But she must go away now. I have to make her go away.

'You go back in, Rose.' My voice sounds surprisingly calm. 'I need a bit of ... air. I'll be fine.' How normal I sound. How composed. But the effort that takes pushes me into a different place, an old familiar place. I know how to play this one; *I'm fine, I'm okay, everything's fine*.

You keep face. You don't let anyone outside the family know that everything is not all as it should be. You practise the lie. You live it, in careful, well-rehearsed phrases and movements, your whole life a symphony that's playing the right music. I'm okay, everything's okay, and all the while your body language, every pore of you is signalling the message loud and clear; *I don't want to talk about this; go away.* Behind my back, Rose picks up the message. I hear her footsteps crunching softly down the path. I hear the door scrape open against the ice. I hear it shut. Then there is only me, my head spinning again, my temples throbbing in a deep, uneaseable pain, my stomach raw and turned inside out; and the pain of the ice on the wall against my hands. And the faint blue above the red streak in the morning sky. And the cold winter air sliding like water into my open mouth, firing my lungs with pain as if I had been running.

He is her father, how could that be?

I know I have to go back there. I have to let myself remember what happened that terrible night, because there is so much I do not remember, so much I have never wanted to recall. I lean my head over the wall. Below me, several feet down, a blank canvas of snow winks up. It is empty and white, gives nothing away, tells no tales. *Everything is buried,* I think. *Everything is smoothed away, covered over.* But I have to remember. Even though there feels like there is no way that I can. I have to pull it all up, draw it all back to me like a fisherman trawls up his nets from the deep.

It starts with a small thing. A speck of black dust that lands on my white hand. A piece of lint from my coat, maybe? It lands on my hand like one of those thunder bugs that kept appearing from nowhere that August. I remember there were a whole lot of them around that particular day. I can feel the sweat starting up, a thin line of perspiration on my brow. The air was hot that day, close. It was close and my shirt was sticking to my back. I rub my temples with my thumbs, easing out the pain, willing myself to remember.

My shirt was sticking to my back because it was hot and I had been digging. I'd been digging a grave in the earth so I could bury Kahn. Something catches in the back of my throat and I turn my head to spit forcefully onto the icy ground. I clench at the wall in front of me, my knuckles white, my jaw tensing. Then I go on. Remembering.

I'd dug him a grave. I'd stacked a whole load of stones on top of it so the wild animals wouldn't come later and get him.

All the while I was doing it, a little clock was ticking in my brain, a little time-piece calculating how long it'd take my father to get back to the house in his jeep; how long it would take him before he dug out my mother from wherever she was. Or to ferret out my brother and rattle him till his bones shook, or whatever it was my father would have to do before one of them gave up the game ...

Pilgrim knew nothing, of course. But Mum - my heart constricted - she was always so crap at keeping secrets. She was always so weak. He'd get to her, I knew that. She'd confess. And then ... what would he do to my mother and my brother when he found out I'd persuaded her to leave with me?

What would my father be prepared to do?

The place where he'd left me that day was a couple of miles from the house. I knew it was going to take me a good long while to walk back. My feet and my body had felt like lead, I remember that now. Finding Kahn like that and burying him had taken every last ounce of strength from me. Knowing that my father had discovered our plans for escape had sapped me of all hope. We weren't going anywhere. We'd be trapped there for life, all of us. *For life.*

And my father was very capable of taking a life, wasn't he? I'd seen him do it, once before. He'd shot a man, at point blank range, right in the chest. I remember the sound of the gun going off, the loudness of it. I remember putting my hands over my ears. I'd have been - what, four years old at the time? - before Pilgrim was born, anyway. The memory is surrounded in black. I closed it down long ago. I only remember the noise. I remember the gun my father used had a little picture of a horse on it.

I remember that he was perfectly capable of taking another

man's life.

Some people said that those men who'd 'hanged themselves' up on Dead Men's Copse had been victims of his, too. Marco told me that when I was twelve. I know that's what was going through my mind as I walked back home that dusty day, the temperatures soaring to the mid-thirties, the electrical charge of an imminent thunderstorm in the air. I'd had nothing to drink all day. I remember my mouth was parched, full of dirt. I remember licking the sweat off my top lip and it tasted salty. I stopped to drink some water from the brook which was green and brown, full of algae, full of buzzing flies and water boatmen. The sky had rumbled, a deep, close-by sound. I'd longed for rain but the air stayed still, charged. No rain came.

By the brook, I must have fallen asleep for a while, racked and exhausted. Scared. I do not know how many hours I slept for. I only know that by the time I opened my eyes again, groggy, my stomach feeling full of bile, the afternoon was already drawing into evening. The skin on my arms felt puckered, cold. I had to get back home, I knew that. I was also scared witless at what I might find when I got there. I did not want to go home. The palms of my hands felt sore, cracked, and it brought back that earlier on I had buried my friend, my *only* true friend, who my father had killed. He'd killed him to spite me. Would he have been prepared to do the same thing to the rest of the family? He was *capable* of it, sure.

But had he done it?

All the while I walked back home my mind was feeling numbed to the point of insensibility with fear but when I got there ... something strange happened. As I rounded the yard, in sight of Macrae Farm I saw his jeep, with the great big dent at the back of it that had been caused by someone who'd reversed carelessly, ramming their car into his. He never found out who did it, but it reminded me that he was not indestructible. That Rob Macrae, too, could be hurt. He could be stopped.

I went into the farmhouse first. I think my mind had been on getting something to eat before anything else. I wasn't making plans as such, but I knew - whatever happened - I wasn't going to be sticking around. I didn't know where my next meal would come from once I left. I had some idea of taking something, sticking it in my pocket.

Mum and Pilgrim had been sitting at the farmhouse table when I got in. It must have been getting on for eleven o'clock, and I remember being surprised - relieved - to see them there. Mum had a black eye but apart from that they seemed intact. My brother's eyes, wide and scared, had taken me in unhappily as I'd walked through the back door. They'd been waiting up for me, I sensed that much but ... they had hoped I would not come?

'Lawrence.' My mother's voice, a mere apologetic croak, had told me all I needed to know. He'd got to them. He'd scared the hell out of them. To even speak to me now was to be a collaborator. I was the new official enemy.

'Lawrence, you need to get out of here ...'

'Get out and go where?' How surprisingly calm I had sounded. Feelings were an unnecessary luxury, I saw it so clearly at that point. I took a glass from the draining board and filled it up to the top with tap water. I remember it tasting faintly of squash because my little brother never properly rinsed out his glass. He only pretended to, and then stuck it on the draining board. I remember how that had amused me for some reason, that faint taste of orange squash in my mouth that evening. It was like a private joke between me and me; the me that knew the truth about the way things were, and the me who knew that all our lives we'd been pretending they were different. I drank the water down. Strangely, I was no longer feeling hungry.

I'd looked at the clock.

'He told us we had to wait up for you,' my mother answered my unspoken question. There were grey lines around her eyes I saw now. We should have been speaking about what he had done to them, *about what he had done to my dog*, debriefing, filling each other in on all that had happened since I'd last gone out but somehow we weren't. Because somehow, I was now on the wrong

281

side of a line that had been drawn down the middle of my family.

'He told you to wait up?' I'd looked from her to my brother and there seemed to be no breath in the room, no light, just a greyness that hung around all the corners, filled up the spaces under their eyes. *He'd told them a whole lot more than that, hadn't he?*

Like what he was going to do to me when I got back.

What he was going to do to them?

'Where is he?' I'd looked at Mum. How did she look, I think, the last time I laid eyes on her? I hadn't taken her in so well. I'd regretted that, after. That I hadn't marked her well enough and I'd been left with no real memory of the last time I saw my mum. I'd been feeling angry at her too, I suppose, for being as weak as she was. For not being strong enough to stand by my side so we could have defeated him.

He was somewhere around the farmhouse, I could sense him. I could smell it as clear as the fear that came off them that he was somewhere in the vicinity. Wherever he was, I was going to find him.

Mum had muttered something beneath her breath then, something that I could have taken to be anything, but I thought I heard;

'He's in the barn.'

Did I really go over and tousle my brother's spiky ginger hair, hug him briefly, or did I only imagine that, afterwards? I know I never said another word to Mum.

'Lawrence,' she'd said, the plea in her voice - it was a mother's plea, I know that now but at the time all I heard was a down-trodden helplessness in her voice that made me feel even madder. It made me feel even more determined to go out and smash something.

It made me even more determined to smash *him*.

'It's late,' that voice came again. 'Don't go out there, Lawrence, He'll do for you. He's sworn it.'

I went, though.

282

I had no weapon on me. Strange as it seems now, my hands, cracked and blistered as they were from the afternoon's digging, felt as strong as a wrestler's hands. They felt powerful and capable of doing anything I wanted them to do. Just then, I didn't have the full measure of my father's strength calibrated right in my mind. The rage I was feeling inside made me the powerful one. It made me feel able to do things I would not normally be able - or want - to do. Pitch and Ranger, two of the Rotties, followed close at my heels as I strode out to the barn. The door was closed by the time I got down there, but it was not locked. I stepped inside. It was pretty dark. I remember I could hear someone stumbling around in there. I assumed he must have been drinking. That would fit the profile all right. Chip and Slash, the Pitbulls, were already there, waiting outside, growling unhappily at the door.

It should have alerted me, that. I see it now. My mind was too focused elsewhere to notice that the dogs were unhappy, sensed an intruder. They'd never have been making those sorts of noises for my father, but I didn't notice that. Their throaty growling, their menace, those things only mirrored my own feelings.

There was precious little light in the barn that night. That should have alerted me, too. *Why didn't it?* If Rob Macrae had been in there, doing whatever he was doing at this late hour, he'd have brought adequate light with him. I didn't stop to consider any of that, that evening. I didn't stop to consider anything.

I didn't want to know.

Seeing those dogs on the loose outside had brought my earlier loss back into sharp focus again. I wanted my Kahn back! Rob Macrae had killed him. Callously, and cruelly, he had killed him. He'd kill me next. He knew by now what my intention had been; he'd kill me too. Was he waiting out in the barn on purpose, I wondered now? So that when he bludgeoned me to death - or whatever else it was he'd got planned for me - I wouldn't be in the house. He didn't like mess in the house, my dad, and those blood-stains - they'd be hell to get out of the carpet.

Then I spotted the tools he must have used to take Kahn

down. The stun-gun and the darts. I saw them, the silhouette of them, up against the wall by the door. I thought of him loading up that gun, aiming it. I thought of my friend, my dear, devoted, big old friend, as his legs must have crumpled beneath him, not knowing what had hit him, not understanding what was going to happen next.

I picked up the shovel that was lying there, handy, near to the door and something snapped in me then. If there was any more blood to be shed tonight it wasn't going to be my blood, that was for sure. It wasn't going to be Mum's or Pilgrim's, either.

Not tonight.

Rose

What am I supposed to do, now?

He wants me to go away and leave him in peace, that's obvious. Maybe he just doesn't want me to see him throwing up? It's messy; not a pretty sight, it's distressing. But what is it that's upset him so?

What on earth can it be?

I don't like to leave him out there all alone in the cold but I have to respect his wishes. Reluctantly, I close the chapel door, giving him his space. The faint warmth from the brazier draws me in, my fingers outstretched above the top of the fire, warming my body, but I can feel my hands trembling.

Was it because of what I told him? Perhaps ... I've triggered off the memory of a time when his father beat *him*, I'm thinking. He's gone into some sort of shock. Seeing him like it, has kind of shocked me, too. It's scared me.

I bend to pick up the ice-filled bucket. I balance it over the fire to melt the snow for water. I need to make him a strong cup of tea, with plenty of sugar. I need to do something, but there is precious little I feel I can do, not until I know what the matter is. Why doesn't he just tell me? I fret. Maybe I shouldn't have told him anything about my dad. Everything was okay up until I mentioned that, I recall now. I was sitting cradled so comfortably in Lawrence's arms. We were both so happy. The memory of what we did last night floods through me again and I recall that I now know what it means to feel *on top of the world*. I was feeling so complete. Everything was so perfect. Lawrence had been happy, and seeing him like it had made my own happiness a hundred times greater.

I had wanted to stay there in his arms. I wanted ... for him to know everything about me. All the things I don't normally jump to tell people about. About my life. About Mum. About what happened to Dad. All those slightly shameful, out-of-kilter things in my life, I'd wanted Lawrence to know them all, to know *me*. He'd begun to let me into his world too, hadn't he? He'd told me about how hard his childhood had been, why he'd had to run away. Was it that, maybe, that brought on his sickness?

I feel a distinct queasiness in my own stomach now. Maybe it's catching. Maybe it's a bug and nothing I told him about at all. Maybe it's something in these decrepit old tea bags? I put one of the tea bags in the cup as the ice starts to melt over the fire. Little chunks of ice start to clink together, move apart. The heat moves up slowly, taking an absolute age. I heap a large amount of sugar into the cup. I know it's not the tea bags. The pain in my own stomach gets worse. It feels like something is gripping my guts from the inside and I know that what that something is, is fear.

I'm going to lose him, aren't I?

He'll come back in any moment. He'll explain. A flood of comforting, reasoning thoughts rush to fill the empty void of panic and fear that has opened up in me; any minute now he will come back in and he'll look at me sheepishly and there will be a perfectly *acceptable* explanation for his sudden sickness. I look at my watch, for no other reason than that the ice is taking so long to melt, the minutes are trickling past too painfully slowly and he isn't coming back. It is 7.45 am

I should be ringing home this morning, I think, reluctantly. I meant to go back home today, didn't I? I'd planned - if the weather had not let up - that I would let them know of our situation up here. I thought maybe they'd be able to send a tractor to clear the route or something. We have no food left. We couldn't have stayed up here indefinitely, I knew that. How I was feeling yesterday, I couldn't have got out of here soon enough. I don't feel like that anymore, though. Last night changed all that. Last night made me think I'd happily live on boiled water and air with him - as long as I could be with him - till the spring came.

Oh Lawrence, what's gotten into you? What's spooked you so?

It is a good twenty minutes later before I hear the chapel door being pulled open, again. I jump up, my heart suddenly thudding. I have his tea ready, with the sugar in it. If he wants it. I'm ready to hear him, if he wants to tell me anything, if he needs to say ...

He will *say*, won't he?

I look at him anxiously as he steps in through the door at last. His face looks grey and drawn. He looks - almost like a different person than the one I woke up beside this morning. It's shocking.

'Please.' I indicate the canvas sacking beside the fire. 'Sit down.' He comes in, but he does not come and sit beside the fire. As soon as he's pulled the door closed, he slides his back down the wall, till he's slumped with his knees up against his chest. I watch as he wipes the faint sheen of sweat away from his brow with his sleeve.

'Are you going to tell me?' Tentatively, I ask the question seeing that he's not going to volunteer it. 'What brought all that on?' I hang my head, aware that it may still be partly my fault, something that my words brought up for him. I hear him swallow, hard. I can hear the grief that he's holding; I can hear it in his breath, in the heaviness in his chest.

'Something scared you?' I whisper at last.

He turns his face away, shakes his head at me, as much to say - *not for your ears* but I feel a surge of desperation coursing through me at that. He has to tell me! He can't leave me like this, not after all we've shared, not after what we've become to one another ...

'Was it something I said?' His hand is over his face now. *Oh*

287

God, Lawrence, what did I say? What did my words bring up? 'You have to tell me,' I say hoarsely. I put my hands on his shoulders and I can feel the juddering of every muscle, every bone, every fibre in his body at my touch. 'Whatever it is, you can tell me. You *must* tell me,' I plead.

'I nearly killed a man, once.' His voice is so soft I can barely make out the stark words he's just uttered. Did he really say what I thought I just heard?

'Sorry, what did you …?'

'I said. I nearly killed a man.' Louder, this time. He looks up at me and his deep brown eyes are pools of remorse.

But I think I am beginning to see what did it. I told him about the person who beat up my dad. He's telling me that he once nearly did the same thing to someone else.

'If you *did* nearly kill someone,' I point out. 'It'll have been in self-defence, right?'

It has to have been; he's no thug. He said it before; he only went into the medical profession because he wanted to spend his life helping people, not hurting them. And, not through his own fault, but he hasn't always kept the best of company. Maybe it was one of those louts up in Bradford he hurt, while trying to protect his Indian family?

'It would have been justifiable,' I say stoutly, ready to defend him. He looks so different at this minute, he looks younger, more vulnerable, more cut up and I know, whatever he once did, whatever else he was once involved in - right now he needs me to believe in him.

'It was not *justifiable*, Rose. What I did to that guy was not justifiable. I told you, I warned you …' he rubs at his eyes fiercely now, 'That I wasn't what you took me to be. The gentle, lovely guy you thought you saw … that's not me.'

'You're *everything* I took you to be.' I touch his hand gently. 'You are caring and honourable and … and good. You're good, Lawrence. And I …' I swallow. 'Well, I think you already know how I feel about you.'

'You don't know me,' he says in a broken voice. 'If you did, you wouldn't feel the way you do. You feel too deeply, Rose, that's the problem. Your feelings won't always steer you true.'

'Try me.' I sit down on the floor beside him and the flagstones by the wall are hard and cold against my legs but I don't care as long as I can be near him.

'They won't. It's better to temper those feelings with a good dose of self-protection, learn to keep your distance a little more.' He looks at me painfully now.

'Like you?'

'I try, Rose. I too once let my blind emotions get the better of me.' He looks at me, his face grey with unease and I wish I could just hug him close. I wish I could make everything all right for him again but I sense, in my deepest heart of hearts, that I cannot.

'You're not going to understand this,' he says slowly. 'You will not understand this nor will you ever ...' his voice catches, 'be able to forgive me.'

'What do I have to forgive?' I whisper. I lean in close to touch his face but shockingly, he flinches back. He does not want me to touch him. He does not want me near. All the intimacy we had gained, my heart sinks, all the closeness we felt towards each other last night, where has it gone, why is he pushing me away like this?

'I don't want to tell you, but I owe you this much, and I'll tell you. You need to understand ... when I did what I did that day ... I started off telling myself I was doing something that needed to be done, but I ending up acting out of blind fear, loathing and rage.'

'We've all done wrong at one time or another. Hurt people that we never meant to do ...' he blanches, and I pause. 'There will have been a reason, though,' I press gently. 'Feelings like that don't just brew up out of nowhere. He will have been ... in the wrong place at the wrong time, that poor guy. But that doesn't make you a monster. You've felt remorse for what you did, I can see that. It's been haunting you ever since?'

'Oh, Rose.' He slips his own clenched white hand into mine, pulls it up to his face. 'You have no idea. You have no idea …'

'Tell me,' I say gently. He says I don't know him, but I need to know him. I need to know everything. 'Tell me what happened.'

Lawrence

'That man I told you I nearly killed the night I finally snapped ...' I look up now as Rose pushes a warm drink into my frozen hands. *When did she get that for me?* I shake my head, trying to concentrate. 'Rose, that was a mistake.'

'Of course it was a mistake,' she says stoutly.

'*I mean*, I thought he was my father, Rose.'

She sits back down in front of me again, her elbows on her knees, just touching mine and I long to be back in the place where I was with her just an hour ago. I long to find some reason not to say what I know I'm going to have to say next.

'Your *dad*?' she says and I see her taking that in, processing it. She's heard second-hand about some of what I'd suffered at his hands but she's never known violence in her life, this girl. There have been other sorrows, no doubt of it; her mum dying, her dad injured and all the rest of the cavalcade of broken dreams but she's never known violence like I have. She's never known what it's like to be hunted. Could she even begin to understand?

I nod.

'He'd tied my dog to a tree,' I tell her in a dull voice. 'He tied him there and left him to die. I knew he'd discovered my plans to get the family away from him. I knew he'd want his revenge. You have to understand ...' my voice takes on a pleading tone. 'I never wanted any truck with my father, Rose. He was a vicious and brutal man and I never wanted to be like him but that night

291

I saw ... *I saw* that the only way we'd ever be rid of him was if I could become *more* like him, better at being Him, more savage and ruthless than even he was.' She looks up suddenly and I catch a glimpse of the look in her eyes, full of sympathy and horror and sadness all at once.

'So I went looking for him.' The memory opens up, a sudden vista onto a long-ago day, how the well-oiled doors at the back of the barn opened obligingly for me, soft as a whisper. 'He would never have heard me coming. It had been raining hard that day,' I tell her softly. I remember the acrid smell of the wet straw, the barn-yard smell hitting me as I let the door close silently behind me. There was only a dim lantern in there.

'I remember being frustrated that there was barely any light; that this thing would have to be done in semi-darkness. Now that I'd psyched myself up to facing him, I wanted to be sure he knew that it was me who was doing it; I wanted there to be no mistake about it.'

Her eyes narrow at the tremble in my voice, because I have already told her *that there was a mistake*, haven't I?

'When I first caught sight of him,' I continue, my voice a croak, 'he was a dim figure at the far end of the barn, he had his back turned to me. His head was bent in a strange, almost apologetic manner that I'd never associated with my father before. It almost stopped me in my tracks ...' For one second, his hunched shoulders nearly made him feel too human. I thought; *maybe this has really affected him, knowing that we were all prepared to leave him this way? Maybe there is some humanity tucked away in the far reaches of his dark heart?'*

She makes a small sound in her throat because I know she does not want to hear what happened next.

'I thought that but then - right at the same second my eyes lit upon the tools he'd have used to take down Kahn. The stun gun complete with the darts he'd have needed to subdue my dog were all there, discarded on one side. There was also a heavy metal shovel lying beside it on the floor. Just in case Kahn hadn't been completely knocked out by the first shot.'

'You hit him with it?' she winces.

'I hit him with it *once*.' I wring my hands together, getting the words out. 'After the first cry rang out he never made another sound. It was so dim I could barely see but I heard the crash as his body fell heavily to the floor. His flailing arms sent the lantern spinning so I couldn't even see him after that but I knew exactly where he was.' She gasps, and I can see how she is affected by this new revelation from me.

'I kept expecting him to get up and come after me, Rose.' I remember how I'd been psyched up for that; his reaction to the fact that somebody had finally taken a stand. 'I stood there expecting him to jump up and lash out with his fists any minute ...'

'And ... he didn't?' Her voice is a whisper. 'He didn't come after you?'

'No. I must have hit him real hard, Rose. Harder than I'd meant to.' The terrible stillness and silence of the body as it lay slumped on the barn floor, returns to me now. I remember waiting there in complete and utter dread after I'd done it, telling myself that my father must surely be faking it. He was as strong as an ox, I knew that. He was faking it so when he turned round and suddenly grabbed my ankles I'd get the same shock as I'd just given him. I wouldn't get away with it, he'd never let me ... But he didn't get back up.

'He didn't do anything. He just ... he didn't move. I thought I'd killed him.' Rose has half-covered her face with her hands at this moment, still watching me. Does she still believe that I am so *honourable and good?*

I think maybe not. I think maybe right now she's asking herself who was the guy she slept with last night, *who was he?* Because he sure as hell wasn't who she thought he was. And we haven't even got to the full truth of what happened, yet.

We haven't got to the crux of my terrible mistake.

'That's when you ran away.' Her voice is a whisper. 'You left the family behind. You thought you'd *killed* him?' She winces, acutely uncomfortable, but still she places her hand on my knee. I know I do not deserve it, but I am grateful for that, for her touch. Her fingers are small, light as snowflakes, but I feel her acutely. *This will be the last time she ever touches me,* the thought falls like a waterdrop from the ceiling, sizzling into my mind. When she finds out what I did, she will alert the whole world to my presence up here; I know she must do. She wanted justice, didn't she? She told me this the day we spoke about her dreams, how she wanted to go to Uni, how she wanted to prove there was still some justice out there. It's because the man who hurt her dad has never been brought to book? She will blow my cover here, yes, and then I won't be able to help Sunny but it's even worse than that.

When she knows ... a violent spasm spirals up from my chest and into my throat, making me cough, making me almost choke ... when she finds out the truth, she will hate me. She will not want to speak to me or even look at me ever again.

But right now, I can see she is still struggling to make sense of what I've told her, she's wrestling with my confession so she can put it in a box labelled 'acceptable' in some form.

'Lawrence, I can't even imagine how bad that must have been for you. How terrible that must have felt ...'

I look away, knowing that I do not deserve her compassion.

'It didn't *feel* bad, Rose.' I catch her eye, wanting her to understand. 'After I hurt him, that's when I *stopped* feeling bad. That's when all the pain I felt at losing Kahn just upped and went.' She looks pained, puzzled. 'I know. I didn't understand it myself at first, but then I saw that maybe I'd lopped some essential part of myself off in order to do what I did.' I pause, and then I say it. 'Maybe it was my heart?'

My mouth is twisting into strange shapes, now, making it harder for me to tell her the rest. 'When I walked out of there that night all I felt was numb. The fact that I'd be leaving my mum and brother behind ... I felt okay about it. They would have to clear up the mess, that was true, but at least now, I figured, they'd be free. I'd saved them. I didn't have to worry about my dog anymore, he was gone. I couldn't afford to grieve for any of them. I had to get away. I'd done it. I'd finally found the courage to take my father on and show him that he could be hurt too.'

I see a new thought cross Rose's mind now. She frowns; she doesn't say anything, but I mark it. It's like encountering a bump in the road, just a little bump where you carry on but you know later on you're going to find you've got a nail stuck in your tyre.

'It should have been my moment of sweetest triumph, Rose, but it wasn't. It was as hollow as a defeat. For a long time I ran through the woods, desperate, *numb*, all I could hear were his last words to me, ringing in my ears … *in the end I have to win, even if it means finishing the lot of you* … I'd taken him at his word, annihilated him first. Sorted it. It was His way though, and that was the problem.'

'That guy in the barn …' Rose's face, so close to mine, her voice, whispering and suddenly tremulous, brings me immediately back to the present 'You just told me he wasn't your father.' It's coming back to her now. That the man was someone else. That that might be significant.

'No.' I look up at her suddenly, aware that up to this point she has been listening intently but now she has moved a little further away from me. Her hand slides softly off my knee. It is a small movement, a slight adjustment in position but it is like a faint powdering of snow blowing off a mountain-top, barely anything at all, a breath of wind, but it presages an avalanche.

It is coming to her, I know. What I did. Who I am, even though I have not come out and said it in so many words. Not yet.

'I never meant to hurt him, Rose. I took the wrong guy down, that's all.'

'That's *all* …?' She has got to her feet shakily and I'm aware of a distance and a faint dread in her manner that wasn't there before.

'If he wasn't your father …' I watch her standing there now, her breathing coming slightly hard and uneven. What is going through her mind? I can see the short puffs of her breath from the light that's streaming now through the little windows. I can see the stray tendrils of hair around her head, like a halo thrown into relief by the fire. She can't quite bring herself to look at me at this moment. When she looks at me, she will see the truth etched into the remorse in my eyes, and I know she fears this. She dreads to know it.

'What was his name?'

'What?' My tongue is so thick in my mouth, reluctant to speak. Now that we've come to it, I find that I have not the courage in me. I can't tell her.

'His … his *name*.' She shakes her clasped hands in front of her, a pleading gesture. 'Tell me his name, Lawrence.' I frown.

It occurs to me now that I never knew what his name was. I shake my head.

'*I'm sorry, Rose*. I didn't even know it wasn't my father till my friend Marco caught up with me.' I stand up, and she backs away from me, her eyes widening slightly.

'You don't know his name?' She doesn't believe that. I can see it in her eyes. She thinks that I *must* know. That nobody can make a mistake like that - and not stick around to see it through, check out the damage, make some amends …

But I'd run, hadn't I? I hadn't waited to find out who he was. If I'd got caught I'd have done time for it, no question. After the years I'd spent being flung in the bunker, I couldn't be banged up again. Not again. I could not be in a place where I could not walk out on a whim and see the sky. Where the smell of stale air is mixed with the smell of fear in the darkness and the door - the door remains shut on you no matter how long or how loud you call out for. Where nobody is coming, no one is ever coming to save you. How could she - a girl like Rose - ever understand that?

Really, how could anyone?

'*It was an accident, Rose*. I got the wrong guy.' She wants his name. I do not have his name, but I know who it was I hurt that night. She knows it too; I can see it in the trembling in her mouth, in the way she's still trying to hold it all in, all the horror of it, her hands clasped into tight fists, hoping and hoping with all her heart that I will say some other name, that it will be some other poor unlucky guy.

'Marco begged me to stay and work it out but after that I knew I could never go back to Macrae Farm. I ran, Rose. I've been running ever since ...'

'Macrae ... *Farm?*'

I knew the minute I said the word - *that word, Macrae* - that my whole life would unravel before me. That then she'd know, as clear as I did, where we stood with one another. That I am her enemy. I am the son of the man who's caused them the most aggravation. I am the man who hurt her father, ruining his life and hers. Oh Rose, Rose ... it was so many years ago and that's not how I wanted things to be. You wanted to know me, and now you know me; forgive me, that is who I am.

'I am so sorry, Rose. I'm so very ...' The words threaten to stick in my throat and choke me but she isn't even listening, anymore. She's just standing there, staring at me with the most terrible distraught look on her face.

The moment stretches out. This moment where I have been thrown into the pit of my deepest shame and humiliation. The day grows darker outside. I can see it, behind her head. The light coming through the windows shrinks, as I wish I could shrink, it fades like a dot on a screen. I think now; maybe her mother was right, *that what we do to others, it comes back to us three-fold*, all the good and the bad and the indifferent, it all comes back to us. I have only been shown the joy of loving this girl so it could be taken from me. I have only been led to feel again so that I might feel the pain of losing her now.

And I do not want to lose her.

She steps up and for a moment all I can feel is shock, that she wants to come so close to me, shock that she is not running away, instead.

And then she slaps me; an open-handed, no-holds-barred blow, right across the face. She slaps me so hard, this small and

297

fragile-looking girl, I don't see it coming and I reel back with the force of it, put my palm to my cheek which is throbbing with the blow. Then she hits me again and the mug of tea she made me goes flying out of my hands. It lands on the stone floor with a clatter, all the tea spreading like dark rain across the floor, and the noise as it bumps and rolls across the flagstones echoes strangely in my ears, *clack-clack-clack* and it feels as if this is not really happening, not here, not now. I feel - as I have so often felt before - that I am not really here.

'Rose.' My voice comes from somewhere deep within my throat, but she doesn't stop. I've got my elbows up, protecting my head, fending off the blows that she's raining down on me, her small fists are sharp and determined but none of it hurts. Strangely, it's only the feral, guttural cries coming from her throat that tear at my heart.

I'm sorry, I never meant to hurt you like this; it was never supposed to have been him ...

She keeps hitting me and hitting me. On my legs, my arms, my head. Pounding me with both arms wherever she can land a blow but I can't feel a thing.

There is nothing I can say that she will hear right now, I know that. I can see it on her face, in her eyes that are shining with a terrible and inconsolable pain. I'm sorry Rose. I'm not who you thought I was, right? Not who you wanted me to be.

I wanted to be him, though.

That guy you fell so madly for. I wanted to be him. When I loved you earlier ... that was like nothing I've felt with a girl before. I've never let my guard down like that. When I loved you, I wasn't a wanted, violent criminal anymore. I wasn't a coward who ran. I wasn't a battered and abused child. I wasn't my father's son. I was just ... me, Lawrence. Fresh as the day I was born with no dark blots on my past and a whole clean page on which to write my future. Oh, Rose, I was just me. A man who a girl like you could really come to love.

I want you to love me.

I lower my arms from my head and her next blow catches me square in the jaw, drawing blood as she opens up an old cut on the ridge of my cheekbone. I groan out loud. I put my finger to the cut and my blood is warm, I can feel the bruise that's already swelling up just under my eye.

She stops. I hear her gasp, and then she's on her knees, facing away from me, but I can see her whole body shaking with sobs, her words muffled by her hands, which she's using to cover her face, but after a time I think I can make out what she's saying.

'I know his name.' She's crying into her hands, over and over. 'Lawrence, *I know his name …*'

Rose

This is too much to take in. Oh God, I can't. I can't take this in! Too many emotions, too many thoughts all swirling round like the flashing lights on a fairground carousel and for the moment I can feel nothing but numbness, confusion. Even though I am very still, my heart is beating very fast. I can hear it whooshing in my ears. Nothing makes sense right now. What did I just do? I hit him. He told me things. I hit him, but ...

I don't understand what's just happened here. All these things he's just told me about the dog that was tied up and the lack of light in the barn and how he'd wanted to get his family away. I hardly heard any of his words, just now; I was trying to follow him but all I could hear was that he was dying inside, telling me them. All I could hear was the beat of it, the stutter and the stumble of his words, strangling him with his own confession, and how he didn't want to be around me anymore, telling me any of it. All I could pick up was the thud of his heart, running away, wanting to get away from me.

Wanting to run.

I don't want it to be true.

But I know that it is true. He's a Macrae. The thought creeps in, trickling like muddied floodwater under a farm gate; Lawrence is the man who attacked my father five years ago and destroyed his life. *Lawrence is the man who has ruined my life.* The realisation is dawning, slow and sure as the sun coming up over the horizon. He has toppled all my dreams down like he toppled that house of those cards of his, *and then he ran away.*

How could you be Him? Oh, God. Of all the people in the world that you could have been, how could you be Him, Lawrence? How could you do this to me? No, no, no. It cannot be him, my heart is crying out. That *coward* who crippled my father, he can't be Lawrence. It doesn't make sense; not the same man who held me so close and showed me that I was not the one responsible for my mother's death; not the man who loved me so tenderly last night, and made that experience so much more than I had ever dared to dream it could be ...

I've just heard the faint *click* of the door shutting.

Has he gone out? Has he gone?

He's gone out, left me. We could not both be in here together anymore, I know that. I could not bear to look at him, or *be* anywhere near him. The pain in my chest is too deep and wide, there is not enough room in here for it all, even though I'm still doubled up, still on the floor, trying to hold it all inside.

You ran, Lawrence. How could you do that? You *ran away*, that's the bit I can't deal with at all.

I couldn't run from what you did, could I? Dad couldn't. After the night you attacked him and left him for dead, my father has never been able to run since. He's barely been able to walk. I don't understand. How could you have done what you did and never stayed behind to see what damage you'd caused, never stopped for a moment to see *who* you'd done it to, even? Oh, I've sat here and listened to the terrible things that have happened to you and my heart has bled for you, Lawrence.

But shall I tell you what it was like for me in the aftermath?

I lift my face, now. My hair is covering my eyes but I can see the dark wall in front of me. I know that he is gone. I can see the thin light from a high-up window making grey inroads into the chapel. I feel ... very raw and very fragile. As if the slightest movement might break me; as if the slightest sound might split my head in two.

Shall I tell you what it was like to go down to the kitchen for a drink one evening and find my father wasn't in the house anymore? To find only the note he'd left me?

'Gone to Macrae Farm' it said. He must have taken extreme care to close the squeaky front door quietly, not wanting to disturb me. He went out after he thought I wouldn't be down again for the evening. I've always imagined he'd hoped I'd never know a thing about it till the morning. He went after I should have been asleep, after there was no chance of me trying to dissuade him, talk him out of it like I'd been doing all week.

I sat in the kitchen for over two hours waiting for him to come back. You won't know that, will you? You won't know what it could have felt like for me, sitting there in my PJs and an old jumper at one in the morning, scared out of my wits at what could have happened to my dad, fretting at why he was taking so long to come home. You wouldn't have known or cared about any of that because you were too busy *running away*.

At quarter past one, I picked up the phone and I called the police.

I was surprised at how little time they took to get there. Half an hour, maybe? It didn't seem very long. Maybe I'd sounded scared enough to worry them. Maybe it was the fact that I'd mentioned the name '*Macrae*' and that was enough to alert them?

I'll never know. They came and they read Dad's note and they went off to Macrae Farm together. They told me to wait there, not to open the door to anyone. Not to go out. By quarter to three, one of them was back at my house. Only one of them. Not two. The lady. If there had been no trouble, they would both have come back. But I didn't need to see her sorrowful face to tell me something bad had happened. I already knew that. I'd known it for hours, being the daughter of my mother that I am. I'd known it as soon as I'd seen his note. I'd felt it, that something really, really bad had happened.

That something that you did.

'There's been an incident,' the kindly policewoman told me.

302

An incident, not an accident. Even at thirteen, and in my muddled state, I'd been able to grasp that. She told me to get dressed.

Shall I tell you what it was like for me, waiting in the hospital corridor that night with no one but the porter to keep me company? The automatic doors kept sweeping back and forth letting the odd person in here and there. I kept looking up at first, half-hoping that some responsible adult might be coming in for *me*, someone to help me. I don't know who I expected; the Clares were abroad when the police tried to contact them. Mrs P hadn't been with us too long at that point. There wasn't anyone left, was there? The policewoman stayed as long as she could. The receptionist came away from her desk for a bit and held my hand. Everyone was so kind. You've never known much kindness, have you?

But the truth is, there are times when kindness can be a terrible thing. When you see it in other people's eyes and you know it springs from a deep well of compassion and pity for you and you don't want to see that pity, you don't want to see that 'Oh God poor girl, look' because it can only mean something really bad.

Do you know how long the hours between 3.30 and 7.30 am can be when you're thirteen years old and your one surviving parent is in intensive care fighting for his life? An eternity. That's how long. At least as long as it took every time for that shit of a father of yours to open the door of that World War Two bunker and let you out. Why didn't you beat *him* up, Lawrence? Why didn't you look your persecutor in the eye before you laid into him and then you'd have seen that you had the wrong guy? All you were creating was another victim - another set of victims - oh, God, *why didn't you check?* How the hell could you have done that to someone and not have checked you'd got the right person? It doesn't make sense ...

What also doesn't make sense - I sink my head into my hands now, berating myself - what doesn't make sense is that I could have had such strong feelings towards a man who was capable of doing what Lawrence did. What doesn't make sense is that there were so many signs and signals that all was not well - he kept telling me himself, he told me over and over, didn't he? - and I never paid any attention to any of them!

I imagined that I loved him.

To think I felt sorry for this ... this coward. I just made him a cup of tea. I held his hands and listened to his story, even though it was hard, because I wanted so desperately to make him feel better.

What a fool, what an easily-duped, stupid, naive little fool you must have taken me for. And you were right. You had me routing for you. You had me totally on your side, charmed out of my senses, trusting as a small bird who'd come to eat out of your hand, didn't you, Lawrence? All the while you knew *you* were the one the authorities must have been looking out for. You must have known it was you. The one everyone was being warned against - '... *don't approach any strangers'.* You. And instead of heeding that warning I let myself fall for you, hook, line and sinker. Idiot, stupid, little fool that I am. How could I have been that naive?

And how ... *how* could you have been so tender and caring towards me? How could you have *pretended* to be such a loving person when it is clearly plain that you cannot be? Nobody that has an ounce of feeling towards another human being could ever have done what you did. Oh, yes, you thought you were attacking your own brutal father - *great* - that makes it okay, does it? It's not okay! It will never be!

Now I think about it - I don't even know if I can believe what he's told me about his dad. Rob Macrae is a complete and utter bastard - everyone round here knows that - but would he really have tortured members of his own family in that manner? Word would have got out, surely? People round here talk about everything because for the most part they have nothing to talk about and yet ...

I put my hand to my forehead which has begun to throb with a deep and terrible pain ... what if it's true? What if Macrae did abuse his family and there were people around here who knew but turned a blind eye to it? Gossip-mongers or no, people round here don't always fall so readily to the side of the truth, the facts of the matter, do they? There were plenty of people willing to stick up for the Macrae's side when it came to the business of Top-fields. Plenty of folk willing to put expediency before the facts.

Well, maybe Macrae *did* torture them. Maybe at fifteen - sixteen, whatever he was, Lawrence had a good reason to want to save his family the only way he knew how.

Maybe he made a mistake, went for the wrong man. My dad was in the wrong place at the wrong time. But still ... Lawrence shouldn't have run away like that. If he'd stayed to face the music - how much better might things have turned out for Dad, I think painfully now. Dad wouldn't have spent all these years feeling so scared. It's the fear that was put into him that's done the real last-ing damage. God, all those nights he used to wake up screaming - I run my fingers through my hair, pushing away the memory - that was *fear*, pure and unadulterated. Fear that I remember Law-rence has felt, too.

But my thoughts return to my own father.

There were treatments he was offered, things he could have tried at the beginning, that Dad never even wanted to try because after he was hurt like that - some part of him fled. Something left the centre of him. I don't know what it was - I haven't the words - but I suspect it was the part of him that would have stood up and made him fight for himself. The police were never able to bring charges but everyone suspected he'd been attacked over the dispute at Topfields. If only he'd *known* that he had never been the intended victim and we were safe - that would have made such a difference to my Dad. I swallow down the pain of knowing this, that this revelation has come all too late, because five whole years have passed since the damage was done. Five winters, icy and wet; five summers, when the flowers all straggled up in the remains of the flower-beds in our garden and the earth kept on spinning like it does, from season to season but me and Dad had somehow got disconnected from it all. Our lives had got spun off their course, and we had no way of knowing how to get them back on track again.

You could have spared us that, Lawrence.

'Rose ...' I thought, somewhere faraway, I heard someone say my name, but there is no one here. Lawrence has not come back in again but, like a spell, it wakes me up. The cold flagstone floor is hurting my knees, I have to move. Painfully, pushing my hands against the floor, I force my body upright. How long have I been kneeling there? I did not know it was so long, but from the pain in my knees and legs, it has been a good while.

Where is he?

I get up, look around me. Part of me thinks; I don't care where he is. I want him out of my life. I never want to see him again, ever. Another part of me frets; if he's still outside, he'll be frozen to the core. He can't have got away down to the valley, not in this weather. I don't want him to have tried it. I don't want to be hearing, in a few days' time, that the police have recovered his body ...

A pang of real fear goes through me at that. My lips feel cracked and dry. I spy the cup which I knocked out of his hand, earlier. I'd pick it up except I don't know if I have the strength to bend and retrieve it right now. I feel like an egg with its shell cracked open. If I bend down I don't know if I'll ever be able to straighten again. I feel my own pulse quickening at the realisation that I hit him. I didn't mean to hit him. I don't know where that came from, and I feel a flash of shame at my own reaction, that I lashed out like that. He didn't try to hit me back, did he? He didn't try to stop me. I wince, remembering that.

Then I bend, suddenly, pick up the tin cup. The movement makes my head giddy but I do it. I cradle the cup close to my stomach. I never meant to knock it out of his hand. I feel a tug of anxiety that forces my gaze towards the door. *Where are you, Lawrence? Where did you go?* There *was* nowhere you could go to. We were trapped up here. Both of us. Is there really only just me left?

I don't want to be here alone.

The fire is burning low again. I drag myself over to it. After a few minutes go by I find the strength to shove another piece of wood into the middle of brazier. There are three bits of wood left now. Just three, unless I can manage to dig out some more myself. There are four crackers and three chocolate liqueurs left. Oh, God! I feel so cold, even in here, standing right by this fire. I need to get back home. I'm going to have to ring them, aren't I? Confess everything. They'll have to send some rescue crew or something up here for me, I can't stay here. And yet ... something is making me put the moment off, stopping me from picking up the phone and making the call. Something I can't put my finger on yet, but whatever it is, it's very strong. The minutes tick by. After a while I manage to put some ice in the pan to melt for water but I don't want any tea.

I realise ...

I want him back. Even though I know that is wrong, that it cannot happen. Even though I know that if he were to walk back in here right now I'd still be mad at him, still be *livid* at him, at how he's hurt me, how he's torn my family's life apart ...

Still, when I pick up the scarf Lawrence left to dry on the back of the pew, I can't stop myself putting it to my face as if it were part of him that's been left behind.

Lawrence

If I could … cut five years out of my life and that'd turn back the clock for her, I would do it. If I could give her father back his dignity and in any way alter what I did that night, I'd do it. But I can't. What's done is done and can never be undone, no matter how much I regret it.

I warned Rose that she didn't know me. She didn't believe me. She believes me now. Turns out I didn't know her, either. *Fucking hell - that it should turn out to be her father I hurt by mistake - how cruel is that? How fucking tragic is that?*

It is somehow fitting, though, because all the pain I delivered that night is back to haunt me in a way I never imagined it would. All along I've been trying to convince myself - she's a girl, just another girl along the road, no one special, no one I won't forget as soon as I'm on the next plane out of here. I've forgotten so many, don't even remember their names because none of them really counted for anything and I thought she'd be the same.

But she isn't.

She's someone special. She's someone that a person like me could never deserve.

What the hell was I even thinking, to imagine I could ever really make a difference to anyone in this world? I don't make any difference. I just create havoc, wherever I go. Even that guy I decked in Sri Lanka - it's caused major waves over there and

Dougie's been arrested because of it. Arjuna says he'll be let off today but what if he isn't? The authorities are after me everywhere - what good could I possibly be to a poor little sod like Sunny who's laying all his final hopes on me? I'm nobody's hero. I'm going to have to let him down, too. I can hardly even muster the energy to remember what I'm supposed to be doing here. I've got too cold. I've got too tired. Maybe my dad was right to throw me in the World War Two bunker all those years ago? He was always threatening that next time he'd leave me there to rot; maybe it would have been better if he had.

I'm sorry, Rose.

I hurt you so bad I want to climb up to the top tower of this broken castle and throw myself off it and die. I would if I thought that would make you feel better.

As I think it, I look up. I've scaled the eastern section of this tower once before, I remember. I did it on a spring day when I was fourteen, as a dare to myself. I did it because I was shit-scared of the thought of it and perversely that made me want to conquer it all the more. Why shouldn't I do it again, now? Climb up there. Get out of her way. A faint memory laps at the edges of my mind; there's a small ante-chamber up there. I think I remember it. It might be somewhere that I could find some shelter? I'm not sure of that at all. I could be wrong, it was so long ago. I rub the sides of my head, which are feeling numb. My ears have stopped burning with the cold but that's not good. That's because I can't feel them anymore. All I really remember is dangling off the edge of that tiny window ledge up there, looking down, the sudden certainty of my own death looming up at me.

I remember that, and how my arms had threatened to give out on me. The climb had been arduous. I'd been up all night and I'd had no strength left in my body. And then something had made me look up. And over the horizon the faint orange sun had been making its appearance over the trees, a new day, and - cheesy as that sounds - I'd suddenly realised that I wanted to be part of that day.

Do I still want to be part of this one? And the next, *without her*, now; knowing how my actions have hurt the only woman I've ever truly loved?

I dig my thumbs into my eye sockets and the darkness beneath my lids lights up with a bright flash of remembered sunlight. A dark shape jumps into the light now, reminding me of Kahn. It feels like him. The one friend I always knew would still be waiting for me when I found myself in this dark space before; the one reason I had to keep living when every last ounce of strength had been crushed out of me. He was what always kept me going, because without me I knew he'd be left to fend for himself, no one would see to him. The dark shape nudges forward, imprints itself more strongly on my mind and in the empty space in this silent courtyard I can almost hear his panting. I can faintly hear his paws, scuffing against the door of my prison, and I can feel him ... waiting; *willing* me to keep going till the time comes when I will be free again. *Don't give up wanting* my words to Rose earlier come back to me now.

Even though it would be much easier to give up wanting.

It would be so much easier to just give up.

The temperatures must be grazing minus-something. I slam my fists together inside my frozen gloves, blowing on the palms of my hands and an old survival instinct kicks in. I need to move. Painfully, I pull first one, then the other of my gloves off. I can't hook my fingers into the nooks and crannies of the walls with these on. I am going to climb up the icy wall to the chamber, and then - and only then - will I give in to this huge urge I have now to sleep. I have to stay alert a bit longer. If I fall, that'll be the end of me, I know. If I stay here, I'll perish anyway.

It has been dark for such a long time now ...

I don't look back but Rose is still trailing behind me. I know she is. I left her at her father's gate five minutes ago but when I stop I can still hear the crunch of her feet against the virgin snow on the woodland floor. It's so damn dark in here. If she comes in

310

too far she'll have trouble finding her way back. Where the hell even is she?

'Go home, Rose,' I shout over my shoulder but now that I've stopped I can only hear her getting closer, her breath coming hard because the air is way too cold.

For God's sake, just go home.

'I can't.'

I swing the torch round and she's standing right there behind me, shaking, shivering from head to toe but she's got a stubborn look on her face.

'You *can.*'

'I can't, because I won't just leave you.'

Has she forgotten? Has she forgotten what I did?

'*Lawrence.*' Now she's caught up with me I feel her small hand slipping into mine, and for a split second I allow myself to remember how good that feels. How delicious it feels to have a companion. Not to be alone.

'Don't go back there.'

'No?' I take her in tenderly. 'You want me to save myself?' I ask softly and my heart expands with hope and joy. Even knowing what she knows, she's worried that I'm going back to Macrae Farm; she still cares enough to come after me …

'Do you love me?' she asks. I feel her fingers tighten against my own and it's all I can do not to take her in my arms again. I groan inwardly, because I do love her. I love Rose more than I ever knew it was possible for me to love someone. I want her more. For a moment I just stand there, watching her: her huge, beautiful eyes, her pale face and her mouth, that mouth that I have longed to kiss since the first time I laid eyes on her …

'*Do you*?' she insists and I pull her towards me, close up against my chest because I want so much to keep her here close to me. I want so much to never have to let her go. And now she's pulling my head down to her, drawing me hungrily towards her own lips again. *Don't, Rose. I need to go. Please don't …*

And then I kiss her.

I kiss her, hard

'God, Rose. You know I love you. Tell me what you want, Rose.' My voice is hoarse, whispering hot breath into her ear and I can feel every fibre of her shudder beneath me when I say it.

'I want ...' She reaches up and kisses me again, her kiss urgent and longing for one sweet, too-short moment before she breaks away, breathless.

'I *want* you to stop running away.'

I laugh, lowly. I wind the rain-darkened strands of her hair around my fingers and hold her face captive, close to my own. 'That's not what I meant. You know that ...'

She turns her head slightly then as the muffled sound of the others, the ones who are still coming, still looking for me along the top lane reaches us.

Who are they? I frown. I can't even remember who they are, but they are interrupting us and I don't want to remember them. I will them to go away and for a moment, at least, they fade.

'You wanted something else a moment ago.' I pull her face back to my own, and I see her swallow. 'You did. Didn't you?'

'Lawrence, if you don't act soon,' she's protesting faintly, murmuring into my ear, '... *it's going to be too late.*' I kiss her neck and I can feel her shoulders relaxing, melting into submission under my touch.

'Too late for ...?'

She takes in a deep shuddering breath;

'Listen.' Her eyes look deep into mine and for a second I catch a glimpse of a determination and a love there that is even stronger than her desire.

'I *want* you to turn yourself in. Just do it. For me. For my dad.'

Jeez. She isn't going to let this go, is she? I pull my face back in disappointment and the angry revving of a tractor ploughing back up the hill chops through the air, cutting through my mood in a flash.

'Do it now and in time you'll be a free man again.'

312

I look at her painfully, at the hope shining in amongst the fear in her eyes.

'I will never be a free man again.' *Doesn't she know that?* She wants me to turn myself in. But her world isn't my world. She thinks it's a simple matter of doing the right thing, seeing justice served and in the end it'll all work out dandy just like in the movies but she doesn't have a clue … I return my gaze to the snowy path at my feet, pull my hand out of hers. I take a step backwards and away from her. Because I have to; the rain is hurrying the thaw along. Very soon the roads will be clear, everything will be moving again. I've got to get going. I see her face fall then, all the energy draining out of her

'Marco said you'd run. And he was right. You *are* running,' she breathes. 'He knew you were a coward.'

Marco never said that.

'He's the one who'd better run. If I ever catch up with him I'm going to ...'

'You're going to *what*?' Her momentary laughter is high-pitched, almost hysterical. 'You know who you sound like, don't you? For God's sake, Lawrence. You never wanted to turn out like your dad and here you are …'

I can feel the little tick going now at the side of my face. She shouldn't say that to me. If there's one thing in the world she shouldn't say it's that.

'Here I am …?' I stop. Turn to face her again, shining the torch on her face but she doesn't flinch.

'A true Macrae,' she finishes softly.

'That isn't true.'

'Isn't it?' She steps up and pushes me suddenly now in the chest. She's a little slip of a thing but she catches me off balance and I can feel myself falling now.

Falling and falling, and the night is so cold and black, it smells damp and earthy, my face feels wet with a little dribble that is coming out of my mouth and then everything is re-set and I am back there beside her.

'*Isn't* it true, Lawrence?'

I can feel my face darkening. I can feel all the troubles I have pushed to the back of my mind re-grouping suddenly, gathering like storm-clouds on a hill-side.

'I am nothing like my father,' I tell her thickly. 'Nothing.'

'…you don't love me, Lawrence. *I doubt*,' the choke in her voice echoes into the stillness, 'that you know what it is to care about anyone.'

'*Go home, Rose*.' I push her away from me again. 'I'm not good for the people who love me. I told you that, I warned you about that before. Forget about me …'

When I walk away from her this time, the crunch of my feet against the snow echoing so damn loud I think that all the world must hear it, I can't hear the sound of her following me anymore.

'You Macraes – you are all cowards and thugs to the last man,' she throws at me at last. 'Even you.'

Even me. I turn heavily onto my side and I'm suddenly aware of the floor in the ante-chamber beneath me smelling frozen and damp. The inside of my mouth tastes sour. God. I sit up abruptly, every bone and every muscle of me aching. Rose is not here with me. Have I been sleeping and only dreaming of her, then? I must have been. I left her … I left her in the chapel, I remember now. I screw up my eyes, angling my watch towards the small pin-point of light that comes through the narrow window to the left of me. My fingers and toes feel numb, which they did not do a moment ago.

Reality seeps back in. I climbed up here. Now I remember. I climbed up here and then I curled up into a ball and went to sleep. By my watch, I must have been dozing for nearly an hour.

Man, the dream seemed so real.

You are all cowards and thugs, I thought she said. *Even you.*

Perhaps she's right.

It's what I've always feared.

Rose

It is too quiet up here.

It is too dark, like a tomb. When I walk over to the other side of the pew to pick up my coat, my own footsteps sound edgy, sinister, make me feel as if there might be someone walking behind me. I have to force myself not to keep looking over my shoulder. I have to get out of here. I know now I have to try.

I'm going to have to make the call back home, aren't I? The one that lets them in on the truth, uncomfortable as it is. I'm going to have to start re-forging my links with the outside world and the family will find out where I have really been, who I have been with. They will find out about Lawrence.

I push the chapel door open, half-hoping that he will be there, waiting, just outside. But he is not. The footprints he made earlier are still clearly visible though, right beside the door. The sight of them makes my heart jolt. It reminds me that only very recently we were still together. It reminds me that hardly any time at all has elapsed since everything we had fell apart. *Where did you go to, Lawrence?* Tentatively, I follow the line of footprints in the snow but they all end mysteriously at the tower ruin. I bite my lip, disappointed; the wind that's got up now must have blown over all traces of his next tracks so I can't see where he went.

He has gone though, hasn't he?

That's the key thing. He's gone and I can't stay up here alone any longer. The morning is misty, dank. A solitary rook is skimming the snow-topped canopy in the valley below. Everything is white, iced over as before and yet ... something has changed. A low humming noise is coming from somewhere down in the valley now. I screw up my eyes to see. Two bright orange tractors, far away still, but definitely visible down at the bottom of the lanes have begun to clear the snow. The farmers are out at last, clearing the country roads. How come I didn't hear them before? I can hear them now! The realisation fills me with a ridiculous joy and relief; it brings a tear to my eye. It means that soon I will be able to get out of here.

It means ... I need to call home.

There are three bars of signal on my phone this morning, but there's a warning flashing too; battery low. On my eighth or ninth try, I get through at last. The phone rings in a crackly, breaking-up way, barely audible at my end. As it rings, I become aware of my palms feeling slippery, heart thudding harder in my chest, *pick up, pick up* ... I feel nervous. It's Carlotta who answers eventually.

'Hello?' she seems to be saying. The line is breaking up, crackling badly.

'It's Rose,' I tell her, shouting as loud as I can into the phone. 'Rose!'

'*Rose* ...?' she says. The sound of my aunt's voice brings a whole chunk of life back into my mind. My normal life; the things I usually have to worry about from day to day. *Is Dad okay? Has everything been okay back at home?* I don't know if I feel ready to reconnect with all that just yet. I don't know if I want to.

'Hello,' she comes back to my silence, her voice as faint as an echo but I can't make out her words after that. I imagine she's asking me when I'm coming home. I imagine she's giving me some news about my dad ...

'I'm not at Shona's!' I shout into the phone now, surprising even myself. 'I've been ... stuck up on the hill. I've been weathering it out at the old ruin ...' I pause, realising that I'm probably giving her way too much information all at once. *Does she even know where this is?* I need to take things a bit slower. It's Carlotta I'm talking to, here. I need to ... calm down.

'What did you say?' she comes back now. I can't make out, down this rotten line, whether she's even heard what I've just confessed or whether she's simply asking me to repeat what I've said. The family *are* going to be shocked when they know the truth though. The sinking feeling I had earlier hits me again. It's not just where I've been, either. It's *who I've been with*.

Lawrence.

Uncle Ty is going to hit the roof.

Dad is going to ... I gulp, filled anew with remorse for what I have inadvertently done ... He's going to be gutted. This is going to feel like a real betrayal to him, isn't it?

If only I had known who Lawrence was! I didn't mean for things to turn out like this. Surely - when I tell the family the whole story - they will understand that I didn't know who Lawrence was.

'Rose?' She comes back now, the line momentarily stabilising; 'Are you there?' There's an edge of impatience to her voice. Now we can hear one another more clearly I get a sudden misgiving over how much it would be prudent to say.

'Yes.' I want the family to know the truth, get it over with. I have to tell them, don't I? The thought occurs suddenly; Lawrence has confessed to what he did and now that I know it, I can have him apprehended. I *need* to have him apprehended, for Dad's sake. For justice. I don't let myself think of how frightened Lawrence was, of going to prison. I don't let myself remember that he's scared of being banged up, away from the daylight. That he cannot bear to be in the dark. I look around me at the empty courtyard and I think; *I need to do this soon, before Lawrence gets away too far. I need to let everyone know he has been here.*

'I've got to ... tell you something ...' I mutter. It's just that I'd also really like to know they're going to be understanding when they do find out.

'Rose, I can't *hear* you,' my aunt's saying irritably now. 'Speak

317

up louder please. *Speak up*.'

I don't want to speak up, though. My throat closes in fear.

It's too soon. This is all happening too quickly and I haven't had time to think of what to do for the best. I know *she* isn't going to be understanding, is she? Carlotta of all people. She will judge me, there's no question about that. If I tell her what happened, she won't give me the benefit of the doubt. She won't think - Rose has made some mistakes, and one mistake has compounded the other until she's found herself in this *unthinkable* position. She won't think - Rose is dying inside now, because the man she loves has done something so terrible there is no way back out of this for either of them. She won't think that. I can imagine what she will think.

Even now, even before I have come to the very worst bit, she'll be thinking; *what else can you expect from Isla's daughter? First the girl runs off. Then she lies to us about where she is, not caring about her dad or anyone else, selfish and untrustworthy* ...

My fingers squeeze tighter on the phone.

'Rose,' she says slowly, deliberately. 'Could you *repeat* what you just said to me, please?'

I stare at the phone.

'I'm going to have to ask for ... everyone's understanding,' I say at last in a croaky voice. 'Even though I know you'll all be mad at me because I haven't been upfront from the beginning about where I was ...'

There's silence at the other end as she must be taking all this in.

This is going to be much bigger than their reaction to me running off, the thought sinks in uncomfortably. They'll mobilise the police, of course. They'll find Lawrence, wherever he is. He won't get to speak to his mum. He won't get to do what it is he risked *everything* to come back here to do - save Sunny. My courage buckles and fails under the weight of it all. If I give him up now I'm scuppering everything that's kept him afloat for the last five years; his hope that he can do some good, his hope that he can put things right for others.

His hope for redemption.

'Where are you, Rose?'

Where am I? I think blindly. *Where am I with all of this?* I haven't had long enough to process everything yet. I haven't had enough time to consider all the ramifications and all the consequences of any actions I take now, any revelations that I make.

'Rose?' A tautness, right over the top of her voice, betrays an instability beneath; her sympathy and understanding are like a thin crust of ice, I think; a veneer that will crack if I try to put too much pressure on it, too soon.

'I'm not at Shona's,' I say again. At some level I'm not even aware of, I have made a decision, it dawns on me slowly. I am not going to mention Lawrence, am I?

Not now. Not yet.

'Look, I've run out of food. And it's real cold. The snow ploughs have started clearing the lanes but the thing is I fell when I came up here. I don't think I'll be able to make it back down without help.'

Carlotta is stunned into silence for a moment.

'There are reasons why I didn't tell you straight away where I was,' I tell her, my voice sinking. 'I knew you'd all worry about me and I thought the weather would break sooner. I'm sorry,' I say as she still doesn't reply. 'I'm sorry I ran out on you in a huff.'

That was a lifetime ago, I think. It was Christmas Day, the day I left home and came up here. That argument I'd had with my aunt - up to this minute, I'd forgotten all about that. But maybe she hasn't. Maybe she's thinking now that our argument was the reason I never came home Christmas night? That I've done all this on purpose? That I've stayed away because I was angry?

'Are you okay, Rose?' she asks unexpectedly.

'Yes. Look. I know it was wrong of me to run out on you,' I admit ... *just as it is wrong for me not to be telling you everything else that I know right now* ... My fingers are shaking so hard I think I'm going to drop the phone. Am I doing the right thing, here? God, am I doing the right thing? He'll get away. Maybe he will get to help Sunny and maybe he won't but I'm not doing anything to help Dad by my silence right now am I?

Oh, my word. I put my hand to my chest, trying to steady my own breathing, fearing she must surely hear that I'm holding something back, fearing that in saying nothing I am only betraying my dad all over again. Only this time I know that I'm doing it.

'I always meant to come back straight away, Carlotta. I only meant to get Dad's meds, and then I fell and I had to stay here. I made a mistake,' I say, my voice stronger. 'I'm asking you to forgive me for that.'

In time, I know there is lot more I will need to ask their forgiveness for.

'*Carlotta,*' I say, uncomfortable when she doesn't come back. Maybe she's still taking in the fact that I've told her I was hurt and I never mentioned it when I spoke to them on the phone? Heaven knows what she's thinking. It's not even what's important ... why has she gone all silent on me?

I stop, sheepish, suddenly realising that the line has gone dead. I try and recall when she last made a response to something that I'd said. How much of what I've said to her has she actually heard? The battery is still holding out - just - but the signal has broken up again.

Damn, damn! Stupid phone! I rush out through the softening sludge, make for the far point over the battlements where we've always been able to get a signal before, but there is nothing. She's gone. Damn it. I put my phone back in my pocket, useless device that it is. I didn't get a chance to make sure she knew where I was, did I? I blink, realising suddenly that I can't hear the sound of tractor engines anymore, either. The tractors that were doing such a fine job a moment ago, clearing the lanes, seem to have stopped. Why have they stopped?

They are still nowhere near here.

They are going to take *ages*.

God, I wish I hadn't even said anything to Carlotta now. I wish I'd saved it all for later. I didn't tell her the one thing they really needed know, did I? I didn't tell her that I'd been staying up here with the man who hurt Dad.

I rub at my eyes, which have begun to feel itchy and sore. Maybe it's because I was crying so hard earlier on, but it feels like I've rubbed sandpaper over my eyeballs. *Shit.*

Everything hurts. Even my leg which Lawrence stitched up, that has not hurt once in all the time I've been up here – that's feeling sore. My head is like an egg-shell. My fingers and toes are frozen to the point of burning and my stomach is cramping with hunger. I turn to look out over the battlements and I stare at the tractors for a long time, *willing* them to start up again but the men must have stopped for their break or something.

For the moment, everything is quiet, again.

I must be going mad.

I just let my best chance of getting help for myself, slip right through my fingers. I just let Dad's best chance of apprehending his assailant slip away too. Why? I can't say. I look down at my red hands, blowing on my fingers, desperately trying to get some warmth back into them. Trying to make them work so when I get somewhere with a signal at least I can dial. There's no signal out here just now. No way to contact them again. When it came down to it, I couldn't give Lawrence away, could I? Not without ... without giving him the chance to do the right thing.

Even though - the thought slips uncomfortably into my mind - he seems to have left me up here alone. Despite him knowing I've got a hurt leg. He'd be aware that - even with the farmers out now, clearing the lanes - I'd find it difficult to get home by myself. He took his backpack with him. If he cared about me, he wouldn't have left so easily, would he? I frown. Has he really left this place now so he can complete his mission for Sunny? I like to imagine so, but ... I pull a wry face, pulling my stiff gloves back onto my frozen fingers - the fact is, *I know his identity now*.

It could be that is why he left.

He didn't want to be caught, I suppose. He's been on the run all this time, in effect. No matter what else he's achieved in his life, he's still been on the run. A renewed surge of frustration courses through me at the thought. Now I know who he is, he must imagine the game is up. That I'd tell. When I get back home eventually and the truth comes out I know everyone will think that I should have told on him. I *know* that's what they will say, how they will react. It's what's making me feel so nervous right now, because I can't be sure I have made the right call. It's what's making me feel maybe I've been conning myself all along.

'Rose ...' When Lawrence speaks my name out loud at last, the shock of it makes me spin round. It makes me drop my phone.

He's standing some way behind me, at the foot of the tower ruin. I didn't see him come back from anywhere. I didn't hear him arrive.

Where did he come from?

I take a step back, even though I am not afraid of him. I am afraid of my own reaction to him, seeing him there again when I thought he had gone for good. Seeing his face look so white, his eyes haunted, remorseful and at the same time so full of ... *desire?*

I turn from him, not wanting to see it, wanting to be mistaken because it would be easier to believe he has no real feelings for me. Much easier. If all he's been doing is using me all along then I can walk away from this knowing for sure what I need to do next. What's right to do. That will be easier than drowning in this whirlpool of disgust at what he's done mixed with my own regret and desire for a man I can never be with.

'Rose I know how you must feel,' his voice sounds gravelly. I know his throat hurts. I know it's costing him to speak. To be here, in this space.

I can't do this. *No.* A sudden panic overtakes me, that we are even speaking to each other again. We should not be speaking, surely, not now I know who he is? He is *verboten*. I don't want to even look at him. I mustn't. I march right past him, ignoring him, but he follows me to the chapel and part of me is glad that he does and part of me is very, very scared.

'Don't follow me, Lawrence.'

He stops, already inside the chapel door. I hear him close it, gently. I hear the small click as it shuts. The small movements he makes remind me of someone who is aching, someone whose every muscle is being held in check, moving quietly and gingerly lest they take up too much space. His presence, so familiar, in the corner of the room, helps my breath to calm a little now. Even though he should not be here. I should not want him here.

But somehow, I do.

I still want what I should not be wanting.

I move a little closer to the fire and the contrast between the cold outside and the heat from being so near to the flames makes my body immediately overheated, the skin on my face feels taut as if it's toasting. I step back a little but my hands are so cold. I remember when he held me before, how everything was perfect. I remember feeling the warmth of his chest against my face. How I was so acutely aware of the strength of his muscles, holding me; how I felt so safely held that I wished I might never have to leave his arms.

I want him so much.

'How could you do this to me?' After such a long time of silence it feels strange to hear my voice again. The wide space between us yawns and closes down as he does not make any attempt to answer that. What possible answer could he give?

'How could you be that person?' I stumble. I turn to look at him at last. 'How could you have done what you did and never stayed behind to see what damage you'd caused ...?'

'Rose, I would give all the world for things not to be like this ...' Something - a guard Lawrence has put in place to protect himself - has collapsed, I feel it.

323

'It doesn't matter *what you would give*,' I carry on over him, my words jarring in the fragile air. 'It's what you *didn't* give that I can't understand. You didn't give a damn about the man you injured, did you? What you did to his life, his family ...'

'It wasn't like that ...' he whispers but I carry on talking.

'How is it you never stopped for a moment to see *who* you'd done it to, even?' My throat hurts but the words still keep on coming out because now I want ... *I want an explanation.* I want an acknowledgement. I see Lawrence is hurting because he's suddenly realised the connection between us, he knows it's *me* he's wounded. But why did he never come back and put this right before?

'Because I couldn't.' I sense Lawrence shifting in discomfort.

'You couldn't?' I bite my lip. He couldn't. Maybe that's true; a small realisation, like a wave lapping right up to a dry bit of sand on the shore, makes inroads into my mind.

'What about *now*, though?' I'm trying to keep the hope out of my voice, not to project too far into the future. He steps out of the shadows a little. I sense him, all of him, wanting something from me, needing something that he almost dares not hope for.

'*Now*?'

'Are you willing to turn yourself in, now?' He makes a sound in his throat, like a gasp. It is so quiet after that I think maybe the world has stopped turning for a bit. I think maybe I'm not even breathing anymore. Maybe he isn't.

'I know you'll think I'm a coward,' he says into the terrible stillness. After the long silence, his voice echoes strangely against the stone walls, bounces around the corners.

'You think so too, don't you?' I say without thinking.

'I'm not a coward, Rose.' He takes another step forward. Then another. He stops when he is still three steps away from me. Not so far away I cannot see the rapid rise and fall of his chest. Not so far I cannot hear the sigh as the breath leaves his lips, or ignore the supplication in his eyes. 'I have faced death many times.' So softly, it's almost a whisper. He has risked his own life to save the wounded on many occasions, I remember now. No coward would have visited the places he's been to, I know that.

'*Rose*,' he moves in tentatively, just touching my elbows. 'No coward would have risked the despair of loving again when love has only brought them pain and unhappiness in their lives.'

I pull a wry face, hardly daring to believe him. *Don't Lawrence, because I cannot bear to want you, to believe you, only to be disappointed again ...*

'I love you, Rose.'

I cannot answer him.

'If I'm a coward, it's because ...' he stumbles on, crushed. 'After all this time, I still can't bring myself to face my father.'

'Or the part of you that is so like him you could lash out at someone and nearly kill them?'

'Like him?' He looks at me, shocked. 'I am not like him, Rose. I never set out to hurt your father ...'

'You never went back to find out how he was, either.' My words come tumbling out, cold and to the point and laced with a deadly cocktail of the truth and I see that bit goes in. I see that hurts him but he's got to hear it. 'You never went back to tell him that you didn't mean to hurt him. Have you never thought ... that it might be something that he needed to hear?'

'For who to hear?' He's looking at me, dumbfounded. It *has* never occurred to him, I realise, not in all this time.

'*My dad*,' I frown furiously at him. 'The man whose life you were aware you had ruined, whose dignity you stole away. Your victim. Didn't it ever occur to you that he might still be living his life, every day - every moment of every day - in dread terror that maybe you'd come back sometime and finish the job? That you'd hurt him again. *That you'd hurt me*?'

'No!' He comes back as I pull away from him forcefully. *I can't bear you to touch me, Lawrence. I can't bear you to be near me. You* have *hurt me!*

325

'No, Rose. Because I put your dad out of my mind years ago.' I look up at Lawrence in surprise, despite myself. 'I had to. I put him amongst the debris of all the other things I couldn't bear to remember; like the wasted life of my beautiful Kahn, the shattered dreams of the life I'd hoped to spend with my family elsewhere. The fact that I haven't seen my mum in five years.' His words tumble out, shining and honest and raw and they silence me. 'The fact that I've never had any contact with her or my little brother in all that time. *My victim* ...' Lawrence steps up to me now, his face twisted with regret and frustration. 'If I ever stopped to remember him it was with regret that he was ever even there that night, because he got in the way. He stopped me doing what I had intended to do, which was to show my Dad that there was *someone* who'd stand up to him. He saved Rob Macrae's filthy hide.'

I gasp, and he steps back. I can hear his breathing, heavy and uneven.

'It was never what I intended, you know that.'

I turn my head away but his fingers are around my face, softly, insistently, drawing me back to him. I would pull away except I find that I cannot, my body suddenly has a will of its own. When he kisses me this time it feels different from all the other times but no less powerful. When he kisses me now I *feel* him, all the different parts of him, merging together like a kaleidoscope of all his memories and fears, everything he has been running from all his life, and all that he still longs for. I know the intensity of his pain and his love. For a moment, all of these things are there on his lips, trembling on mine. I feel it in his body which he has pressed close to me again, so close that we might for these few minutes have become one person, not separate anymore. In the urgency on his lips, there is something else, too. I know he wants me to understand what happened. He wants me to show some compassion. Lawrence needs me to forgive him and I ... I cannot hold out against him any longer.

What happened to my dad - it was never what he intended.

My hands reach up tentatively to his shoulders, to his neck. I kiss him back, softly. His mouth opens slightly in relief and wonder and I take in the slightly bewildered gratitude in his eyes, feeling myself momentarily giddy, almost faint with a sense of my own immense power.

'I have to forgive you, Lawrence. You know I love you.' I whisper the words into his ear and for a few seconds they feel like a blessing, like cherry blossom falling softly through the park on a spring morning.

'*You can't imagine, Rose*, how much you saying that means to me ...'

I think maybe I do know. Unexpectedly, it has released me, too. We don't have to be enemies anymore, do we? Whatever happens next, I can still love him. I *do* love him, I don't have to deny it, even to myself. My fingers reach up to twine around the short hair at the nape of his neck, wanting to touch him, wanting to remain in physical contact because I am aware that, now I have said the words, I feel a pensiveness. An apprehension. Because there is only one way forward from this and I know it is not a way he will relish.

'The thing is - Dad never even knew who you were,' I whisper. I can feel my whole body trembling.' He never knew why you wanted to hurt him so badly.'

'I didn't. I didn't want to hurt him ...'

'Then ...' I look into his eyes, hope lighting for the first time since I learned the terrible truth. 'Then I need you to come back with me and tell him that.'

Lawrence swallows. His hands come up to seek my own now. For a moment I feel his fingers, warm and loving, just as they were before, clasping mine.

'I can't do that, Rose.'

He can't. My stomach sinks but I keep my eyes on his, don't let him wriggle away.

'You can't. You mean you *won't?*'

'Please try and understand.' His voice, when he eventually speaks, comes from a very faraway place and it occurs to me suddenly that he never expected things to go this way when he came back in here just now. He came back in here to let me know his intentions, to execute a sense of duty that way.

'I heard from Dougie while I was in the tower.' Lawrence casts his eyes upwards and I realise where he's been hiding out all the time. Dougie. I close my eyes for a second and the name is like some bird arrived from foreign shores, a thing out of place here. *Dougie,* I think, *your boss from the place you have told me you've already left.* What has Dougie got to do with anything important, with anything that really matters?

You heard from him, I raise my eyebrows questioningly ... *and?*

'He told me that he's back and that ... as long as I have things sorted out with my family, he hopes to have positive news for me this afternoon.' Positive news. I look at Lawrence blankly.

'What about my dad?'

Lawrence swallows. I see a fleeting look of panic cross his face.

'I have to save Sunny,' he repeats.

'He still matters, then ...' I mutter under my breath. My fingers tighten in his. *Sunny.* Of course. That's who he came here for, isn't it? That's who he's risked it all for. I don't know why I imagined my concerns would take any precedence over what Lawrence originally came here to do.

'He still matters, Rose.'

I pause, then I lift my chin up. 'Because he is You, right?'

'He's me?'

'He's you. A different version of you. Someone you might have been. If you save him ... it's like saving yourself from the World War Two bunker.' My eyes come challengingly up to meet his. 'You have to do it because nobody ever came to save you.'

There is a moment's silence after that.

Lawrence looks down. His hands slide out of mine sud-

328

denly and he sits down, right there, on the floor at my feet as if his legs have just given way beneath him. I stare at the top of his head as his hands go up to cover his face and I wonder; *what did I say, what did I just say that you didn't already know? Wasn't it obvious?*

A few minutes go by in silence. Then I can hear his shuddering breath and I know that he is quietly crying. I feel a lump in my own throat.

'I'll help you,' I say after a little while. 'If you trust me to, I'll help you to do the right thing and save yourself, Lawrence.'

He makes a movement with his head, gulping down his tears and I can't tell whether he's accepting my offer of help or whether he's just re-affirming that he's got to go. I sense how conflicted he is. He had a mission to accomplish here, and time is running out. If he's going to succeed in helping Sunny, he can't stay here any longer.

But if he has any hopes left of doing the right thing by my dad, *and saving himself* - he can't afford to go.

An arc of tiny sparks shoot up from the brazier into the dark air now, bright moments of deep yellow and red igniting my memory. The hot hazy air over the fire wavers for a bit. My eyes water and I clench my fists. In the smoky haze over the brazier a shape forms, stretches out, dissolves; I can see a man running. *It's him*, isn't it? The thought catches at my throat, puts me suddenly in touch with my grief at losing the man I have been so in love with. For a split second, I'm standing in the stiff breeze with Mum, on the edge of Topfields again, scattering primroses, *Titsy, totsy …*

And he - I turn to look at him at last - Lawrence, the man I was destined to love and then hate and then to lose - he's back here again when he shouldn't be. Back in the place that will be the ruin of him.

Doesn't he know that?

Lawrence

I know Rose is right.

Yet I cannot bear to think I will not be able to help Sunny; that after coming all this way, I will fail him at the final hour. When that call from Dougie came in, woke me up with a jolt in the tower, it gave me a kick-start again, made me remember why I came. To hear that surprised hope in his voice, that maybe something could come of this after all when I've suspected all along he's never really believed it - that was a vindication of all my fragile hopes. When I lift my eyes, stare at the chapel door, the possibility of what I might yet do is still within my grasp.

Travelling alone, I could be at Macrae Farm within the hour. I could seek out my mother. I could get all the i's dotted and the t's crossed on the documents Dougie needs. Sunny could still be on that flight out. It could happen.

Yet now Rose is asking me to consider someone else and I cannot ignore the significance of that. Now that she's put him into my mind - I rub my face, taking in deep gulps of breath, trying to come back into myself - now her father is in there, I cannot get him out. Why did you remind me of him, Rose? The forgotten one. I didn't want to remember him. *'He never knew why you wanted to hurt him ...'* That's what she said, isn't it? Her words clawed more deeply into me than she will know. I thought I saw him, cowering there, terrified, bewildered, in some deep and unused corner of my heart. A place I never go to. I've been too scared of what I'll find there. Me, perhaps? The part of me who still believes I am a coward. The part of me who still believes maybe I deserve to be locked away somewhere and forgotten. Could Rose ever love *that* part?

Could I?

She's kneeling by me, still. Her fingers are in my hair, I can feel her, the gentle pressure of her fingertips as she massages my scalp. I am grateful, but I can't bring myself to look at her. I reach my hands up at last, pull her fingers away from me.

'This is never,' I say to her after a while. 'Never going to work. You know that, don't you?'

'What isn't going to work?' She edges herself around to the front of me.

'You, me.'

She makes a small sound, like a strangled laugh, then.

'I've always known it, Lawrence.'

I look up at her, a little shocked. She believes I'm him, then? Her soul-mate. The one she can never be with.

'Yet still you ...' I'm not even sure what my question is. Still you comfort me? Still you're talking to me? 'You didn't tell them about me?'

'You heard me just now, talking to my aunt?' She's only just realised that. I heard some of it, not all of it. I heard the tone of her voice, how she hesitated, answered only carefully. I didn't hear her spilling out everything she knew. I didn't hear her give me away. I watch her pulling apart the thin leaves off one of the branches we brought in yesterday, stripping it carefully as if it were a very important task, a task she must get just right.

'I didn't mention you,' she breathes. 'What you do next ... it has to be *your choice*,' she says shakily. 'Anything else won't count. The police marching up here and dragging you away, that won't count. The judge throwing you in jail for five years - that won't count. The only thing that'll count now is if you come back with me, of your own volition, and tell my dad what he needs to hear.'

'What will your family say, when they find out?' I look at

her curiously. *Strange*, I think, how now we are in this space, *talking about what will happen next, how things might pan out*, I find that is not something that frightens me. It isn't what the world will do to me next that I am really scared of.

'Will they demand an eye for an eye?' As my father would. *As he will*, when I am taken in. When I am no longer in a place that is out of his reach.

'Uncle Ty and Carlotta will want you to face the penalties of law,' she comes straight back. 'They'll want to see you go through due legal process. I believe that's the only thing that'll satisfy them.'

'And your father ...?'

'My father ...' She sucks in her lips and her shoulders hunch ever so slightly; here we are talking about someone whose wishes matter a hell of a lot more than *Uncle Ty and Carlotta* without a shadow of a doubt. Here we are talking about someone whose happiness is so close to her core we might be talking about Rose herself. 'What will he say?' Her large eyes flash open wider, scanning me apologetically, and then she frowns a little, looks away. 'I really don't know, Lawrence. All I know is what he needs *you* to do. I don't know what will happen after that. It's an unknown.'

An unknown. There's a kind of comfort in that. A gentleness, a hint of kindness that reminds me of Dougie, and Mr and Mrs Patel and all the other good people in my life who've helped me along the way.

'So,' I say to her after a while. 'Do you think that maybe, with my help, and the fact that the tractors are back on the lanes again - you'd be able to make it back to Clare Farm today?'

She stands up, slowly.

Then she smiles a small smile, stretching her hands out to me, helping me up.

Rose

What are we going to say to everyone?

We are so near to Clare Farm now that I think, if I were standing at my own bedroom window looking out I would see us coming down the hill. To my surprise, we have made it back in well under an hour. Lawrence helped me, piggy-back style where the snow was deepest, along the top lane. I thought it was going to be real tough going but when we got to the middle stretch we found a good long section where the lane was completely cleared and I could walk it by myself easily. It felt so strange to be able to see the actual path beneath my feet. The fact that it was still there. In the forty-eight hours or so since I've been away I'd come to believe maybe the real world had completely gone. I couldn't remember what it was like to see the sticks and leaves poking out through the hedgerows, mud on the ground, *life* in the air.

And it is not only the air. To my surprise, we've come across people on our way down, too. A couple walking their dog hailed us loudly from the clear stretch.

'A bit trickier further down,' they warned cheerfully. I saw them smile as Lawrence set me down on the path, imagining we were just any ordinary young couple - young lovers - out to play in the snow.

Lawrence smiled at them briefly and they went on their way but ... somehow, coming across them seemed to break some kind of spell. It brought home that we really were on our way back, and everything that would mean for each of us. Maybe that's why so much of the way we travelled in silence, each churning over our own thoughts? After the couple went by, I got in touch with how sad I was feeling. Those two were together and that's the way they were going to stay but it wasn't going to be like that for *us*, was it? When Lawrence held out his hand to hold mine on the last stretch home I was thinking; are we going to be holding hands like this when we turn up at Clare Farm? Am I going to introduce him to everyone as the guy who helped me get back home or as my boyfriend or as ... I squeeze my eyes tight shut for a moment, not even wanting to *think* the next thought that threatens to come into my head. Do the family have to know who he really is? *Do they have to know straight away?*

'Hey.' Lawrence swings my arm in a wide arc now, calling me back to him. 'It's going to be okay, Rose.' I gulp, suddenly, aware of an apprehension that's been growing ever since we left the ruin.

'What do you want me to tell them about you?' I blurt out suddenly. 'I mean, how much should I say?'

He stops and turns to face me for a moment. In the hours since I got up this morning, the dank mist has slowly lifted. There's a brightness and a promise to the day that was not there before.

'Tell them what you have to.' I feel his hands squeeze mine lightly. 'Don't tell any lies on my account. But I think, Rose ...' He hesitates and I feel a tug of anxiety in my chest at what is coming, at all the unknown excruciating moments that are coming up in the next few minutes, the next few hours and days;

'I think maybe it'd be better if we turned up at your house separately ...'

I look at him carefully, at his eyes that are watching mine so candidly. My first, treacherous thought, that he intends to get away the minute we separate - *that he's only come this far with me because he wouldn't leave me on my own* - is assuaged. He wouldn't do that to me. Of course he won't.

'Why?' I say painfully. What he's suggesting makes a kind

of sense to me, even before I ask it. I need to reconnect with the group. I need to make my explanations. I need to see Dad, prepare him for what's coming. The thought makes me nervous again; it makes me feel afraid. I don't know how Dad is going to react to all of this, do I? I've had ages to get to know Lawrence, to appreciate who he really is, what he's about, but Dad might still perceive him as a threat. The shock of it, Lawrence turning up at his door suddenly, it might all be too much for him. No, I need to go first, pave the way, that makes sense. I feel a sudden raft of doubts crowding in now. I've made the assumption that this is what Dad needs; this'll be the thing that will reassure him, let him sleep in peace again at night. But what if I'm wrong?

'We'll find a way, Rose, to tell them everything we need to say. Both of us.'

And then they will take you away from me. I feel a rush of tears come into my eyes. I wipe them away brusquely before Lawrence sees. No time for that now, is there? We've got to get back and face the world now. We've got to be brave.

And the world ... like the sun, just starting to peep over the edge of those clouds - it's already here. We're not alone anymore. A middle-aged couple, out with two kids in their early teens and a younger child, are climbing the snowy part of the hill, all of them with sledges in tow. I think I recognise her as one of the local primary school teachers. Some way behind them, three men in their twenties are throwing snow about. Their laughter crackles into the still morning air. And now the sound of the tractors starts up again. They are so near. There's one on the lane just ahead of us. It's stopped, but the engine is making an almighty noise. There's a sense, unquestionably, of everything waking up, of a world slowly coming out of hibernation. And again I feel a sense of regret, that this fragile, frozen world we've been inhabiting these last few days, it's not going to last. I feel my sadness that what we had is slipping away and in truth I don't know if - out in this noisy, demanding and judgemental world we're now going back to, our feelings for each other can survive ...

'They'll take you away from me,' I say out loud.

Lawrence puts his head down, pulling me back onto the journey again, making me move.

'Think about what we're going back to *restore*, Rose,' he tells me. I see his eyes are glistening, too. *Your dad's dignity*, he means. *His peace of mind.*

At what price to you, though? I think. But I can't stop this. I know that. This is the way it has to be. But boy ... is it difficult. I want to throw my arms about his neck and hug Lawrence to me. I want to breathe in the scent of him, feel the scratchy bristles on his face with my fingers, just *feel* him, one last time ...

'Hey, fella.' A man's loud voice slices right through our last bit of private space and we both look over to see who's calling. One of the tractor-drivers is calling Lawrence over.

'You look like a strong, healthy young bloke ...' The man is jovial, smiling. He does a double take, then, observing the grey tired lines around Lawrence's eyes, taking in his obvious fatigue. '*She been keeping you awake, fella?*' His laugh rings out over the brightening air. He seems quite pleased with his innuendo. I put my head down, but I can't help seeing that in front of the tractor there are two other men and a woman. A large tree cracked right in two has fallen across the lane and the tractor can't make any further progress till it's cleared. I notice, with a little jolt, that the woman and one of the men are wearing high-visibility green jackets that say 'Community Police Service' on them. They smile over at me and my boyfriend and the woman rolls her eyes at me, a fellow female in the presence of raucous men - *silly joke, eh?*

I pull a smile back. I'm sure it looks like a grotesque grin but it's as good as I can manage.

'All right?' her companion addresses me now. 'How's your dad?'

I freeze. 'Good,' I say. This man recognises me as my father's daughter but I don't know him. All I know is he is a community police officer and Lawrence is standing here beside me. My heart is suddenly thudding very fast, very loud.

'We need to get back to him, now ...' I look at Lawrence significantly, offering him the chance to get away but he stands fast, remembering our previous agreement that I go in first.

'You not staying to help, then?' The tractor man looks at me with mock disappointment.

'I'll stay.' Lawrence comes between us. 'Rose fell. She's got stitches in her leg.' He turns to me now. 'Can you make it from here, Rose?'

I start to shake my head but he looks at me warningly. He knows very well I can make it back from here. He wants me to go. I look at the community police and back to him again with growing distress. I don't want to leave him here with them. What if they start asking innocent questions? I know right now they don't realise who he is. Even if they've been on the look-out for him, any photos they have must be at least five years old. And they'd never, ever, expect to see their wanted man travelling back down the lanes with *me* of all people, would they? The fact that he's just showed up with me, makes Lawrence safer, if anything.

'Go home, Rose,' Lawrence urges. 'This could take a little while ...' He indicates the fallen tree. 'These things aren't easy to shift, believe me. It's okay to go on ahead of me.' He wants me to, it's what we've agreed and I know I should just go.

'What?' he smiles ruefully. 'You don't trust me?' The others are all aware of us and I know it. They're getting back to their log-clearing operation but they're not talking amongst themselves anymore, all acutely aware of *our* conversation and it feels like a too-public moment. I let out a breath.

'I promise we'll send him back to you in one piece, princess.' The tractor-driver pipes up and they all smile. I have to plaster a smile on my face, too, at that.

'Sure,' I say and there's a sudden murmur of camaraderie amongst the others.

'Everything will be fine,' Lawrence promises. Before I go, he reaches down to kiss me. One last time. His lips on mine are like the marzipan and apricot layer of a cake at Christmas; his lips are like a promise of spring, green shoots of narcissus peeping out from under the ice. His lips say he loves me, I can trust him and he will be down soon but I know that when he does ...

Everything will not all be fine.

Rose

When I reach for my house key in the bottom of my coat pocket, I'm aware of a slight surprise that it's still even there. Of course it is there. Just like all the other everyday things of my life will still be here. I wait for a few seconds before putting the key into the door. I know what I am really worried about but I tell myself the best way will be to take things one step at a time. For now, all is well. I am about to walk back into normality. Safety. The known.

In a moment I will open the front door and the same warm smell of cherry polish will greet me as it always does. The same slightly-damp carpet smell. The scent of whatever's cooking in the kitchen will waft down the hallway. When I walk through, the windows at the back will be steamed up because the seal on the glazing is going. The large pot of red poinsettias that Mrs P bought us from the market will still be sitting on the table in the hall, the leaves starting to slightly curl at the edges by now. And Dad ... I let my mind go up the stairs to where his bedroom is; I imagine him still sitting there in his chair by the window.

He'll have been waiting for me to come home, I think.

Everything will be normal. The only thing that will have changed is me. *I've* changed. I'm not the same person I was when I left here two days ago. I'm not, am I? My fingers run over the jagged ends of my house key. All the things that I still have to tell them at home, all the uncomfortable truths I am going to have to speak jostle like nervous ghosts at my back, making me jumpy. I insert the key into the keyhole and turn it. Push the door open. I walk inside. I feel ... strange. I don't feel normal.

When Uncle Ty appears suddenly out of the sitting room now, my heart gives a jump at the look of surprise that crosses his face.

'Rose!' he says, his eyes opening slightly in amazement. 'You're back. Is everything all right?' *Is it? You tell me ...*

'How's my dad?' I get out.

Ty frowns ever so slightly, and my heart tightens. *Don't tell me anything bad ...*

'He's doing fine,' Ty says.

I search his eyes for clues of what Carlotta might possibly have made of the jumbled conversation we had this morning, but he just looks surprised to see me so soon.

'The lanes are clear, then?' I nod, trying to get my brain to engage my tongue to speak.

'They're clearing them. Someone helped me back,' I say. I wait for him to ask who; the doorway to the beginning of everything they are going to need to learn. I'll tell them little by little, I decide. They don't need to know the truth about Lawrence all at once. But Ty is still staring at me. When I turn to the mirror in the hallway I can see immediately what he's so taken aback by is my *appearance*. My clothes are rumpled and look slept-in. All I've had to wash in for the last few days has been those small bucket-fuls of melted snow we had. My hair is tousled and untidy, and I appear to be juddering with the cold, even though I'm feeling really hot on entering this centrally-heated space.

'I got ... a bit cold walking back,' I tell him through chattering teeth.

'You walked? Good *God*, girl, I know this bit is still snowed in but when you mentioned someone had brought you home just now, Rose I assumed you meant you'd come at least part of the way by car.' Ty takes me by the shoulders and marches me in a no-argument manner to the bottom of the stairs. Whatever his misgivings about my dishevelled state, he's clearly holding them in check till the needs of the body are sorted out.

'Look, have a hot bath, love. Get changed. Then come down and we'll talk.' That's it? I hesitate, longing for the chance. It would be an easy escape if I could do that.

'I can't talk just yet. I've got a ... friend coming over soon,' I say. 'The person who brought me back. He's just stopped to help some people move a tree.'

'He's coming here *now*?' Ty blinks, taking this in. The news of a third party about to arrive shifts something in him, I sense it. His own priorities suddenly swing a little closer like horses on a carousel.

'Ah. The thing is - as you probably have guessed - there is something you and I really need to talk about, Rose.'

I squirm. Is this thing he's so keen to get off his chest about *me*, my being away these past few days, where I've been and who I've been with ... or is it about Dad? I'm not sure which one I'm looking forward to talking about least.

'You said Dad was fine,' I say tightly.

'Fine is a *relative* term, Rose.' Ty pauses for a second. 'He could be a lot finer. I think you know that. I had a chance to put together some proposals for his future while you were away and we need to make space to discuss them.' In one way, I feel relieved. He doesn't want to bring up where I've been then, this is not about me. Then I feel my face growing hot at the uncomfortable thought; is this what they've been concerning themselves with, these past few days? Googling care homes for Dad and working out costs and ... and what not? What does Ty mean about 'proposals for Dad's future?' I don't like the sound of that at all. I don't like the fact that they've come up with these proposals while I was away and without consulting me first.

'He's not going into a care home, Ty.'

'*Rose*,' Ty persists. 'I need you to be open to discussion on where we go next. I need you to keep your Dad's best interests in mind.' Ty clears his throat. 'I *need*,' he continues, 'for you to be on side with this or else we're never going to persuade my brother to do what's in his best interests. Understood?' My heart sinks at the implication. I am not going to like what he has to say next, am I?

'Hey,' he pats my hand firmly. We both turn to look as Carlotta appears from the kitchen now, carrying a bowl of soup. The flavoursome smell of it makes my mouth water and I realise I'm suddenly gazing at her soup like a famished person.

'I heard voices in the hallway,' she says. I look down at the floor to escape her frank open-mouthed stare as she takes in the state of me. 'Rose! Where have you *been*?' She plucks at the sleeve of my arm, a little bewildered. 'Has everything been all right? I mean,' she swallows. 'I realise you probably had to sleep on somebody's couch, but you look ... really rough.'

Of course, I must look rough to her. I suck in my lips. They're going to think the same of Lawrence when he eventually turns up, too. They're going to think I've been hanging out with tramps under an archway ...

'Conditions weren't all that great,' I admit. 'At least we had a roof over our ...'

'Would you like this soup?' Carlotta virtually pushes the bowl into my hands. 'I haven't touched it yet.' She shakes her head slightly at my uncle. She suspects something's up. She's a woman; she *knows* it.

'Thanks,' I get out gratefully. 'If it's okay with you guys - I'll have it upstairs.' I look up and the peace and quiet at the top of the stairs, *my own stairs, in my own home*, beckons enticingly. I'm half-expecting my aunt to demur at that, to come up with some objection at food being eaten in bedrooms, but she doesn't.

'I'll need to check in on Dad, too,' I say half-heartedly. *It's not that I don't want to see him, it's just that I'm dreading ...*

'Listen love, your dad's been *fine* and in any event I believe he's asleep right now,' my aunt pats my hand firmly. 'Get changed. Get dry. *Then* we can all speak.' Aunt Carlotta isn't really all that bad, I think, in sudden wonder. Ty seems to relent slightly at her intervention but now that I've got the soup in my hands, wobbling so precariously as I start going up the stairs, the *something that we need to talk about* that he mentioned is preying on my mind.

'Your aunt's right,' Ty concedes. 'You need to get yourself sorted first of course. It's just that ...' He stops himself in time as he goes automatically to look at his watch, 'If you're expecting company it's important we speak sooner rather than later. The girls want to leave ASAP as you'll appreciate, and once word comes through that the Bentley's sorted ...'

Once the car is road-worthy they'll be keen to be on their way. I've barely arrived back home and soon they will be off. In some ways it feels like a relief but I know it really isn't. It feels - very unsatisfactory somehow, as if some opportunity I've barely even imagined yet, might have been missed. I take another step up the stairs. The hot soup wobbles slightly over the edge of the bowl, lapping at my fingers, and I make a real effort to steady it.

I've only been back a short while and already I feel bombarded. I was worried about how I was going to tell them about everything but now it feels as if maybe my family were waiting to ambush *me* with all their concerns the moment I walked through the door ...

Ty wants me to persuade Dad to let them put him into Forsythes. I can't imagine that it's anything else. My uncle seems so set and determined. Like my dad could be at times, I remember; it's a family trait. I hear Carlotta come and stand behind him as I go up; together they make a formidable team, solid, unbreakable. *I'm about to lose the only boy who I ever wanted to be my boyfriend*, the thought slips into my head; *and now they want to take the only other person who matters away from me, too ...*

I continue up the stairs without another word. Right at this moment I haven't got any words left. I have to change out of these clothes. I have to talk to Dad before Lawrence gets here - that's more important than all this care-home stuff that Ty and Carlotta will want to speak about, I tell myself. All that can wait. Lawrence is coming. And what Dad has waited to hear all this time has already taken long enough.

I change quickly, tie my hair back. I don't even drink the soup. When I go into Dad's room, he is sleeping in his chair and his hands are cold. I have to tuck them in under the blanket like I always do. I kiss the top of his head and my heart, my heart is bursting with so many things when I come up from the long, gentle hug that I have given him while he sleeps. Oh, Dad. I don't know if I'm doing the right thing, here.

All I know is; if you can't let Lawrence speak the words he has to say I don't see how we are ever going to move away from this tangled mess we've allowed our lives to get into. I don't know how we are ever going to move on.

Now I'm standing here beside you, the clock on the bedside table ticking comfortingly, your favourite curtains - the ones Mum sewed so many years ago - half-drawn, only letting in a little bit of light, I'm not so sure anymore if you'll even want to move on. If you're ready for it.

'*Will you please give him a chance, Dad*?' My plea sounds so loud, even though I am whispering in the quiet bedroom air. I stop to take in my father and his breath is so shallow, the rise and fall of his chest so undetectable, that I have to touch him, just to make sure he's still breathing.

'Will you give Lawrence a chance?' I lean in a little closer. 'Or are you going to fear and hate him straight away just like your people did to Isla?' His breath halts altogether now and I stop talking. A few moments go by, while I wait. Then he lets out a long breath all in one go, and I can't help wonder if, somewhere deep in his sleep maybe, he *heard* me. He needs to hear me.

There are so many things he needs to hear. The unspoken words that Ty still needs to speak twist uncomfortably in my stomach. The family are going to say you need to leave. I know you won't want to. Because of Mum.

But maybe - I stroke his head tenderly - *maybe if things had been different*, if you'd never walked those two miles to the hospital on that clear, cold afternoon eighteen years ago and you'd never laid eyes on me, your only child, or made that decision to give up your old life for me and my mother - then you'd never have come here in the first place. You'd never have felt you had to be the guardian of it. Imagine that. If he'd had his way, Macrae would have torn those woods down for development nearly two decades ago. Everyone would already have forgotten they were ever there. There'd be a whole bunch of families bringing up their kids on 'Topfields' Drive and 'Topwoods' Road and they'd never stop for a moment to wonder where the *fields* or the *woods* went. They'd never stop to wonder what wildlife might have been sacrificed for the homes they now lived in. Nobody would care.

Isla cared, passionately, but ... Isla's gone, Dad. When I went back into her room just before Christmas, I knew it then. She's gone. Perhaps it's about time that we made plans to leave, too?

I pick up my bowl of soup and turn to go downstairs, leaving him to his peaceful dreams for just a few moments longer. Sam told me just before I came in here that he hasn't slept all night and he's only just dozed off. It would be cruel to wake him.

He's going to find out the truth soon enough.

Rose

'Darling, what we've got to do here, is persuade your dad it's in his best interests to sell Clare Farm.'

I *knew* something like this was coming; I could feel it.

I'm sitting on the edge of one of my own sitting room sofas, feeling warmer and drier than I have in days and yet I'm finding myself more uncomfortable by the minute. This feels wrong. It feels wrong to me that we should be talking about selling up behind Dad's back while he's asleep upstairs. It feels wrong to me that Lawrence wanted me to come on ahead so I could speak to my Dad first and I haven't managed to do that, but I'm still down here talking about these other matters. Lawrence is going to be here any moment and then I'll have even *more* explaining to do and all Ty cares about is getting his own point across ...

I try and keep my mind on what Ty's so desperate to talk about.

'Dad won't sell up,' I tell my uncle tightly.

'Hear me out please, Rose.' A small edge has crept into Ty's voice now. *Maybe he's not feeling too comfortable about all these 'proposals', either?*

'We've been looking into things on your dad's account while you've been away.' He glances at my aunt. 'I understand you'll probably feel ... we haven't been of much use to you before, but I hope you'll appreciate that what I'm going to put forward next is something that has your father's best interests at heart.'

346

I fold my arms, sit back on the sofa and the cushions behind my back feel suddenly very soft, as if I'm sinking into them. They aren't supporting me at all.

'Being stranded here with my brother these past few days has been a complete eye-opener for us, Rose. I'm ashamed to say it, but now I see quite how bad things have been for Jack I only wish to goodness we'd got involved in his care programme a whole lot sooner ...'

I can feel my breath coming in huge long waves in my chest. As if no matter how much air I suck in there is no way to get enough into my lungs. I'm waiting, waiting and listening and yet it feels like he's taking a very long time to get to what he wants to say.

'You want him to go into a care home,' I say in a strange breathy voice at last. 'You've seen the level of care he needs and you think that's why I was asking you for help? You think ... I want to go and study and maybe I need you to fund his care in some way ...?' Why does my face feel as if it's gone a bright pink colour right now? Why do I feel as if what Dad's brother wants is going to take precedence over anything *I* might want or say?

'That isn't what I want.' I grip the side of the sofa and haul myself upright though I still feel as if I'm sinking. 'I know we haven't had a chance to speak properly yet, but that was never what I wanted. It isn't what he wants either.'

Ty and Carlotta look a bit sheepish at that. I get the sense they're both feeling a little cowed.

'I appreciate that.' Ty leans over and the sudden gesture silences me. 'I've been doing a bit of research on Jack's behalf. On the Internet and such. I've been putting out email enquiries all over the place. Everyone's off for Christmas, of course. But I did manage to get through to the father-in-law of a work colleague of mine. He sustained some terrible injuries in a crash a few years back but he's come through.' He smiles.

'The thing is, he tells me, sometimes there's a lot more that could be done to get people mobile again than they realise. He's going to put me onto the guy - Dr Singh - who successfully treated him, in the States.'

'What are the chances, though?' I look at him sceptically. 'This guy Singh - I guess he'd have to see all Dad's notes and stuff before we'd know if he could help?'

'Naturally, he would. I found a link to his website yesterday evening. All I can say, Rose, is that it looks promising.' His eyes on mine are intent. 'From what I've read, it looks like they've been able to make monumental progress in some cases. I think he's just the right person who might be able to offer hope to Jack.' Hope? For Jack? I feel my heart leap but there is something else coming, I can feel it ...

'*But*?' I perch on the edge of the sofa, waiting for the catch with baited breath. My uncle exchanges another glance with his wife who's remained remarkably quiet up to this point.

'It means Jack would need to go to the States for up to a year.'

'*A year?*' The States. The words seem to fly right over the top of my head. I can't take them in.

'While they carry out the tests and procedures and implement their recovery programme. It's possible that there's a lot they might achieve for him, Rose. Imagine it. If he could walk properly - what a difference it could make.' He lets that sink in for a bit. 'Look, it's a long shot, I know. You have to realise that nothing may come of it, nothing at all ...'

'And if he goes for it, it means we'd have to sell Clare Farm?'

'This is where some tough decisions are going to need to be made, Rose. Singh's research is part state-funded, but a lot of it comes from private donors and patients are required to pay a proportion of their costs. We'd help out as much as we can, of course but, frankly, it would entail you selling the family home for your dad to even have a look-in.'

So that's why he wants us to sell Clare Farm? Not to pay for Forsythes, but to pay for the treatment?

'It's a gamble, though?' I say slowly. And Dad won't want to

348

sell up. Uncle Ty doesn't understand that bit. It's not just because we have no other assets - and Dad would naturally be worried about how I'm going to live - it's because of what'd happen to the land if we did move out.

'Life is always a gamble, Rose. Don't you think this one might be worth the risk?'

I don't answer him. Maybe it is a good idea. If it worked it would be beyond my wildest dreams, give Dad his life back again. It might. But it's not what *I* think that's going to count, here. Dad would have to be persuaded and when it comes down to it he can be every bit as stubborn as my mum was. And if we went for it - gambled our house in the hope of Dad getting better - there's one thing that wouldn't be in question at all. Macrae would develop the land if we left here. *We* might lose everything, but however it turned out for us, he would certainly win.

And then there is Lawrence. I turn my head slightly to the sitting room door, still waiting for the doorbell to go, waiting for the moment to come when I can get it over with, take Lawrence upstairs and then Dad - *oh God, if only Dad will listen* - he'll find out he doesn't have to worry anymore. I get up, feeling suddenly jumpy again, nervous. *Oh, when is Lawrence going to get here? What's taking so long?* I don't want to sit here any longer. I can't.

'This is all ... great news,' I choose my words carefully. 'Potentially. I'll talk to Dad, okay? See what he feels about it.' From their faces, I can tell they already know what he feels about it. They're banking on me to persuade him differently.

And I ... I'm banking that Lawrence will still be along any minute. That he'll do what he promised he would. That he won't wimp out. That Dad will take it all okay. I've been sitting here talking to my uncle and aunt for a good half hour, I realise. Might he be awake yet? I need to go up and find out. *Life's always a gamble, Rose,* My uncle's words return to me as I make my way to go back up the stairs again.

I'm hoping this one will be worth the risk.

Rose

'Dad,' I shake him gently. 'Dad, I'm *back*.' There is a length of shiny golden tinsel entwined around the handlebars of his chair, I see now. A Christmas touch. I didn't put that there. A small pang goes through me, both of sadness because of the things that I have missed out on, and gratitude that other people have been here to look after him, to make his chair look Christmassy ...

He stirs in his sleep, a brief smile crosses his face and I stop shaking him. He's ... happy, where he is right now. I need him to wake up, to talk to me, but - should I just let him sleep; leave him to his dreams, his few moments of peace?

No.

Because we've been sleeping for long enough, the two of us. Maybe it's time to wake up and face some truths?

'Dad.' I crouch down and shake him more urgently now. 'Wake up. It's me, Rose. I'm back.'

'You're back.' He opens his eyes and a flash of pure warmth and love crosses his face. 'I saw you coming down the hill and then ... you were gone again. I thought it was a dream.' He sounds a little sad.

'It wasn't a dream,' I say. 'It was real.' My face colours at the thought that Dad must have been watching us, coming back down together. For how long? Did he see Lawrence, too? He must have. The thought flitters through my mind; did he see us holding hands? Did he see it when Lawrence bent to kiss me as we parted?

350

'I got your meds, look,' I rush on before he mentions it, if he did see him. 'Do you want to take one now? The locum said you could take one as soon as I got them.'

He holds out his palm and I place one of the little red tablets in it. I hand him the water beaker and he swallows it down.

'That's better,' he says. As if it could ever have worked so quickly. He makes me smile.

'You *could* be better, you know,' I put in hesitantly. I bend, busying myself suddenly with tucking the blanket back around his legs. I don't want to speak just now about the fact that I have been gone for a few days. That when I left, I went feeling in a huff with Carlotta. It seems so petty and pointless now. Is he even aware of the manner in which I left? 'Uncle Ty has been telling me about some treatment you could go for,' I bring up instead. 'Do you want to do that?'

'In the States?' There's been some discussion about this while I was away, just as I thought. Dad looks away now, immediately uninterested. His gaze stretches out over the huge mounds of snow in the garden.

'It's been snowing all the time you've been away, Rose. I slept through most of it. Every time I woke up and looked out - there was more of it.' There's a soft wonder in his voice now. A child-like wonder as if he's forgotten all the other years of his life we've been snowed in. What else has he forgotten?

'Ty tells me there's a consultant in the States who he believes might be able to help you with your condition.' As I say the words to Dad, for the first time, the magnitude of them begins to sink in. When Ty brought it up earlier, I was too surprised, too well-defended to take it in fully. But here, in this quiet, private space with my father, the full reality of what it could mean, dawns on me. 'Will you at least agree to have an assessment?'

Dad looks at me listlessly.

'You know I won't.'

'*Why*, Dad?' I straighten, then walk over to sit on the window ledge, blocking out his view so that he's forced to look at me,

351

concentrate properly on what we need to talk about. 'Why won't you even consider it? You think there's something noble about being in your condition?' I frown, feeling a sudden desperation at his predicted stubbornness, at the fact that he seems happy to carry on like this, for nothing to ever change.

'There isn't. There's nothing noble about it.'

I didn't come up here to talk about the neurologist Ty has discovered, I realise that. I came up here to tell Dad about Lawrence, to help prepare the way for him but I have no words right now, no grounds for dialogue of any sort if he really doesn't want anything to change ...

'Staying here and giving up on all hope for yourself because of that bloody patch of land Mum cared so desperately about ... you might as well be stuck in a burrow under the tree roots like she was. What difference does it make?'

I have no idea where all those words came from. They just surged up from a deep unconscious well of frustration at him. Frustration that we never really speak. Frustration that I could never speak to Mum because she only ever listened to what she wanted to hear. That I've never really been able to speak to him either because since she died and he got attacked, he's felt somehow too fragile; I've felt that if I said the wrong thing I might somehow break him in two.

Except ...

I didn't let Lawrence get away with not hearing what I had to say to him, did I? I made him stay there and hear me, everything that I felt, all the horrible, painful, difficult things that I needed to say to him, I made him listen to me. Dad will, now, too.

'What difference did it make to *you*, that I let my brother open up Mum's room and use it, Rose?' Dad comes back softly. Oh. So he knows then. He does know why I left on Christmas Day. How I left. I bite my tongue.

'I got upset, yes. That was before I realised that my upset - it was never really about the room. Never about the room at all. Maybe I was like you - I thought I could lock up my grief over losing Mum and throw away the key forever. I don't need to do that anymore. *You* don't, either.'

Dad doesn't answer me but I need to make him understand there *is* something that could make a difference to his life. If he chose it. If only he wouldn't be afraid. If only he could be open enough. I'm aching to tell him about Lawrence but we haven't finished speaking about Mum yet, have we? There are more words yet, tripping up over my tongue now that they've suddenly somehow been released ...

'Why won't you go for treatment, Dad? *Why*? Is it guilt? Is that what's keeping you here now? You cried when you lost Mum but you ... you never did anything to stop her wilting away. You never lifted a finger to try and help her, did you?'

'Is that what you think, Rose?' he comes back surprisingly forcefully now. 'I'd have done anything for your mother. Anything in my power if she'd only let me. She didn't let me though. She never wanted any medical intervention ...'

As you don't now, I think. I cross my arms over my chest.

'And you just let her get away with that?'

'I let her ...' His voice is starting to wobble. '*I let her* because I made a promise when she married me that I'd never force her into doing things my way or living her life *my* way.'

I throw my hands up in the air.

'Why? What a stupid thing to promise. In this case you were right and she was wrong. You should have forced her to ...'

'I promised it the day you were born,' he cuts across me now, stopping me in my tracks. 'I swore it on your life. I had to or she'd never have agreed to come and live with me.'

'You swore it ...?'

'So that I could be near *you*, Love.' His voice is trembling now and I can see what a terrible, horrible mistake I've made in assuming what I have all these years; that he hadn't noticed how sick she was.

'I never foresaw what it might come to. How could I have known that? But never once think I turned a blind eye to how

353

sick she was because I didn't care! It seems she'd been sick like it before, growing up, she told me. It was some tropical disease she'd contracted as a teenager. She'd had to go through all sorts of unhelpful interventions at the time and she swore she would never do it again. That was her choice and I couldn't compel her.'

'She didn't get sick because of being under the damp tree roots then?'

He gives a painful smile.

'It wasn't the trees that killed her.'

'And you?' Chastened, I come back to him at last. 'Are you prepared to go through some treatments that might help you? If we sell this place and the Macraes get the land after all this time … so be it. Is it worth giving up your life for?'

'I made her a promise, Rose, that I wouldn't give up on the home we'd made together.' He shoots me a regretful look.

'One promise that cost you her life. A second promise that will cost you yours. And what about me? Don't I figure in any of your decisions? Doesn't what I think and want and feel matter to you? She's gone, Dad. I'm not. I'm still here and I still need you to be here.'

'You really think …' He holds out his trembling hands – 'Anyone can get these to work again?'

'I think you need to trust that they might.'

He seems to consider it for a moment, then;

'I was the one who made the undertaking to stay here, Rose. You didn't. You don't need to stay here with me, do you?'

'You know I do! I can't leave you, can I?' I get up from the window ledge and push my hair back in frustration. 'You're as good as blackmailing me into helping you keep a promise that needs to be broken now, one that should never have been made.'

'I need some air,' Dad's saying, and I know that our conversation has to end because he's gasping now. I can't keep going on at him like this. I need to back down.

'Here you go.' I go and fetch him his nebuliser, which has been placed by his bed. 'You're supposed to have this by you at all times,' I rebuke gently.

'I keep dropping it,' he says. He holds his hands out and his fingers are trembling uncontrollably. *He's not fine.* My eyes fill with tears again. He's not. I wipe the tears away roughly. Right now I feel so frustrated with him that he won't let me - or anyone else - help him. I feel so frustrated that he won't let me tell him everything I know. Oh, I could tell him all the things that have happened over the last few days and how they've affected me deeply; how I really believe his injuries were the result of mistaken identity but could Dad ever bring himself to believe that too?

He won't believe me.

'You still need it by you,' I say. I don't know what else to do. And Lawrence isn't here yet. Maybe he's never even coming?

The thought makes me realise I need to get on with the things I still need to do. I don't want to keep hanging about on tenterhooks, doing *nothing*, just waiting ...

'Dad, I need to get something proper to eat. I need to run a bath and chill for a bit. Will you at least *think* about what I've just asked you? Will you do that?'

He looks at me blankly. It's a look which says nothing but which I suspect masks a lot of his own tears. He doesn't answer.

'Oh, what's the use?' I mutter as I walk over to the door. 'What's the use when what it boils down to is - you're as stubborn and hell-bent as Mum ever was? Nothing I say is ever going to make any difference to you, is it? Nothing I say is ever going to get you to shift. I might as well face it.'

'Rose ...'

I keep on walking. *I tried, Lawrence. I knew he wouldn't want to hear any of it.* I can feel the hunch of my shoulders, as I walk away, holding in the pain of my defeat. When Lawrence comes in - *if* he ever comes in - I will just have to take him upstairs and we'll explain it all to Dad together.

'I really need to take that bath now ...'

'There's something else,' Dad admits in a small, almost hesitant voice as I reach the door. 'Something came for you while you were away, Love.'

What now?

'I think it - might be the letter you were waiting for. Your Uni letter. Matt Dougal spotted it over at next door's - he was up there dropping Pilgrim off, apparently. They were going to throw it out. He insisted on bringing it over for you ... it came just after you left here, Christmas Day.'

My letter? 'Where is it?' I can feel the blood draining from my legs at the thought. It's here then? It came.

'It's on the dresser. Over there.'

I never saw it when I came in. I wasn't looking out for it. My letter. Oh, God.

I go over and pick it up without really seeing it. Is it the one? My heart is going ten to the dozen. Will it contain the offer I've been longing for? I know he's expecting me to tear it open but something perverse in me doesn't want to do that right now, even though I know he's waiting. I put it in my pocket and I hear his quiet gasp of disappointment behind me. I don't want to open it because I've finally realised the truth.

It doesn't matter, does it? It doesn't matter what that letter says because Dad is going to be stuck here for the rest of his life, and I will, too.

Rose will have figured out by now that I'm not coming.

I look up as the couple with their teenagers and the guys we saw larking about on the way down arrive to lend a fresh set of hands.

'Bloody rain,' the older guy grins at me. It's only intermittent at the moment, sudden blowy gusts but it seems to have ruined their sledging plans. I see one of the younger guys look over at me curiously. He'd be about my age. He reckons he knows me, maybe, but I'm not hanging about to give him the chance to find out. I've been here the best part of an hour already. I look back at the fallen tree. We've got the damn thing most of the way off the path now. I need to get on.

I make my excuses to the group and the tractor guy comes up with something generic about me being in a hurry to get back to my girl. *If only you knew the truth*, mate. I give him a high-five and he seems satisfied that I've done my share. The community police lady makes some regretful noise about '*mince-pies and coffee at hers when we're done*'. She assures me I'd still be welcome to join them. I tell her I wish that I could, and it's almost true. It'd be better than where I'm going now, that's for sure. She smiles at me from under her lashes the way some women do and it occurs to me - with some regret - that if I hadn't spent the last five years living practically as a hermit I'd have done all right with the ladies.

But right now, there is Rose. And Rose's dad. She'll still be

357

waiting, I know. And I did promise her. She might even have told him by now. I feel a small curiosity at that; at how her old man might have taken it, the thought of *me*. How exactly might she have put it to him? And then - would she have told him all of it, I mean, the bit about her and me, or would she have left that part out? I don't want to go down there to Clare Farm and that's the truth. It's a few short minutes from the lane, that's all. But all the way down, this scenario keeps flashing into my mind; if Rose has spilled it all out - to Ty and the rest of her family, the relatives will all be baying for my blood by now. They'll have called the fuzz. The police will be there, probably, waiting for me or they'll be on their way. I shrug my collar closer up against my face as I walk. If they take me in now then I'll never get the chance to speak to her dad like she wanted me to. If they take me in now, I'll be throwing all Sunny's chances away for *nothing*, Rose.

I stick my hands deep into my pockets as I walk, making myself keep going straight down, because my legs don't want to go this way anymore. I can hear my own heart racing, feel it pulsing in my chest and my throat, feel all my limbs trembling with adrenalin, because I shouldn't be here, I don't want to be here, risking discovery with every moment; I'm ready to run. And now that I'm standing here in her front yard I cannot find the courage to knock on her front door. The door of their home. I take off my gloves and my palms are sweating underneath, all clammy and wet. The long icicles, like frozen daggers reaching down from the guttering along the front, remind me of prison bars. I want to pick up a brick and knock them all off, free her somehow from the prison I have put her in, free him, *free myself*, but I don't touch them.

Where are you, Rose? I scan the upstairs windows, desperate for some glimpse of her. I stare at the closed front door, at the trail of footprints outside which she must have made so recently, the edges of it being melted away by the rain. The downstairs curtains are still drawn, even at this late hour. A thin line of smoke struggles up from the chimney breast but there's a wind getting up now, pushing it this way and that. I can hear the hissing of the rain as it lands on the frozen ground, the uneasy sound of the gusts blowing through the trees. And then there's a faint rapping on the window.

When I look up, my first hopes that it might be her are immediately dashed. It's just an old guy, sitting at one of the upstairs windows, probably wondering who I am. An old guy.

I swallow down the bile that comes up to my throat then. In any other place, I wouldn't have recognised my neighbour; we never had anything to do with the Clares, but I know who he is. Without knowing his face, I know my victim. His action, calling me back by rapping at the window, has stopped me in my tracks, sent a shot of fear right into my core. What does he want? What could he possibly want? Does he know who I am? He can't know unless she's told him. It was dark that night five years ago and I've grown up into a man, changed beyond all recognition. No, he can't know me unless Rose has said - but what does he want?

He raps again, insistently now, loudly. I can make out his gnarled hands in their fingerless mittens. They look like a child's hands might do, poised beseechingly at the window. For all that he can rap at me, he can't actually *do* anything. He can't move. He's helpless. His mouth, twisted in strange shapes as he tries to form some words I cannot hear, make him look grotesque somehow, remind me of a ghost at the window. Now he's got my attention he makes a quick motion with his head, '*come up here*'. He wants me up there? It's what I've come for, after all. It's him I've come to see, at her behest, but ...

No.

The fear that grips me now is like nothing else, it's like nothing in this life. Now that I've seen him I realise he can't possibly want me here, not me, no matter what she thinks. He's calling me because he doesn't know who I am. She hasn't told him yet, has she? He doesn't know I have no business in his house. Besides, I have no time. I have not the will. Why should I go up to him? What for? I didn't want to. When I was with her, she made it seem so clear, what I had to do but now ... I need to wake up, get myself out of here. It's the only way. I turn my back to the old man, my sodden boots sinking into the slushy snow and he raps one more time.

This time, just once. Forlorn, as if he realises he is going to be ignored and I feel a shot of anger on his behalf. Why the hell has he been left all alone? Abandoned. Forgotten about. I feel a sharp pain go through my heart at the memory of what that feels like. *Where's Rose*? Surely one of his people could go up to him. He doesn't need *me*. I turn back, unwillingly, and he makes eye contact with me again.

Up here, he beckons, his mouth opening and shutting like a fish, gagging and gasping. Oh, I see what it is. He can't catch his breath, can he? Fuck, *fuck*, there isn't time ... there isn't time for him and there isn't time for me, either.

And yet, here I am, taking the steps on the fire escape up to his door two at a time. The fire-door, leading in to his bedroom, is stiff - is clearly never, ever used. Perhaps surprisingly, it is un-locked. *Quick, calmly,* my professional training kicks in, *check his vital signs, what does he want, what does he need?* I step inside, my heart hammering loud as a steam train, into his room. Blinking in the dim light, I take in his bed which is unmade, the wilting chrysanthemums in a vase, two unfinished mugs of tea on his cabinet. I take it all in at a glance, in a millisecond, and then the nebuliser that's fallen to the floor, well out of his reach. I pick it up and insert it into his mouth gently, my hand supporting the back of his neck.

'Nice and easy does it, sir. Deep, long breaths, you know the way ...' and he's gulping in the puffs, his eyes tight shut with the pain and the effort of it till the nebuliser does its work, opens up his airways and then suddenly - there he is, he's back. All done. Easy-peasy. I look at him and I see he's looking at me expectantly, his hair parted neatly to one side in an old-fashioned kind of way. He looks so harmless, and gentle, her father. So helpless.

'Damn thing slipped from my hand,' he says. His voice,

cracked and faint but still well-heeled, comes as a shock. It's not the same voice I hear coming at me sometimes in my nightmares. 'Would you be so good as to open up that window for me, young man?' he asks shyly.

'The … um …?' Who does he even think I am, I wonder? He doesn't know me? I glance at the window and it's one of the old-fashioned types, a sash window. The sill is wide and deep, would have been painted white once, a long time ago. I can see the cracks in the wood from here. Like him, the whole room feels worn out.

'It's cold,' I warn.

'That's what they always say.' His voice is beguilingly gentle. 'It's *cold*. But it's been a while since I last felt the crisp air on my face.' I look at him, guilty, as he continues; 'Not been out of this house since September.' Then he adds, frowning. 'We are still in December, aren't we?'

I nod. Go over and attempt to pull up his window a few inches. The radiator just underneath it is working overtime, boiling to my touch. The window pane doesn't budge.

'There's a catch,' he says, and his words dance around inside my brain, shocking me, making me think this might be some kind of trick. *What's the catch? That the police are waiting for me downstairs? That someone else is waiting to take me in?*

'Where?' I say but I spot what he's talking about even as I ask it. It's a little wooden catch. As I undo it, I think; what am I even doing here? Going out of my way to open up the window for this guy. Someone will see it, or they'll hear it go up. This is what Rose wanted but all I can think right now is that if they catch me here I'll be flung in jail for sure. *What am I doing?*

I need to get out of here, yes, but for some reason I don't move. He breathes in long and deeply, the moment the outside air surges in; to me, it is merely cold, to him it is fresh, a relief from the stale air in his room which is musty and smells of some sort of liniment. I stand by the radiator, enjoying the warmth while he enjoys the cold. After a while, he says a shocking thing;

'Have you ever been in prison, young man?' I blanche. 'No, no of course you haven't.' He smiles apologetically. 'But it must be like this, no?' He indicates his own body. 'No chance to do … all the things…'

'I can imagine,' I say dumbly.

'Years ago, I'd have told you …' He points to his wheelchair - 'something like this was my worst fear. Always a very active man, you know. Not having freedom of movement - been the worst thing.'

'I'm sorry.'

'They say it's cold, but the real reason they won't open up the window for me is that my suspicious sister-in-law doesn't trust I won't topple myself out of it.' He delivers this all with a small smile.

'Any reason why she shouldn't?' I ask, cringing.

'None whatsoever, young man.'

I glance towards his bedside cabinet.

'Look, do you need a drink of water or something? I've got to …'

He smiles. 'No, thank you. Saw you come back with Rose just now.' He leans forward on his chair curiously. 'I saw you brought my girl back to me. I want to thank you, for that.' His voice wobbles a bit, betraying his feelings. I lift up my hands depreciatingly, uncomfortable at his gratitude. Uncomfortable, in fact, at being in his presence at all and I feel a wave of shame wash over me.

'No problem.' *You have nothing to thank me for; everything to blame me for,* I think. 'Rose not around?'

'Gone to have a bath,' he observes. 'You look a bit cold, too. My daughter didn't ask you in?' I give a non-committal shrug. I glance through the window and I wonder; has this man had enough air yet?

'Sir, I'm sorry but … I've got to go, okay?'

'She wasn't at Shona's, was she?' He puts in unexpectedly and when I turn to look at him again I get the strangest sense of déjà vu. It's his eyes - they're like her eyes, aren't they? Like hers. I didn't expect them to be. I never saw his eyes last time our paths met. If I had ... if I'd only looked him in the eye, things would have worked out very differently.

I turn away, not wanting to see his eyes; take in the frayed edges of his off-white bedroom curtains instead, the worn tread-marks on his carpet. I don't want to see that, either. Dilapidated, that's the best way to describe it. I'd imagined Rose as living in a beautifully-kept house, somehow; clean and modern and whole-some. Maybe Clare Farm was like that, once? This place looks so sad, worn-out. Is this what I've brought them to?

'Look, I really need to be getting on ...' I turn to close his window but he stops me.

'Not yet. Please, just a little longer.' I can hear the plead-ing in his voice and it stops me in my tracks. He can't get many visitors up here, I imagine. 'When the wind comes from the right direction you can smell the sea from here if you take in a lung-ful of it.' He breathes in again, so deeply I wonder if he wishes I could smell it through his nostrils, as if he could make me feel it through his own experience.

'I know,' I say. I know how the air up here can sometimes smell of the salt-sea breeze. 'When the wind blows in strong enough it can bend back all the stalks of wild grass so far it's like a giant hand sweeping over the top of the field. I used to love watching it do that ...'

'You used to,' he picks up.

'I used to.'

'You're from around these parts, then?'

'I was, once.' I admit.

'You know my daughter?' he gets in softly now. I shake my head. Then I nod. I do know her.

'I haven't known her long,' I admit.

'You seem to have made quite an impression for such a short acquaintance, if you pardon my saying so.'

'I'm not quite sure what you mean, sir.'

'The way she looked at you when you two were together on the lane. I was watching, through the window, you see. I like to watch the blackbirds come and scramble for the remains of the toast.' He points out of the window and I see what he must have seen, his viewpoint; 'I saw you two ...' He makes a motion with his hands, as if to say - *I saw you two part.* 'You have feelings for each other, don't you?'

I give a strangled laugh. What can I say? *Don't get your hopes up!* I'm a non-committal kind of guy, that's what I should say to him, throw him off the scent, but I don't. Now that I'm here, something in me wants to keep on having this conversation. I have no place here, no place at all in this family's affairs and yet here I am, feeling as involved as a thread that's been woven deep into the pattern of their lives. I *am* involved. She wanted him to know just how much. Because she thinks that will help him. I'm still looking for the courage ...

'Am I right?' He looks at me openly, asks me man to man. 'Does she care for you?'

'She cares about *you*,' I tell him now. 'She's ... she's told me all about you,' I carry on talking, even though I can hear foot-steps, downstairs. There are other people in the house, I have to remember that.

'She cares about me and I'm all she's got left but ...' He gives me a significant look. 'The things that matter change, don't they?'

'Sir?'

'She's cross at me right now ...' He lowers his voice conspir-atorially, 'because I won't agree to leave here to go and try some new-fangled experimental therapy in the States. My brother's been trying to persuade me to go. And now her.'

'Could it ... could it help?' I take in this new information with a growing sense of wonder. There is something that might help him? Something that could wash away all the badness I brought into his life?

He opens his hands in a 'who knows?' gesture.

'Do they think it might?'

'I'd have to be assessed for suitability but … they *hope*,' he says wryly.

'And you?'

'I don't know. It *might*. But I can't go unless I sell this place. And I won't sell this place while I live. Won't give them …' He indicates with his head up towards my father's farm. 'The satisfaction. I promised Isla I'd never let those trees be torn down. Rose thinks I'm just a stubborn old fool and the truth is, I think she could be right. My daughter needs to move on and … I need to move on too.' He gives me a sad smile. 'Trouble is, I don't have much to move on to, do I? Forgive me,' He says, suddenly self-conscious, 'I shouldn't burden you. You can see I don't get many people to talk to up here …'

'You could move on to a life with better health?' I feel a surge of hope rising in me at the thought of it. 'You've got to try, haven't you? For both your sakes.'

For my sake, too …

'Maybe … I am just too old now.' His voice suddenly sags in the middle. 'And too scared.'

'I know you are scared. She told me.' I look directly at him, 'About how it was after you got hurt. How you still have nightmares over it …' Rose's father is looking at me so closely I get a sudden shock to my system. Does he know me? Christ.

'What's your name?' he demands suddenly.

'Lawrence.'

'Speak up, young man.' He indicates his ears.

'*Lawrence.*'

He smiles. 'Thank you for bringing my daughter home safely to me, Lawrence. Thank you.' His voice cracks. 'For bringing her home.' He's been so worried about her, I can feel it in his voice. Because he loves her so much and he feels he can't protect her anymore.

'Sir, I know what happened to you that night …' I swallow, realising that I am about to go somewhere maybe I shouldn't go at all. But she's right; he's got to know that he doesn't need to be scared anymore. 'I just need you to know that Rose is safe. That you're both safe. No one is going to hurt you ...'

He's silent now, taking me in. Then;

'Would you indulge an old man for a moment, Lawrence? Answer me one question?'

'Sure.' I swallow.

Is there any reason you know of in particular why I should *hate* you, Lawrence?'

'Why you should hate me?' The question sends a series of shock waves surging through my system. This innocent-seeming, harmless old man - why has he asked me this? What does he know? And ... what could he possibly do about it? 'I like to play reggae music very loud,' I say stupidly. 'I love dogs. Especially very large, noisy dogs. I hate cats. I love fast, flashy motorbikes but I can't currently afford to buy one. I have just lost my job ...' I look at him wildly. *Are these all reasons why you might hate someone*?

'I don't ...' My words are tumbling out, one on top of the other, jumbled, unstructured as a house of cards when it all comes crashing down. 'I don't get on very well with my own father. I ... I don't like him very much, sir. In fact, I can't stand him.' We are coming to it, aren't we? Slowly, like a prairie dog circling a wounded deer we are coming to it. 'He's a bad man.' *He and me both*. 'As a consequence of that, I haven't seen my own family in years.' I stop, feeling my whole body trembling, hearing my own heart thudding in my chest. I am young and strong and he is old and weak, but if he learns the truth now, I know the tables will be turned and he will have the power to take me down.

'For how many years?' he asks softly.

'Five years.'

'Five,' he says and I think I can see water beginning to gather behind his eyes. '*Five years*.' And the unimaginable truth is starting to dawn. Something about him seems to shrink in now and he goes very silent.

'I try my best to be an honourable man,' I continue unsteadily, my voice perceptibly slowing down, 'but I haven't always done

366

the right thing. On occasion,' I croak. 'I have done some very bad things.'

The silence between us now becomes thick and gloopy. It feels like the darkness when I'd take Kahn out on a chill autumn night and there'd be the smell of decaying leaves in the air, an unwholesomeness, as if the earth were calling everything that was stagnant back to herself ...

I bend down now, kneel beside his chair,

'Bad things. Including one thing for which - yes, I believe you would have every reason to hate me.' He blinks, saying nothing, but I see a solitary tear roll down one weathered cheek. For a moment, his hand moves, flutters in his lap, but the rest of him seems immobilised and I feel a stab of pain at my own handiwork. *I never meant to do this to you.* The sight of that tear rolling down his face catches at my heart and I feel the swell of water behind my own eyes now, a burning at the back of my throat. *I never meant to hurt you.*

I lay my hands over his.

He stiffens, and when he takes in a small breath now his whole frame feels shocked and so very fragile.

'What did you do, Lawrence?' he says. I feel his hands, thin and weak as they are, turn surprisingly quickly to catch hold of my own in his lap. And I want to run; like I have never wanted something so much in all this life.

But I won't.

Not until I tell this man something that I should have told him years ago.

367

'Sir.' I lean down and look into her father's eyes. 'There's something I need to say to you ...'

'My name is Jack,' he tells me unexpectedly. I didn't know his name. This man, whose life I ruined, he has a name. It brings a lump to my throat. He has a name and he has a loving daughter and he likes to smell the sea breeze and feel the wind on his face ...

'Rose has told me about you, Jack. How you're a good, family man. A loving father. She told me a little about her mother, too, how it all turned out that you were up there at Macrae Farm that night, how you got injured, trying to get that land back. She told me that you never knew why it happened. How that's affected you deeply ...'

I know why it happened though. It happened because I made a mistake. It happened because the man who lives next door to you is a psychopath and five years ago I was young enough and foolhardy enough to think that I could stop him. I take in a breath and go for it.

'Look, it was never you who was the intended victim of that attack. You need to know that. That bit was a mistake. The police - they never found ... they never caught up with ...' My voice catches in my throat, 'but I know, *I promise you* ... he's never been a free man since the day of that attack either. Just like you.'

His fingers close almost imperceptibly tighter around mine

368

now, his eyes close for a brief second but when they open they are directly on my face.

'*You*, Lawrence?' he says. I stare at him for a moment. Then I look down, a brief nod. I cannot bring myself to say the words. I don't have to say the words. I hear that small strange sound now, at the back of his throat, and there is no mistaking that *he knows*. He knows who I am. He knows what I did.

It's going to happen now. Any minute now, it'll all come crashing down, it dawns on me. This whole fragile life that I have created for myself; this life in which I am someone good, someone who does the right thing by others; this life where I am not someone who is hated for who I am and for the one thing in my life I have done that I regret beyond all else ...

'*You*?' He says again, and I am back in the space where I told her the truth, disappeared almost to nothing, shrunken to almost a dot on a page, waiting for his howl of anger, waiting for the scream of fear and shock to reverberate right through the house that I have come right into his private space, disturbed the sanctity of his home like this but he doesn't sound angry. He sounds, instead, so *sad*.

He sounds so full of disappointment. I can't understand it. This isn't what I expected his reaction to be. The truth is, this feels much worse.

'You are the man who did this to me?' I can't lift my eyes to his. I can't. My eyes are glued only to his legs, his stick-thin legs that someone has wrapped so lovingly in a red chequered blanket.

'I didn't mean to hurt you.' My throat and nose are full of phlegm, so bunged up now I can barely breathe, let alone get out the words. 'I *meant* ...' I close my eyes, hard, wanting to stop whatever it is that's happening in my chest and my belly. 'I meant to hurt *him*. To teach him a lesson. Only him. Not you. I thought you *were* him.'

'Your father?' His hand on mine feels so strangely warm. His hand is like a little bird's foot, warm like a pigeon which once landed on my hand, a little thing, so fragile and trusting. 'You

369

thought I was him. You wanted to hurt *him?*'

'Rob Macrae.' I bring myself to look sideways at him now. I feel the tears that have wet my face without my even noticing. 'Your enemy. Mine. My father. I wanted to ...'

I can't say it.

At the mention of my father's name his fingers lift slightly on my hand. He makes no other movement but I know, I can *feel* him, making connections in his mind when I tell him that. So many connections, they fly around like leaves in a dust-bowl. Who I am. What I am. What we are to each other. And then me ... what I suddenly appear to be to her, his daughter, that's there too, all whirling around in the mix.

'So. Rob Macrae is your father,' he says. When I look into his eyes - so like her eyes - I am waiting to see the gates go down, now that the truth is out. For all those hundred-and-one ready-made assumptions about the person I must be, to slot into place. I am a Macrae. I am the thug who hurt him. What more does this man need to know about me? What more do I need to say?

'And yet ...' he says hesitantly. 'My daughter loves you?'

And you. Enough to want to bring us together, I think. If this man could walk, he'd get up and leave this room right now I am sure of it. If only it were possible for him to do so, he'd move away from this unfamiliar and difficult place, he wouldn't stay here. Not in this place, where his truth is being challenged so un-comfortably, this place that should not exist; where the currents of two opposing rivers converge, run confluent with each other.

'She *loves* you,' he says again, and I can hear the bewilder-ment in his voice, the upset. Because by all rights, such a thing should not be possible - should it? For a while there, he'd been prepared to love me too, I know it.

'I don't ask your forgiveness.' My words sound so strange. I can hear this whooshing sound in my ears and the whole room seems suddenly a little darker, a little yellower. Now the entire household outside of this room, all the sounds I have been so acutely aware of up to this moment, all the little noises I've felt so keenly they could have been my own heartbeat, every breath, every movement ... they've all gone quiet, I can't hear them anymore. No ticking of the radiator. No footsteps moving about on the creaking floorboards, no sounds of water rushing away down household drains, no more cracking as the ice on the roof starts to shift and melt, no hushed voices. No breath. Only now ... through the partially-opened window, I can hear the raindrops pattering outside, I can hear them spitting and sizzling on the snow. I don't ask for his forgiveness. Right now my whole body has gone numb. The only part of me I can really feel is the part where he's still holding my hand. It's the only part that's still got a pulse, I don't know where the rest of me has gone.

What would it take for him to forgive me, anyway?

An eye for an eye? A prison sentence?

'I know I ... have never lost the proper use of my legs.' I wipe my face again. 'I never got sent down. But there are so many ways in which a man can be imprisoned. Right now ...' I glance uneasily towards his door, because I know our time alone in here together is nearly up. The voices coming from the hallway - female voices - are slightly raised now, tense. I can't hear what they are saying but the household is on the move, I sense this much.

'Right now I've got my nemesis coming to me. Does it help you to know that, Jack?'

'Your nemesis,' he repeats softly and his eyes are pained, full of an unexpected concern for me that haunts me, humbles me. 'What shape would that take, Lawrence?'

He presses my fingers when I don't answer.

'She cares for you,' he says, and I can hear the edge of his voice shaking. 'You matter to Rose. I know that much. And ... she matters to me, too.' He says feelingly. 'She brought you here?'

'Yes, sir.' My mouth feels dry, like a lizard's mouth in the desert sun. He considers this for a long time. The fact that she brought me. The fact that I have come. The minutes - they could be mere moments, but they tick by so slowly they feel like hours. He can't get up and walk out but he could call out to his family

371

and they'd soon come running in, I think now. They would get me well away from him. He doesn't have to stay here and listen to this. He doesn't have to stay ...

'Does she know what else you are planning ... your *nemesis*?' he comes back after a long while.

I shake my head, slowly.

'She asked me to come back here. We didn't discuss anything further.'

'No?' His eyebrows raise a fraction and I see a host of conflicting things surge up in his eyes now. Understanding, that I want to somehow put things right. Concern, *fear*, that I mean to go back. Curiosity. Compassion. I see all these things, the colours of them merging and pulling apart into separate thoughts in his mind while he considers what's best to do next.

'What will your father do to you?' he asks me at last and for some strange reason it does not feel out of place for him to ask it. Still, I feel a little surprised - honoured even - that he cares. My hand, still in his, feels comforted and warm. How strange this is. How unexpected. I do not want to move it.

'He'll kill me, probably.' I let out a humourless laugh.

'Don't go, then,' he says simply. The edges of his eyes are crinkled up in an unexpected sadness for me. 'You didn't mean to do this to me, did you?' There's a new strength in his voice now - a strength in *him* - that I didn't suspect would be there. 'I won't derive any satisfaction from you getting yourself hurt, Lawrence.'

I shake my head now. I don't want to get myself hurt. That isn't why I need to go.

'I have to go. I do not want to do it. But I need to face him, Jack.' I didn't know till this moment that I still had to do that, but I see now that I do. I see now that my reasons for coming home were way more complex than my desperate need to find a sponsor for Sunny. 'All you need to know ...' I lean a little closer to his chair. 'From the bottom of my heart, is that I have never stopped paying for what I did to you that night, Jack Clare. And I am truly sorry.'

'Lawrence,' he shakes his head, regretful, as I straighten now. In a minute I am going to make my way back out through that fire-door. I want to go before Rose comes in and stops me. I want to go before anything *else* happens to stop me. They're going to take me in, now. I know this. They're going to catch up with me and then I'll never get the chance to face my father - do what I never did five years back; what I should have done then.

'All *you* need to know,' he gives my hand one last squeeze before I let his go, '... is that the only person left who needs to forgive you now, is yourself.'

I haven't opened the letter yet.

It's here. In the bathroom, propped up on the shelf where I keep my nice soaps and my dried starfish and all the shells I collected during walks along the beach as a child. It seems appropriate, as it's the culmination of everything I've been aiming for all this time.

For me, it is potentially the greatest treasure of all. And yet - even if I have an offer I'm still back to the original problem. Without my dad being willing to shift, I can't go anywhere.

I lie back in the hot water and listen to the tiny bubbles of the soap suds as they pop all around me. I would love to be able to enjoy the heat of the water soaking into my skin and wish that I could just block out everything else; that I could stop being so hyper-alert for the sounds of the door going, for any sign that Lawrence has at last arrived. I've got my towel on the side, ready for me to jump out the minute I hear anything. But nobody arrives.

The minutes tick by. The heat from the bathwater, normally so comforting, is doing little to help me feel better right now. It's only making me feel too hot. I try and untighten my shoulders. I try and relax. I must change what I let myself think about. Not Lawrence. Not Dad. Not the letter. But as I sink down I see the hot steam rising up from the bath has smeared the mirror over. *It'll cause the paper to become all damp*, I think. By the time I open the letter all the writing will be smudged and almost illegible like the hand-written scrawl in the top corner.

Urgent – please reply by the 30ᵗʰ December.

The 30th of December. Today is the 27th, I think, and time is rushing by ... Damn it! *Why* won't Dad give the States a chance? More importantly, why hasn't Lawrence turned up yet? It can't have taken them all this time to move just one tree - can it? I know he said it would take a while ... The sound of someone knocking sharply at the bathroom door goes right through me now.

'Hey,' Sam says, and I can tell her face is close up against the door. 'Who's in there?'

'It's me.' I sit up, abruptly.

'*Rose*?'

'Of course,' I tell my cousin. '*Who else?*'

'It's just that ...' She sounds a teeny bit put out. 'I was about the use the bath,' she says after a bit. 'We're planning on leaving soon, haven't you heard?'

'I heard,' I say. The rapidly-cooling bathwater is dripping down my arms now. They're going; the sense of regret, of lost opportunity, that I felt earlier, returns softly. They're going and very soon all that'll be left is me and Dad.

'If you're in the bath,' my cousin adds as an afterthought. 'Then who has Uncle Jack been talking to all this time?'

'Talking to himself, most likely.' I think: if his meds haven't kicked in yet, it's entirely possible.

'I heard more than one voice in there,' she insists.

'Maybe he's got the radio on?' I'm not really paying attention to Sam anymore, all I'm thinking is that I can't let them go and let Lawrence go and for *nothing to have changed*. Things have got to change! Lawrence should have turned up by now. I could always get dressed and go back out there and find out what's going on.

Or maybe I could just accept that he's changed his mind,

he's chickened out, and he's left me here to pick up the bits and pieces of my life as best I can. The thought makes me very angry. It makes me feel that perhaps what happens to me in my life really isn't all that important to him. Maybe he doesn't care about putting it right with my dad as much as he cares about running away? And now I think about it, Dad's not very much better, is he? He's too scared to move from here. He's too scared to let *me* move.

And I am letting him do that.

Oh, sod it. What am I playing at? I stand up abruptly, the water going all over the place as I rise. I wrap the large bath towel around me and step out onto the linoleum floor, the water pooling into messy puddles at my feet. I go over and pick up the letter.

Maybe if what I've got in here is an offer ... I should just take Dad up on his suggestion and go do it anyway. Let him sort himself out. Whether that means via help from Uncle Ty or a trip to the States ... maybe I need to step out of it all, take a step back, just like Lawrence seems to have done out of my life. I need to make the decision for myself, that this is what I am going to do. I am going to leave. *I am*. Everything else is going to have to fall in place. I trust that it will.

I rip the envelope open now. My fingers, all tangling and useless, feel thick as balloons, and the letter inside, thinner than I'd expected, slips to the floor.

As I bend to retrieve it, my last-chance ticket to the life I've dreamed of, I feel a sudden panic that it cannot be what I want. It is too thin! I got pawed by my gross neighbour, for this, the memory comes flooding back. I went out in a snowstorm, prepared to risk getting mauled by next-door's dogs. *You were wrong, Lawrence,* I feel the swell of bitter tears gathering in my throat. *You told me that I'd make it. That I wanted it bad enough and I'd get there and I believed you.*

I believed in you so much I thought you'd make it too. I believed that you'd save Sunny and that you'd come out of it all intact somehow, someway, and that there'd be a place for us in this world. But none of those things are true, are they? I ignore the sharp rapping at the bathroom door, now. *Go away*, Sam!

Dad is the only one who should be here with me, to witness this, I think regretfully. I left him alone in his room, came away with the letter but I shouldn't have done that. He wanted to be here with me for this moment. Dad knows ... he's one of the few people who really understands what getting this offer would mean to me. What it'll mean if I don't.

I won't study Law.

I will never walk over the bridge in the spring and watch the lazy boats punt gently up the Cam when the petals are falling like snowflakes from the cherry trees. I will never take my books on a sunny day and lie out with my friends on the grass at Howard Court like I saw all those other students do. I won't sit in one of the fashionable coffee-shops, watching the tourists go by, or spend a Sunday evening sitting on the stone wall outside King's chapel, listening to the choir sing. I won't leave Merry Ditton. Because this paper ... this paper is too thin.

And yet, despite everything, I can't entirely let go of this crazy hope that things could somehow turn out all right. I bend to pick up the paper, turning it over to read the words on the other side as I do. Now that I dare to properly look I can see that it *is* from Downing College, I can see that by the letterhead. A rejection?

I don't actually read it, though. I catch just one, solitary word, on my way up.

That word is 'pleased ...'

'Hello? Hello *Rose?*' It's Sam, she's back. 'I've just gone and checked,' she says in a low voice, 'and I can definitely hear Uncle Jack talking to someone in there.' She sounds spooked. Why doesn't she just knock on his door and check? I wipe my eyes again and my face feels hot, steamed up from the bath and I can't properly concentrate. I just got my Downing College offer. *OMG! I just got my offer!*

'Rose?'

'I'm ... just looking at the letter that arrived for me,' I say. There's a moment's silence as she takes this in.

'It's from the University, isn't it?'

I place the letter over my heart, hardly daring to believe it but I know that it is true. And now I have to reply to them! And soon. Did they mean by email or by post? What do I need to do next? Oh God, oh God. ..! I skim over the letter, looking for clues but I can barely see the words in front of me, I can barely read, I can barely *think* any more. I put my clothes on then, in a hurry, dragging them up impatiently over my still-wet skin and then, in amongst my frantic rush to *do* something, take some action and do it quickly, I suddenly realise;

When I reply to them - what am I going to say?

I mean, I don't know yet if I can honestly go. Not really. I feel like someone who's bowled a bowling ball right bang down the middle of the lane, a sure-fire to knock over those ten-pins all in one go and what happens? The ball slows down and stops dead right in front of the gate. I go and unlock the bathroom door, my letter getting damp in my hand.

'Let's have a look at it then,' Sam demands. I hold it out to her now and she reads it slowly and thoroughly. When she's finished, a small smile crosses my cousin's face. 'Well done,' she says quietly. 'I'm glad that you got the offer you wanted.'

'Thank you.' I smile at her and I'm aware that the relief I'm feeling is coming off me in waves. She steps forward and gives me a little awkward hug. She's happy for me, I know she's happy, but I can *feel* what she's thinking as clear as if she'd actually said the words out loud. I wipe my cheeks with the back of my hand and she steps away a little, her eyes crinkling curiously.

'I mean to find a way to go ...' I tell her.

'Will you persuade Uncle Jack?' She shrugs, and in that one little movement I get a whole back-story from her, a sure sense that her parents haven't just mooted the whole States issue with my dad - they've done their darnedest to persuade him; they've already *bent over backwards* to convince him. She doubts I'll get any further than they did. 'Maybe now that you've got your offer?' she says, a little doubtfully.

'I'm thinking maybe ... once he knows what *my* plans are, he'll shift his own,' I tell her. As I tell her this, it seems to become clearer to me, in my own mind. I can't wait around for Dad to come around anymore. No matter what the temptation is to stay here and rescue him from the uncomfortable consequences of his own decisions. I mustn't. He has options, after all.

'That's brave of you,' she says. I'm not sure if that's what she's actually thinking, or whether she feels that would be the wrong thing to do, an unthinkable thing to do. Then she lightens up suddenly, a dimple forming right there, in the corner of her cheek and she looks at my letter again. 'You're very lucky.' This time a little wistfully. 'I wish that I might get such a chance. I don't think I'd get a look in. Maybe I can come and stay over in your room some weekend though?'

'Sure, you can.'

'All right, girls?'

Her mother appears beside her now, coming up the stairs folding one of her blouses as she goes. She looks at my letter which Sam holds up for her to see before handing it back to me and her eyes widen a little in surprise.

'*Congratulations,*' she says and I can see that she really does mean it. 'It's all the more remarkable when you consider the circumstances under which you have achieved it.' I feel a flush of pleasure at that. 'Have you told Jack yet?'

I clear my throat.

'I was just going in to him now ...' This doesn't feel right. Two people know already and Dad isn't one of them. He should have been the first to know. He wanted to be the first, but I was so *mad* at him ...

'I could have sworn you were already in there with him,' she shakes her head. 'I thought I heard him ...' She looks towards his door, slightly puzzled. 'It's not Ty. He's still downstairs. We were both waiting for you to come down, in fact ...'

There's something else, isn't there? Something in her expression looks cut up, hurt. For the tiniest of moments, standing there in the corridor with Carlotta, I catch a glimpse of the desperation beneath the tautness around her eyes. As if she has to hold the whole world together with her being; orderly, tidy, perfect. As if any sign of weakness or imperfection in her could mean that the sun might never rise again of a morning, that the moon could fade in the night sky and the tides stall.

'I came up to tell you I've just had a call on my mobile from Matt Dougal. The Bentley's repaired,' she informs me now. 'And now that the roads are passable enough we won't be sticking around for too much longer ...'

'No. Of course not.'

'I came up here to let you know but - Rose ...' She glances at Sam as if not sure if she should proceed with my cousin in front but then she says it, anyway. 'There's a bone I need to pick with you. I'm sure there's some perfectly reasonable explanation for it, but until I know what it is I'm left feeling, well, frankly, uncomfortable.'

'Yes?' There's a cold draught running through the upstairs hallway now, I can feel it, chilling the damp skin on my arms and legs. A draught like a window's been left open somewhere but I know that with Carlotta in charge here, no window would ever be left open. The draught makes me shudder but right now it's the discomfort in her eyes that is troubling me the most.

I get the feeling that I am about to be called to account. All the things that I haven't told the family yet since re-entering the house. All the things that I knew, when I came back here, I was going to have to tell them...

'The thing is, when I spoke to him just now, Matt Dougal didn't seem to be aware that you'd spent Christmas at his house.' She stops, and I can hear from her voice how upset she is. *Didn't she hear me tell her that over my mobile? Didn't she hear me, then?* My stomach tightens. 'I haven't said anything to your uncle yet,' she continues breathlessly. 'If you weren't at Shona's ... I thought I'd come up and find out from you first. What's been going on, Rose?'

A feeling of shock, of imminent discovery, trickles like a rivulet of cold water from the top of my head right down to my toes. Suddenly, ridiculously, I feel like I want to laugh out loud but I know if I do I'll only alarm her further.

'You're right of course.' I can feel my eyes watering, keep my head down. 'But there is a ... a perfectly good explanation.' She looks relieved at that, I can see her shoulders visibly relax. An explanation is forthcoming. Her discomfort is about to be assuaged and everything is still all right with the world ...

'It's just that ...' I look her straight in the eyes. 'I really, really want to go and give my dad the good news ...' I glance at the letter in my hand. 'Do you mind if I come back to you in a bit?'

'Oh. Well - of course,' she understands. 'Naturally. First things first, eh?' She pats the letter in my hand. 'Jack's going to be thrilled. And *proud*,' she brings herself to add. I stare at her for a moment. That last is as near as I'm ever going to get to an acknowledgement from Carlotta. I feel a warmth spread for a moment in my stomach, a feeling of pleasure at the thought that my aunt might ever actually *approve* of me.

It's mixed with a sadness at the thought that she won't feel so approving once she discovers what the *perfectly good explanation* for me not being at Shona's is …

None of them will.

I left Jack's room by the same means which I entered it, closing the fire-door carefully behind me. I did not run. I walked out of there. My head was full of a clarity I have not known before, my whole body buzzing with a lightness, as if he had given me a blessing of some sort. I think maybe he had. It was as though, after all this time, Jack had given me permission to take up my life again. He had offered me some sort of truce, some sort of peace and I knew I wasn't going to run anymore. But I still had one more thing to do before I earned it. One more thing.

As I arrived at Macrae Farm a few minutes ago, the key was still ensconced in its usual place behind the large flowerpot out front. The burglar alarm was disarmed with the same code - my father's first car registration. Nobody was in, my father's jeep gone from the drive. Nobody here to greet me, the prodigal son returning at last, soaked to the bone because it had begun to rain in earnest as I walked down here, frozen to my core. Hungry. Scared. Sad.

When I got in so easily I had a moment of hope back there that maybe my mother would be in the house after all and the men would be out. That I'd be able to see her for a few minutes alone, at least. Entering the hallway, I wanted to see her again. I wanted it so much it hurt but I got the picture pretty quickly that she wasn't in. Her coat wasn't on the rack. Nobody's was. The house was so quiet, so dark. Two of the older dogs had been left inside, off the chain. They sniffed around, curious for a bit, but then they slunk off. Dogs don't bother me. They never have. So I stole up here like a thief in my own parents' house, into my father's room. The door has not been locked. He's expecting no intrusion, no trouble, today. He's not expecting me.

Walking in here now, into my father's close and darkened study, it feels like walking back into yesterday. The black leather-topped desk, tidy and polished, still stands by the window. The photocopier and the fax machine still occupy the same corner. The curtains are the same heavy mustard-coloured drapes. He's got the same ugly fake Georgian table-lamp sitting in the corner. The certificates and photos from Rob Macrae's boxing days, signed and framed, are still hanging up there on the walls.

I see his father's carriage clock has gone; he's got one that doesn't tick so loudly now. I go over and touch it, let the tips of my fingers run softly over its ornate lacquered top - not a speck of dust here anywhere - and then I catch my fingers back quickly, because everything in here is his, chosen by him, touched by him, placed here by his hand.

I do not want to have any part of it, *be* any part of it. I never have. I never will. I take in a gulp of breath now, had not realised that I had stopped breathing. My eyes dart back to the table-lamp in disgust. He hit me with the metal end of that, once. The sight of it still there, when in my mind I have smashed it to pieces a thousand times, both enrages and upsets me. I look away quickly.

Nothing much has changed here, has it? There's still that same fug in the air. The smell I associate with him; of his tobacco and his too-bright aftershave and all that thick furniture polish trying to cover up the smell he carries always on his fingers, the lingering taint of pig blood from the slaughterhouse. The smell of it unearths memories that I have worked for years to bury; strips away all the years in which I have grown into a man, a decent man, doing a job that helps put people together, instead of tearing them apart.

I lean down now and pull open his under-desk drawer. It

jams a little. Maybe he doesn't use this one so much anymore. The gun is still in there. He really is a creature of habit. I take it out and examine it, feel the weight of it in my hand. It's a Colt 1908. The tiny picture of the dancing horse on the side always fascinated me as a child. I used to think it must be intended for shooting horses but we never had any of those on our farm. I've seen my father point this gun at his lackeys on more than one occasion, though. He used to terrify the life out of them. *A man's fear is like a curse on him*, he used to say. *It's the easiest way to control 'em. Make him scared enough and a grown man will cry and beg like a baby, even the hardest of them.* I know he enjoyed that. I wonder if he'd enjoy it so much if he ever saw this thing pointing towards his own snout?

I tuck the colt into the waistband of my jeans, hidden under my top. If it comes to it, I intend to be prepared.

I am so focused on the task that the buzz of my mobile phone going off all of a sudden feels like a drill-saw cutting into the space around me. Who the heck is it?

Who the hell is that now? And what can they have to say that could possibly matter? I think; he was always on about installing CCTV in every room, wasn't he, my dad? He could have been in the house all along, watching me from some hidden vantage-point. The thoughts that start coming in now, they're all crazy, paranoid thoughts, but for the moment, my heart is pounding so hard I can't think of any other explanation, nothing else will come in at all, just that he's found me. He knows I'm here. *He knows ...*

I wipe the thin band of sweat forming across my forehead with the back of my hand. Then I pick up.

'Yes?'

'Hello, son.'

Son? I don't answer for a good few seconds. All I can think is; *my father's got hold of my mobile number somehow. This is some kind of game on his part. He won't just come in and face me; he needs me to be scared ...*

'Lawrence?' The voice comes again, and this time I know

who it is. Dougie. Ah, God. The kindness I always hear in his voice does something to me inside; it opens me up a chink, reminds me of the person I am when I'm away from here. But I can't afford to be that person right now. Not now, when I need to be strong. Not here. 'Everything okay, son?' It is not okay. I swallow.

'Sure.'

'You're at home, right now?' He's imagining me in some cosy domestic scene; I can picture it in the nostalgia in his voice. A bead of sweat trickles down from my forehead and onto my cheek. It itches like a mosquito walking across my skin and I want to swat it off. I want to stop this panicky sweating. I want to get back in control of my breathing again.

'Yeah.' I say at last. '... I'm at home.'

I look around me, taking in my father's old favourite picture of himself with a broken and bloodied nose the day he won his biggest fight. The last time I sat in here I was just a young lad and yet, ironically, I felt so much more up to the challenge of facing him, then. I used to come in and sit on his chair on occasion, whenever he was out. I used to let myself pretend. Let myself think about what it was that needed to be done. How the day must surely come when I would be big enough and strong enough to square up to him. How the time would come when I no longer felt afraid at the thought of doing that. And when I did ... it would stop the fear I woke up with every morning, that each day might be my last; that he might, on a whim, decide to finish all three of us. Because none of us mattered to him, I knew that, we were only there to serve him. Back then, my mind was beautifully clear. Now it is not. Back then, I thought that I would one day know how I might win this game. Now I know I cannot.

'I'm at home,' I say again, and I hear my old boss clear his throat. He was expecting to make a breakthrough today, he said. He's going to tell me now that Herr Lober has come through for him and I need to fax those documents through, stat. Only I can't fax any documents through. I have no sponsor. My mother isn't here. I've been through the house, and by the looks of it, she's been gone a few days. There are no signs of her presence any-where. No Christmas flowers in the dining room. No tree up. No special food in the fridge. I don't know where she is but - she's not here.

'Lawrence.' I can hear Dougie's out breath, the relief in him, all those hundreds of miles away. 'Listen up lad. I've a confession to make.'

'Yes?' I almost want to laugh out loud when he says that. *He has a confession?*

'When I told you to go home ... that I'd be able to send Sunny on through after you - you knew that was only ever a real long shot, right?'

'What's happened, Doug?' I feel my heart sinking now; sink-ing into a long, cold bath which is freezing the heart out of me. 'You were expecting good news today. You told me that earlier.'

'I am going to be honest with you.' Pause. 'There was never any real chance that Sunny could get on that Aid Abroad flight ...'

'*What*?' I push my hands through my hair, pacing the room now, my heart going faster. I can hear it, beating in my chest. '*Why*? And - in that case - why did you send me back here?' He's lying, he's got to be. I don't know why. But he's lying ...

'I sent you back because I thought I'd rather sell you a false promise than see a caring, talented guy like you flung pointlessly into a jail cell for a few years. I wanted you back home, Lawrence. I wanted you out of Jaffna. Convincing you we could save that boy was the only way I could persuade you to leave ...'

I stare at the phone for a minute. Wipe my mouth with the back of my hand. 'There was never any chance?' I say it, and I know it's true. This time he isn't lying to me. 'All that talk of Herr Lober ...?'

'Oh, it was true we applied to him, but there were so many protocols that needed following, lad. If Sunny had been the heir apparent himself it'd have been a job to get him on that flight ...'

'So ... what's happening to him?'

'To Sunny?' He gathers himself. 'They needed to release his

387

hospital bed yesterday. More urgent cases were coming in every day. It was decided he'd have to take his chances back in the camp …'

'Pretty damn poor chances, Dougie.' My voice is laced with disappointment. 'You know full well what'll happen to him out there.'

'I know,' he says faintly. He's practically squirming with discomfort, at the deceit he's laid on me. I'm so let down and disappointed with him I feel like hanging up right now. Except … the fact is, I've been leading him up the garden path, too. There was precious little chance of me ever getting to my mother in time, persuading her …

'I know what the implications were for Sunny. Once he was turfed out of hospital, the chances that sooner or later he'd be back, needing an amputation were almost a certainty. Up till this afternoon there was nothing I could do about it, except now …' he breathes. 'A miracle has happened.'

A miracle. I close my eyes and press my thumb into my eye socket. What miracle? He's grown another foot?

'One of his relatives has come in for him. She spotted his photo hanging up on the fence, apparently. She didn't recognise him from the lists we compile because they'd used the wrong surname for him. But she's definitely a relative. We've had confirmation of it this afternoon, she's his older sister, Lawrence.'

'His *sister* …?'

'Arjuna said if you hadn't paid for the fliers of Sunny then she'd never have known, could never have come forward …'

'I didn't pay for any fliers …' I get out.

'Apparently you did. Arjuna saw you do it. The day when you were on your way out of the camp with him. Apparently you stopped and emptied out your wallet. Gave the lot to the guy who puts up the photos.'

All the rupees I had left. I remember now. I gave them to that guy *for himself*, because Arjuna told me how the man had fifteen relatives left he somehow had to feed. How he only made

388

fifty rupees for himself for every missing person he posted up there. I knew I wouldn't be needing the rupees anymore. I gave them to him. I didn't mean him to put up any fliers for Sunny ...

'And his sister saw the picture?'

'She came looking for her relatives and she saw it. She's taking him to her home in Colombo where he'll be well-looked after. He's going to make it, Lawrence. He's going to make it after all. And you ... you're back with your family, and ... I take it you're working things out?' What can I say to him? He wants it all to have come out good for me.

'We're working things out,' I get out at last.

'I was like you once,' I hear Dougie say in a low voice. 'As a young man, I fell out with my folks. But the day we resolved our differences was the day that changed my life.'

'Dougie ...' I start.

'You're a good lad, Lawrence,' he says over me. 'Damn it, you're one of the best workers I've yet had the pleasure of supervising out here.'

'Thank you.' I wipe my eyes with the edge of my sleeve and I know that this is all wrong, this phone call coming in now. It makes me vulnerable. It reminds me of the kindness I have known in my life and that makes me weak. I can't face my father when I'm feeling like this.

'If you can keep your nose clean,' he can't resist adding, 'You'll go on to do great things some day, I have no doubt of that.'

'I'll be in touch, Doug.'

Ah, God. I appreciate what he's tried to do for me but it's not going to work out the way he was hoping. It's not; it can't. And yet ... I have come home. I am here. I have met Rose and I have been to Clare Farm and spoken to my victim. I'll admit - seeing Jack Clare sitting in his chair unable to reach even that window, that did something to me inside. My overriding feeling wasn't the remorse I'd expected to feel. It wasn't the guilt. Seeing my unintended victim sitting there I felt - *I felt* - where it was my actions five years ago had really put me; it's put me in exactly the same place where Jack is. I've run and I've run but in the last five years I've never once been a free man. I never will be till I face my father.

My nemesis.

So; maybe it's all been worth risking? I am going to wait. I go and sit down in the soft leather swivel chair. The one that still has the imprint of him on it, like me; like anything he's ever touched. Except - Rob Macrae won't touch me ever again. I lick my lips and my mouth is parched. My left ear has started up buzzing and throbbing with an old pain. I inch the colt further down into my waistband. To steady my trembling hands I take out my playing cards from my pocket and lay them out on the desk. Then I build them up, three pairs abutted against each other, lay the roof-cards along the top, taking my time, willing my heart to stop hammering, willing my fingers to be steady. In my mind, I'm humming that tune that Rose sang to me when I called out in my sleep in the chapel. I don't know where that tune came from all of a sudden, but it's here, it helps to calm me.

By the time he comes in, I am ready.

'I said you'd be back.' He's here. Five years older, a little paler, a little greyer, flabbier around the jowls than he was but the hardness around his jaw and his eyes, it's the same. I blink, feeling the old churning in my belly.

'I *knew*.' He leans his arm against the door jamb and his rock-hard biceps form a square block of muscle that I can't take my eyes off; '... that sooner or later you'd come crawling back with your tail between your legs.' I see a small self-satisfied smile cross his face. 'And here you are.'

Here I am.

'I'm here to put things right,' I say and my eyelid twitches in the corner of my eye. The impulse which I always get in my father's presence - fight or flight - is kicking in now, hard. I stand up coming away from his desk, involuntarily take a few steps back towards the window.

If he went for me, could I take him? Not here; not like this. The time I tried to tackle him before, I had the advantage of the cover of darkness; I had the element of surprise. I had the unstoppable fuel of my hatred and my grief. Now I only have my feelings of regret, of wrong-doings that need putting right. I have no desire to add to them.

I look up at my father slowly, my eyes drawing level with his as he speaks again.

'Get tired of running, did you?'

I lick my lips, a dry white foam has formed in the corner of my mouth.

'I'm tired of running now.' To my surprise, as soon as the words are out of my mouth, I know them to be true. He gives me a strange, slightly disgusted, look.

'You'll be wondering why I never came after you?' He's come inside the room with me, now. If there's anyone else outside, I have no idea. Right now, in here, it's just him and me. He never did come looking for me, did he? I used to wonder why. His promise stayed with me long enough though; *I'll hunt you to the ends of the earth ... even if it means finishing the lot of you ...* When I left here, for a few weeks I slept in the open, under park benches, in doorways. But when I took to sleeping in houses at last, places that had an address he could potentially discover, I remember I slept sitting up in the wardrobe for months. I used to sleep under the bed with a knife in my hand.

It took me a long time before I let myself know that he wasn't out there somewhere, lurking in the shadows, waiting for his chance. I look at him warily now, watch him lower himself into the soft leather chair I've just vacated.

'Why didn't you?' I feel the twitch go in my eye again and I rub at my face, willing it to stop.

'Didn't need to, son.' He jabs at the air with his index finger, and then at his own heart. 'I'm already in there, aren't I? Inside of you.' His certainty makes me wince. 'You take me wherever you go, just like I always took my old man. I know that.'

A wave of cold goes over me but he's right. For months after I left here, just the memory of him was enough to keep me awake into the small hours. When I slept, it was enough to invade my rest, drag me out of deepest sleep in a fitful sweat, crying out. Just like the time Rose heard me, comforted me. He's hunted me to hell and back, haunted my dreams just as he promised me, without ever leaving his doorstep. And I in turn ... I've haunted Jack's. I bite my lip.

'Once a Macrae ...' He opens his hands, leaves the sentence

392

unfinished, and I know that he's goading me. 'You're mine, Lawrence. Blood of my blood. That's why you had to come back.'

I'd blocked out the memory of his voice, I realise now. His voice has the power to set off little jangling nerves of worry deep in my brain. Like the broken shards of a beer bottle being shattered in a dark alleyway, it sets the blood surging through my limbs, heightens my senses until every extremity is tingling with an electric rush of fear.

I am not like you. I never wanted to be yours. I take in a deep shuddering breath. *I used to dream that my mother would tell me she'd cheated on you before I was born just so I could hope it was some other man who fathered me, anyone but you ...* She's never going to tell me that now, though, is she?

'Where's Mum?' I look at him suddenly. Not here, I know that much. But where is she?

'I sent her away a couple of days ago,' he says slowly. 'Didn't want your sudden appearance here unsettling everyone again, upsetting the applecart.' *My sudden appearance ...*

'Marco told you I was back, then?' Of course. It makes sense. How else would the police have known to look for me if someone who knew hadn't alerted them? Bastard.

My father shrugs.

'He still works for me, Lawrence. And, no,' he answers my unspoken question. 'Your mother didn't know you were coming back. I told her to take this Christmas off, spend it with her sister like she's always wanted to. She was happy enough to go. She never will know you were here unless I decide she should. *If* I decide it.'

'If?' I've been leaning with my back against the window, watching him. I'd like to stand up now, to walk over to his desk and lean forward over it and just tell him what I've come here to say, get it over with, but my legs won't support the idea of standing.

'Depends on you, son. What you've come back for?' He looks at me and somewhere deep within that hard, blank face, I fancy I can see a small something opening up; his hope?

'I came back because ... I needed some help.' There's something very painful about admitting that to him, even though it was never him I wanted the help from. Needing help means you are vulnerable. Needing anything – or anyone - means you are vulnerable. And damn it, I have fallen in love with Rose; I have never been more vulnerable in my life than I am right now, and I know it.

'*Help! He needs help!*' he mocks, in a little falsetto voice. Then;

'What kind of help?' He's suddenly serious again, back into business mode - *let's see what we can sort out here ...*

'Money? Protection?'

'Can you protect me from the cops?' I throw unwillingly at him now. I don't even know why I say it. The words come out of their own accord, maybe because what I said to him just now is true. I am tired of running. I am tired of always hiding or being hunted. It would be good to stop.

'Word's clearly out that I am back. As soon as the highways are cleared this place will be crawling ...'

Why am I telling him this? I'm going to get thrown into jail, I know this now. Jail is the very least that's going to happen to me. Unless ... a tiny, unformed hope that hasn't a chance in hell, rears its head now, a hope as remote as the chance that I was ever going to be able to save Sunny from his fate; only this time the hope isn't for Sunny, it's for me.

'Can you save me from a prison sentence?' This brutal man who I once tried to hurt; he isn't going to be interested in saving me now, is he?

'Of course,' he says unexpectedly, a faint pleasure creeping into his voice, and something else, something I did not think to hear; *a pride*.

'Of course. I can protect you from anyone. Anything.' A strange frisson of something goes through me at that; an echo of something, a memory of what it might feel like to be truly protected; safe from harm.

'You're a Macrae,' he reminds me. 'We look after our own.' And I am one of yours. I swallow. He opens his hands in a gesture of curiosity.

'What are they after you for this time?'

'What *for*?' I stumble. He knows what for. He must do. 'I hurt Jack Clare. You know that,' I begin but he's shaking his head brusquely.

'That was five years ago, son,' he dismisses that in an instant. 'I meant; what have you done now? What's really brought you back?'

I open my mouth to tell him and then I shut it again. Sunny's story will be totally irrelevant to him. There's a glitter of anticipation in his eyes and I know he's waiting to hear I'm guilty of something even worse than what I did to Jack. But I am not. The Sri Lankan guy will recover, and I do not need any help in that regard.

'There's nothing else. I never meant to hurt that man the way I did ...' I look at my father painfully. 'I never should have done it. I never meant ...'

'He shouldn'a fuckin come up here, Lozza.' My father shrugs my remorse off as easily as he'd swat an annoying fly off his back.

'He shouldn'a come begging and bothering me. Stupid fucker. Don't cry about it.' He stands up suddenly, pulling his jacket down and the huge rings he always wore, knuckle-dusters shine menacingly on his fingers. 'If it makes you any happier, you did me a big favour, know that? Got him out of my hair ...'

'I didn't ...' I choke. 'I didn't do it for that reason. I did it because I ...' I stop. His eyebrows go up. Just a fine arc of red hair on his shiny white forehead.

'Because ...?'

I don't go on. My face is burning. *I wanted to stop you,* I think. *Because of what you did to our family. Because of what you did to my dog.*

'You wanted to get your own back on me, right?' His voice

is so soft. It's like the whisper of a dark wind, bending back the branches of the trees in the night, bending them back so hard that in the morning when you look all the branches have snapped ...

'I wanted to put the fear of God into you.' I breathe. I don't know why I say it. If he doesn't already realise it was him I was after that night I went for Jack Clare, then he should learn it now.

'I know,' he says, with the faintest of smiles in his voice. 'You failed, though.' *Just as you will always fail in any transaction you engage in with me,* his look says. *I win, Lawrence. After all this time, you've come crawling back wanting something, needing something. Just tell me what it is. Tell me, sell me your soul and let's do the deal because once I let you have it, you stay here just as I always intended for you to do and you're mine.*

'I can protect you,' he says. I look at him, my eyes glittering with dislike;

'I went for you and ...' I choke a little as the words stick in my throat. 'You're still prepared to offer me some sort of protection against the law?'

'Total protection,' he says confidently.

'You don't care? What I did? *I hit that guy with a metal shovel ...*'

'As far as I'm concerned,' he shrugs. 'That was the one time in your life you ever proved to me you had any balls, son.'

'What I did to Jack Clare - that wasn't balls,' I say, my heart thudding in my mouth. 'That was rage and sheer fucking hatred and ... I'm not proud of it.'

'Come on.' My father dismisses my qualms with a shrug. 'You squared up to someone you took to be your old man. All lads do that some time or another. It shows me you have something in you that your brother never had. It shows me that you're the only one capable of taking over this business after I retire.'

'No.' I look at him in horror, shaking my head.

'You said you were here to put things right. Well. I'm offering it all on a plate to you now, Lawrence.' He looks me candidly in the eye.

'Pilgrim is a good gofer but that's all he'll ever be. He isn't as clever as you, he hasn't got your guts or your abilities.'

'What *abilities*?'

'You've stayed clear of the fuzz all this time haven't you? Without any help - that's no mean feat. Truth is, Macrae Enterprises could be yours for the taking once I step down.' He spreads his hands in a magnanimous gesture. 'If you want it. We can sort you out with a water-tight alibi and nobody would ever touch you for what you did. *Yes*,' he smiles. 'It can be done. You could work for me! In the meantime, you'll run things under my direction, learn the trade and how things are done.'

I just stare at him. How could he have got hold of the wrong end of the stick so badly?

'You said you were here to make amends,' he prompts. 'Here's your chance.'

'I'm not proud of what I did that night,' I get out. 'I'm here because I want to make amends. *To him.*'

'To him?' My father looks a little taken aback. 'Who?'

'I want you to give Jack Clare his land back.'

There's a long, dark silence while he takes in the implications of this; I can feel him, moving a whole load of pieces across the chessboard of his mind. He takes in that I am compromised; racked with guilt. He takes in that I have somehow found the courage to risk coming back here. He takes in that I'm worn out with running and that I desperately need help, but clearly not enough to take what he's offering me in exchange for it.

He takes in that I still, after all this time, reject him.

'I've come back here for one reason,' I tell him again. 'To put things right. I want you to sign the land back over to the Clares. We never should have taken it. I'm not here to talk about coming home. I'm not here to accept any offer of protection from you for what I did. Just the land, to make it right, and then I'll go ...'

'Just the land.' He opens his hands, nods, his mouth pursed as if he's considering my words very carefully. A small light has just come into his eyes and I seize upon it, sensing his slight shift in attitude towards me. What is this new thing I'm picking up?

Respect?

For one brief moment I entertain the fantasy that my father might actually be proud of me for being man enough to take this stand. That he might - *like Dougie was* - be proud of me for believing in a goal so much that I'd put the attaining of it before my own comfort or safety.

His next words pop that bubble in an instant.

'You've come for the land. And just ... how did you intend to persuade me?'

I stop, open-mouthed, not knowing how. I don't have any leverage, do I? All I ever had was the forlorn hope that some small

398

part of him might be glad to see me after all this time. Because I am his son. Happy enough to buy me peace of mind the only way I will ever now get it.

'Jack Clare is real sick,' I beg. 'He could go away from here and get treatment but he won't go because he's scared you'll develop the land. If we let him have it back - that would be an act of atonement. It would be an act of *mercy*.'

'Of course,' he agrees. 'But you and he and I all know that land is potentially worth a lot of money,' he prompts. 'You're offering me a business proposition of some sort, I take it?'

I hang my head, recognising the fool that I've been. My father doesn't know about mercy. He doesn't know about love. He's not interested in any transaction in this world that doesn't have some underlying commercial value to it.

'I know about that man you killed,' I tell him at last. 'I might only have been a young lad but I know ... you buried him in the mound behind the pens, didn't you? I saw you do it.' My father bangs his fist on the desk suddenly, gets up and leans over it now, his eyes looking fit to bulge out of their sockets.

'Don't go there, Lawrence,' he breathes. 'Forget about Jack Clare. Topfields is my property, now. It is mine, do you understand me?'

'You can keep everything,' I say. 'I won't tell anyone. About all the other things you have stolen, all the other people you have cheated and hurt. What you did to the family. *What you did to me*. I'll say nothing. I just want that land signed back over to Jack.'

'Fuck you, Lawrence. You wouldn't have found me as easy to take down as that muppet you surprised that night, son. I'm not him,' he warns me. 'I'd have broken both your arms, and then some.' He looks at me and a sudden sneer twists his face.

'I still could.' I stand very, very still. He's come up and he's just inches away from me now.

'I just might. You've grown, boy, but you haven't grown that much. I could still knock your lights out and don't you forget it.'

'I didn't come here for that,' I breathe, but I can see he's barely listening to me anymore.

'No. You came here to threaten me. Don't you think I deserve a little more respect than that?' I flinch backwards, but his breath is coming hard and fast. I recognise the signs. How he used to work his way up into a rant and then from there the punches would start flying. 'All my life I've slaved away, dirtied my hands, *slaughtered pigs for a living* so that you three could have a roof over your heads. Don't you think I should have some acknowledgement from my family for that? Is that it? Nothing for Rob Macrae?'

I look at my father in fear and disbelief. He's mental, that's what he is.

'No matter what I tried to do for you, you always let me down.' He twists his neck now and I can see the veins bulging.

'Don't come a step closer,' I warn.

'Why couldn't you have just worked with me, boy? All those things you took so much to heart, everything that you and your brother thought of as terrible punishments - I was trying to instil a bit of discipline into you, that's all. Life's hard. I was trying to teach my kids to roll with the knocks. *To become men.*'

'Men like you?' My throat closes up. If he touched me now, could I take him? I am famished and exhausted. He's that little bit older and I'm that bit bigger, swifter, but still I know I could not. Not after seeing what I did to Jack Clare; I could not.

'I'm a *free* man, Lawrence,' he taunts. 'More than can be said for you, eh?'

'More than can be said for any man who works for you, either ...' His face twists into something very ugly now; something I recognise from long ago and I recoil.

'You never saw any value in me, did you, boy? You've never respected me. Even your mother saw that.'

'My mother only ever saw what she wanted to see ...' *Didn't she ask*, I think suddenly, *didn't she even wonder, why he sent her away this Christmas? She could have worked out it was because I was back ...*

400

'Your brother saw it. He accepted me. Not you though, eh? You were just a bad apple through and through – you always had to throw everything I ever did for you, everything I offered you, back in my face.' He takes a small step closer to me and my fingers creep down to close around the barrel of his gun under my jumper. Could I do it? I've never shot anyone in my life before though if anyone deserves it, it's got to be him.

'You must have known that I would never let you out of here.' He shrugs his arms out of his jacket and underneath I see he is wearing only a thin white shirt. Slowly, he unbuttons the cuffs. He rolls up the sleeves and then he begins to dance and feint around me, jabbing at the air once or twice, as if he were back in the boxing ring, grunting and lunging. His eyes are little black circles now, his forehead down, focused, getting ready to go in for the money shot and then ... he's hitting my forearms, left-right, right-left, hitting them like a machine with military precision and fireworks of pain are exploding deep inside my biceps; suddenly, I get a real shot of clarity.

This time, I think, *he really is going to kill me*.

My head feels giddy now, as if the room is spinning. I put my hands up and a flurry of rain spatters against the window. I feel the warm stickiness of bleeding coming from my nose. Through the glass I can see the massive oak by the farm gate is still groaning with snow, a few of its boughs are broken, sagging almost to the ground with the weight. Then I look downwards as my blood splashes over the parquet floor, darkening the wood effect. It is already so dark. How much darker can it get in here? How much darkness is there, left?

'You must have known,' he's saying softly now. 'That I would never let you go.' He's pulled me by the shoulders round to face him again and now he punches me, just once, hard in the midriff. Next, in the middle of my forehead, my head jerking backwards like a crash dummy in a smashed vehicle and the room has become so dark, I can barely see I can barely think I can barely breathe then - *bang* - his fist smashes deep into my chest and I crumple like a straw.

'What did you really come back for, eh? What?'

'Dad.' My brother's horrified face is at the door suddenly now, watching us. How long has he been out there, listening? Does he know that my father was poised to hand the whole kit and kaboodle over to me in his stead? That I only had to say the word? Pilgrim used to wait outside the World War Two bunker for hours, when he was a kid. I used to hear him, talking to Kahn. He used to wait for me at first, before he grew old enough to realise I wouldn't be out any time soon. Hearing my brother's voice now, I don't know what gives me the strength to look up but when I do, I see him swallow, his Adam's apple bobbing. He's grown from a boy into a man while I was away, I hardly recognise him. He's a man, but he's Rob Macrae's man now. Still, I can see he wants my father to stop. He puts his hand to his face and it's obvious that he's scared.

'*Dad* ...'

'Get. Out.' Fists still clenched, Rob Macrae turns to slam the door shut on my brother with his foot.

'You could have been someone,' he mutters. 'A winner. Like me.'

Someone like him. No. Never. I taste the bile in my mouth at the thought of it, of us being lumped together, father and son, because I reject him. While his back is still turned I pull the gun out from under my jumper. I loathe him. Everything he is and everything he stands for, just like I always have.

And now this is going to end.

402

'Hey,' I say. I've just knocked on Dad's door tentatively. I realise he's probably been expecting me to come back in for a while now and I'm not proud of keeping him waiting. I know it took even longer because I got hi-jacked by Sam and Carlotta but still, I'm surprised to see that in the time it's taken me to have my bath and get dressed, he's taken himself back to bed. That's not like him.

I go and perch on the edge of his duvet.

'Hey,' he says. When he lifts his eyes to me, something's immeasurably different about him but I can't for the life of me fathom what. Unless what we were talking about earlier is still playing on his mind? I put the offer letter down on the bedcover in front of him. I don't have to *say* anything. He can already see that I'm grinning from ear to ear. I watch him as he reaches out uncertainly from under the warmth of his cover to pick up the letter with both hands.

'You're *in*?' he says. I know he can't see without his specs. He's just pretending to read it but I can feel the thrill of relief, the joy in him, at the news, echoing my own. I lean in tight for a hug. 'I knew you'd make it,' his voice is all wobbly. He wipes away a tear. That's when I notice that his eyes are already puffy, the sleeves of his PJs wet. He's been crying? Is that my fault? I feel a pang of guilt.

'What's up, Dad?'

403

'I'm happy for you,' he says gruffly, blowing his nose, but he's not getting away with that.

'What is it?' I shuffle a little closer along the bed.

'This is about what we were talking about earlier, right?' I bite my lip, wishing now I'd been a little more careful with him. I'd only just got back. He's probably been worried sick about me, because that's what he always does, and the first thing I did when I arrived was go and lay into him over how I thought he'd just let Mum die without making her seek medical aid. How stupid of me. *How very thoughtless …*

'No.' He shakes his head forcefully, stares at my letter but I know he isn't seeing it.

'It helped clear the air though, right?' I look at him entreatingly now. 'You came out and told me a whole load of things that we'd never spoken about before. Like - I never knew about Mum's illness as a teenager. I always thought she'd contracted that sickness by being under those trees. It would have helped me more than you could imagine if I'd only been told about all that earlier, Dad.'

'I'm not upset because of anything you brought up about Mum's illness,' he says thickly. *What then*? I raise my eyebrows.

'It's not what I said to Carlotta before I left the house, is it?' I look at him apologetically. 'I wish you'd spoken to me before you let them have Mum's room, that's all. It would have given me a bit of time to adjust. Maybe I wouldn't have got so upset with my aunt about the way they flung all Mum's things about …'

'Rose. You and I would never have got round to clearing out Mum's space, would we? I know … they were careless,' he comes in sadly. 'But we'd have left it all there as a shrine forever. I told your aunt to clear the things out, love.'

'You *told* her to do it?' I look at him, taken aback.

'I told her to do it. Because they needed the room. Because I didn't want to keep alienating them forever when it's perfectly clear that we need them, you and I. We need them on our side. But, look, that isn't what's really affected me this morning.'

404

Oh. My feelings of upset at him fade away as quickly as they'd come. He didn't let them destroy Mum's space because he didn't care. He did it because he was trying to be prudent. For my sake, I suspect, more than for his own.

'Rose.' He pats my letter now. 'I've decided to go and give those chaps in the States a whirl, the medics my brother's been nagging about,' he tells me now. 'Give us both the chance of a new life, eh?' He will? I can scarcely believe what he's telling me; that he's changed his mind. It's what I'd hoped for, what I'd dreamed of. There are no guarantees. He knows that. But life is full of gambles …

'What about the trees?' I get out. 'Your promise to Mum?'

'You're more important than the trees,' he admits. 'So am I. I think she'd understand that, don't you?'

Thank God. He holds out his arms for a hug. All I can think of is; we're going to be moving out of here at last, then. After all this time? It feels so strange to think that could be true. Now that it's coming so close, I even feel a little sad. We're going to walk away from here, this place where I was born, this place where my parents once built their new lives around the unexpected child they'd had. The wrench for him is going to be *huge*, I see that more clearly than ever, now. For him more than me, because this is what he's spent his life building up. For me, Clare Farm is where I launch from. For a split second, my fingers reaching out to touch the wallpaper behind his back, the paper I once helped him put up, I think; I can't ask him to *do* this, to leave this familiar place in the twilight of his years. It isn't fair. He really shouldn't have to be put in this position now. It's not right.

'Rose, *Rose*, don't cry.' He pats me gently and his hand on my shoulder is familiar and comforting. 'I want to do this.'

'No, you don't.' I wipe my nose. 'You're only doing it for me. You don't really want to leave Clare Farm and all the memories you shared here with Mum. I *know* you don't.'

'In some ways, Rose, I *do*.' His eyes look very sad, suddenly. 'The past can be a very painful place to remain trapped in, no

405

matter how pleasant it was at the time ...' In the quiet space that follows I'm suddenly aware of the sound of running water coming from everywhere outside. The dripping of the icicles along the guttering, the lashing of the rain against the windows. Everything has changed. Suddenly, with a turn in the weather, everything outside that was soft and quiet and still, it's become busy, charged with movement; it feels as if real life has taken over the reins, got back in charge again.

I still don't know where Lawrence got to, do I?

All that time we spent together, everything we shared, it's beginning to feel like a dream to me now. A lovely dream that you awake from only reluctantly, clinging to the last vestiges of sleep for as long as you can but all the while you know you can't bring that dream with you, back into the real world. Is that how Dad feels about Mum, now, I wonder? Is that how he's decided it's time for him to move on?

I smile at Dad, softly and I see that there's something else;

'I *have* been mulling over something we brought up earlier,' he confesses at last. 'What I said to you about how it's been for me, loving your mum, how I had to make sacrifices, *big* ones ...' He's choosing his words carefully. 'In order to be with her.' He looks at me pointedly but I don't say a word, not sure yet where this is leading to.

'I don't know if you ever realised it but for me, falling for someone who fell so far outside my own social milieu, I've felt I've needed to fight everyone and everything around me for years just to honour my feelings for her ...' He lowers his chin. 'People didn't *approve*, Rose. But that didn't change how I felt about her. It couldn't and it wouldn't.'

Am I actually breathing now? I think not. I cannot.

'What I'm saying is; I think you already have some idea what I'm talking about, don't you, Rose?'

'Because I've had to fight for her too?'

'Rose, I'm talking about *you*,' he insists. 'You and that young man I saw you arriving back with. You are in love with him, I take

406

it?' I baulk at his directness. If he saw me with Lawrence this is the first time he's mentioned it. He could only have glimpsed us anyway. How could he go so far as to think I'm *in love*? I feel a flutter of panic in my belly now, because we are coming to it. Everything I've got to tell him that I haven't yet told him. We are coming to it, and right now.

'I ...' I stall. 'I've only known Lawrence a few days, Dad.' Does he know from where? I put my hand to my mouth, trying to figure out how much he could possibly have deduced from that one glimpse of me and Lawrence that he got. *How much does he know*?

Does he realise - as Carlotta clearly has - that I haven't really been staying with Shona at all over Christmas? I've tried to be discreet since I got back, but it looks as if I've not pulled the wool over anyone's eyes. I was going to tell them all, of course I was. I just wanted to give Lawrence enough of a chance to come in and square it all with Dad. But he hasn't. I feel my heart sink. He hasn't turned up and that makes me feel like a fool for caring about him, all over again.

'You're in love with him,' Dad insists. 'But he's in trouble, yes?'

'Why do you say that?' I flare. So; Dad saw me and Lawrence together. 'Just because I didn't invite him in, you jump to the conclusion ...' I can feel my face flaming now. *I can't tell him, I can't; if Lawrence hasn't come back and spoken to Dad himself, then that leaves me vulnerable and alone in all of this.*

'What else have you concluded?' My voice assumes a hurt tone. Dad folds his arms over the top of his duvet. He takes me in quietly.

'I suppose - just because you saw me arrive back with Lawrence, you're *imagining* that ... that I spent the last few days with the guy, right?' My voice goes up a notch. 'You're imagining that I've fallen madly in love with him, only ... I never invited him back in to meet all the family because you'd all be mad at me for running off and because he's someone you'd all disapprove of?'

'You've got a better imagination than me, Rose.' There's a sad smile in his voice now. 'Tell me; just how much of all of that is the truth?'

I stare at Dad.

Carlotta's told him what Matt Dougal said about me not being with them. She must have. God, I look away from him, not knowing how on earth I am going to answer him. Right now my face feels so hot I think my skin is melting. I get up and stalk over to the window and pull it up, feeling as if I'm gasping for air. The window lifts easily because the catch hasn't been put back on. An echo of something being not quite in place here, reverberates in my head. I turn to look at him slowly. He's still waiting.

It is *all* the truth, I think. The words don't want to come out, though. I open my mouth to say them, but nothing comes out.

'He's just been in here,' Dad says to me at last.

'Who?' I go and sit on his bed again. I perch there right on the very edge like a bird on a telephone line just poised to fly away at the slightest alarm. '*Who's been here*, Dad?'

'Your lad,' he says quietly. 'Lawrence. He came up through the fire-door.'

He ... he came through the ...? I look towards the door, shocked, but it is closed now. I'd thought he'd come up the normal way. I'd imagined ... I'd have to introduce him to everyone and then ... afterwards, he'd go to my uncle and maybe hand himself in or something.

'*When?*' I breathe, even though I know it could only have been very recently. *He came up while I was in the bath*, I think. *He came up this way so he could see Dad and avoid seeing everyone else. Even me?* 'I mean ... when did he go?' No. I don't mean that. What do I mean?

'What did he say to you?' I grasp my Dad's hands suddenly, wanting to know everything, wanting to hear *everything* ...

'I think he wanted to face his victim, Rose. I think he meant somehow to make amends ...'

'*Dad.*' My voice nearly gives out. He knows! 'When was he

408

here?'

'He left within the half hour, not so long ago. I got the impression ...' Dad presses my palm now. 'From all he knew about us, that maybe you'd asked him to come?'

I nod, my eyes down.

'Did I do the wrong thing, Dad?' I ask apologetically. 'I didn't mean for him to come in without me. *Dear God* - were you scared?'

'No, Rose,' Dad pats my hand. 'There's nothing to be scared of, is there? I see now what he did was a mistake. All this time, there never was anything to fear ...'

'Can you forgive me?' I say in a small voice, 'For falling in love with the man who hurt you? I didn't know who he was. I went out to get your tablets and I got trapped up in the ruin by the weather. He was there too. I fell in love ... with the person he's become since he did that horrible thing to you. I thought you'd never understand ...'

'If not me, then who would ever understand it?' he asks sadly. Because of Mum, he means. Because when love comes it is bigger and wider and stronger than all the rights and wrongs of the world, and maybe it can heal them all?

'The *family* aren't going to understand it,' I remind him shakily. The fact that Dad has taken it so well is a miracle. I don't hold out any hope that the others will.

'The family will have to come to terms, Love.'

'They'll want him taken to court, Dad. They'll want justice to be served. And ... he's scared of prison. That's why he ran in the first place. His father used to lock him up, you know. He used to beat him and lock him up in the darkness ...'

When I look up, Dad's got a very strange expression on his face now. *What is it*? Oh, God.

'What is it, Dad?' I feel a sudden fear catch in my throat now, seeing that look in his eyes. 'Where has he gone?'

'I don't think you're going to be able to keep this matter from your uncle or from the police very much longer, Rose. In fact, I wouldn't advise you to do so. He's gone to Macrae Farm.'

He's gone back home then? It's far too late for him to do anything for Sunny now, surely? He knew that when he agreed to come home with me. He made his decision. He came and saw Dad. Yet he has still gone on to Macrae Farm. My heart sinks another notch. *Why did you feel you had to do that, Lawrence, why?*

When I stand up now, my legs barely keeping the weight of me upright, I don't even get to the door before it's opened abruptly by someone else from the outside.

''Scuse me for barging in,' Ty is opening the door even as he's knocking on it. 'I'm told *you two* have just received some very good news ...?' His hands grip mine for an instant, and he smiles into my eyes. He's so genuinely happy for me that I get a small rush of happiness inside. *It's not all bad, things aren't all bad* ... some things in my life are very good right now. But until I get over the hump of what I still need to confess to them, *until I know what's happening to Lawrence*, how can I be truly happy?

'It's all very sombre in here,' Ty notes. He pulls me towards him now, for a brief bear-hug, catching me by surprise. He smells of the outside; of cold air and melting snow and fresh tree-bark, and he's got a cheerfulness about him, a purposefulness I haven't seen on any of them since they first arrived. I can see little spots of rain glistening on his expensive cashmere jumper, and little chips of wood. He follows my line of gaze.

'I've just been out replenishing your stocks.' He brushes the wood-chips off his sleeve, winking at Dad. 'Seeing as we used up a load while we were here ...'

'Very kind, old chap.'

'You're welcome. And this is one clever girl you've got here, Jack ...' My uncle pulls up the wicker chair from the window and seats himself down beside the bed, now. He sits down right on the edge of it, like a man invigorated, a man who knows he's going to be up and away at any moment. He will be. The car is fixed,

411

Carlotta already said it. It'll be parked on a clear road further along the valley, just waiting for them all to come and jump into it with their bags, resume their journey. Right on cue, his wife and daughter sidle in behind him now. I can see they all look smartened up and keen to go; they've got that 'ready to go out there and face the world' air about them.

But they can't go.

They have to stay here and help me save Lawrence from his family. They have to stay here and listen to me tell them the whole truth, first ...

'Car's all ready then?' Dad takes in that this is a farewell party, even as I do.

'Indeed it is.'

'Here you go, my love,' Ty makes to give the chair up for his wife but she perches on the arm of it instead. Sam plumps down on the other arm and they both glance over at me a little apprehensively, anticipatory but saying nothing. They're waiting for me to 'fess up about where I've truly been; they're a little curious but aren't expecting anything *too* untoward. I go and sit back down on the bed, trying to work out what'll be the best way to explain it all to them, knowing that I mustn't delay anymore. I open my mouth and then, before I can say it;

'So ...' Ty leans in a little nearer to Dad's bed. 'Has Rose's offer made any impact on your decision to pursue getting possible treatment in the States?'

Dad smiles at him, but I see his smile is tight. He's worried, I can feel it.

'I've decided to give the States a go,' he says in a crinkly voice.

'Fantastic!'

'But there is something else.' *Sorry Love,* Dad's glance says to me before he turns to face them all.

'Rose has got something she needs to say to everyone. Something important.' He grips my hand a fraction tighter as he adds. 'This is not going to be easy for her, so I trust you'll all hear

412

her out before you say anything. That's all I ask. That you hear her out.'

I look from one of them to the other at their slightly puzzled faces, at the anticipation growing in the room that all is not as well as it appears to be. I reckon Sam and Carlotta think they have a good idea what this is about. But they don't, not really. It takes so long for the words to form in my mouth that the smile in my uncle's eyes fades to concern. By the time the words come out they sink like bits of ice in a cold lake, nobody is expecting me to say anything good ...

'I haven't been at Shona's these past few days.' My voice, when I find it now, is surprisingly clear. 'I've been ... with someone else.'

I feel my aunt shift on the arm of the wicker chair. She shoots me an encouraging smile, only slightly tense, waiting for that *perfectly good explanation* ...

'The thing is, I discovered who Dad's attacker was. He's been staying here, in Merry Ditton ...' If they had been expecting me to say anything at all, I know that is not something that would ever have crossed their minds. Not that. *Anything* but that. There's a collective gasp in the room as they take my words in.

'The police knew he was planning on visiting locally,' Ty blurts out before I can say anything else. 'They contacted this house soon after I got here in fact. They informed me it was him they were on the look-out for, to be aware ... I didn't say anything to you, Jack, because I didn't want you to worry unduly, but I never thought Rose would be out ... By the time anyone thought to *tell* me she'd gone,' he glances angrily at his daughter. 'We assumed she must have gone on to her friend's. An assumption which she herself confirmed a short while later.' Dad looks pained, but I'm more aware of my uncle now, his eyes narrowing, as he makes connections in his mind that are nowhere near the truth. 'Did you *know* of this, Rose?' He turns to look at me in faint horror. 'Did you go out in search of this man yourself?'

'No. No! I had no idea it was him. None at all. *At all*,' I say

413

emphatically. But that doesn't allay the darkness I see forming in his eyes now.

'Then ... where have you been?'

Shit. This is the moment I have known would have to come, ever since I arrived back. The moment where they find out the truth, and I know they are not going to like it. Not one little bit. Dad's fingers tighten in mine encouragingly.

'I've been with him, Uncle Ty.' I look my uncle directly in the eye now. 'The man they're after. I've been with him ever since I was forced to shelter up in the old ruin after I left here, waiting for the weather to break.' How easily the truth slips out. It is not as difficult to say as I'd feared. It is the truth, and I must not be afraid, just as I didn't want Dad to be afraid anymore and he had to know the truth.

'Dear God.' My aunt's hands go over her mouth. There's a small, stifled noise from Sam.

'Start from the beginning.' My uncle's face has gone very white. He's having trouble taking in what I've just said to him, I can see it in the conflict in his eyes. 'So you ... you left here and were forced to find shelter ... where?'

'The old ruin,' I say again. His hands go out to his sides in confusion.

'And this guy happened to also be up there? This *man*?' He looks utterly shocked.

'He was sheltering, like me.' I can hear my voice trembling but I don't take my eyes off his.

'Sheltering,' he nods, very slowly, letting the implications of what I'm saying sink in. 'And you didn't think it might be important to *tell* us any of this?' I open my mouth and shut it again. 'Especially knowing as you did there was a man the police were warning about?' He glances at Sam briefly, as if wondering if she might be complicit in all of this. I see her shake her head, shrink back a little. 'Instead of which, you pretended to be at your friend's house, correct?' I give a small nod.

'I lied.'

414

'You lied. You were up there with him for *two days*, Rose. You phoned home more than once.' Uncle Ty is very still suddenly, intent. I see him glance at my aunt and then he swallows, pained.

'*Why*?' The change in tone in his voice, so quiet now, soft, suddenly concerned for me, jars even more than his fury would. 'Why would you do that? Unless ... what did he do to you, Rose?'

'What did he do?' This time I find it more difficult to level my gaze to his.

'He hurt you?' Ty stands up and moves a little closer to me, his ear so near to my face now, willing me to say all the things that it would be acceptable for him to hear. That I was coerced into this. That my complicity - saying nothing up to now - it's all down to some form of Stockholm syndrome. It's a psychological self-defence protection mechanism. That I am not really an accessory after the fact, protecting a known wanted man ... I shake my head, slowly.

'He never hurt me,' I say. I don't look up. A single tear-drop runs down my cheek, splashes onto my father's hand. 'He never did anything to hurt me.'

'He's. .. he's made you say that, right?' Ty stands back abruptly, and the suddenness of the movement jars right through to the core of me.

'No.'

'He made you promise not to give his position away so he could get away from here without detection - he's *threatened you*, said he'd come back and hurt Jack again?'

'No!' I can't stand this any longer. 'No he hasn't. He didn't.' I look directly up to face my uncle now, even though I'm trembling, even though I can feel every fibre of me wired with fear at what might come of it.

'He didn't, Uncle Ty! He didn't do any of those things you just said. He didn't threaten me. He didn't hurt me. He didn't make me do anything I didn't want to do.' I look at Dad for support, waiting to see if he'll say anything, back me up and tell them

415

about Lawrence coming here, tell them that *he* knows Lawrence is not so bad ...

'The only things he did for me were *good* things, helpful things, even though in order to do them he knew he'd be putting himself at risk.' I stop, taking in the shock on my uncle's face. This is not what he expected to hear. Not what he *wanted* to hear.

'He saved my life, Ty. He picked me up and took me to shelter when I fell and lost consciousness in the snow after I left here. If it weren't for him coming out to me I'd have frozen to death.'

'He saved you?' Sam's biting her nails fiercely now. She looks from me to her parents but right now neither of them seem inclined to respond.

'He risked his own position to take me into shelter. He stitched up the wound in my leg ...'

'You're telling us you let him perform some procedure on your leg?' Uncle Ty splurts. 'What is he ... some sort of medic, now?'

'He's a paramedic.'

'That's what he said? And you believed him. Rose, Rose ...' Ty turns round and for a moment or two paces the room. 'People like that don't *become paramedics*, Rose. Don't you know this? Haven't you lived next to those Macraes for enough years to know what kind of people they are?'

'Not him,' I say staunchly. 'He's different. He saved me. He even came back here to speak to Dad, to let him know how sorry he was for what he did ...'

'He was sorry.' The words shock my uncle into silence once again. They push him away from the kind-hearted, generous person I know him to be. I see his fists clench. 'He told you he was sorry and you let him convince you to bring him back ... *here*, Rose?' He looks furious suddenly. More than furious. 'Have you *any idea* of the danger you were putting yourself - all of us - in?'

'It wasn't like that,' I say as he steps in front of me, glowering.

'You brought that ... *thug* to the house where my brother lies

416

vulnerable in his own bed. To the place where my own wife and child are currently sheltering ...? You let him persuade you to do that?'

'He never persuaded me.' It's my turn now to look shocked. 'You need to stop jumping to conclusions. You need to just stop and *listen to me* ... It was I who persuaded him to come. He didn't want to come back here, *why would he*?' Ty raises his clenched hand to his mouth and Dad's hand tightens in mine.

'Rose was acting in my best interests, Ty,' he warns his younger brother. 'She alone knows how much I have suffered these last five years. She knew how to release me from it, and I thank her for that. I thank *him*,' his voice wobbles, 'that boy, for having the courage to come back here and say to me what he did.'

'I see,' my uncle looks away now, looks down at the floor but I can tell he doesn't really see. He is way too angry. He doesn't see at all.

'And ... where is he now?'

'He's gone,' Dad says. 'He left here a good hour ago ...'

My uncle's face is a picture. *You let him go* ... every inch of him is saying, but he doesn't voice the words out loud. He says nothing, nothing at all for a good few minutes while he struggles to come to terms with what he should do next, what part he should play in all of this, if any.

'Then we will leave,' he gets out at last. His back is suddenly stiff, his whole posture has changed from what it was before. 'You clearly don't need us here anymore, and if your long-running feud with your neighbour has been resolved by this Jack, then ... I can only say I'm happy for you.'

'Not yet,' Dad says, and there's something in his voice that even Ty still recognises as the voice of his older brother. 'You can't leave yet, because it's not over yet.'

'No?' my uncle throws at him, but no matter how antsy his tone I can feel that he's been thrown by the things he's just learned. He doesn't want to believe there can be any good in Lawrence. But he has to acknowledge that *we* think so. That there might be something worth salvaging there.

'Lawrence is in danger, Ty,' I step in now. 'He's always been in danger. From his own people, that's why he never came back here after what he did.'

'Oh?' My uncle steps back a pace. 'You know where he is, then?' I can hear little strange breathing noises coming from my aunt, now. Out of the corner of my eye I can see my cousin trying to comfort her, telling her that it's okay, everything's okay ... even though from the shock in her voice she clearly doesn't think it is.

'Where is he, Rose?' Uncle Ty crouches down, beside me. His hands on my knees feel like the weight of all the world, every authority figure I have ever known, the police, every judge and jury in the land, what I imagine them all to be ...

'Okay, Rose. Okay.' He slides his mobile out from his jacket pocket. 'He didn't hurt you. Or threaten you. But now you're ready to shop him. Just do it. Where is he?'

I put my hand on my uncle's arm, my face hardening.

'I'm not doing this to shop him, Ty. I'm doing it because it's the only way I can save him.'

'Are you sure that's how *he'll* see it?' He slides my hand off his arm. 'Don't bank on it, Rose.'

I stop, taking in the truth of his words because I know Lawrence won't want me to do this. He won't want me to call the police on him right now, to betray his whereabouts. But at Macrae Farm, everything works according to Rob Macrae's rules. I know that as well as Lawrence does. I know he cannot come out of this in any good way. I don't know what else to do.

'He's gone to back to Macrae Farm.' What else can I do? *What else?* I can feel my aunt and cousin looking at me in shocked curiosity now, a thousand questions milling uncomfortably in their eyes.

'What ... must it have been *like*, being up there,' my cousin's voice cuts through my thoughts. 'What was it like, *being* with him?'

She cannot know that. She cannot even guess. How I have

418

been with him, in what way. And what that was like. I shake my head at her and my uncle goes out into the hallway, calling the local police station. I can hear him, even as she keeps asking me questions, shaking my hand to get my attention when I don't answer. I'm only half-listening to her, I can hear Ty telling whoever's at the end of the line that there's been a breakthrough and this is urgent. They need to come out and arrest a suspect immediately. *That's great,* he's saying, *thank you. Thank you, we'll expect you any minute then ...*

'It must have been a terrifying ordeal for you,' Carlotta's actually got tears in her eyes. 'Terrifying. Once you knew who he was. I don't know how you got through it, Rose, I really don't.'

'It wasn't ... terrifying,' I begin. I turn to Dad and his eyes say - *Slowly and steady does it, my love.* He gives a tiny shake of his head. I don't have to tell them everything all at once, he's saying to me. One little bit at a time.

'Right. Best get your coat on, Rose.' Ty's back in the room, his face still looking like thunder but there's an underlying confusion, a hurt and a feeling of puzzlement in there too, now; it's the feeling that the two ends of the rope that go to encompass the world as he understands it don't fit together anymore. Things are no longer as they should be. Something is broken.

'They're sending some men out to Macrae Farm and they want us out there too.' His voice sounds cut up. He doesn't quite look at me as he speaks.

'Us?' I look at him in alarm. He's just told me to put my coat on, hasn't he? I didn't think to ask why. I didn't want to know why.

'You,' Ty corrects. 'They want you to be present at the time of arrest. But I'll come with you.' The thought of it is worse than anything else. Me being there at the end, when they get to him. I don't want to be there. I don't want to be there and Lawrence knowing that it was me who betrayed him to the police.

'They want you to identify him as the man you've been with. The man who's confessed to you. He *did* confess it all, I take it?' My uncle pats me perfunctorily on the shoulder. 'Come on

419

now, Rose. Cat got your tongue? You're the girl who wants to go off to the halls of learning to study the law! Here's your chance to see a bit of justice in action, *to make it happen.*' He's business-like, suddenly driven, and I get a glimpse of what this means to him, as well. The chance to see Lawrence brought to justice is something he's been waiting for, for a long time, too.

'Come on, Rose,' he urges as he sees me hesitate. 'We need to get there before his family spirit him away again.'

'They won't, though. They won't protect him.'

Uncle Ty shoots me a dark look, then. A look that tells me I'd better just get my coat on and shut up. He's not entirely convinced of my innocence in all of this, I can tell. He's not happy that I kept so quiet about everything I knew right up till this point, that I've wasted all this time, maybe even allowing the perpetrator a chance to get away. He doesn't understand it.

'These people will close ranks, Rose. Don't you doubt it. *Families* stick together in times of trouble.' His eyes are laden with reproach. 'Don't you know that, Rose? Don't you know that's how it goes?' He shakes his head at me and I can feel his anger and his huge upset at me with every breath, with every tiny movement of his shoulders as we go downstairs and he shuffles his coat on again, pulls on his boots.

'Lawrence made a mistake,' I tell him once he's standing there, ready to take me as soon as the police come. 'He made a terrible mistake and then he stayed away for five years and made it all that much worse. He never came back until now, to see how he might have helped put things right ... but now he *has*. He did. At least you have to give him credit for that much?'

I feel him sniff, in a hurt way, in the darkness of the downstairs hallway. He doesn't want me to be understanding. He doesn't want me to be forgiving, or for Dad to be. He doesn't see how that's the only way any of us are ever going to move on.

'You've pretty much stayed away for those five years, too ...' I remind him in a small voice and I can feel his intake of breath, though he says nothing, doesn't even make a slight move at that comment. 'And it's only now that you've had a chance to see Jack over Christmas, that you've started to look into how things might be put right for him.'

'*I* didn't put my brother in this situation, Rose,' he reminds me acidly.

'But *families stick together in times of trouble*, don't they, Ty?'

He doesn't answer, but I feel something go in, then. Something sticks. Maybe part of his fury at Lawrence - his unwillingness to see that this boy has any good in him at all - comes from his own guilt at not doing more for his brother beforehand? The discomfort he feels at his own inaction. I don't know. I pull my own spare coat down from the rack and put it on.

And then we stand in the hallway for the longest fifteen minutes of my life, waiting for the crunch of footsteps outside in the drive, waiting for the sharp knock on the door to let us know, the police have arrived.

Lawrence

They say when you come to the end of your time you get a flashback of it all. Your whole life scrolls before you like a slide-show, every last moment of it. I had no idea those pictures could come so fast and yet be so clear; that it might even be possible to feel those things over again and all so keenly. The night Kahn first came home; all velvet paws, ungainly walk, curious and unafraid. My heart swells again at the first sight of him. How I loved him, how I knew that he would be mine even though he'd never been intended for me.

My brother and I are throwing scraps to the pigs. They are so noisy and so big. They smell! He's scared of them. I tell him he mustn't be. That he mustn't be afraid. I don't know where my mother is.

The moon grows big, over the hill, a harvest-yellow moon and the fields are ripe with corn. I'm walking with some girl. The first girl I ever kissed. The first time I ever realised what it was all about. I want to stay there but the scenes are shifting so rapidly, my life rushing away like grains of sand through a timer and now there is this huge flash of shock, the sound of falling masonry, the smell of fear in my nostrils as my sanctuary is being torn down around me.

But no matter, for here is Mrs Patel. She is feeding me rice and lentils in her busy kitchen. The whole house smells of pungent spices, there is no escape from them, not in the hallway, not in the sitting-room, not even in the crowded utility space where she hangs out their washing and they have placed a small put-you-up bed for me. I'm studying in there. The feel of the paper beneath my fingers is smooth. For the first time in my life I'm studying because Mrs Patel insists that I should. In a strange, uncomfortable way, I am happy in there, in my little room.

My father jolts me now, swings me round over his shoulder like a rag-doll, interrupting the flow of my life, jolting me back into this world, startling me. I don't know quite where I am. I cannot remember how I got here and I do not want to remember. I do not want to come back. The pictures of all my life, they were so beautiful. So much more beautiful than the place where my body is now. And I am tired. I am hurt.

So hurt. I cannot move. My arms hang limply down over my father's shoulder. I force one eye open, and the ground beneath me is blurred, everything is dimmed. The afternoon is cold, I can feel it on my back. I think; we are out in the yard. Snow and black pebbles crunch beneath my father's boots and when I try to remember how I got here my brain hurts. It hurts as if selective parts of my memory have been wiped clean and I know I should not try to bring them back.

I slid the colt along the floor towards him. I know I did that. That was the last thing I did. To show him; I could have killed him but I chose not. That I am not like him. The last act of my life, I think; it will be my last. I can hear the noise he made in his throat when he saw that I'd taken his gun. And now, every last nerve buzzing, I can still feel the coldness of the gun barrel as he stuck the colt to my head, pressed it in, tight. I can feel the veins in my head throbbing at the memory. How it hurt. How the sound of the empty click as he pulled the trigger back, released it, sounded like an explosion in my brain even though the gun was empty. I think I remember him laughing. How his laughter sounded coarse and cracked, hacked into phlegm by years of tobacco abuse.

As if my victory in *not* aiming that gun at his head and shooting it was an empty one. The gun was not loaded; I could not have hurt him.

But I know my gesture was not empty.

My head hurts now, it hurts so much but I still cling on to one thing; I know that when I chose to put that gun down, slide it back over to him - *in that moment* - I became my own man. In that moment of surrender, I chose to claim the only victory that I still could. I chose not to kill him. Not to be the brute he's always wanted me to be. And when he stopped laughing, his face going down at the sides in a strangely-rapid change of sentiment, I saw that he knew it, too. He knew that he had not really won anything at all.

And I saw his face.

And I *knew,* that if I would not be that man, then he would not let me live. And now - for so many reasons he would never understand - I have every reason to *want* to live. I want ... oh God, there are so many things I still want. I want Rose. I want my life back, the life I could have still had. All of it. All the places I haven't yet been, the times we could have had together. It is so cold. I want to see the sun in the sky again, but ...

I made my choice. It is time to go to the place where he cannot hurt me, where he cannot reach me any longer. And I am so nearly there.

My eye closes and my blurred view of the yard scrolls into rain, warm rain, and I'm cycling on a borrowed bike down some muddy camp road in Jaffna. The afternoon I arrived was so quiet but it exploded into action in less than an hour. I didn't know what to do. Fresh out of training, what did I know? There was so much noise, people shouting, people running everywhere. They brought the broken bodies in and we did what we could. I helped them, I was brave, I tried to save them. And then the sun is rising over the forests on some sparkling golden morning and I am breathing it in, just me, alone. The air smells of the bright exotic flowers of Asia, it smells intoxicatingly sweet. On a morning like this, I don't know how there can be anything but peace in this world.

424

And then at last I am standing in my sanctuary again, with Rose, my arms wrapped around her. There is a stillness and a peace in the quiet snow lying on the ground at our feet. The air is shrouded in a cold mist, but her body pressed against mine is so warm. The forgiveness in her heart is like a golden light that has freed me. She and her father - they have both freed me. I see that now. No matter what happens next, nobody can touch me now. The pictures stop. Now that I am at the end of it, I'm not sure, looking back on my life, what it was all about, what it was all *for*. Did I help anyone? Did I make it right? I know, in the end, I did help Sunny. But there were so many moments, there, touched with joy and sadness and, in the end, real love.

Maybe that's what it was all for? That's what everything was leading to; that I should know Rose, that I should love her.

That I should know that she loved me.

That is the one last thing I think before the darkness comes.

Rose

'Rose Clare?' The policewoman who comes for me and Ty doesn't look very much older than I am. I see her eyes, bright blue, flicker over me curiously and then she gives a small encouraging smile as I step out into the bright glare of the day.

'I'm Ty. Her uncle. I'm the one who made the call ...' Ty stumbles out behind me. She gives him a courteous nod. *Thank you, we're dealing with this now*, she seems to say.

'I'm DC Pauline Bright. My colleague DC Milton is waiting for us in the car. I'm going to need you to accompany me now but there is no need for you to worry, Rose. We only need for you to identify Mr Macrae. You'll stay in the car the entire time and we will be with you every step of the way.'

Her face is laden with sympathy but when I assure her that 'I'm not worried about *me*,' she only nods, still smiling. I know she hasn't taken that in.

'You can walk?' She looks at me solicitously. 'I understand there was some minor injury sustained?'

'I fell,' I tell her. 'A few days ago. Lawrence stitched the wound.' She doesn't seem to take that in, either. She turns her face away, a little; speaks into her walkie-talkie.

'Witness secured. I'm bringing her up now. Uncle attending. Over.' The driver responds with something that is lost in static. A bright breeze hits my face as I come out properly into the yard, my boots squelch into the softening snow. I know Carlotta

426

and Sam are standing back, watching us from the door. When I turn round I glimpse them, strangely formally-dressed, looking cold and scared.

'Would have thought this amount of snowfall would have lasted a few days more, yet, eh?' This last comment is aimed at Uncle Ty as we follow DC Bright out onto the road.

'It's the rain we had earlier,' he says. His voice doesn't sound like him. It comes from a very strange and faraway place and I know he's still thinking about what I just said to him in the hall; about how he's only really taken an interest in Dad's welfare now, five years after the event; about how he's hung back all this time and not done anything to help. She turns round to look at him and he adds;

'The rain must be melting the ice,' as if it needed further explanation.

'It's good that it's clearing now, though,' she comments. 'And that you two have come forward so quickly. Before he can get away again. Never mind, eh?' she glances back at me. 'He'll be behind bars before long and then you and your Dad can rest easy at night, Rose.'

'We don't want him behind bars,' I mutter. I see a shadow cross her face at that. But Uncle Ty shakes his head at her.

'She's upset,' he says.

'Some people take it like that,' she nods. 'Some people take it hard. It's understandable.'

As we get nearer to the police vehicle I see the tractor Lawrence helped on its way before by clearing the road, is back. It's now been requisitioned as a road block, by the looks of it. The tractor-driver gives me a frankly curious stare as we all troop past. I ignore him, but I see now that while we can still travel up, towards Macrae Farm, no vehicles will be travelling away from it with the tractor in place. Not today. Not by this route, anyway.

I squint up the lane and the afternoon has opened out into a strange glaring brightness. For now, the rain has stopped. The wind has moved the clouds on, rain and snow-clouds alike. The sun is threatening to break through. I can see birds, wheeling here and there, large seabirds forced inland by the weather. I can see a robin redbreast perching on a hedge.

'According to the information we have, the suspect was last seen headed out towards Macrae Farm. Is that correct?' The driver turns to his partner as she opens the door for me and Ty to get inside. We climb into the back. It is a non-marked vehicle, not a patrol car. It is dark in the back but as we get in I can see a load of dog hairs sticking out of the rug that covers the seat. It smells of dogs, not like I'd somehow expected it to smell, all military and sparkling clean. I don't know why I expected that but I did. As we move off, I wish I could roll down the window for some air. I feel suffocated, suddenly, being in here. I don't know how I expected this to end, but it wasn't like this. *Not like this ...*

'All right, Rose?' The driver is a middle-aged bloke, kindly-looking like she is. *They all know my name*, I think. They keep calling me Rose, as if they knew me, as if they knew me well. I know they're trying to help. I need their help. But I truly wish that I did not. I wish I hadn't had to do this, call them in like this. Because calling in the authorities brings with it a ring of inevitability about how things must go from here. The pattern of events from now on, they must follow in a certain line, from which there can be no deviation. The police-guy, DC Milton, nods, friendly-like at my uncle and uncle Ty breathes in deeply through flared nostrils and there's this whole sense, as we're being driven along in this car for these first few minutes that we're all on the same team in this. Me and Ty, we're the wronged party and these officers are here to help see that justice is done and the villain is caught and we're all on the same side, only ...

That isn't why I wanted them brought in.

'The plan when we arrive is to wait till they bring the suspect out of the property. We will then proceed up the top drive in order for you to view him, Rose. You will remain within the safety of the vehicle at all times with me and DC Bright, is that clear, Rose? All we need for you to do is to ID him when the team

428

bring him out. If this is the guy who confessed to injuring your dad. That's all.' It won't take long, I know. Not by car, and especially now that the lanes are clear. It's just ... I can't help feeling somehow that we are running out of time.

'I need some air, please.' My voice comes out high-pitched and I know they take this as a sign that I'm scared.

'No need for you to be frightened at all, Rose.'

'I'm not scared about what you think I am.' As soon as he's wound the window down and I can breathe, I find my voice again. 'I'm worried about what Lawrence's family are going to do to *him*. That's what I'm worried about. You have to understand. He never tried to hurt me once in all the time we were together ...'

'There'll be a chance for a full de-briefing from you later, once we take you back to the station, Rose. Your job right now, is just to identify the lad.'

They don't want to hear it, do they? They don't want to know. I sit back and fold my arms and close my eyes now. As we move on slowly up the lane, I breathe in the oily scent of dog hairs on the rug. I breathe in deep like Uncle Ty and now I catch the scent of stale coffee and the whiff of mints and the bright orange sunlight streams through the window onto my closed lids for a moment, reaching me inside the car. Warm orange tones mix with darker shadows, the feeling of people moving about, blocking my sunlight but nobody in the car is moving. A sudden panic grips me. I get the overwhelming sense of somebody running.

Somebody *is* running.

Not here, not near the car. This is nothing to do with any of us. It is *him*. It's Lawrence. I know it's him. I open my eyes with a jolt.

'He's not at the farmhouse,' I croak.

'What's that?' DC Pauline Bright looks back at me curiously. Uncle Ty looks uncomfortable. He doesn't say a word.

'Lawrence isn't in the farmhouse because they've taken him somewhere else.' I lean forward in my seat, feeling a churning sickness in the pit of my stomach. I know what I am saying is true.

429

I do not know *how* I know it, but I do. I know it more certainly than I have known anything in my life. And I know we must act on it. Now. The officer stops the car momentarily while he examines his notes.

'That isn't the information that we have, miss.' He looks at me. 'I thought you said ... your uncle said - that you had information he was headed back home, Rose?'

'That's where he was going. But that isn't where he is, now.' I open the door of the car and step out. The day around me is blustery and bright. I can see the tail end of a bright yellow vehicle - an ambulance - parked further up the lane. It seems to be just waiting there. Waiting for trouble? At the front of our car I can see DC Pauline Bright as she steps out of the vehicle, after me. She looks slightly alarmed. She doesn't know what I'm doing, why I'm saying this. She doesn't understand where I'm coming from. How it might be possible to know something when you have no idea *how* you know it, what has informed you. My head is drawn immediately to the right, to the clump of trees further on and upwards, at the bend on the road. Towards Topwoods. I get a strong smell of wet earth in my nostrils now. I get the damp smell of tree roots and rotting vegetation.

'There,' I point. 'I've got ... I've got *a hunch*,' I tell her. The police know about hunches, I think. They *must* know. You see it in the cop movies all the time.

'Rose ...' she looks at me. 'Why there?' Her colleague makes a motion; *get her back inside the car,* but she stalls, playing along for a bit.

'Dead Men's Copse,' the words come out before I even think them. 'That is where they're taking him.'

And then, before she can stop me, before anyone can stop me, I make a run for it up the lane. When I reach the wooded area I dash into the darkest place between the trees that I can find, so they won't be able to catch me so quickly. They won't be able to delay me.

'Rose ... come back!' Ty is calling after me now, following

behind her, following me, but I have a head start on both of them. And I know ... I know where I am going, something keeps pulling me east, further into the woods, onto the wet sludgy path under the darkness of the trees, something is compelling me to plunge forward blindly because I know he will be here. I know they are taking him here. I *know* it.

I can make it, reach him, if I can just keep going ... But for a second, I have to stop, bending over while a pain like a vice-cold clamp has got hold of my lungs. I have to catch my breath. My leg feels like a needle-sharp spear has just split the skin. It hurts! But I have to keep going, the other two are still trailing behind me, I can hear them, the police lady and Uncle Ty, they keep calling me. Very soon the vegetation crowds in, the path peters out. Old blackened brambles with withered berries and yellowing leaves are all that cover the ground in front of me.

And it has gone very quiet.

Something smells bad, here. I stop. Behind me, I hear the other two stop, even as I do. I hear the crashing sound of their footsteps pursuing me through the trees come to a halt. Ahead of us, there is a large tree. An old oak, that stands proud above all the others. I know which tree this is. I've heard about this tree before; it's the one those men are said to have hung themselves from. And there are two people, I see now, standing still at the bottom.

One of them is Rob Macrae. I believe the other one is Pilgrim. Pilgrim is making some strange, weeping noises in his throat. Noises that catch in my stomach, filling me with fear. They are both looking upwards. I can't see, at first, what they are looking at. I can only feel their awed silence, something in the way they're both standing there, not moving anymore; something in the frozen space, in the terrible silence, between them, sticks a cold spear right through me.

They have done something very bad.

I let out a scream, and my voice pierces the dank air, it pierces the silence so loud a host of black birds fly up from their perches on the surrounding trees, croaking and cawing and scattering a shower of snow drops as they go. And I walk, step by frozen step, closer to the bottom of the tree. And look up.

And I see what they have done.

They have hung him from the tree.

Lawrence. *My Lawrence.* I can see his boots, covered in mud, but they are clearly his. I can see his head, hanging downwards, his face all battered and bruised. My hands go up to my mouth, but no other scream comes out. It stays stuck inside me. Oh. God. How could this happen? *How could it really happen, in real life?* It is like a bad dream. It is like a movie that you switch off when you get to the bad bit. It is what I had hoped so hard I'd never get to and yet ... I always feared I would. Now everything about the day goes far away. All the noises round me, they're muted. Like I've been put inside a box, suddenly, a box which muffles all the sounds and blurs the sight of what happens next because I cannot bear it. Uncle Ty and DC Bright arrive. I see Ty's face, shocked and horrified as he turns to look at me. I see him scramble onto Pilgrim's back, standing up tall on his shoulders and take the rope from around Lawrence's neck. He brings the body down and lays it gently, tenderly, on the woodland floor. I see his shoulders shaking, and after a bit I realise that Ty is crying. I see DC Bright stooping, feeling for a pulse. She doesn't find one. I see her glance at her watch. I see the other police constable arrive, his face dark, determined, angry when he sees what's been done here.

'He didn't win,' I hear Rob Macrae's voice as the handcuffs are put on him and his other son. That's it. No remorse. Nothing.

'No. You won't either, mate.' DC Milton says. I can see Pilgrim is weeping. I see it all from behind the muffled grey glass of my box.

And me ... I go and kneel down beside him now. I lay my head on his chest and close my eyes and wish that I could be in whatever place it is that Lawrence has gone to. That I wouldn't have to be here anymore, without him. Because what is the point of being here, if he is gone? What would be the point of a single moment more on this dark, painful planet when people like Rob

Macrae can live on and yet men like Lawrence must die? What is the point of it all?

To have lost him like this after I already lost him once, it is too cruel. It is not right. Why couldn't we just have been together? Why couldn't we have had a chance? *Why couldn't I have the one thing I wanted more than any other thing?*

'Come on, Rose. You need to stand back now ...' The lady constable is saying gently. 'You need to let them do their work ...' And the men from the ambulance that the police have had on standby in the lane are there already, opening up his collar, inserting some tube into his mouth, pumping his chest, trying hope against hope that they will bring him back to life. I hardly dare to believe that they will succeed.

I only know that I will love him till I die and then some. I'll love him till the ends of time and then some more. And nothing that Rob Macrae or his like can do will ever change that.

Rose

Ten months later

'Hey, stranger!' Shona's voice at the other end of the phone is only slightly reproachful. 'I haven't heard from you for *ages*. I haven't seen you since you flew back for my wedding ...'

'I know.' I've got a little red sachet of Demerara sugar in my free hand and I'm turning it first one way and then the other on the café table. I can feel the little granules of sugar as they run past my fingers through the paper. It's strangely soothing. The waitress clears the table next to me, glances over surreptitiously to see if I've finished my coffee yet. I'm sitting in the open market square and I can see all the stall-holders beginning to pack up for the day. Tired shoppers are starting to gather, searching for a free space. I catch her eye and she gives me a tight smile; *whoever it is you're waiting for, they clearly aren't showing up*, she's thinking.

'I've only just been back in the UK for five days,' I pause, back on my phone call. 'I'm sorry I didn't make the christening, Shonie.'

'I didn't expect you to fly back from the States twice on my behalf,' she huffs. That bit is understandable. There's a moment's silence and I imagine her adjusting the position of her baby boy on her lap. Thomas Tyler Moore. I hear a quiet sound at the other end I take to be a baby burping and Shona is back.

'How *is* your dad doing, Rose?'

434

'Amazingly well,' I breathe. It's true. 'He's surpassed everyone's expectations. Carlotta isn't even going to need to go out there and take my place.'

'He's mobile?' Her surprise is palpable.

'With a stick, currently. But yes. They reckon with time even that may go.'

'*How?*'

'It's complicated but ... apparently a large part of the body's malfunctioning is sometimes to do with a person's system having gone into shock. Dad was very lucky. If there is no intrinsic lasting damage, sometimes things can be kick-started back into health again.'

'That sounds ... miraculous.'

'It's not a total fix,' I warn. 'But it's going to make a huge difference to his life. Huge.'

There's a slight pause and then she ventures.

'I see the house sold a few months ago. I heard you got a fair price for it,' she notes. 'And you ... you're back in the UK permanently now? It's so weird to think you're in the UK and you aren't *here*. How's Uni going?'

'Frenetic. Amazing. It's Fresher's week,' I tell her. I'm trying to sound as enthusiastic as I'd like to feel. I've been throwing myself into it as much as I can, making the most of the opportunity, determined to put the past behind me.

'Tell me everything.' She gives a deep conspiratorial laugh. 'Been on any hot dates yet?' I feel a flash of sadness at that. A group of Freshers, jostling together, are looking over at my table hopefully. The autumn breeze lifts the paper napkins from their holder, sends a bunch spinning out all over the ground.

'I've had an offer or two,' I admit, but my voice sounds flat. It's not like she thinks. Shona is unusual, the marrying kind, but people aren't exactly pairing off here. 'Everyone is ... really friendly.' I peer into the froth inside my empty cup wondering why I even rang her just now, knowing full well as I did that she'd interrogate me, knowing that this is the real reason I haven't properly been in contact with her for months. I could have emailed her from the States but I didn't, I couldn't bring myself to.

She interprets my silence the only way I know she can.

'You haven't forgotten him yet, have you?' I bite my lip. *No*, I think. *I never will.*

'Maybe I wanted him too much,' I admit unhappily. 'I'm not supposed to want anything that much or I'll never get it.' I never learn, do I?

'You wanted your Cambridge offer very much, I take it? *You're studying Law at Cambridge Rose*! You got that,' she points out.

'That's true ...'

'You wanted to get out of Merry Ditton.'

'I *did*, but ...'

'You wanted for your life to change and for some great news that would come along and help your dad ...'

I put my hand to my mouth. I see suddenly that I have got everything I'd wished for that night I went into my mother's room and made that spell. I got the offer letter. I got the hope I'd wanted, for Dad. I found my soul mate. All of these things. Everything I wished for, I got.

And everything is transient, changing as the seasons. Nothing that we get, can we keep. The tears run blindly down my face, I feel so sad. I feel so angry. After all we try so hard to strive for, we get to keep *nothing*!

Except maybe love.

'Shonie, I'm so sorry, I've got to go.' I don't want her to hear me weeping. I'm still in public, here. I don't want her to remind me of any more things that will make me weep.

I pull up my texts as soon as she's gone and check the most recent one from *unknown* this morning. The one which asked me to come out here and have coffee at this time, this place. I've handed out my number to so many random people over the last few days, I have actually no idea who it is should have been turning up today. It could have been any number of people. I came

436

here because whoever it was had signed off L. x

    L.

I run through a list of possible names in my head. Linda, Louise, Lorenzo, Lee ... A tear-drop falls into my cup making a big splash right in the middle of the froth and the waitress looks at me sympathetically as she bustles past.

'Can I get you anything else?' she asks helpfully. I look up.

'Not just yet. I'll be leaving in a second ...'

I push my chair out as she hesitates, collecting my cup. As I bend to pick up my bag, I'm aware of someone coming and sitting softly down opposite me while my head is still lowered. I see his trainers slide in under the table and I feel a flash of annoyance. Whoever it is, they haven't even waited for me to go. I'm going to tell him, when I sit upright again, that he can bugger off because this table isn't free yet. I'm not going anywhere. I'm still waiting for L. But he's placed something on the table, for me. I see it the moment I look up.

It's a white paper giraffe, fashioned delicately out of one of the napkins that went flying before.

A giraffe.

I catch his eye now and the shock of it, seeing him actually sitting there in front of me after all this time, it catches so hard in my throat I can't even speak. I just stare at him. The dappled autumn sunlight catches the fine lines under his eyes. It catches the hint of auburn in his now very-short, almost shaven, hair. His face is clean-shaven, too, how I have not seen him before. He looks somehow, much younger.

'*Lawrence,*' I say, and my voice cracks.

It has been many months. Seven months, I know, since the case came to court, and I have not even been in this country. I swallow, trying to come to terms with it all. At the fact that after all this time he is here, sitting right in front of me, right now. I'd wanted to see him before I left for the States with Dad but some-how a whole load of red tape had grown up between us. Nobody seemed keen to make it easy. I'd learned from a hospital volunteer

437

that he'd spent a lot of time in recovery after they resuscitated him. He'd been in intensive care for weeks. By the time he came out me and Dad had left the country but I knew from Ty that Lawrence had pleaded guilty to causing injury. Still, he never responded to any attempt from me to contact him at all. When I flew over for Shona's wedding I'd tried to reach him again but he never replied. I came to believe he didn't want to. I told myself he must have a lot going on, with his own recovery and his father's and Pilgrim's upcoming trials. I knew he must have had a lot to cope with. The volunteer wrote to say he asked for my understanding, for my patience. He never wrote to ask for it, himself. The months went by and my patience turned to resignation. He was so unwell, so tied up, and I was so far away, so taken up with all the new things Dad had to be learning ... I gave up expecting him to contact me.

I gave up hoping for it.

I don't know if I even *want* him here in my life anymore.

I lean forward, and the sting of bitter tears are there again, waiting, in the back of my throat. Still, I cannot speak. I lift up the giraffe he has placed in front of me, which was starting to slide across the table with the breeze. It seemed so sturdy, standing there, but when I pick it up, I feel its papery legs fluttering delicately beneath my fingers. It could blow away in an instant. I could crush it with little more than a careless look.

'I heard you were back.' His eyes are glistening strangely. 'Your cousin Sam sent me a postcard.'

She did?

'*I* sent you postcards,' I remind him. 'And letters.' My fingers run over the smooth papery legs of the giraffe. 'And emails.' I even tried to call him, once or twice but he didn't make it easy. He never came to the phone.

'I got them. I still have them. Rose, I'm sorry. I wasn't in a place to reply,' he says. I can see from his face that this is true. I glance at his neck and the pink burn-mark is still faintly visible on his skin. I blink, and a tear rolls down my cheek. I stand up abruptly and the chair scrapes noisily behind me, making everyone turn to look. He looks down and I see him brush something from his cheek as he does so.

'Are you free?' I whisper.

'I got ten months custodial sentence.' He pauses awkwardly, then adds. 'They took into account my circumstances Rose. They were lenient. Most of my time is being served at an open prison facility. I'm - on leave this weekend. I heard about Jack's recovery, Rose, I came to seek you out, hoping that you still ...' His voice fades away. He's kept himself apprised then, all this time? He's known what's been happening in my life? 'As long as I'm back by nine pm ...'

He stands, then, his hands seeking my hands as I move in towards him, blindly, hungrily, remembering what I have had to endure, being without him for such a very long time. I didn't know ... wasn't at all sure whether it would ever be possible for us to take up where we left off. I know it now, though. I know it without either of us having to say another word.

'And yes,' he whispers into my ear, our hips bumping companionably as we move away together, undeniably a couple, and the Freshers who snatch up our table snigger something about 'getting a room'.

'I *am* free, Rose.' In the only way that really matters, he means. In his heart, *in his soul.* The autumn wind blows back my hair as I walk across the empty market square with him now. Only the flower-seller remains, smiling hopefully at the passers-by, his yellow dahlias standing proud in their plastic buckets. They remind me of a day long ago in a forgotten spring, a stiff breeze in a field and a bunch of yellow cowslips that called me first, titsy-totsy, to my love. But that is gone now, long past, what should have been our fate. And I know that I, like him, have also been set free.

The End

439